37INK

SIMON & SCHUSTER

ALSO BY
SADEQA JOHNSON

The House of Eve
Yellow Wife
And Then There Was Me
Second House from the Corner
Love in a Carry-On Bag

KEEPER *of* LOST CHILDREN

SADEQA JOHNSON

37INK

SIMON & SCHUSTER

New York Amsterdam/Antwerp London
Toronto Sydney/Melbourne New Delhi

An Imprint of Simon & Schuster, LLC
1230 Avenue of the Americas
New York, NY 10020

This book is a work of fiction. Any references to historical events, real people, or real places are used fictitiously. Other names, characters, places, and events are products of the author's imagination, and any resemblance to actual events or places or persons, living or dead, is entirely coincidental.

First 37 INK/Simon & Schuster hardcover edition February 2026

37 INK/SIMON & SCHUSTER and colophon are
trademarks of Simon & Schuster, LLC

Interior design by Lewelin Polanco

Manufactured in the United States of America

5 7 9 10 8 6

Library of Congress Control Number has been applied for.

ISBN 978-1-6680-6991-2
ISBN 978-1-6682-2742-8 (Int/Can Exp)
ISBN 978-1-6680-6993-6 (ebook)

For my father, Tyrone Murray—
my forever example of love.
I am because of you.

PROLOGUE

Mannheim, Germany, 1946

A hand pounded against the front door. Startled from her morning prayers, Sister Proba clutched the cross hanging around her neck, hoping it was just the wind. But then she heard it again.

Rap, rap, rap.

Wearing only her thin nightgown, she quickly got to her feet and grabbed her robe.

The knocking got louder and more aggressive as she moved down the winding back stairs, draping her veil over her wispy hair and pinning it in place. At the bottom of the steps, Junior Sister was dressed just as haphazardly, brow furrowed with concern. With only a look between them, the two nuns moved down the long hall, passing the dining room, and then through the foyer.

After flipping on the light in the small vestibule, Sister Proba looked through the peephole. She touched her forehead and then made the sign of the cross before unlatching the door.

Under the portico stood a woman with pasty skin and slightly wrinkled clothes. Streaks of dried tears stained her hollow cheeks.

A child's legs wrapped around the woman's waist, and tiny arms were tightly fastened against her neck.

"Help me," the woman croaked.

The nun stepped aside and ushered the pair into the parlor, where Junior Sister was already at work starting a fire.

"I cannot keep him." The woman's eyes were filled with shame.

The child stayed fitted around her so tightly, it was hard to see where one began and the other ended. Sister Proba gestured for the woman to take a seat.

"My father banished me from our village." The young woman repositioned the boy in her lap, and when he faced forward, his sweater was a size too small and his thick hair unruly. It was just as the nun had suspected.

Mischlingskinder.

The two nuns exchanged a look but said nothing.

"He threatened to sell him to the traveling human zoo as an exotic for twenty-five deutsche marks. My son would be kept in a cage and put on display." She wrapped her arms more tightly around the brown-skinned boy. "We ran away to a shelter, but the conditions . . ." The woman dropped her eyes. "Deplorable."

The billows made a whooshing sound as Junior Sister stoked the fire.

"I have found work as a live-in housekeeper, but I cannot bring a child. You are my last hope. Please, take him."

Sister Proba stood and reached for the boy, who was so sleepy he didn't put up a fuss. "Write down the usual information before she goes," she directed Junior Sister, then squeezed the frail woman's shoulders. "May God be with you."

The boy grew heavier in Sister Proba's arms as she ascended the steps to the second floor. This child would be number twenty-two at the orphanage. All occupation children, all of mixed-race parentage and a result of war.

The large dormitory room smelled of babies' breath and pillow drool. She lay the sleeping boy down on an empty cot and tucked the gray wool cover around him. Just as she turned to go, the boy lifted his head and clutched the hem of her robe.

"Mummy?"

"Shh, go back to sleep. You are safe," she cooed.

But the boy wouldn't be mollified. "Mummy. Mummy," he said, louder this time. The child next to him stirred, then the one in front of him. Harmonious cries of "Mummy. Where's Mummy?" echoed throughout the room.

"Go back to bed, children, it is okay." The nun moved from one child to the next, tucking them back under the covers, rubbing backs, and whispering sweet words of affection.

Still the boy would not be pacified. He pushed off the bed and started running across the floor. "Mummy. Don't go. Please, no!"

Part I

When I discover who I am,
I'll be free.

—RALPH ELLISON

CHAPTER 1

Prince Frederick, MD, September 1965

SOPHIA

On the morning of her first day of tenth grade, Sophia Clark lay in a damp nightshirt, cowering at the sound of roof rats eating through the plaster walls of the farmhouse's kitchen. Through the tiny window, she could see that it was still purple outside, and although she wanted to stall a bit, she could hear Ma Deary's nagging voice, *If you want to eat, then you got to work.* The sole rooster in the barn began to crow like he was being paid to warn farmers within a five-mile radius that the sun was coming. Although his *cock-a-doodle* was the constant start to her mornings, today his cawing plucked against her temple.

As her eyes adjusted to the dark room, she touched her forearms, inflamed with welts that had sprouted like blades of wheat. Her throat felt parched, but when she reached for the mug of water she had placed on the milk crate beside her bed, she discovered that it had been tipped over by the wild flailing of her limbs through the night.

Sophia rose carefully to avoid hitting her head on the low ceiling. Her bedroom was so small she couldn't even cuss a cat without getting fur in her mouth. It really wasn't a bedroom. More like a space meant for storage adjacent to the kitchen. Ma Deary had forced her into the tiny space so her night screams would stop waking the rest of the house.

Stepping out of her faded nightshirt and into threadbare overalls, Sophia fastened them at her shoulders with safety pins. Then she used the rubber band on her wrist to tie back her ginger hair. As she opened the door to the kitchen, she stomped her feet to scare the rats into their hiding place.

Sophia moved to the sink and turned on the faucet. The basin was tarnished with rusted copper streaks. The pipes shook, then sputtered out brown water. After about fifteen seconds, the water ran clear, and she dipped her mug and drank. From the front bedroom drifted the hard snorts of Ma Deary, which somehow harmonized with the soft snores of the Old Man. Sophia gritted her teeth.

She shuffled across the scuffed plank floors to the back of the house, where her twin brothers, Karl and Lu, were curled head to toe on a mattress that smelled of piss no matter how many times Sophia sprinkled it with baking soda.

"Boys. Time to get up," she coaxed, but when neither moved, she pulled the blanket, pocked with moth holes, down to their waists.

Karl tugged the covers back over his thick head and mumbled, "Five more minutes."

Sophia tapped his back. "Can't, bud. Today is the first day of fifth grade, remember?"

"We gotta do chores on the first day a school?" Lu sat up, rubbing his hazel eyes. "No fair."

"You know the men aren't here to help, and we gotta take care of the chickens and the cows before we head off to school. Now move it." Sophia shoved the blanket to their ankles to show she meant business. Both boys groaned, and she understood why. They were dog-tired.

The summer had been hard as shoe leather on all of them. In the past, Ma Deary's brother, Uncle Wayon, had hired recently released convicts in conjunction with a government program to do some of the more strenuous work on the farm. But this past spring, Unc had spent all of his time in D.C. chasing tail—Ma Deary's words, not Sophia's—and had forgotten to reapply for the program before the May 15 deadline. So all fifty acres had fallen on Sophia and her brothers. While their classmates had enjoyed lazy lake swims, the kids had worked their tails off.

They spent each day with their backs crouched, hauling heavy buckets of produce, grinding tubs of feed, dragging sprinklers across the massive fields, feeding the animals, and fighting with faulty machinery under the merciless sun. In the evenings, they heaved debris until their shoulder blades screamed, and shoveled animal manure until what little they had in their stomachs threatened to come back up. Before bed, they scrubbed every surface clean, and disinfected the farm tools and equipment until their heads were dizzy from the smell of Peridox, a concentrated cleaner which prevented bacteria, viruses, and the outbreak of disease.

For the past three months, Sophia and her brothers had labored twelve-hour days, and now that school was starting, she wasn't sure how they would manage it all.

"Hurry, boys." She flicked on the light. "Time's a-wastin'."

When she was satisfied that the twins were slipping into their sweatpants, Sophia went through to the kitchen and pushed open the screen back door. A cool breeze caressed her cheeks, and the burst of crisp air awakened all her senses.

Her older brother, Walter, sat on the porch in a corroded metal rocking chair, chewing on a piece of straw. "Morning." He tipped his wide-brimmed panama hat to her.

"How'd you sleep?" Sophia dropped in the seat beside him while reaching for her mud-caked boots.

"Nothing like breathing in all that fresh open air." He smiled, showing off the gap between his two front teeth. Walter's skin was so tanned that his nose was peeling. When it was hot like it had been, Walter preferred to sleep in a hammock outside rather than on the sagging sofa in the living room of their two-bedroom house. "You?"

Sophia shook her head and pulled her shirtsleeves down over the red marks on her arms, but she knew that Walter had already seen them.

"The dream again?" He wrinkled his brows with concern, but she changed the subject.

"Any word from Unc? He knows today is the first day of school, right?"

"He'll be by soon." Walter stretched his long legs out in front of him and then stood.

"If you don't see those boys in the next five minutes—"

"I'll wrangle them and send them your way."

Sophia mumbled her thanks as her boots sank into the soft earth. She could smell the morning dew and could already hear the dawn chorus of hens summoning her to the coop. As she rolled back the barn door, the stench of chicken feces and ammonia greeted her. *"Buck-buck-buck-badaack,"* clucked the hens.

"Morning to you too." Sophia sneezed while picking up one of several white pails stacked next to the pallet of hay.

Along each side of the barn walls were wooden raised coops stacked in rows of three and four. Each contained individual nesting boxes for the nearly five hundred hens that Sophia was responsible for. Some of the boxes cradled brown eggs abandoned by the hens, already out foraging the barn for food.

Sophia collected the eggs off the floor, from the empty nests and the dark corners where some hens liked to lay them, and put them atop the hay she'd collected earlier. There were always a few broody hens who honored their motherly instincts and refused to move from their nests, and she gently scooped them up and out of her way to secure the eggs. As she gathered eggs from nest to nest, rotating full pails for empty ones, Sophia tried to let the squawks of the hens drown out the talking picture that had been playing through her head all morning, but the noise just kept getting louder.

Sophia had never told Ma Deary or the Old Man about her school counselor, Mrs. Brown, pulling her from the school's breakfast line to meet the white woman in the pillbox hat.

The visit had taken place on the first Monday after Christmas break, last school year. Sophia's toes had still been cold from her walk to school when Mrs. Brown invited her to sit in her office. Every person at W. S. Brooks High School was Negro, and Sophia remembered being taken aback to see a white woman with gold rings on most every finger smiling up at her.

Mrs. Brown had introduced the woman as Mrs. Winston from the Prosser Foundation, explaining that she had come to Brooks High School searching for the brightest Negro student in the county to offer the privilege of attending an elite boarding school to continue high school education. Sophia had been selected along with Kathy Baker and Alonzo Morton to sit in the library and take the three-hour placement test.

"Today? Without studying?" Sophia sputtered, but Mrs. Brown assured her that she would be fine.

"There is nothing to prep. It's a standard test."

They were each ushered to a different table in the library, given two pencils, a question booklet, and a bubble sheet. Once the exam had concluded, the three students were lined up outside of Mrs. Brown's office and called in one at a time for an interview with Mrs. Winston.

During Sophia's interview, Mrs. Winston offered her a cup of peppermint tea and shortbread cookies on a paper doily while asking questions about her family life, education, hobbies, and future aspirations.

Sophia got stuck on the notion of hobbies and told the woman frankly, "There isn't much free time on the farm. 'Cept maybe a quick game of catch in between milking the cows and composting the dung."

Mrs. Winston's stricken look made Sophia wish she had made something up. She left school that day with a small bag of goodies that had included a keychain with "West Oak Forest Academy" on it and a brochure slathered with pictures of smiling students in brightly decorated classrooms holding brand-new books. The glossy pamphlet provided a portal into a new world that Sophia had never imagined existed. On the farm, she had told only Walter. To which he'd smiled and said he'd pray on it for her. She didn't have the heart to share the idea of West Oak Forest Academy with Ma Deary: She would be the weed to Sophia's seedling, choking out the life of her dream and depriving it the light to grow.

What had gotten Sophia through her gruesome summer days cleaning the horse stalls, watering and feeding the chickens, cows, cats, and goat, collecting eggs on top of eggs, and harvesting and grinding corn for feed, was knowing that at the end of each night, she had the shiny pages of the school's brochure waiting for her. Against Sophia's will, hope had seeped in, and a deep yearning had taken root. Her whole body had begun to crave a life away from the farm.

But as the metal handle of the pail dug into the crevices of her dry palm, the reality of her life brought her back into the barn, and Sophia chided herself for being so foolish. Attending West Oak Forest Academy had been nothing more than a pipe dream.

Finished with pulling the eggs, she lifted the garden hoe hanging from the wall and scraped the roosting bars from left to right until all the waste had fallen to the ground. While she swabbed the bars with a sponge she kept soaked in vinegar, Karl and Lu entered the barn with the chicken feed and fresh buckets of water.

The boys were fraternal twins but looked nothing alike. Karl was tall and big-boned, with skin the color of toast, and had inky eyes. Lu was short and willowy, with eyes so see-through he reminded her of a kitten.

Sophia wanted to give them the job of carrying the eggs down to the mudroom, but she didn't trust them not to break them.

"Lu, while Karl fills the feeders, you grab the pitchfork and turn the bedding in each nest. If it looks soggy, just replace it with clean straw from the pallet."

"Why can't I feed the hens?" Lu whined.

"You did it yesterday," said Karl.

"Boys, we don't have time for arguing."

"He started it," said Lu.

"It was you," said Karl.

"You have twenty minutes, so make haste. We still gotta milk the cows." Sophia headed for the barn door and then remembered, "And don't forget to close up all the nests so the chickens can't get back inside."

Sophia lugged two pails of eggs at a time to the small mudroom at the back of the farmhouse. It was more like a shed with a refrigerator and a long aluminum prep table. It took her several trips to get all the pails inside. Sophia then examined each egg, checking for cracks, and then wiped them all down with a clean rag before placing them into the cartons.

Satisfied with her work, she stacked the cartons in the refrigerator. The Old Man would carry some to their local customers in town later, but the bulk of the egg production was delivered to three restaurants in Washington, D.C., on Thursdays, just in time for the weekend rush.

Next she had to milk the cows, the chore that she abhorred most. As she rounded the corner to the milking parlor, she hoped the cows were in a good mood.

Inside the parlor, she found Walter already perched on the milking stool, cleaning the cow's udders.

"Don't you have to water the fields?" she asked.

"I'll do it after this. You go get ready for the first day of school."

"You have school too, Walter." Sophia put her hands on her hips. "Just 'cause you're a senior don't mean you can skip."

He swatted at a fly in the air. "I don't need to go on the first day. It's more or less the same. 'Sides, I promised Unc that I'd have the milk ready for the morning pickup. He said he should have two or three hands by tomorrow, and then I'll go."

Not having to fool with the cows would give her time to freshen up before the three-mile walk to school. "You sure?"

"Go on, now." He turned his face back and started lubricating the teats.

Walter did not have to tell Sophia again. As she headed back to the house, she couldn't understand how Walter could be so content with farmwork. Sophia could not wait to grow up and wear classy dresses with high heels and perfume like the pretty girlfriends Unc brought around.

Sophia washed her hands at the spigot that ran on the side of the house. Cracked and calloused, her fingers looked like they belonged to someone twice her age. The Old Man was already out on one of the tractors—she could hear the motor chugging from around back—but Ma Deary continued to snort and snore.

As Sophia set the eggs to boil, she thought lovingly of her television mother, Margaret Anderson from *Father Knows Best.* Margaret would never let her children go off to school without presenting a beautifully set dining table, covered with bacon, eggs, toast, and freshly squeezed orange juice. Sophia rolled her eyes in the direction of Ma Deary with disgust.

She walked down into her bedroom. An octagonal window the size of two fists let in a stream of sunlight. There were no electrical sockets in her room, and the only other light that came through was when she left the kitchen door ajar.

Sophia pulled her school skirt out of the trunk in the corner.

Last school year, the skirt fell below her knee, as required. She must have grown at least two inches over the summer, because now the skirt stopped above her knee. Seeing that it was all she had to wear, it would have to do.

The farm sat a ways back from the main street, so Sophia and the twins traipsed through uncut grass for a quarter of a mile before reaching Double Oak Road. Sophia checked her brothers for ticks, then the three walked along in single file. After dropping the boys off at the big red barn that had been converted into a lower school, she walked the last mile alone to the high school, feeling her stomach slip from a loose loop into a tight knot.

W. S. Brooks was a single-story brick building that sat back on a large lot with a smattering of white ash and hickory trees. The grass smelled freshly mowed, and the high-pitched laughter of classmates reuniting after summer rang out loud. Sophia pushed her hand over her head, not sure why she had even wasted time with the brush and comb because the morning humidity had already puffed up her hair like a horse helmet.

As she crossed the parking lot, tugging her too-short skirt, she saw upperclassmen wearing their first-day best, posted against freshly washed vehicles, shooting the breeze. A group of sophomore boys tossed a football while blushing girls flashed their teeth, thirsting after the attention their two-hour morning routine deserved.

"Orangutan," a shrilly voice called out.

Sophia's shoulders stiffened. It was Maxine and her dreaded triad of flunkies. She picked up her pace.

"Don't pretend like you don't know your name all of a sudden." Maxine spoke louder, and her acolytes scratched under their arms while producing monkey sounds: "Oo-oo-ah-ah."

Sophia didn't have to look at them to know that all four girls had on brand-new A-line skirts, starched white blouses, and two-toned flats, with their hair pressed to a shine. Their flowery fragrances contrasted with her own aroma of egg yolk and the rotten-plant residue stuck to the bottoms of her shoes. The girls were on her heels by the time Sophia had reached for the school's front door with a trembling hand.

"Don't fall asleep in class this year, either. Wouldn't want the boogeyman to get you," Maxine hissed in her ear and cackled while the flunkies chorused their monkey sounds.

Sophia was about to run away from them like she had all last school year, but something deep inside of her rooted her to the ground. She turned and looked Maxine dead in the eye. "And don't you eat lunch. Might be a razor blade in your sandwich."

Maxine looked so stunned that, in the time it had taken for her to recover, Sophia was already down the hall ducking into her first-period class.

She had been assigned to eleventh-grade chemistry even though she was technically in tenth grade. While her teacher went over the year's objectives and what they would master, a student entered with a note for the teacher.

"Sophia Clark, report to the principal's office," her teacher said.

The knot was now so tight in her stomach, Sophia thought she would throw up. Swallowing hard, she gathered her things. It seemed like every eye in the room turned to watch her get out of her seat. Her knees wobbled so much that, right before she reached the door, she tripped over her own foot and grabbed the doorknob to catch herself from falling. The kids roared with laughter.

"Now, class, settle down." The teacher slapped her palm three times against her desk.

Sophia moved through the deserted halls, wondering if she was being summoned because Maxine had told on her about the razor-blade comment, or if one of the hall monitors had reported her for dress-code violation on account of her too-short skirt. If it were the comment, she would deny it, and if it were the latter, she would assure Principal Travis that the short skirt was an accident. She'd say that her mother had bought the wrong size but would take her shopping over the weekend. Which was a bald-faced lie. Ma Deary never took them shopping. She simply brought home clothes from the hospital's lost-and-found box and told them to choose whatever passed as fitting. Unc's latest girlfriend had given Sophia what she wore now, probably out of sheer pity. She had looked Sophia over and said, "Sugar, you are way too pretty to be dressed like an old maid."

The school's office had a small reception area with a desk and two bookshelves.

"For heaven's sake, Sophia?" The white-haired receptionist looked up from her ledger.

"Yes, ma'am?"

"Mrs. Brown's just about had a cow trying to locate you. Head on back now before you give that woman a full-fledged heart attack."

Sophia breathed a sigh of relief. Mrs. Brown would be easier to talk to about her circumstance than the principal. When she reached the end of the hall, she could hear Mrs. Brown's heels click against the vinyl-plank floor. Mrs. Brown was wearing a plaid blazer with a pleated skirt, and as she removed her reading glasses, her mouth hung agape. Sophia bristled. She could tell by the look on the woman's face what was coming next.

Detention.

Mrs. Brown was the first lady of First Samuel's Baptist Church, and very no-nonsense about girls looking and behaving like young women: no short skirts, no fingernail polish, no earrings bigger than a hatpin, and no foul language permitted under any circumstances. Sophia was in violation of at least two of the hard-and-fast rules and braced herself for the consequences.

"Sophia. Why are you here?"

"A student pulled me from class with a note," she stuttered.

Mrs. Brown's dimples deepened as she shook her full head of Shirley Temple curls. "I mean here at Brooks High School. Did you not receive my message?"

Sophia touched her forehead. So she was not in trouble. Which meant that there was no detention, leaving ample time to get her evening chores done before the sun went down. It was near impossible to work in the barn in the dark, and she always worried about stepping on chicken snakes.

Then Mrs. Brown's words registered. Sophia asked, "What message?"

Mrs. Brown lifted a file folder from her desk with "Sophia Clark" written in red ink. "Your application to the Prosser Foundation was accepted. You've passed all the necessary tests and have been admitted to West Oak Forest Academy."

Sophia blinked her eyes, not sure she had heard correctly.

"The school's headmaster has called countless times looking for you. He said two letters were mailed out to you over the summer. I even called and left a message with your mother."

"I got in?" Sophia asked, stunned.

"Yes. You did it. Congratulations." Mrs. Brown's lips were stretched so wide with laughter that Sophia could see the gold crowns wrapped around her molars.

Sophia put her hand to her mouth as she sank into the chair opposite Mrs. Brown. Why hadn't Ma Deary given her the message?

"They were going to give your spot away to a boy from Richmond, but I told them that I would have you there before class tomorrow morning." Mrs. Brown slid the folder across the desk to Sophia. "I am certain that it was your mother I spoke with on"—she spun her chair toward the calendar hanging behind her head—"July 29, 1965."

July 29 had been the one day, all summer long, when Sophia had been away from the farm. Unc and one of his girlfriends had taken them to the bay for a picnic and a swim on Walter's eighteenth birthday. Sophia thought to lie to cover for Ma Deary's negligence. She usually had something at the ready, but right now she was drawing a blank. She fidgeted with the hem of her skirt around her fingertip.

"Something told me to stop by your house, but I got so busy with the prep for the new school year." Mrs. Brown beamed. "Well, in any case, you've already missed a few days, so it is imperative that your parents drive you first thing tomorrow." She shuffled a few more papers. "Here's the packing list. You can head on home to prepare. Oh, and I almost forgot."

Sophia watched as Mrs. Brown reached under her desk and then handed her a silver gift bag tied with a white bow.

"A few of us in the office got you this. To get you started."

Underneath the shiny tissue paper was a white cotton nightgown with a matching robe and a pair of fuzzy slippers. A package of new panties, knee socks, and a pair of gently used loafers. Sophia could not remember ever receiving a gift, let alone one packaged so beautifully. Not even on Christmas.

"I had to guess your shoe size. I sincerely hope they fit. You will be given a school uniform upon your arrival, so you don't have to worry about that."

"Thank you," Sophia breathed, weightless with glee.

"Your parents won't have any issues getting you there tomorrow, will they?" Mrs. Brown eyed her pointedly. "I'd take you myself, but I have a meeting with the superintendent on the terrible condition of our textbooks."

"No, ma'am." Sophia swallowed hard.

"Good. Here is my telephone number. Call me if you have any problems at all." Mrs. Brown stood, and before Sophia knew what was happening, Mrs. Brown had swept her into her arms. She was big-breasted, smelled like peach cobbler, and her embrace was as comforting as anything Sophia had ever known.

"I don't know how to thank you." Sophia couldn't remember the last time she had been hugged, and she didn't want to let go.

Mrs. Brown patted her shoulder. "Doing your best is thanks enough. Now go on. Make Brooks proud."

Sophia picked up her bag of goodies, and as she walked out the door, Mrs. Brown called behind her, "And for the love of God, do something with that hair."

CHAPTER 2

Lourdes, France, July 1950

ETHEL

Ethel Gathers rode the train to Lourdes, France, desperate for a miracle. She clutched her rosary beads, knowing that a healing encounter with the Virgin Mary was as likely as Pope Pius XII inviting her to the grand dining hall at the Vatican for dinner. Still, she had no choice but to believe. Dr. Burroughs's letter with her diagnosis was like energy radiating from inside her purse, and she found herself patting the top of her bag, trying to suppress the dissemination of his memorandum, which stated that Ethel was unable to bear a child.

As the wheels of the train churned and clacked beneath her feet, Ethel kissed the crucifix of the rosary and then made the sign of the cross before draping the multicolored beads across her cotton gabardine skirt. She had already prayed the full rosary three times over the past six hours while riding through the woodlands of France, but she did not feel at peace.

Since she had arrived as a newlywed in Mannheim, Germany, three months earlier, Ethel had rarely left their apartment. She had no friends, did not speak German, and whenever she ventured outside to do more than on-base shopping, she found herself disoriented on the streets. With her husband, Bert, working long hours in the field, she was often alone, and the solitude had begun to unravel her. She found herself restless and had started to lose weight. It was Bert who suggested that she join the other army wives on the trip to France.

"I'll miss you"—he'd pecked her cheek as he produced the pamphlet—"but it'll do you some good, darling, to make some friends and see a bit of the world while we're over here."

Now the women were traveling from Mannheim, where they were stationed with their high-ranking officer husbands, on a spiritual pilgrimage to the Sanctuary of Our Lady of Lourdes, where St. Bernadette was said to have had eighteen visions of the Virgin Mary. Ethel had agreed to the long journey because she believed that the Blessed Virgin Mary, mother of all, could heal her womb and change her fate. *For we walk by faith, not by sight,* she reminded herself as she reached for her leather-bound diary resting in the empty seat next to her.

As a reporter at large for Baltimore's *Afro-American,* Ethel had been assigned a feature on the living conditions of the Negro military stationed abroad. She picked up her pen, with the notion of writing about the mistreatment Bert had shared with her of the Negro soldiers by the white military police, but after starting and stopping, starting again and stopping, she had managed to write only one lackluster paragraph. Capping her fountain pen, she abandoned the idea, at least temporarily, and looked out the window. She saw a clear, bubbling stream running down lush green hills into an open valley. The burgeoning blue sky held just a small trace of clouds, where two birds soared and circled each other. And then the train shunted through a lavender farm so purple and wild that Ethel could smell its soft powdery scent. Never had she experienced a rolling landscape that changed like a picture show, but even with so much beauty, Ethel had begun to feel her knees stiffen. They had been on the train for nearly seven hours. Perhaps she needed to stretch her limbs and walk a bit.

Ethel rose from her seat and made her way down the aisle toward the lounge car for a refreshment. As she passed through the railcar, she saw the other wives. While there were no segregated cars in France, she noticed her companions had managed to separate themselves. The whites sat on the right front side of the railcar. Ethel had sat in the center, on the left side. Julia Jones, the only other Negro wife on the trip, sat behind her, though she'd been sleeping the whole way.

The scent of burning cigarettes reached Ethel at the entrance to the lounge car, which was filled mostly with French and Spanish patrons eating on white china plates and sipping from champagne and highball glasses. Two young boys wearing knickers played checkers at one of the tables while their parents cackled over a board game that Ethel did not recognize. Sitting alone on a velvet sofa was a dark-haired woman with olive skin and striking blue eyes. She was the American wife who had coordinated the trip, but Ethel couldn't recall her name.

"How do you do?" The wife tilted her chin while taking a long drag from her cigarette.

"I'm well. You?"

"Positively exhausted of this train, that's for sure," she said, exhaling.

Ethel chuckled. "That's why I came for a beverage. Ripe for a change of scenery."

"Where are my manners? Please, have a seat." The woman gestured to the spot next to her.

Ethel hesitated for only a second before smoothing down the back of her skirt and taking the offered seat.

"Any idea how much longer we have to go?" Ethel sat her envelope purse in her lap. The classical piano music felt good against her ears.

"I think about thirty minutes more."

A waiter appeared in a stiff black uniform. Ethel ordered a cup of English breakfast tea and the woman a gin fizz.

"Please, tell me your name again?"

"Ethel Gathers. My husband, Albert Gathers, is the army chief warrant officer."

"I'm Dorothy. Dorothy Hansen." She exhaled. "I'm married to Lieutenant General Skip Hansen. I'm glad you were able to join us. I've run this trip for three years straight. It was designed so that the new wives who arrived on base had the blessing to be fruitful by the Virgin Mary."

That was Ethel's hope, but she could not tell Dorothy. Instead, she said, "I have always wanted to take a religious pilgrimage."

Dorothy smirked. "Well, hallelujah! You are the first. Most of the women are along for the adventure and the promise of a soak in the hot thermal baths that the Pyrenees Mountains are famous for."

"Well, that sounds delightful too."

The waiter returned and poured their respective drinks. "How long have you been in Germany?" Dorothy said as she sipped.

"A little over three months. Still trying to get my bearings."

"Living abroad is an adjustment, but you will get used to it. I have come to appreciate the cultural experience. Back home I was forced to be so closed-minded." Dorothy released the swivel handle of her belly-skin handbag and pulled out a book. "I think this will help." She turned the book over to Ethel. The cover read *The Army Wife* by Nancy Shea. "It's been a life saver for me. Outlining all the dos and don'ts that come with this gig. You are welcome to borrow it."

Ethel wanted to refuse the book—she had enough reading to do for the article she was writing—but she recognized the book as an olive branch and decided to accept it. "Thank you, that's very kind."

"Don't mention it." Dorothy waved her comment away. "On this side of the pond, we have the freedom to get to know each other. Let's take advantage of that." She pinned Ethel with her blue gaze until both women couldn't help but smile.

There was something refreshing about Dorothy, and Ethel found herself saying, "I'd like that, and I'll be sure to return the book when I am finished."

At Gare de Lourdes, Ethel disembarked to blaring rail announcements in French and the smell of unflushed toilets. She touched the beaded necklace at her throat, hardly able to believe they had finally arrived. Dorothy led the group down the platform, through the station's doors, and onto the street.

Tiny cars were scattered along the curb, and Dorothy pointed to the red passenger van waiting for them to the left of the entrance. As the women giggled their way onto the van, Dorothy confirmed the party with a head count.

Julia Jones slid across the leather seat next to Ethel. Julia had a square face and small eyes that reminded Ethel of Eartha Kitt. She smelled like maple syrup, and her hair was tightly curled.

"Well, this is the most exciting thing I've done in a long time, I must say." Julia whipped out a black compact stenciled in gold with hummingbirds and flower petals. She powdered her cheeks, forehead, and nose as the van came to a traffic stop. "Have you traveled much?"

"Back home a bit," said Ethel, touching her bangs. "But this is my first time in France."

"Mine too," cooed Julia.

"Your compact is stunning." Ethel pointed.

"Thank you. It was my grandmother's. Wouldn't believe it was made in the thirties," she said, dropping it back into her purse. "Mama said to hang on to it, might be worth some money one day."

The town of Lourdes sat in the foothills of the Pyrenees Mountains, and as the van drove west toward the religious attractions, Ethel could hear the gargle and flow of the Gave de Pau babbling through the center of the city. The van twisted past what looked like gingerbread houses and storybook shops sandwiched by piney hills and jagged mountaintops. The driver parked at the tip of a slim pedestrian-only street. The aromas of frankincense, myrrh, and balsam greeted Ethel as she followed Julia off the van. The white wives pivoted around one another, just far enough away from Ethel and Julia but in earshot of Dorothy's voice.

"Ladies, there's lots to see here," bellowed Dorothy as she smoothed down her rose-printed swing dress with oversize black buttons. She wore a bold red lipstick, with a matching scarf tied at her neck, and short black gloves. "You can visit the shrine, wander the cathedral, shop the vendors. Whatever you decide, please go in pairs, and make sure you are back at the van by three o'clock."

Instant chatter burst between the wives as they looked to one another for confirmation on where to start, but Ethel had no plans to be confined to a group consensus. Without consulting anyone, she let her navy flatties carry her through the pedestrian plaza, where she inhaled the collective joy of people pulsing with belief and hope.

She joined the queue to see the shrine of Lourdes alongside Catholic nuns in long black habits, crippled men in wheelchairs, elderly couples stooped over wooden canes, young adults giddy with possibility, elegant European women carrying Hermès bags, and small children asleep in prams.

Ethel closed her eyes as the line of people shared in the collective singing of "Ave Maria" in a bevy of languages uniting into one. Ethel felt so warmed by it all that sweat beaded her brows.

"It's beautiful, isn't it?"

Ethel turned to see Dorothy remove her cat's-eye sunglasses. Julia Jones and a woman with blond curls stood beside Dorothy. Ethel had gotten so wrapped up in her personal mission that she had not realized the three women were behind her in line.

"I've never in my life experienced a crowd pulsing with this collective energy."

At the entrance, racks of white candles set up in the shape of a Christmas tree burned brightly in front of the grotto of Massabielle. In the center of the grotto stood a statue of the Virgin Mary, surrounded by green trailing flowers. The line of people moved at a steady pace. The three wives chatted behind her, but Ethel prayed the Hail Mary again and again under her breath.

When the four women reached the small cave, people slowly slipped into the walkway surrounded by thick layers of stone. The air of the grotto cooled Ethel's balmy skin, drying her sweat almost in an instant. Against the wall rested a glass prayer box, and she mumbled another Hail Mary as she removed Dr. Burroughs's diagnosis from her handbag and dropped the slip of paper into the box. She then mimicked the stout man in front of her and ran her hands along the grotto's stone.

As her fingertips brushed the smooth rock, a staticky feeling pulsed deep inside her. Ethel felt a glowing warmth flow through her belly. Her arms tingled, and her chest heaved up and down. She blinked several times at the white mist that appeared just in front of her. Then a raspy voice uttered, "*You have much to offer others.*"

It was so loud and clear that she wondered if anyone else had heard it. Was that the message she had come for? Had that been the Virgin Mary herself? Ethel had not realized that she had stopped, stalling the line with her hands outstretched on the grotto, until she felt a hand on her elbow.

"Ethel?" Dorothy asked. "Are you feeling all right?"

Ethel took a deep breath and nodded while the words continued to thread through her. *You have much to offer others.*

Praise be.

Ethel staggered out into the light of the day, trying to cloak and swaddle what she had experienced in the grotto.

"Well, that was an uplifting experience for sure," said Dorothy, tugging her gloves back on. They had moved to the right of the crowd and into a small patch of shade.

Julia added, "I must say, I feel like I have just prayed a month of Sundays and received the promise of all my blessings."

Ethel stood silent with her hands folded in front of her. Her mouth was dry, her body heavy, and she wished she had something to lean against.

"Ethel, honey?" Dorothy crinkled her brows.

"Yes." Ethel shook her head, trying to find where they were in the conversation.

"You look faint, dear." Julia peered at her. "Do you need some water?"

Ethel remembered the empty bottle she had tucked in her purse. "Yes. Let's head over to the spring and collect some of the holy water."

"There's holy water too? I should have studied up on the history of this place before we arrived," said Julia, chuckling.

As they walked, Ethel's head began to clear, and she told the ladies that the Lourdes water had flowed since the apparitions in 1858 and was reputed for miraculous healing. What she didn't say was that she had planned to sip a little and sprinkle drops on her belly each night before bed.

Once the four had collected the holy water, Dorothy and her blond friend decided to explore the town and extended an invitation. Julia complained about sore feet and said she would wait it out inside the van. Ethel declined and walked north toward the Basilica of Our Lady of the Immaculate Conception to pray in gratitude, for she was convinced that she had been healed.

CHAPTER 3

Prince Frederick, MD, September 1965

SOPHIA

Sophia's walk back to the farm seemed like it took half the time it usually did. Despite the extra weight of the gift bag, and being chased down the road by the full blaze of the midmorning sun, she felt agile on her feet. She had spent most of her trek home turning the conversation with Mrs. Brown from one side of her mind to the other. Mrs. Brown said that she had spoken to Ma Deary, but Ma had never uttered a word. Had someone else answered the telephone? One of Unc's girlfriends, perhaps, and she had forgotten to give Sophia the message? And where was the acceptance letter? she wondered.

Even without all the details, her insides bubbled over with excitement. She was so tickled with possibility that on more than one occasion she found herself skipping down the road, twirling, and laughing herself silly. She had done it. Sophia was the best student at W. S. Brooks High School and had been admitted to one of the most elite schools in the state of Maryland.

As she slipped off the main road onto the grassy path that led to the farm, Sophia's thoughts wandered to the pages of the school's brochure. The campus was sprawling, and the library was a building unto itself, unlike Mrs. Brown's closet-size room with two shelves of tattered books. The dormitories had real beds, not a mattress in a storage room. No rooster to wake her before the sun or laying hens ready to peck her hand to bleeding. No more hauling hay, making soap, or feeding animals.

Sweaty and out of breath, she finally glimpsed the house. The slates of plywood that Walter had used to patch the shingles were cracked and curled from the weather. He must have run out of either wood or time, because there were two big bald spots with no shingles at all. The exterior of the house was mostly a dull, chipped yellow, except for the siding along the backside of the kitchen. That was half gray. Last summer the Old Man had gotten it in his head that the house needed a coat of paint, but he'd brought home only one can, and that one wall was as far as he'd gotten. The windowpane in the front door had a hole in it as wide as her foot and had been covered with plastic and reinforced with tape. No one used the front door, anyway. It jammed all the time, and if a person pulled too hard, the whole house seemed to rattle. If Sophia didn't live in the farmhouse, she would suspect that it was abandoned. As much as she wished she had received the news from West Oak Forest Academy sooner, she was suddenly glad that Mrs. Brown had not stopped by to deliver it after all.

Ma Deary's Rambler was parked in the dirt patch just to the left of the house. When Sophia saw it, she reminded herself to slow down. *You can't cross a bridge before you reach the river.* When she opened the door to the kitchen, she saw that Ma Deary was still asleep. She worked the four-to-midnight shift at Freedman's Hospital as a nurse, and the hours she spent at home were mostly in her bed.

Sophia listened for snoring and then removed her shoes, tiptoeing over to the short cabinet that doubled as the stand for the black-and-white television set. It had a catchall drawer for loose buttons, small tools, safety pins, pencils, scratch paper, and mail. The drawer was stuffed to the gills, and Sophia had to rattle it a bit to pry it open. At the top of the pile were stacks of bills, a few with the words "Final Notice" blazed in red, two postcard advertisements, and then she saw it: an envelope crested with "West Oak Forest Academy" in navy blue. The letter had been opened, and when Sophia held up the document, she spotted a coffee stain in the top-right corner. She heard the mattress springs creak as Ma Deary sat up in bed.

"Rusty?" she called out to Sophia, her voice hoarse with sleep. Ma Deary had given her the nickname Rusty on account of her hair; Sophia despised the name. She was the only redhead in their family. In second grade, two boys had yelled, "Get away from her. She's Satan's daughter. Run!" Sophia hadn't known who Satan was, and when she came home crying to Ma Deary, asking why she looked so different from everybody, Ma Deary just barked, "Stop asking dumb questions. Just be grateful for what you've got." And that was the end of that.

Sophia held the letter between her fingers as she watched Ma Deary push up from the bed. She pulled on a pin-striped duster robe. Her big breasts flopped from side to side as she stuffed her feet into teal slippers. Her hair was in pin curls, covered over by a silk headscarf.

"Why aren't you in school? It can't be three o'clock yet. Feels like I just put my head on the pillow," she said, and then leaned her torso forward and let out a "pfft." Sophia could smell the sour cottage-cheese odor of the flatulence instantly, and she waved her hand in front of her face.

"'Scuse me," Ma said, shuffling toward her closet.

"Mrs. Brown sent me home."

"What for?"

Sophia held up the letter. Ma glanced at her, tsked her teeth, and then went back to thumbing through her wardrobe.

"Ma, have you read this? Mrs. Brown said that West Oak Forest Academy is one of the best schools in the state, and I got in."

"Who said you could apply?" she snapped. "Ain't nobody notify me, 'cause I would have told them not to waste their time." She inspected her uniform and, when satisfied, hung it on the closet door.

Sophia exhaled and made her voice softer. "Ma Deary, I'm the only one in the whole school who was selected to go. It would be foolish to pass this up."

"Rusty, we're barely making ends meet 'round here. Y'all eating us outta house and home as it is."

And you inhale anything that's not nailed to the table, Sophia thought, but she didn't want to get popped for being smart-mouthed.

"Says right here that my tuition is fully covered by the Prosser Foundation. All you need to do is get me there. They'll put me up, give me a uniform, and I'll receive a top-notch education."

Ma Deary walked into the living room, scratching the pit of her right arm. Then she looked down at her fingernails and flicked something white in the air. "The school you go to is fine, and we need you working this here land."

"But Unc told Walter that he'd have two or three new hires by tomorrow. They could take my place." Sophia's voice cracked. She could feel her dream of going to West Oak Forest Academy slipping away from her.

Ma Deary sucked her teeth. "Umph, he's been saying that all summer long. I'll believe it when I see it." She walked to the kitchen, opened the cabinet, and reached for her tin of Maxwell House coffee.

"But if he does, can I go?"

Ma Deary spun around so fast, it caused Sophia to jump two steps back. "Rusty. That fancy school ain't nothing but a pie-in-the-sky dream. They don't want no ragamuffin like you. You've got as much in common with them fancy white folks as I have with Lady Bird Johnson. Now, please."

"But—"

Ma Deary picked up a spoon and slapped it in her hand and then pointed it at Sophia. "Not another word. Now, since you want to be home, go on down there and harvest some corn so you can feed your brothers tonight and forget all this foolishness."

Sophia's eyes burned as she pushed past Ma Deary and stomped her feet out the back door. She ran barefoot up the hill, past the chicken coop, to the back half of the farm where they planted all their crops. A few weeks ago, Sophia had put in rows of collard greens, broccoli, spinach, and romaine. The cornfield had a slight slope, and the path between the two fields was wide enough for a tractor to pass through without harming the crop.

Sophia grabbed an ear of corn as if it were Ma Deary's head, bent it straight down until it snapped, and then ripped it from the stalk with all her might. That woman didn't have an ounce of love for her children. Why had she become a mother, anyway? To make them work until their fingers bled? Sophia grabbed another stalk. Bend, snap, rip, bend, snap, rip. She was holding seven ears in her arms before she realized that she had forgotten the wheelbarrow back at the house. She threw the corn to the ground, bent over at the waist, and screamed, "Ahhhh," so loudly that she startled a flock of mourning doves, who took off into the sky.

"Whoa."

Sophia turned to see Walter coming through the field on his old Schwinn bicycle.

"Rusty, what's the matter?"

She could no longer support herself and crumpled to the ground. Then she told her brother all that had happened at school with Mrs. Brown and then Ma Deary.

"She's an evil witch. I'm tired of working like a mule, Walter. I got this on my own merit. I want to go." Her eyes felt bloodshot.

"So then go," Walter said, straddling his bicycle.

"On what? The back of your wobbly bike?"

"Don't talk about Lucy." He patted the seat as he climbed off, carefully propping the bicycle on its kickstand. "She'd get you there, we'd just have to leave right now for tomorrow morning." He chuckled, folding his legs beneath him, joining Sophia on the patch of grass.

Walter's overalls were covered in motor oil, and Sophia knew he had spent some of his morning under the hood of one of the spotty tractors again. He reached in his pocket and pulled out a piece of wrapped peppermint.

"Where'd you get this?" She took the candy and placed it in her mouth. The menthol flavor cooled her.

"The girl who works at the General Store is sweet on me." He smiled, popping a mint into his mouth.

"Seriously, I have to get to the school tomorrow, or all is lost. And Lucy won't get me there."

Walter ran his hands over the grass until he found a yellow buttercup. He picked the flower, placed it beneath his chin, and smiled at her. "Lucy won't. But Ma Deary's car will."

Sophia snorted. "Ma Deary wouldn't give you the keys to her Rambler to drive me to the General Store, let alone a boarding school that she said I couldn't go to."

"That's why we're gonna steal it."

Sophia looked at her brother with her hand shading her eyes from the sun. His gaze didn't waver. He was serious about this. Could they really pull it off?

"How are we going to steal the car without Ma knowing?"

"You let me worry about that. Just be ready at first light."

"What about the twins?"

"Maybe you being gone will force Ma to take care of them. If not, they've got me."

"It can't be that easy. What if we drive all the way up there and they want parent signatures or something?"

Walter leaned back on his elbows and narrowed his eyes at her. "You want to go or not?"

Sophia pulled her knees to her chest and rocked. "I'm scared," she confessed after a long pause.

"God wouldn't have opened this door for you if He didn't want you to rush through it."

Walter was the only one who talked about God on the farm, and Sophia felt the hum of possibility slowly creep back up her spine. If she didn't at least try to get to West Oak Forest, she knew she would regret it for the rest of her life. What did she have to lose by going for it? She stood, dusting her legs off. She could feel the swelling of at least three mosquito bites on the back of her thigh.

"You gotta make those boys go to school. I don't want them messing up their education on account of farm chores. Make sure Unc gets the workers here to help. You can't do it all by yourself, Walter."

"I will. Promise."

Sophia looked up at the clouds and sighed. "Then I want to go."

When Sophia returned to the house, her arms filled with corn, Ma Deary was already dressed in her white uniform, smearing a tube of brown lipstick across her full mouth.

"I'm heading off to settle some business 'fore my shift starts. Make sure you check the corn for bugs, then set it to boiling."

She moved past Sophia, smelling like lily-of-the-valley perfume, without so much as a touch. As soon as her Rambler pulled onto the road, Sophia went out back for the big metal washing bucket that she'd been using to clean all the laundry since the wringer washing machine had broken down last summer. The Old Man claimed he would fix it, but he was waiting on a part.

Sophia dragged over the hose and filled the tub with water. The few items of clothing that were suitable for her to take, she immersed in the homemade lye soap mixed with 20 Mule Team Borax. While they soaked, she decided to follow Mrs. Brown's advice and do something with her hair. After rummaging around underneath the bathroom sink, she found two unopened boxes of Ogilvie Sisters magic color. She had watched Ma Deary apply the dye to cover up the grays sprouting around her temples. After reading the instructions, Sophia decided that she would combine both boxes to color her entire head. She would go to West Oak Forest Academy with a fresh start, and no one would ever mistake her for an orangutan again.

CHAPTER 4

Philadelphia, PA, May 1948

OZZIE

The sun had gone down on the annual Memorial Day block party, but the smells of charcoal, barbecue sauce, and smoke still ruled the air. The women of Ringgold Street were covering leftovers of chicken, chitterlings, pig feet, creamy potato salad, and collard greens with tinfoil while pushing children with pound-cake and oatmeal-cookie crumbs in the corners of their mouth into the two-story row houses.

First thing that morning, all the cars had been cleared off the narrow one-way street, and Mr. Raymond's Teletalk speaker had been placed in the middle of the block. The mothers had insisted that the day start with the gospel sounds of the Blind Boys of Alabama and the Dixie Hummingbirds; the young folks took over in the afternoon, swinging in a circle to Louis Jordan's "Boogie Woogie Blue Plate"; and now the men were winding it down with homemade hooch and a game of tunk to Fats Waller's "Ain't Misbehavin."

Ozzie, who had made the mistake of guzzling three cans of Schmidt's, sucked on an ice cube, trying to sober up, while keeping an eye out for Rita. His head felt heavy as he tried not to think about this being his last evening at home. His final moment with Rita. In less than twenty-four hours, he would arrive for basic training as a volunteer for the United States Army.

Ella Fitzgerald's "In a Sentimental Mood" crooned through the speakers as the screen door across the street finally slid open. Ozzie rocked forward, steadying his chair on all four legs as Rita's red ankle-strapped sandal hit the top step of her limestone front steps.

She had gone inside to change her dress after some little kid had spilled cherry water ice all over her. With her curls pooled on top of her head, her long neck was left bare. The sky-blue shirtwaist dress she wore was cinched with a crimson patent belt, matching her sandals exactly. When she saw Ozzie watching her, she dipped her chin at him and batted her lashes in the way that made his heart swoon. Then she waved him over to an empty card table with a set of checkers.

"You doing all right?" she asked, fingering the chips.

Ozzie nodded, intoxicated by her smile. "How you feeling, pretty mama?"

"Can't believe it's your last night," she said, pouting, and Ozzie longed to lean in and kiss her, but there were too many people out on the street.

The mothers had taken their seats with fruity drinks in Styrofoam cups and bowls of potato chips, tee-heeing over neighborhood gossip. His uncle Millard was teaching backgammon to a woman who had wandered over in a short skirt from Oakford Street.

"Got everything all packed?"

Ozzie told her that he did as Mr. Mel, the chubby man who owned the corner store, stopped at their table. He removed his hat and held it in his hand. Ozzie stood, pulling himself to his full five feet and eleven inches, his broad shoulders erect like two boulders.

"Son, I just wanted to let you know how proud we all are of you. Takes a strong man to volunteer. We're countin' on you to go over there and show them. Make sure they know that the Negro man is just as heroic and capable as the white man."

"Yes, sir." Ozzie's chest swelled two sizes. People had been treating him with respect all day, but this was the first time it had happened directly in front of Rita.

"Brought you a little something from me and the missus." Mr. Mel handed him a paper bag filled with Chick-O-Sticks, licorice Snaps, Red Hots, and Squirrel Nut Zippers, all of Ozzie's favorites. "Just a little token of our appreciation for you serving, son."

Ozzie shook Mr. Mel's hand, and then the older man wandered over to the tunk table.

Rita beamed. "Aren't you the celebrity?"

"It's been like this all day. The block mothers made me a quilt, and a few women from Bucknell Street came 'round asking me to talk some sense into their knucklehead boys."

"Well, I'm proud of you too." Rita touched her foot to his shin under the table. Her stroke sent a tingle up through Ozzie's thigh, settling in his midsection. Rita and Ozzie had been going steady for over a year.

"I could say the same about you, college girl."

"Somebody's got to change these laws and fight for our daggone rights."

Her Southern drawl tickled him. "You'll make a fine lawyer."

"First in my family. Got to, after what they did to Uncle Maceo." She stood gingerly and wandered over to the women's table.

Two years ago, her uncle Maceo Snipes had been shot in the back by the Ku Klux Klan after he'd cast his vote in the Georgia Democratic Primary. He'd been the first Negro in Taylor County to vote.

"Once I'm a lawyer, no more Negroes will die because they don't have colored blood at the hospital," Rita said, having returned with two Styrofoam cups containing a tip of clear liquor. "That's the first law I'm going to work on." Her uncle had dragged himself three miles to the hospital only to be told that the hospital had no blood for coloreds.

"Hurts my heart still, to think that Uncle Maceo died from wounds that could have been easily treated." Rita turned somber. After her uncle had passed, waiting on a blood transfusion, her parents had worried over her safety and sent her up to Philadelphia to stay with a great-aunt.

"I have no doubt in my mind that you're gonna be amazing at whatever you set your sights on."

"Glad you know it."

Ozzie raised his cup, tapped it to Rita's, then downed it. The clear liquor made him cough. "What was that?"

"Corn liquor." She smirked.

"I gotta keep my eye on you, pretty mama. Trying to get me drunk so you can have your way with me?" He eyed her until she blushed.

"Now, Ozzie." She giggled. "I've enjoyed these last few weeks with you." She pushed the black checkers across the table to him and started setting up the red ones.

"I'm sorry it has to end. I never get tired of spending time with you." Ozzie pressed his ankles on hers, boxing her legs in from both sides. Fever spread through his torso. He knew the warmth was partially the effects of the liquor, but it was mostly Rita.

Ozzie and Rita had spent every weekend since Easter Sunday taking in bits of the city together. They had gone to the Lakes for a picnic, walked through the department stores in Center City, and even saw Pearl Bailey perform at the Pearl Theatre on Ridge Avenue. The only thing that they hadn't done was *it*. Whenever they came close, Rita reminded him in her sugary Georgian lilt, "Now, Ozzie, why buy the pig when the sausage is free."

Ozzie, who had two older sisters, knew to respect her way of thinking, but man, he wanted her. Rita was fine. Thick legs, deep-set eyes, and smooth caramel-colored skin that always smelled sweet like honeysuckle; when she slid her folding chair closer to him, her fragrance didn't disappoint.

Rita had jumped two of his checker pieces when Ozzie spotted redbone Harold Lowery and two of his friends strolling down the block. He turned his chair so he could keep them in sight. Harold and his crew lived on Reed Street between Twenty-Third and Twenty-Fourth, where the homes had wide front porches, sturdy wicker chairs, and a view of Wharton Square Park. Harold was a preacher's kid, and his father drove the only Cadillac Series 62 that Ozzie had ever seen up close.

Those boys had gone to Southern High School and Ozzie to Bok High, their rival. Ozzie and Harold had played basketball against each other for the past four years, and the tension between them never seemed to simmer down.

Harold wore double-pleated slacks and a windowpane shirt that looked like it came straight from the Sears, Roebuck catalog and was then taken to the tailor for the perfect fit. His hair was naturally soft, and he had a toothpick placed in the side of his mouth.

"Rockstar Rita." Harold eyed her up and down. Also sharply dressed, his boys stopped just behind him.

"Harold," she said dryly.

"I heard you comin' to Lincoln in the fall. My stomping grounds. Happy to show you around." His words slurred just enough to let Ozzie know that he had also had a few tastes.

"Won't be no need." Ozzie put his hands on the table, studying Harold. No man with liquid courage was gonna walk along his block and talk shit to his woman like he wasn't sitting there.

"What you say to me?" Harold finally acknowledged Ozzie's presence.

"I don't stutter."

"Mmmm. I also heard that you volunteered. You know you ain't gonna be much more than the white man's flunky. Don't you?"

Harold looked down his nose at Ozzie like he was scum staining the whitewalls on his father's Cadillac.

Harold's two cronies laughed in unison. It echoed menacingly in Ozzie's head. Rita slid closer. She probably thought the gesture was the best way to diffuse the steam rising between them. But as she touched her elbow with Ozzie's in solidarity, Harold took a bold step forward. Like a man used to getting what he wanted.

"Like I said, Rita—"

"Fall back, partner," Ozzie warned, feeling that *tick-tick* pulsing through his veins. All day he had been fawned on and respected, and he wanted to keep it that way.

"Say, Rita." Harold looked her over again. "What you with that black-ass coon nigga for, anyway?"

Suddenly the music stopped, and Ozzie was out of his seat. "Who you calling a black-ass coon?" They were now nose to nose.

"You the only one out here. So black I can barely see you this late at night. Need to go get my flashlight." Harold laughed and turned to slap hands with the boy next to him, but before their palms touched, Ozzie had punched him in the jaw. Harold stumbled, and his friend put an arm out to keep him from falling.

"Oh my Lord," Rita shouted.

"Whoa," called Uncle Millard, moving quickly between the boys.

One of the women at a nearby table shouted, "Jesus, y'all acting like park apes."

Uncle Millard grabbed Ozzie by the waist, pulling him back and pushing him toward the house. "Somebody get Harold some ice. Ozzie, inside, now."

Ozzie stumbled up the front steps. His knuckles ached, so he pushed the front door open with his elbow. When he glanced back at Rita, she rolled her eyes and stalked away. The disappointment on her face made him feel like the biggest loser in the world. Then he saw his mother, Nettie, charging through the door behind him, and he felt worse.

"I guess it ain't a South Philly party 'til somebody start fighting." Nettie was barely five feet tall, but her voice boomed like she was a giant.

Ozzie trudged behind her through the living room, past the sofa and two armchairs, through the dining area where the table and buffet dominated most of the room, and then back into the flower-wallpapered kitchen.

"What's gotten into you, son?" His mother reached into the icebox and pulled out an aluminum ice cube tray.

"Nothing."

She removed several blocks, then dropped them into a dish towel. "Don't tell me nothing when you out there scraping in the streets like you ain't got good sense. I ain't raise you to be like that."

Ozzie leaned against the sink, wishing the *plink-plink* of the drippy faucet would drown out his mother's tongue-lashing.

"You on your way outta here. What? You need to leave your mark?"

"He was being disrespectful."

"Them white boys in the army gonna be real disrespectful. What you gon' do then?" She grabbed his hand and rested the homemade ice pack on his inflamed knuckles.

"Ouch." He winced.

"Just hold this here till the swelling go down some." She smelled like a combination of sweat and sugar, and despite her ire, her hands were gentle. "Look a here, son." His mother grabbed his chin, forcing him to make eye contact. "Leave that hooch alone. Ain't no good ever come from the bottom of a bottle."

"I didn't even have that much." He wiggled his face away from her and stepped back, clutching the ice. The kitchen was hot enough without her breathing down his neck. It always came to this with his mother. Any bad decisions that he made, she blamed on the liquor. His father had scarred her something good.

Big Otis hadn't been home in months. If his father ambled through the front door at that moment, it wouldn't be without his bottled best friend. Scotch was his poison, but he'd drink whatever he could wrap his fingers around, and Nettie was the one burdened with cleaning up Big Otis's missteps.

Nettie folded her hands to her mouth as if in prayer. "Let me say it like this. You gon' have enough to contend with over in Germany. Leave the booze alone, or that liquor gon' be the death of you, son. You mark my words." She fixed her eyes on him until he sighed, dropping his shoulders in compliance. "Promise me, Ozzie." She looked him deep in the eyes.

Ozzie knew how hard his mother worked to keep food on the table. He had volunteered for the army to make something out of his life but also to make her proud. With Ozzie gone, she'd still have his two younger brothers to clothe and feed. Both of his older sisters had jobs, but the earnings were barely enough to keep the lights on and the rent paid. Ozzie had already planned to send her a portion of his pay, but he knew that him staying away from booze was what would really help her sleep at night, especially with him so far away.

"Okay, Mama. Promise."

"Good." She kissed his cheek. "Go on and get some rest now. Millard's comin' back for you first thing to take you to the train station."

"I'll be up in a minute, Mama."

"Don't forget to lock up," she said, making her way through the narrow house toward the stairs.

By the time Ozzie heard Nettie's bedroom door close, both his anger and his buzz were gone. All he could think about was patching things up with Rita. He was leaving town at first light, and he needed to see her one more time before he left.

When he opened the front door, he saw that in the time he had been inside, all of Ringgold Street had been restored. Tables and chairs put away, cars parked, garbage collected. Tomorrow morning, the women would be out with buckets filled with bleach, scrubbing their front steps, sweeping the sidewalks pristine clean.

Ozzie closed the door quietly behind him and started walking. He had wanted to knock Harold down a size for as long as he could remember. Ozzie was sure now that his message to Harold was crystal-clear: *Leave my girl the hell alone.* Still, he didn't like that Mr. Rich Boy would be up at Lincoln University, breathing the same air as Rita.

An orange-and-white cat darted past him as he ducked into the alley. He stepped over thick patches of weeds, shattered glass, and old cardboard boxes, holding his nose against the smell of piss. When he reached the back of Rita's row house, her second-floor bedroom light was on. Ozzie threw a stone at her window.

A few seconds later, she pulled up the shade and stuck her head out. Her hair was down, and she twisted up her lips in disgust, then closed the window and turned off the light.

This was not how he had envisioned his last night at home. He paced the alley, crunching sticks and debris beneath his feet. Had she gone to sleep? At least ten minutes had passed. He picked up another pebble, but then he heard a click unlocking the back door, followed by her footfalls toward the high wooden fence that stood between them. She unlatched it. "What are you doing here so late?" She folded her arms across her waist.

"I needed to see you."

She was still wearing her sky-blue dress, and it was unbuttoned at her throat. Ozzie yearned to press his lips against that spot right below her ear.

"Why you let your temper get the best of you like that?" she hissed. "You know Harold's daddy is the type to be knocking on your front door with the police, trying to press charges." Her sweet drawl was always more pronounced when she was angry.

"Stop stewing at me, baby, please." He moved in closer and tugged her into his arms. To his surprise, she didn't resist.

"Stop doing stupid things."

"You calling me stupid?" He held her at arm's length.

She widened her eyes. "I said you do stupid things. I'm worried about you."

"I can take care of myself and you."

They took the few steps to the iron patio love seat, and Ozzie tipped her chin and kissed her long and deep, the way he had been pining to all day. Her breath was hot, and it pained him to know that this was the last time he would hold Rita for the nearly four years he'd be away. He ran his hands from her shoulders down to the supple mounds of her breasts. They caressed, necked, and petted, and even though Ozzie knew they had reached that point at which he needed to be a gentleman and pull away, he couldn't make himself stop. Rita put her hands on his chest and pushed him softly. He knew what was coming next. It was time to say good night.

"Come inside," she said, her eyes hooded.

Ozzie could barely control himself from panting out loud as he followed her through the dark kitchen. Rita held his uninjured hand as she led him down the creaky steps to the basement. He had been down here only once, to relight the pilot on the hot-water heater. Tonight the cellar was cool and smelled like freshly laundered sheets and damp cement. A sliver of moonlight pooled through the jalousie window. Against the far wall was a green satiny sofa.

Rita sat him down but didn't look at him as she spoke. "Listen, Ozzie. We haven't talked much about what's coming next."

"What do you mean?" He reached for her hand, but she pushed his away.

"I mean, four years is a long time to be apart. It would be naive of me to expect you to be faithful."

Caught off guard, he shook his head. "What do you mean? I don't want no one else but you."

"Men go away, and they don't come back. Especially in the military."

"Baby, I'm not going to war. My job is to help a country in ruins get back on its feet."

Rita finally looked up at him. "You're embarking on one of the greatest adventures of your life. Most of the dudes around here haven't even been to Atlantic City. This means something, and I want you to be at liberty to live it to the fullest without worrying about me."

The meaning of her words registered, and Ozzie's jaw tightened. "Are you breaking up with me?"

"My mama always said if you love something, set it free. I'm just giving you permission to fly, Oz."

But Ozzie didn't want to live without Rita; she was his axis. When he opened his mouth to protest, she cut him off. "We'll still be friends, and we can write."

"I don't want you to be with anyone else," he hissed.

"Staying together across the globe is an unrealistic expectation on both our parts," she said in a tone that conveyed finality. Rita had never been a woman who minced words, and for every way Ozzie tried to convince her that it could work, she had two counterpoints on why they would fail.

Defeated, he asked, "Why won't you try with me?"

"If we are truly meant to be, we'll find our way back to each other." Her eyes looked sad but decisive. "It's for the best. The last thing I want is to end up resenting you." She leaned in to kiss him.

Ozzie wanted to resist her touch, but he could not. Even as she crushed his heart, she remained his weakness. Their time together was running out.

Rita placed her forehead against his and whispered, "Before you go, I want to give you a goodbye present."

"What's that?" He couldn't think of anything that he wanted more than her.

She gazed into his eyes. "All of me."

Ozzie's stomach quaked. "You sure about this?" His voice came out husky and sounded so needy that he was almost embarrassed.

Rita took his face in her loving hands. "Come on here. Let's have a night that neither one of us will forget."

Ozzie gently lowered her against the sofa. Goose bumps prickled her skin as he peeled away her dress. Then he painstakingly savored every inch of her body, slow and deliberate.

CHAPTER 5

Prince Frederick, MD, September 1965

SOPHIA

Sophia lugged the red plaid Olney train case, stolen from Ma Deary's closet, up the steps from her dugout. For once, she was pleased to hear the rhythmic snores and snorts of Ma Deary and the Old Man. It confirmed that they were dead asleep and made it easier for her to tiptoe out the back door undetected.

She hadn't told the twins she was going away. But she'd squeezed them extra hard before they'd gone to bed last night, reminding them not to skip out on their homework. It was breaking her heart to leave them behind.

The dewy scent of morning greeted her as she crept onto the back porch, and the air was foggy. Careful not to step on anything that would crackle, she trod onto the overgrown path that led to the main road.

"What happened to your hair?" Walter leaned against the white oak tree.

"I dyed it." She fingered the nape of her neck. "You don't like it?"

Walter shrugged. "I liked it just fine before."

As he led her through the grass, Sophia heard a barn owl hissing and screeching, sounding like a terrified woman, and crickets rubbing the edges of their forewings.

"I don't know how you sleep out here," she whispered to Walter. "So creepy."

"The sounds don't bother me none."

But then Sophia thought she heard a rustling coming from behind them, just below the evergreen bush. She held the travel case in her arms like a football. She didn't know if she should hide or run. Her heart seemed to move down into her stomach. It was over. Ma Deary or the Old Man had gotten wind of their plan. They would make Sophia stay and work the farm. When she turned, she braced herself to come face-to-face with one of the grown-ups, but what she saw was a startled fawn.

"Come on." Walter continued.

They hiked a little farther, until they reached the small clearing where he had hidden Ma Deary's Rambler.

"How in the world did you get the car all the way out here?" Sophia asked, placing the train case in the backseat.

"I pushed it in neutral so that the engine wouldn't wake the house."

"All by yourself?"

He stretched his arms above his head, then cranked the engine. "You owe me."

Sophia settled in her seat, filled with gratitude for her older brother. She had never felt much tenderness from Ma Deary, not even as a child. When she fell, it was always Walter who picked her up and bandaged scraped knees.

They pulled onto the main road. Ma Deary's car smelled like her lily-of-the-valley perfume. "You sure you know how to get to the school?"

"I studied the Old Man's map last night." Walter rolled his window down a crack for fresh air. Sophia looked over at the gas gauge and thanked her lucky stars that it was Tuesday. The Old Man had a ritual. He filled up both cars and the tractors every Sunday night. The Rambler had close to a full tank.

The morning was well underway when the Rambler coasted through the wrought-iron gates welcoming them to West Oak Forest Academy. The lawns on either side of the road were so manicured, they looked like thick carpet. As they drove through the circular roundabout, Walter let out a long whistle between his teeth, pointing out the fleet of expensive cars: Ford Thunderbird, Mustang, Jaguar, Plymouth Barracuda, Buick Riviera. "You're going to school with some fancy folks, Rusty."

The grounds were green, wide, and expansive beyond what her eye could see. "This place looks bigger than our entire county."

"I doubt that. But it does sit on one hundred and seventy acres of land," she said, quoting from the brochure.

The pea-size knot that had been in her belly when she woke had grown to the size of a beefsteak tomato. Her mind had taken up a steady chant. Ma Deary was right. She wouldn't be able to keep up. Why hadn't she listened? She should have been feeding the hens and pulling the eggs, milking the cows, and preparing breakfast for the twins.

"We should turn back," she said, panicked. "Stop the car. Please, Walter! Let's go home."

Walter had located the administrative building at the center of campus. It was distinguished by white columns and a grand double staircase.

"Seriously, Walt. I'm not kidding." Sophia grabbed her stomach. She hadn't eaten anything for breakfast, but she could feel the bubble of bile coming up. "I don't think I can do this."

Her brother pulled into the parking lot and killed the engine. "Rusty, listen to me. You belong here. And it's not because you dyed your red hair black."

"I can't do this," she insisted.

"Opportunities like this come up for kids like us once in a lifetime. If you go home, they might not open this door for the next Negro from Prince Frederick."

"I'm overwhelmed. It's too much."

"Look at me."

Sophia turned in her seat.

"You are Sophia Clark. You have earned this. Now go. 'Cause I'm not taking an ass beating for nothing." He pressed a dollar bill in her hand, leaned across her seat, and pushed her door open.

She knew her brother was right. They had come too far for her to turn back. "Can you at least walk me in?"

"Not in my overalls, Rusty. I don't want to make you look like a country bumpkin. Now go on, get." He gave her his gap-toothed smile.

Sophia carried her bag up the formidable stone staircase, looking around to see if anyone was watching her. There was a squat Negro man trimming the hedges, but he was focused on the task at hand. She pushed the double doors open and stepped into the cool lobby, following the sign to the administrative office. Behind the desk sat a pale woman with tendrils curled around her ear.

"Can I help you?" She took in Sophia with her thin lips set.

"Yes." Sophia's voice squeaked. "I'm Sophia Clark. A new student here." She held out the papers that Mrs. Brown had given her. Last night Sophia had forged Ma Deary's signature.

The woman silently picked Sophia apart with her blue eyes before accepting the paperwork. "You from that program? The Prosser Foundation?"

"Yes, ma'am. Tenth grade. I've just arrived."

"Don't you have any parents?" the woman said, looking past Sophia.

"They work in D.C. and just dropped me off to get ahead of traffic," she said, repeating the lie that she and Walter had concocted.

"Where's your birth certificate?"

Sophia paused. Mrs. Brown hadn't told her to bring it.

"You're not supposed to start school without a birth certificate," the woman said.

Sophia stuttered. "I . . . must have . . . left it in my mother's car."

The woman wheeled her chair to the file cabinet behind her. She spun around, thumbing through the second drawer. What if she told Sophia she had to go back home? She was sure Walter had left. The woman turned toward her desk with a sheet of paper that she pushed toward Sophia.

"We need that birth certificate, but I'm going to go ahead and let you get settled. Here's your room assignment and your class schedule."

The woman looked over at a young brunette with white ribbons in her hair, standing against the wall. "Patty, will you show Sophia to the W5 dormitory?"

Patty shook her head violently. "No, ma'am. My parents told me I cannot talk to any of the Negro students."

The woman pursed her lips in a way that conveyed to Sophia that she was satisfied with Patty's answer. She pointed. "Well, if you go down the steps and make a right, you'll come to a path. Walk past the tennis courts, and on the other side of the pool, you'll see a big bush. Then go to the left, and the dorms will be right there. Can't miss it. Big old brick building. Room 202." The woman said this loudly, like Sophia was hard of hearing.

"Thank you," Sophia said. She walked back to the door, where she had strategically left her train case out of sight because it was tattered and the handle frayed. As she moved through the double doors, she heard the woman mutter, "God help us. The founding fathers must be rolling over in their graves with all this desegregation stuff. Just doesn't make sense."

The directions were so awful that, by the time she finally located the dormitory, sweat had stained her only white blouse. Ma Deary's platform Mary Janes clicked loudly against the porcelain-tiled floor. As Sophia read the numbers on the doors, she could still smell manure on her despite her water-bucket bath. She felt the grime of dirt underneath her fingernails, even though she had used a piece of cardboard to clean-pick them on the drive over. The farm was not easy to wash off. It was like a bloodstain. She could blot it, but it never quite went away.

According to the numbers, she had made it to the correct floor. Room number 202 was the last one on the right. Now that she was standing in front of the brown wooden door, she wondered what to do next. Should she knock or just open it? She decided to do both and rapped twice while turning the knob. The door scratched against the floor, and the hinges creaked. The room was sunlit, spacious, and smelled of lavender. On the left was a bed made with blankets folded and tucked neatly around the edges of the mattress.

"Hello," Sophia called.

On the right was a shapely girl stretched out on the bed, clutching a book. Her wavy hair was neatly parted down the middle and gathered in two ponytails. When she saw Sophia, she swung her feet around and sat up.

"Hi. I think we are roommates?" Sophia made it sound like a question, but it was most definitely a statement. Her name was tacked to the door.

"It's nice to make your acquaintance," the girl said formally. Then she stood, wiped her hand on her dark gray skirt, and stuck out her hand. "I'm Wilhelmina Pride, but my friends call me Willa."

Her palm was as soft as cotton, and Sophia was painfully aware of how callused and dry her hand must have felt in comparison. "Nice to meet you, Willa. I'm Sophia Clark." She opened her mouth to say her friends called her Rusty. But that wasn't true. Now, with her new black hair, at her new school, she would be known only as Sophia.

Even though Sophia stood in her best skirt and blouse, she paled next to her new roommate. Wilhelmina had startling green eyes and looked well kept. Even in the drab school uniform, she still looked like well-to-do was her everyday attire.

"Are you a freshman?" Willa asked, breaking the silence.

"No, sophomore."

"You do realize that you've already missed the welcome parties and the first two days of class? Did you have a long way to travel?"

"Sort of." Sophia couldn't tell the truth of why she'd arrived late and was glad when Willa changed the subject.

"Well, I've been hiding out here during my free period because some of these white people are positively crazy. Lunch is at eleven-thirty if you are hungry. Have you received your schedule?"

Sophia pulled it from her bag and offered it over.

Willa scrunched her nose. "We don't have any classes together, but let's meet at the foot of the girls' building and walk to dinner together, and I'll introduce you to the others."

"What do you mean?"

"The other Negro students. There are five of us in total."

"On this whole gigantic campus?"

Willa nodded. "They didn't tell you?"

"Tell me what?"

"We are the first Negro girls to ever attend Forest. The boys started last year." Willa slipped into her leather saddle shoes. "Since I have arrived, I've been feeling like Rosa Parks." She smirked. "But as my mother says, the first must open the doors for the next."

"Do you know where I can find my uniform?"

"It's in the top of your closet. If it doesn't fit, you'll have to go back to the administrative office for an exchange."

"Thank you." Sophia stood.

"I need to stop by the library before my next class. I'll see you at dinner." The door closed with a click.

Sophia sat down on her bed gingerly, afraid of messing it up. Her brain was on overload, trying to understand all that she had done in just a few hours. She had moved from one end of the state to the other without parental consent. Forged her way into Forest. Had Willa said they were the first Negro girls to attend the school?

Sophia and her brothers had sat around their black-and-white television about five years before, watching a little girl named Ruby Bridges being escorted to elementary school by federal marshals. Watching this take place on television was one thing, but Sophia didn't consider herself a front-liner. She had come here to get away from the farm, not to break barriers. To receive an education so that she could grow up and work in an office. She was barely strong enough to keep the twins from ripping each other's hair out. And what was she going to do about getting her birth certificate?

As she rose to unpack her suitcase, she tried not to worry about any of it. Though there was one nagging thought that wouldn't leave her mind: Ma Deary would be waking up soon. Once she found out that Sophia had escaped, would she drive to the campus and demand that she return home?

CHAPTER 6

Philadelphia, PA, May 1948

OZZIE

Ozzie could still smell Rita's honeysuckle scent on his fingers from the night before, and the knowledge that she no longer belonged to him hurt like an open wound. When he'd told her that he didn't want to picture her with anyone else, she'd replied, "Then don't think about it," as she had nestled her head in the crook of his arm and their warm bodies lay tangled. "Whatever happens in Germany, just leave it there. If we find our way back to each other, it'll be with a fresh start."

Ozzie chewed his lip at the memory as he let the music on the car radio wash over him. Uncle Millard was driving his Vagabond-blue Oldsmobile down Dickenson Street. As he turned left onto South Broad Street, Count Basie's "One O'Clock Jump" came over the AM station WHAT. His radio system was so sophisticated that when he hit a small pothole, the station stayed put. Uncle Millard reached for the knob and turned the radio down low.

"I was listening to that," Ozzie said.

"I ever tell you how I came up to Philly?" Uncle Millard spoke at the same volume whether he was indoors or out: loud.

Ozzie stayed quiet. He knew Uncle Millard didn't expect an answer, because whether he'd told him before or not was irrelevant.

"You know that redneck down in the country who took advantage of your mama, putting Sissy in her belly?"

Ozzie ground his teeth. Mama didn't talk about that. What they also didn't talk about was how his older sister, Sissy, left the house most mornings before dawn to travel by foot, bus, and trolley two hours from the belly of South Philly to her job at Strawbridge, a department store on Old York Road nearly to Jenkintown. Sissy with her milky skin worked in the ladies' hat department, which, despite grumbling from the NAACP and other civil rights organizations, had a strict policy for their workers: white women only. If her manager only knew the rest of their family.

"Well, I stabbed him."

Ozzie turned to look at his uncle. Uncle Millard was one of the coolest men in the family. Smooth toasted-brown skin, pearly white teeth, and hair conked like Nat King Cole's. He drove with one hand on the steering wheel, the other dangling a Pall Mall.

"Went into a blind rage the moment I found your mama crying, lip busted, with her dress torn. Killed the bastard on his own front porch. Before his body stopped shaking, I had cut through the woods and hopped the train to Philly." Uncle Millard tapped the ashes of his cigarette in the ashtray.

"You jiving."

"Serious as a heart attack." He rocked his head. "Shit. I was so scared that I left my damn knife in him."

"Evidence?" Ozzie said, wide-eyed.

"Yeah, but more importantly"—Uncle Millard took a drag—"it was the best knife I ever owned. A Fairbairn-Sykes commando knife. Won it off some dude in a game of poker. She was a beauty too. Double-edged stiletto, and I used to wear it strapped to my left ankle." His face lit up like he was talking about his woman. "Anyway, I was on the next thing smokin'. Got up here and changed my name. Been on the run for damn near twenty years. Always watching my back."

They had reached the Philadelphia & Reading Terminal Railroad Station, and Uncle Millard pulled to the curb at the corner of Eleventh and Market. The front of the station was noisy with pedestrians.

"I never knew that." Ozzie turned in his seat.

"You don't want that life, youngblood. You gon' over to Germany to make something out of yourself. Don't let that temper of yourn get the best of you, like it did last night."

There it was again. Everyone was worried about his temper. "I hear you."

Uncle Millard got out of the car and unlocked the trunk. He rounded Ozzie's side of the car with his B4 U.S. Army–issued garment bag. "Osbourne Philips" was stamped in black with his serial number. When the bag had arrived, Ozzie could tell that it had been used previously, because he could see the traces of the name Luke under his, and one of the inside zippers was jammed.

"Do you? 'Cause I ain't trying to lose you to no bullshit. Promise me you'll keep your head."

"I will, don't worry about me," Ozzie offered, and then they clapped hands before Uncle Millard pulled him into a tight hug.

Ozzie started for the train station. When he reached the gold framed doors, he turned. "Uncle Millard? What's your real name?"

"Awwww, nephew, if I told you, then I'd have to kill you." He winked and then slid back behind the wheel of his car, tooted his horn twice, and pulled off.

Ozzie spent the next several weeks in basic training at Fort Dix near Trenton, New Jersey. When he completed his training, he was put on a bus and driven to the New York Port of Embarkation. When he arrived at the ship, it teemed with hundreds of troops reporting to duty. Everyone looked young, most barely out of high school. Ozzie noticed that some of the men's faces were flushed with excitement and adventure, while others looked worried and homesick, even though they were still on American soil. Ozzie felt somewhere in between. He knew that he wasn't going to Germany to fight; World War II had ended nearly three years prior, so he wasn't overly concerned with dying. But it was the first time in his life that he'd be all alone, no family, no friends, no Rita, living abroad, so far from everything that was familiar to him.

Despite his best efforts at studying the German-language book that his favorite English teacher had secured for him, he was worried about the language barrier, the taste of food, and what his living conditions would be as a Negro man stationed in the U.S. Army abroad. Ozzie understood Uncle Millard's warning, and though he was going to Germany with the intention of behaving, he also had the expectation of being treated civilly.

"Step up," called out a thin-nosed sailor. "Keep moving."

There were two lines, one for the white troops and a separate one for the Negroes. The fishy fragrance of the Hudson River was amplified by the heat of the day. The troops were all dressed in their khaki cotton summer uniform and low-quarter shoes. Ozzie could feel sweat trickling from his head to the collar of his shirt as he walked up the gangplank with his B4 bag in one hand and his M1 olive helmet in the other. The boxed lunch he had wolfed down on the ride made him feel queasy, and Ozzie knew that it was more nerves than indigestion.

As the troops filed onto the massive ship, they were met with navy personnel who checked off their names and called out their enlisted berth information. The ship was confusing, with compartments and passageways going in every direction. As Ozzie moved with a group of men, he could hear the hissing sound of steam, pipes rattling, and machinery grinding then halting, grinding then halting. After getting turned around, Ozzie found the narrow hall and then took the ladder down to the mess hall, as instructed. There the men were met by a Negro man wearing oval glasses.

"Welcome home, soldiers," he said.

Ozzie looked around the tight mess hall, which had tables and chairs and very little walking space.

"I'm Sergeant First Class Marshall, your platoon sergeant. I know it isn't ideal, but because the ship is over capacity, this will be your home for the next two and a half weeks."

"'Scuse me, Sergeant Marshall, but where we supposed to sleep?" asked the string-bean-shaped man standing next to Ozzie.

Sergeant Marshall pointed to the racks above the table. "Let me show you how this works," he said, then motioned to the ten men who had gathered to help with pushing the tables back and folding the benches. He then pulled on a chain that dropped down racks along the wall, each stacked three bunks high, with very little space in between. The sleeping racks were held up by white posts and metal chains. The cots were metal frames with stretched canvas.

Sergeant Marshall pointed to a pile in the corner and instructed each man to pick up a white sheet and a coarse blanket. "There are twenty bosun's lockers. You have six cubic feet of storage for everything that you own. When we run out, which we will, the remaining men can use seabags as storage."

The mess deck, converted into a berth for the Negro soldiers, was cramped and far smaller than the images Ozzie had seen in the recruitment office. He couldn't help but wonder how much more spacious the white soldiers' quarters were. He counted the racks. There were eleven suspended on metal chains with three bunks each. He'd be sharing the mess hall with thirty-three other men. The space was long but not very wide. Men started claiming their racks, and Ozzie moved through to the closest rack and claimed the top bunk. He could see that the bottom bunks hung right above the folded tables and would feel like sleeping in a coffin. Ozzie had slept in a two-bedroom house with his family of six, seven on the rare occasions when his father made it home. But no matter how tight it got, they were family. Already, he could smell the ripeness of men who had traveled on crowded buses and trains with no air-conditioning.

"First meal is at zero six hundred, so that means you need to be up and your racks stowed by zero five," Sergeant Marshall said. "Once you are settled, you may go to the weather deck. The colored section is marked." Marshall turned and made his way back up the ladder.

After Ozzie stowed his belongings in his locker, he then moved his body sideways and squirmed past the men to the ladder. On the deck above the mess hall, he found the head. Two wash basins, two shower stalls, one urinal, and one seated toilet for all thirty-three Negro men. They had just boarded, and already he could smell that the latrines needed ammonia and bleach.

Up on the weather deck, Ozzie found the rows of wooden benches marked "Coloreds Only" and dutifully took a seat. The clouds streaked through the open sky, and fresh air gave him a small sense of peace. As he pulled a canteen of water from his waist, his thoughts drifted back to Rita. He wondered what she was doing and if she'd be true to her word and write him a letter. Ozzie was so preoccupied, he had not noticed the three leggy women until they were blocking the setting sun.

"These seats taken?"

Ozzie inhaled a whiff of talcum powder and wondered how the women had managed to smell so good on a ship that already smelled funky. "No, help yourself," he said, gesturing.

The three women chattered on, but Ozzie could feel their eyes darting back and forth between one another and him.

"Where you from, soldier?" asked one of the women, leaning forward. She wore an Army Nurse Corps cap over big curls.

"South Philly."

"I'm from Baltimore. My name is Clara Thompson, and these are my fellow nurses, Della and Celestine."

The three women were various hues of brown, with Clara's skin being the richest, a velvety sepia tone. She had deep-set eyes, and he couldn't help but notice how they danced when she smiled.

"Ozzie Philips," he introduced himself as two of the men from his berth walked over to them.

"Thomas Morgan. Pleased to meet you ladies," one man said, waving. Morgan had a stocky frame, as if he had played running back in high school. Melvin Thornton nodded hello while shuffling a deck of cards.

Before Ozzie knew it, the men and women were exchanging Negro geography. Who grew up where. Whose family knew whom. Then they heard the loud blast of the ship's horn and felt the slow motion of the ship drifting away from the port. As they sailed away from America, from everything that they had all known, Ozzie watched a band of seagulls soar into the air. He tilted his face to the clouds, breathing in the salty scent of freedom.

CHAPTER 7

Mannheim, Germany, April 1951

ETHEL

Ethel smoothed her white gloves against her Peter Pan collar and then made sure her Jelly Belly tropical bird pin had not shifted from where she had placed it over her heart. As she pressed the doorbell to Dorothy Hansen's home, she glanced at the handwritten invitation, having the sudden need to confirm that the tea party's theme was indeed birds. When she did, she noticed for the first time that the tea had started at two o'clock. She turned her gold Bulova watch. She was thirty minutes late. Ethel was never late, but recently she'd had a hard time getting out of bed. Menial tasks like the dishes and vacuuming had been taking her longer than usual to complete. She just could not muster the energy. Was lethargy a symptom of pregnancy?

The wooden door swung open, and Dorothy Hansen greeted her with a toothy smile. "Ethel!" She wore a red gingham dress with large pockets, her hair pulled back tight into a ponytail.

Ethel followed Dorothy past the coat rack and through the foyer. Dorothy's four-bedroom house was the most spacious living quarters that Ethel had seen since arriving in Mannheim, and it was twice the size of her home with Bert. Dorothy had two school-age children, and as Ethel passed fingerprint paintings, "I love you Mommy" drawings, "Mathematician of the Year," and "Student of the Month" certificates pinned to a corkboard in the hallway, her daily longing for children fluttered inside of her. Her menstrual cycle was one day late.

The living room was airy, with two curry-colored sofas and a matching recliner. A few folding chairs were threaded in between. There were about ten army wives seated, all wearing jewelry or clothing that highlighted the bird theme. A few of the women, Ethel had traveled with on excursions to Frankfurt and Munich.

Dorothy Hansen had been arranging monthly teas, luncheons, and socials so that the wives of the higher-ranked husbands could get together to discuss books and charity work, and brainstorm on different ways they could be useful to the army and their husbands while living abroad. Today's tea was being held to discuss ideas on how to uplift and support the Women's Army Corps, and as Ethel crossed the room to sit beside Julia Jones, the only other Negro wife invited, she tried to follow the conversation already in progress.

"We all have a role to play while here. We must make ourselves useful."

"God did not bring us this far just to do the shopping and ironing. We could do that back home."

"The WAC needs our support."

"Especially the Negro WAC, who have the humiliating job of caring for the prisoners of war. We need to do something that will raise their morale," said Julia Jones while throwing her two-month-old baby girl over her shoulder, tapping her back lightly. Two other women had small children on their laps. Three toddlers played blocks on the carpet.

Ethel waved hello and apologized for being late as she took her seat. One of the few women who hadn't come around to the idea of mixed company at these teas scooted her chair a bit more into the corner, away from Ethel and Julia. Ethel ignored her.

In addition to being in this group, Ethel and Julia had started the Negro wives of Mannheim, which met on the second Friday of each month. Those women's meetings were a social space where the Negro wives could relax, discuss issues that pertained to their families, and form community. Most of those women's husbands were privates or first-class privates, and they looked to Ethel and Julia, whose husbands were chief warrant officers, for guidance on how to navigate living abroad.

Dorothy came around with a platter of cucumber sandwiches, scones, tea cakes, biscuits, and jam. Ethel didn't have much of an appetite. But to be polite, she took a sandwich. While sipping her black tea, she felt something wet slip between her legs and frowned.

"I'll be right back," she said to Julia, then excused herself down the short hall to the powder room just off the kitchen. As she closed the bathroom door, one of the children started to wail. Ethel pulled away her layers and wiped. The sight of the crimson streak staining the toilet tissue made her gag.

She was not pregnant. Again.

It had been a full nine months since she had visited the shrine at Lourdes, and she had thought that her stomach would be full by now. Ethel had been faithful. She had prayed her rosary beads, read Scriptures, fasted, doused her belly with holy water, and asked the Virgin daily to bless her womb and make her fruitful. But Old Lady Flo had found her again and again. In this moment, Ethel didn't know if it was the presence of so many children in Dorothy's home, but she felt tears prick her eyes.

Suddenly she didn't have the strength to return to the women, but staying in the bathroom too long would be impolite. Ethel pulled herself together, padded a handful of tissues between her legs, tucked her blouse in her pencil skirt, splashed cold water on her face, and pinched her cheeks. When she entered the living room, the talk had veered away from the WAC to the accomplishments of the school-age children. Ethel just couldn't sit through it all again. She looked around for Dorothy but didn't see her.

"I need to leave, female problems," she leaned in and whispered to Julia.

"I'm sure Dorothy has a belt she can lend you."

Ethel put her hand to her chest and whispered, "I'm just not feeling well."

"You were already tardy. Now you're going to leave me here with them alone," Julia hissed while rocking the baby. Ethel knew how Julia felt but would have to make it up to her.

"I'm sorry, but I'm so nauseated. Please give my apologies to Dorothy, and I'll call you later. Promise." Ethel squeezed Julia's knee, picked up her wooden box purse, and scurried for the door.

Ethel hastened away from Dorothy's with the thought of going back to her unit apartment, throwing a blanket over herself, and curling up in a ball. But she could not let herself sink into the clutches of another dark hole. She had done that twice in the past six months, and it had worried her sweet husband when he could not lift her from the gloom.

Ethel had never shared her plans for a miracle baby with Bert. When they had started dating, she had revealed her illness and shortcoming with him. It was her second marriage, and she didn't want any unnecessary misunderstanding between them. After her revelation, Bert kissed her hands and spoke. "Just be my faithful wife, and I'll die a happy man."

The sentiment, while sweet, never completely soothed her. It was Ethel who wanted more, and she could not understand what she had done to make God so angry that He would withhold something so crucial as motherhood. Ethel was such a good person. She was faithful. Always put others' needs before hers and had a big heart. She gave of herself because she had lots to offer. Wasn't that the vision she had received? So why was she still unable to heal her womb and carry a child? It felt like the worst of punishments.

The tears stung her cheeks. She walked and wandered, and by the time she took stock of where she was going, she realized that she had marched in the wrong direction. In some parts of Mannheim, all the tiny streets looked the same. Ethel could not read many words in German, so she often relied on landmarks to get her from one place to another. On this walk, nothing was recognizable.

The wind blew, ruffling her candy straw hat, and as Ethel reached up to make sure her pins remained in place, she saw two Catholic nuns dressed in long black robes across the street. They were sandwiching a thin line of eight or nine little children holding hands. The sight of them stilled her. Ethel craned her neck to see into the faces of the sweet little boys and girls, noticing right away that their complexions ranged in color from sand to storm.

They were Negro children.

Without thinking, Ethel started following them from her side of the road. After about five minutes, she crossed the cobblestone road to walk directly behind them. She fell in step with the shorter of the two nuns, who took up the rear, tasked with guarding the children from behind.

"Sprichst du Englisch?" Ethel asked. It was the first phrase that she had learned and the one she used most often. The short nun pointed to the taller nun at the front of the line.

"Danke." Ethel's heart galloped as she slipped quickly past the children's miniature faces to the front of the pack, where she walked alongside the older nun, who held her head up like the person in charge.

"Sprichst du Englisch?"

"Yes, I speak English."

"Hello. My name is Ethel Gathers."

"Hello, Ethel. I'm Sister Ursula. Do you live nearby?"

"I'm not sure. I seem to have lost my way."

"Do you need help?"

"I'm all right. Where are you going with these children?"

"We are the sisters of St. Hildegard and live just up ahead. You are welcome to come with us."

Sister Ursula reached for Ethel's hand, sending a calm wave through her entire body. After a few more steps, Sister Ursula turned down a small alley and pulled a key from her robe, unlocking a metal gate. It squeaked and moaned as she pushed it open and ushered the children through.

"Eins, zwei, drei," she counted out loud until she got to eight. The shorter nun locked the gate behind them and then said something in German that must have translated into "Go play," because the kids scattered throughout the courtyard, roughhousing with one another and laughing. The sounds of their return brought more children into the courtyard from inside the two stone buildings. A younger nun rolled a baby pram out, and Ethel watched her sit with three smaller ones underneath a wide-branched tree. Some of the children wore tattered clothing. Most were dressed in items too big or too small, and none of their outfits had been paired in a way that suggested anything beyond necessity. A few went barefoot, but most wore sandals or badly scuffed shoes.

Ethel watched, speechless. Sister Ursula had gone off and returned with a glass of water, which she offered to Ethel.

"What is this place?"

Sister Ursula had intense eyes, and a gray strand of hair had come loose from her habit. "This is St. Hildegard's children's home. We take in the orphans who have been left behind."

"Left behind by whom?"

"Whomever. The war was difficult on many."

Ethel looked around and then back at the nun. "All of the children appear to be mixed-race."

Sister Ursula nodded. "It is unfortunate, but some of the American fathers have moved on, and the German women cannot always keep their children."

"Why not?" Ethel touched her stomach. She had known about Negro soldiers taking up with German women, even seen a few mothers with brown-skinned babies in the streets, but she hadn't known they were being abandoned.

"The mothers lack the support they need to raise these children. Most lose their jobs once their situation is known and they had some privileges revoked."

"What a shame."

"We do all that we can to care for them." Sister Ursula motioned for Ethel to follow her.

"My husband is an officer. He told me that when Negro soldiers apply for permission to marry German women, the U.S. military almost always denies it."

"I wish the two countries could work together and put the welfare of the children first. It's having a devastating effect on all of us."

Ethel stood beside Sister Ursula. Two boys about ten years old tossed a baseball. A boy and girl held hands while peering at her quizzically. The children all looked clean and fed, but many of the little girls' hair looked matted and uncombed. Ethel felt the urge to scoop each one up in her arms.

Instantly, Ethel heard, *You have much to offer others.* Could this be it? Was it her calling to aid these forgotten children? Ethel had worked at a beauty parlor to pay her way through college. She had not worked as a beautician in many years, but it was a skill she could put to good use now.

"Sister Ursula. I am stationed with my husband near the new Benjamin Franklin Village. Would it be possible for me to volunteer and help with the children?"

Sister Ursula's blue eyes glowed. "We are always looking for volunteers."

"Wonderful. I will return tomorrow morning."

"We look forward to it." Sister Ursula touched Ethel's hand in gratitude, and Ethel felt a wave of tranquility pass through her body again. She left the orphanage with such a lightness that it did not dawn on her until she had walked several blocks that she had no idea how to get back home.

CHAPTER 8

The Atlantic Ocean, August 1948

OZZIE

Heat pulsed beneath Ozzie's skin as his upper body flashed into a cold sweat. Another wave of pressure from his stomach traveled up through his esophagus. He reached for his emesis bag and retched out chunks of pink. It was the tomato soup that someone from the mess hall had delivered to him in the infirmary, and in its regurgitated state, it stank.

The metal door creaked open. Ozzie heard footsteps and then felt cool hands on his forehead.

"They've got you men crammed in here like pigs in a stall." She tsked her teeth.

Ozzie looked up and saw Clara Thompson, the nurse he had met on his first day at sea, peering down at him. His breath tasted pungent, so he didn't open his mouth to speak. The small room had been like a hot pot marinating the funk of the five sick men and their waste, but Clara moved from touching him to the next man, seemingly unbothered by the heat or smell.

After a quick round, she returned to Ozzie. "Brought you some raw ginger. Chew on this awhile, and then I'm going to give you some tea."

Ozzie had been curled up on the bottom bunk and wanted to sit up straight, but his stomach curdled when he moved. He hated to appear weak and downtrodden in front of a woman he vaguely knew. But when he tried to rise, Clara put her hand on his shoulder and then eased him back onto his stiff pillow.

"My mama used to say a hard head makes a soft behind. Now let me do my work, soldier."

She stood watch as Ozzie eased the square piece of ginger into his mouth. It tasted spicy and felt like straw between his teeth. The ginger burned the back of his throat when he swallowed, and the taste of it lingered on his tongue and opened his nostrils. Clara passed out raw cubes to the other four men in the tiny infirmary and then poured tin cups of water for each of them. While they chewed, she took away their emesis bags and returned with new ones.

She knelt before Ozzie with a cool cloth and wiped his brows, face, chin, and neck. After taking his temperature, she checked his pulse and then pressed her stethoscope to his chest and listened to his heart.

"Am I still alive?" Ozzie whispered out the side of his mouth, hoping the ginger improved his breath.

"Barely." She grinned. "But I won't let you die even if you do suck at tunk." They had played cards up on the weather deck before he had fallen ill.

"Backgammon is more my game," Ozzie managed.

"I think what you need is some fresh air."

"How long have I been down here?"

"Three days, which is long enough. Now chew on that ginger. I worked hard getting it away from the men in the kitchen."

Clara stood and once again moved from patient to patient, checking vitals. From his bottom cot, Ozzie couldn't help noticing her hips move beneath her wool army skirt. Watching her made him think of Rita, and what he wouldn't give to have her curled up beside him, making it all better.

"I'll be back in the morning," she whispered to Ozzie. "If your emesis bag is empty, I'll get you up on deck. The air will do the rest; now, keep chewing the ginger." She pressed a pill in his hand. "Take this in about an hour. It should do the trick."

Ozzie didn't remember much after taking the pill Clara gave him because it knocked him out cold. He wasn't sure how much time passed before he heard the door open, and in breezed a whiff of Clara's powdery scent.

"Rise and shine, soldiers," she called.

Clara went through the nurse's formality of checking each man's vitals and giving out ginger and tablets of medication. She saved Ozzie for last. With a hand on his forehead, she declared, "Fever is gone. Let's go get some air."

Ozzie felt steadier on his feet than he had in days. After a stop in the washroom to freshen up, he followed Clara down the corridor and up the stairs to the main deck. The blast of air felt good as he made his way to a bench where two men from his berth sat with their water canteens. One tipped his hat. Ozzie took a deep inhale of the salty air. The blue sea was wide and expansive and stretched farther than his eyes could take in.

"See what you've been missing? It's breathtaking, isn't it?" Clara pushed a loose curl from her eye.

Once they were seated, Clara pulled out some dry toast wrapped in waxed paper. "Chew it slowly," she instructed.

The air moved through him like magic.

"Is this your first time on a ship?"

He nodded. "You?"

"No. I've been to England and France."

"Really?" Ozzie swallowed the bread. "What'd you do over there?"

"I served with the Six Triple Eight Central Postal Directory Battalion. Our mission was to clear a two-year backlog of mail for American soldiers stationed in Europe."

"Ah, I read about you ladies in *The Philadelphia Tribune*."

"Really?" She beamed.

"Lucky me." He put his hand over his heart. "A Women's Army Corps handpicked by Mary McLeod Bethune has nursed me back to health."

Clara smiled even brighter. "So you do know about us."

"Sure do," he said. Leaning back on his elbows, Ozzie asked, "What was the hardest part for you?"

Clara looked up at the sky. "The work conditions were awful. The warehouse where we sorted was often unheated and the lighting poor. But I'd say the worst was returning mail addressed to soldiers killed in the line of duty. No one ever wanted that job."

"How long were you stationed out there?"

"I left home in January '45 and returned in spring '46. When I got back, I enrolled in nursing school. Now I'm returning to Europe as a WAC nurse."

Ozzie stretched his legs in front of him. "All I keep thinking about is all those white people in one place."

"They are far nicer than the ones on this ship. Trust me."

"I just really want a job that makes a difference," Ozzie confessed.

"What is it that you want to do?"

"Intelligence. Gotta brain for strategy and logic."

Clara looked him over. He saw something in her eyes that suggested she knew something he didn't. "Just be careful. There is a lot of freedom in Europe, but don't forget who you are."

When the ship arrived in Bremerhaven, Germany, Ozzie had been at sea for eighteen long days. It took over two hours to disembark all the soldiers with their possessions. He had lost sight of Clara in the shuffle and regretted that he hadn't said a proper goodbye.

"Man, I have never felt so happy to feel solid ground." Morgan stomped his feet.

"I could kiss the cement," replied Thornton.

Ozzie shoved his bag over his shoulder. Already he missed Rita, despite their breakup, and the familiar rhythms of his life in South Philly. "I just hope the journey was worth it."

"Shiiit. I come from the Mississippi Delta, and anything here is better than being down there," Thornton said matter-of-factly.

It was dark out, and a salty breeze gently whipped at the back of Ozzie's neck. His uniform felt soggy and was in desperate need of a wash.

Sergeant Marshall walked several paces in front of the men, then turned to face them, calling, "Fall in!"

The thirty-three men in Ozzie's platoon took their place in the accountability formation, lined up by squad, facing Sergeant Marshall and waiting for his next order.

"Parade!" shouted Sergeant Marshall. "Rest!" The platoon snapped from the position of attention to listen to their platoon sergeant's orders.

"We are heading to Kitzingen, just south of Würzburg, to the basic training facility for Negro troops. There you will receive orientation and training before being dispatched to duty. Grab your equipment and follow me to the bus. Platoon, atten-SHUN! Fall out."

The soldiers broke from their ranks, and Marshall led the way to a fleet of service buses. He located their bus, and the soldiers filed onto the vehicle, stuffing their bags on the rack overhead and beneath their feet.

Ozzie found a window seat. As the bus pulled away from the dock, the men started off with rowdy chatter, but after a long stretch on the autobahn, the motion of the ride lulled most of them to sleep. Ozzie had been snoozing deeply when he was yanked back by Sergeant Marshall's voice shouting "good morning" and prompting them to look out the window.

As they drove through the center of town, Ozzie watched the locals walking along the streets. Many had sullen eyes, and he saw kids in shabby clothes who were so skinny and frail that they looked as if a heavy wind would be the end of them. As the bus slowed near a footbridge, people brightened and waved their hats in the air. A few shouted, "*Willkommen!*"

"They are welcoming us." Marshall waved back, and a few others did the same. Ozzie held up his hand and waved too.

Morgan whistled. "Man, I can't wait to get to know some of these honeys."

"Yes, Lawd. I heard the girls here hunger for that Coca-Cola in their ice cream." Thorton slapped Morgan five, and several of the men chimed in with more bravado.

As the testosterone-charged conversation revved, all Ozzie could hear was his mother's final warning: *Don't you go over there messin' with no white women. Ain't nothing on the other side of that but the devil's luck.*

The bus slowed at the mouth of the military base. There were two military police stationed at the gate, and after a few words with the driver, the gates opened and the bus drove through.

"Welcome to the Kitzingen Basic Training Center for Negro Troops. We are the spark plug of the entire Negro population in the European Command," Sergeant Marshall said, pride gleaming from his face. "Now, let's get you gentlemen settled so we can show them what we can do."

The sleeping arrangements were one long open bay-style room with several bunks, a far better arrangement than what Ozzie had on the ship. Once the men had unpacked their things, Marshall gave them a tour of the facility. They went through the Army Education Center, the Kitzingen library, the tailor shop, Tent City—which housed the telephone switchboards and all communications—the chapel that held both Protestant and Catholic services, and the basketball courts. They ended the tour at the rifle range.

"This is what I'm talking about. When do we get our weapons?" one man asked, pulling an imaginary trigger before blowing away pretend smoke.

"Soon enough, but first things first. PT starts tomorrow morning at six a.m."

The next morning, after a three-mile run and a shower, Ozzie moved through the chow line at the mess hall. Famished, he piled his plate with eggs, sausage, and what the men called shit on a shingle, which was nothing more than creamed chipped beef on toast.

Satisfied, Ozzie's squad reported to the classroom for the aptitude test. It was a two-hour exam, but Ozzie finished with at least thirty minutes to spare. As he walked from the classroom, Morgan fell in step next to him.

"How do you think you did?" Morgan asked, his stocky shoulders bunched around his ears.

"It was pretty basic."

"Yeah, I agree. Nothing challenged me much. Where do you want to be assigned?"

"Intelligence. You?"

"I'm hoping for adjutant general. I'd like to advise on military policy and procedures. Handle promotions, transfers, discharges, and that sort of thing."

"You don't want to get your hands dirty?"

"I'm a thinker. Combat would be a waste of my talent," Morgan said. Ozzie felt the same way. He'd rather read a book than swing a weapon.

They walked down the hall and up the steps to the library to wait for the other men to finish testing. The room was narrow, with one wall of floor-to-ceiling books, several stuffed chairs, and a coffee table with stacks of American newspapers. Ozzie found the *Pittsburgh Courier*. Even though the newspaper was dated May 5, 1948, nearly three months prior, he flipped it open. Morgan grabbed an outdated issue of *The Chicago Defender.*

One by one, the other men from their unit filed into the library, some looking at magazines, others in small groups whispering about how they thought they'd done on the test.

"Gentlemen, may I have your attention." Sergeant Marshall had walked into the library and stood with an almond-colored man decorated in stripes and ribbons. "This is Lieutenant Lonnie W. Hill, assistant adjutant of the Kitzingen Basic Training Center."

All the men in the library stood and saluted the lieutenant.

"At ease, gentlemen. I wanted to welcome you all to the best training center in the European Command. You are here at a monumental time," said Lieutenant Hill. He wore his tie tucked inside his button-down shirt, and a single wedding band adorned his thick ring finger. "This just in from Washington: President Truman has signed Executive Order 9981, which mandates the desegregation of the U.S. Armed Forces."

Ozzie blinked, wondering if he had heard correctly. The other men seemed equally stunned by the news. The room was so quiet you could hear a hatpin drop.

Lieutenant Hill held up a piece of paper and removed his glasses from his shirt pocket. "It reads that 'there shall be equality of treatment and opportunity for all persons in the armed services without regard to race, color, religion or natural origin.'" Laughter and joy emitted from the soldiers like water rushing from a dam. "This is progress, men. Congratulations," finished Lieutenant Hill.

Ozzie could see tears sparkling in the lieutenant's eyes.

"We've come a long way. But there is still much work to be done. A celebratory dinner will be provided at five p.m. Enjoy this moment in history."

Once the lieutenant and Sergeant Marshall left the library, the men roared. A few beat the table with their fists.

"We need to go out tonight and celebrate," said Thornton. "Shiiit. This is the real deal."

"My grandfather told me stories about his time in the army in World War One. Segregation was so bad that he wasn't even given a pistol to fight with. All he could do was clean up, cook, and be caddy to the white man. Now we get to be equals. I need to have a drink for him." Morgan scratched his chin and headed toward the crowd of men talking loudly and making plans. When he returned, he said, "Sounds like there's a club that will welcome us. Down next to the footbridge."

"I'm in like Flynn," Thornton said. "Philips, you down to roll?"

Ozzie reveled. He was serving his country at an age that would go down in history. This was what he had volunteered for, to make a difference. To show people what the Negro man could do once given the chance. With the military now desegregated, the dream of securing that position in Intelligence seemed a little more within reach.

"Yeah, count me in."

"Man, I'm about to boogie with like three, four gals all at the same time," Thornton bragged.

"Ain't no woman going to be studying you. They'll be too busy checking me out." Morgan popped his collar.

"Watch me work."

"Fool, you can't even dance!"

"What you talking about? I move these feet like I'ma Nicholas brother."

Ozzie and Morgan laughed, which only egged Thornton on. "They performed at my local juke in Mississippi once, and I memorized all their flash dances. I came to show you." He hiked his pants and tapped his toes.

The men taunted and teased each other until they reached the club with the blinking neon sign. When they walked into the bar area, there were already a handful of Negro soldiers Ozzie didn't know, sitting at the counter, chatting with ivory-skinned women. Even though he had heard that German women would be at the bar, Ozzie was caught off guard by the way the ladies smiled in the soldiers' faces. There were other women sitting in pairs at tables, and their gaze roamed over Ozzie and his friends, pleading for an invitation to dance. Ozzie scanned the L-shaped room but didn't see any white men anywhere. He scratched his head at this new world that he had entered.

"A far cry from America," Thornton said, putting Ozzie's thoughts into words. "But I heard the local clubs do all they can to keep us separated from the white soldiers."

"How?"

"By the music they play. Tonight, it's blues."

"Well, first round's on me," Thornton said. "What will it be?"

Morgan ordered a whiskey, Ozzie a club soda.

"Don't you want something in it?" Thornton looked at him, perplexed.

Ozzie felt a little itch in the back of his throat, but he ignored it. "Naw, just the soda." He intended to keep good on his promise to his mother. The bar smelled of beer and roasted nuts. The swing jazz playing sounded familiar, and it furthered Ozzie's good mood.

"I'm going to ask one of those wallflowers over there to dance," said Morgan, pushing out his chest.

"I'm coming too." Thornton stood.

Morgan turned. "Philips, you getting in the game?"

"You go ahead. I'll watch the table."

The club had swelled, and as the music snapped up-tempo, the Negro men stepped to the German women like ducks on June bugs. Laughter and movement suggested that everyone was having a good time. Ozzie drank his club soda and sucked on ice cubes as he observed his new friends leading the ladies onto the dance floor. Watching Thornton gyrate and Morgan sway made Ozzie wonder what Rita was doing up at Lincoln. Had she replaced him with a college boy in a Greek sweatshirt? What he wouldn't give to kiss her on the lips at that moment. Share the news of the military desegregating and his renewed sense that his future was bright. He craved the sound of her voice in his ear and replayed their time in the basement again. He had expected to receive a letter from her by now, but he had not.

Suddenly, Ozzie felt a burst of cool air and caught the sounds of rumbling voices. They got louder and louder, and he stood to see what was causing the commotion. He spotted six sour-faced white men with buzz cuts who looked annoyed to have wandered in on the wrong night.

"What the hell?" The hot-faced, burly leader's words slurred in a way that suggested he was drunk and not opposed to starting a ruckus. He pounded his fist on the bar. "Shut this party down now," he said to the bartender. "These niggers are in violation. I don't care what you think Truman signed. Ain't nothing change around here."

"Please. No trouble," pleaded the mustached man, wide-eyed behind the bar.

Ozzie looked to Morgan and then Thornton, who both stood in front of their partners with their feet spread apart and hands wide at their waist. The three exchanged a knowing look that said, *If these guys make a move, we are on them like stink on shit.* Ozzie inched closer to the burly man disrupting the scene. Ozzie couldn't stand racist bullies, but what he despised even more was being disrespected in front of women. It was why he had sucker-punched Harold, and why he hadn't taken his eye off the troublemaker from the moment he had stepped foot inside the bar.

The mustached man behind the counter held up a wooden bat. "Leave. Now." His accent was heavy, but his words rang clear.

The burly leader looked around the room, taking in the sight of all the Negro men and white women, and then spat on the floor in disgust. There was a frail woman with pink lips sitting alone on a barstool. He grabbed the woman by the arm and pulled her close to him. "What do you want with these filthy animals? Dance with me, pretty."

"Stop." The woman squirmed in his arms, trying to get loose. The man spun her out so hard that she stumbled backward. Ozzie caught her before she fell to the floor.

"Nigger lover," the burly man shouted.

Ozzie didn't think twice as he pushed the woman behind him and looked the burly man up and down.

"You need to leave, now," the mustached man said to the troublemakers, and then patted the bat on the bar in a way that suggested he meant business.

The burly man's laugh was raspy and defiant. "What the hell are you going to do? That your whore?" He directed his words to Ozzie.

From the corner of his eye, Ozzie saw Thornton and Morgan flagging him on both sides. His heart was racing. He didn't want to fight these white boys. Nothing good would come out of it. But he wouldn't be disrespected either. The tension in the room was too thick to cut, even with a butcher's knife. Before Ozzie could answer, the mustached man stepped from behind the bar, bat in hand.

"The *polizei* are on the way," he said. "You." He pointed at the white men. "Leave now."

The burly man spat on the floor again, eyed Ozzie one last time, and then backed out the door. As they exited, one of his friends called out, "Girls, leave those darkies alone. They all have tails between their legs!"

Ozzie felt his temples pulse, and as he moved to follow the men, Morgan grabbed him by the arms. "Naw, man. They ain't worth it."

Ozzie opened and balled his fist as the rage bubbled inside him. The music all of a sudden sounded off-key. The earlier spell of celebration and glee had been broken. People found their drinks and seats; some of the women reached for their sweaters and purses.

The short blonde who had danced against Morgan all night patted his cheek. "That's why we like you better."

"The white American soldiers are mean," her freckled friend added. "And rude."

"Thank you for saving me," said the frail woman Ozzie had caught. She smiled invitingly at him, but Ozzie couldn't hear what she was saying beyond the thunder in his head. His jaw had started to ache from clenching his teeth. It wasn't right. The Negro man couldn't have anything. Not a good time. Not a victory on the day of military desegregation. Not a single breath of freedom. And most certainly not a white woman. Not even across the ocean.

CHAPTER 9

West Oak Forest Academy, September 1965

SOPHIA

Having opened the wrong closet, Sophia now stood frozen, enamored by Wilhelmina's department-store wardrobe. To the left there was a neat row of wool and cashmere sweaters in a confetti of pink, green, yellow, and blue. On the right, a line of ruffled blouses, hip-huggers, and A-line skirts in varying patterns of plaid, pinstripes, and floral checks. At the bottom on a metal shoe rack were kitten-heel pumps, Mary Jane strap shoes, tennis shoes, and furry satin slippers.

Draped on the bed in contrast were Sophia's meager belongings. A pair of faded Wrangler jeans, black pedal pushers, a Sloppy Joe sweater, and two passable blouses, all hand-me-downs from Unc's summer girlfriend.

The generous gifts that she had received from the school counselors were folded neatly and packed away in the chest of drawers opposite her bed. Then Sophia remembered her uniform and located it at the top of her closet. It was in a simple brown bag with her name written on it in blue.

Sophia made sure the door was locked, then changed into the stiff pleated skirt and crisp white blouse, which, to her relief, fit perfectly. She could not bear returning to the office and asking for an exchange, not after the way the receptionist had treated her. Against the door hung a full-length mirror, and when Sophia looked at herself, she felt almost pretty in her new clothes; she liked her shiny black hair and the way Ma Deary's Mary Janes hugged her ankles. Maybe things would work out for her here.

She checked her school timetable and realized that she had twenty minutes before her afternoon classes began. While packing up the school supplies that Mrs. Brown had given her, she decided it was better to be early so as not to call attention to herself.

Outside, the day was still warm, and she hoped she could make it to class without sweating. Sophia had a good sense of direction and wound her way back to the admissions building with ease. From studying the brochure, she had learned that the boys' school, Donoghue Hall, was on the right, and the girls', Campbell Hall, on the left. Boys and girls interacted fully only during meals.

Sophia walked up the sprawling stairs to the three-story brick building on the left. The white halls gleamed as she followed the numbers on the wooden door to her physics class. When she entered the sunlit classroom, she was taken aback by the neat rows of beautiful maple desks with matching ladder-back chairs. There were only three other early arrivers, with their noses inside of books. The teacher, a long-faced woman with a mole on her chin, pursed her lips from behind her desk at the front of the room. A chalkboard filled with scientific notations and metric multipliers loomed behind her head. In the top right corner, her name was written in cursive: Ms. Meacham.

She brought her hands together. "You must be Wilhelmina."

"No. I'm Sophia," she said, fiddling with the stiff hem of her new uniform skirt.

"Right, the other one," Ms. Meacham said to herself. "Well, here's the syllabus for the year. Help yourself to a textbook from the back shelf, and sit anywhere you like. Let me know if you have any questions." She slid a packet of papers across her desk.

The back of the classroom was lined with two bookshelves. With the heavy physics textbook in her hand, Sophia picked a seat by the window. The pages smelled freshly inked and crisp, and the spine cracked just a little when she opened it. What a stark difference from the textbooks donated to Brooks High with whole chapters torn out and obscene language scribbled in, courtesy of the all-white students who had used the textbooks first at Calvert High.

A cluster of about five girls entered the classroom, talking loudly and giggling. Sophia kept her head down, careful not to look up and make eye contact with any of them. Even though she didn't see them, she could smell them. Powdery hair spray, fruity lotion, and floral perfume.

"There she is. The one I was telling you about," and as if it had a mind of its own, Sophia's head snapped up and she made eye contact with Patty, the brunette wearing the white ribbons who had refused to show her the way to the dormitory. Patty grabbed the arm of the friend closest to her and steered the group to the corner of the room, on the opposite side of Sophia.

"Don't pay them any mind." A girl stopped next to Sophia's desk with a forearm crutch strapped to each arm. She had a thick braid tossed over her shoulders. "I'm Nancy, by the way."

"Sophia."

"Nice to meet you." Nancy put all her weight on one of the grip handles and stretched out her free hand to Sophia. "I'm new this year too."

The teacher cleared her throat, and all the students who were up and about got to their seats. Nancy lowered herself in the chair beside Sophia.

"Good afternoon, ladies. Please turn to page seven in your textbooks, and I will explain the notes up on the board."

Once her physics class was dismissed, Sophia sat through literature and then Latin. Her last class of the day was applied mathematics. All afternoon, her teachers had been polite, and the curriculum felt doable. If the day seemed long, it was because she had been hungry for most of it, and she was happy to find Wilhelmina waiting for her in front of the girls' building when she descended the stairs.

"How was it?" Wilhelmina asked, leading Sophia down the path in the direction of the dining hall.

"Not too bad."

"Good for you. Claude Portis, one of the boys who started last year, told me that he had a terrible first day."

"What happened?"

A group of boys in letterman jackets strolled passed them, and Wilhelmina lowered her voice so that only Sophia could hear her. "He was cornered in front of the boys' building by six huge football players. Since he played too, he assumed they were teammates coming to welcome him to the school." Wilhelmina grimaced. "Instead, they pushed him around and called him Sambo and other nasty words, then chanted for him to go back to Africa where he belonged."

Sophia opened the door to the dining hall as Wilhelmina continued, "Poor thing ran into the bathroom crying. It took three teachers to pry him out of the stall."

Sophia gulped. "Wilhelmina, that's awful."

"Tell me about it. And please, call me Willa. Wilhelmina is such a mouthful." She repositioned the strap of her leather bag on her shoulder.

"Sorry. Willa, I mean." Sophia pinched herself for forgetting.

Willa led the way, moving like a girl who was confident and completely at ease. As Sophia walked slightly behind her, she found herself pushing her chest forward and trying to imitate Willa's poise and sureness.

The school's dining hall was expansive and mirrored the nice restaurants that Sophia had gone to with the Old Man on fresh-egg deliveries. The cafeteria at Brooks High was merely a room with three laminate tables, plastic chairs, and plates of food that looked and smelled like an afterthought.

"This is the cold food station." Willa pointed. It was piled high with sandwiches, a variety of cold salads, and sliced fruit. "On the other side are the hot stations," she said. "That's where I'm headed."

The hot stations were filled with burgers, hot dogs, french fries, spaghetti, meat loaf and gravy, mashed potatoes, green beans, and cabbage. Sophia's mouth watered at all of the choices. Then she remembered that she didn't have any money.

"I can't pay for this," she whispered to Willa, who had grabbed two brown trays and was handing one to Sophia.

"Your parents have already paid for it." Willa looked at her incredulously. "The meals are included in our tuition. And it's all you can eat, even the dessert." She pointed to another station on the far side of the room.

Sophia's face blanched with embarrassment. She should have known that and felt silly for being so ignorant. Behind the counter of one of the hot stations stood a cinnamon-colored woman wearing a black hairnet. Her lips were painted fuchsia, and she had a pencil tucked behind her ear.

"Welcome. What's your name, sugar?" She dished a piece of juicy meat loaf onto Sophia's plate.

"Sophia Clark."

"Well, folks call me Miz Peaches 'round here. You look like you've been skipping a few meals," she said, spooning two helpings of mashed potatoes and then a heap of cabbage onto Sophia's plate. "Here, baby, don't forget the corn bread. Just came outta the oven."

"Thank you."

"You're welcome, sugar." She flashed her deep dimples. "Anything you need. Anything at all, you come find Miz Peaches. Hear?"

"Yes, ma'am."

"Willa, you be sure to show Sophia how we do things 'round here."

Willa chuckled. "Will do, Miz Peaches."

The two girls plopped down at a big table overlooking the tennis courts. Students buzzed around them, filling plates and catching up with friends. Sophia took in their leather bags, new shoes, preppy jackets, and decorated hairdos. They were carefree and comfortable. How could Sophia find solace in this new space when everything was so different from what she had experienced at Brooks High?

"This school has so much of everything," she blurted.

"That's exactly why my parents sent me here. My father always tells me you must be with the best to be the best." Willa sipped her lemonade. "What made you choose Forest?"

"I guess you can say Forest chose me." Sophia told Willa about the program that she'd applied to and how she had received the scholarship to attend.

"That's cool." Willa squirted mustard on her hot dog. "Before you arrived, I thought I'd be the lonely only. At least we'll have each other. I'm glad you're here."

"Me too."

Willa took birdlike bites of her hot dog while Sophia had to restrain herself from lifting her dish and slurping the food down. Everything tasted delicious. It was the best meal she had eaten in a while.

"Evening, ladies." A wide-framed boy, about six feet tall with a close-cropped fade and dark-rimmed glasses, sat down at their table.

Willa made the introductions. "Sophia, this is Louis Clark."

She touched her napkin to her mouth. "I'm Sophia Clark."

"Wonder if we're kin." Louis took a good look at Sophia. "Where are your people from?"

That was a weird question, one she did not have the answer to, though she thought about it often. Her people were Ma Deary, the Old Man, Uncle Wayon, and her three brothers. She hadn't known grandparents on either side of the family. According to Ma Deary, they had all died before she was born.

"It's just us, and we all you need," Ma Deary would insist whenever the questions of extended family came up. It was even more painful in her elementary years, when she had to draw her family tree with a mere seven people and present it at school next to kids going back with two and three generations of relatives.

She gave Louis the only answer she knew. "Southern Maryland. How about you?"

"I come from a long line of proud Virginians. Grew up in Norfolk, not far from Norfolk State University."

"Louis was the first of us to enroll here," Wilhelmina supplied in between nibbles.

"I was here a whole semester before Max and Claude joined me in the spring." He bit into his corn bread.

"Was it scary being here all alone?" Sophia asked.

Louis winced, but then he turned to her and smiled. "Like Dr. King, I've done my best to keep it peaceful. We'll just leave it at that."

Willa blurted, "Louis is being modest. He already told me that a blue-blooded boy spat on him in the quad and he chased the boy into the principal's office."

"Was the boy punished?" Sophia looked from Willa to Louis.

Louis swallowed a forkful of cabbage. "After a small deliberation, he was given detention. I haven't had any trouble out of him since."

Willa cracked up, like it was a story she had heard several times but still got a kick out of. Sophia dropped her fork, suddenly having lost her appetite.

"Are the other guys still at basketball practice?" Willa asked.

"Far as I know."

"I want you to meet Max and Claude, our other two," Willa said, but Sophia had stopped listening. She didn't want anyone chasing her, spitting on her, or anything else. She had seen on television how the police had thrown nightsticks, powered fire hoses, and let loose dogs on the Negro youth, same age as her, who had marched in the streets of Birmingham, Alabama.

"Don't look so worried." Louis patted Sophia's hand. "You'll be fine. Just remember that you are here to learn, so give it everything you've got. We have all committed to doing whatever it takes to be at the top of our classes. The best revenge is to outsmart them."

Sophia nodded, but a heavy fatigue came over her. Though the conversation continued between Willa and Louis, it became increasingly difficult for Sophia to concentrate on what was being said. Maybe she didn't belong here after all. Perhaps Ma Deary had been right and Brooks High School was good enough. At least there she didn't have to contend with the hatred of people. But then Sophia stopped herself as she remembered being tormented by Maxine and her crew with monkey sounds and slurs about her hair.

Louis broke into her thoughts. "Do you play sports?"

"No."

"Well, we are required to play two sports a year. The sports fair is being held now on the lawn in front of the athletic center. Hopefully, you'll settle on something that you like." He popped the last of his corn bread in his mouth before sauntering out of the dining hall.

Sophia and Willa walked the quad and then headed to the left, toward the athletic center. There were folding tables set up advertising all the fall and winter sports. Many of the tables had enticing snacks: Rice Krispies treats, vanilla frosted cupcakes, and chocolate chip cookies. Willa made a beeline for the tennis table, leaving Sophia looking around alone.

The thought of doing anything that required hand-eye coordination made Sophia absolutely nauseated. She and her brothers had played ball, but that was a healthy competition between the four of them. Nothing serious, just a way to pass their little pockets of free time. She stopped at the track-and-field table. She could walk for long periods of time, between her work on the farm and the three-mile walk each way to school, but she was not interested in running until she made herself sweaty and dizzy. She stopped in the middle of the quad and was looking around for anything remotely interesting when a tall man wearing a tweed baker-boy cap waved her over.

Sophia looked around to make sure he was talking to her.

"Hi, I'm Alastair Fletcher," he said, his accent sounding like John Lennon from the Beatles. "What sport do you play, mate?"

"Sir, I don't play sports."

He had a whistle hanging around his neck and was wearing blue jeans, which struck her as odd for a teacher.

"Where are you from?"

"Southern Maryland."

"Farmland, then?"

Sophia wrapped her arms around her waist. Could he smell the wet earth, chicken feed, damp milk, and manure on her?

"Yes."

"I knew it." He slapped his hands together, grinning and pleased with himself. "I can always spot them. I grew up on a ranch west of Manchester, England. Let me share a fun fact with you: Farmworkers are excellent at basketball."

Sophia looked at the posters on his table and saw girls wearing uniforms and holding balls. "Why is that?"

"Because farmwork makes you fit and strong, and I bet you are tight in your core." He sized her up. "You are the perfect height for the sport, and look at that wingspan."

He pointed to her biceps, which were toned from lifting the chicken feed, pulling out the manure, heaving jugs of milk and buckets of eggs, and lugging firewood. But Sophia shook her head, unconvinced.

"Really, it has something to do with strategy, IQ, and some other facts. This is only our second year having a girls' basketball team, so everyone is fairly new. You'd be perfect."

"Okay," Sophia heard herself say. He was convincing, if nothing else. She knew nothing about tennis, and since she had dribbled a ball before with her brothers, it was a better alternative than running track.

"Brilliant. Then it's settled." He handed her a pen and a form to fill out. "We start on Thursday. See you then."

The showers in the W5 dormitory were communal; Sophia waited until she thought the last girl on their floor had padded back to her room before venturing out. She hadn't wanted to run into anyone. The last thing she needed was for any of the girls to see the red welts on her arms from her night terrors.

Fresh white towels were piled on a rack against the wall, and Sophia took one on her way into the shower. Each stall contained pumps labeled with shampoo, conditioner, and liquid soap that smelled like coconuts. Underneath the running water, Sophia felt her body sigh with relief. The water was hot, ten times better than the cool-water bucket bath she was accustomed to taking on the farm. She lathered herself generously with the coconut-scented soap and worked the suds underneath her nail plates. After she'd finished and dried, she slipped into the white nightgown her counselor had given her. The material was smooth against her skin and the most luxurious piece of clothing she had ever owned. She twirled like a princess and then floated from the stall, feeling pleased with her appearance.

As she stepped out into the community bathroom, Patty stood with two other girls at the row of sinks, holding her toothbrush. "Oh my God, whose grandmother did you rob for that old thing," she said, cackling and pointing to Sophia's nightgown, which buttoned up to her neck and grazed her ankles.

Sophia's head dipped as she shrank an inch. The three girls at the sink wore paisley gowns that sat above their knees, with three buttons opened at the chest.

"She looks like Granny from *The Beverly Hillbillies,*" another teased.

"And that hair. It looks like she stuck her finger in a socket," said the last girl, with a tone that sounded like she'd refuse to be outdone.

Sophia didn't know what to say, so she turned and bolted from the bathroom. When she reached her bedroom door, she checked to make sure they hadn't followed her. Then she took a few beats to catch her breath before entering. She didn't want Willa to know what had happened, but that conversation was easy to avoid. Willa had a sleep mask pulled over her eyes and her hair covered with a silk scarf, and she was buried under her covers.

Sophia quietly climbed into her own bed. The duvet cover was plush, and the twin mattress was softer than she had imagined. She curled herself into a ball and faced the wall, still a bit shaken. She had not been in the habit of praying at night. Ma Deary didn't care one way or the other. But Walter always prayed, so she thought she'd give his God a try. She needed something to soothe her and to believe in.

Walter's God, she thought. *Please don't let me have a nightmare tonight and wake up Wilhelmina . . . I mean Willa. Pretty, pretty please? And don't let Ma Deary come for me. And make Patty and her friends leave me alone. Oh, help me figure out this basketball thing too, but most importantly, no nightmares. And if I start dreaming, help me wake up before I start screaming. Please and amen.*

Sophia pushed her head deeper into the pillow, hoping that was enough for Him to grant her wish, because the last thing she wanted was for Willa to find out that she was rooming with a freak.

CHAPTER 10

Mannheim, Germany, April 1951

ETHEL

Bert left earlier than usual to oversee a shipment of materials scheduled to arrive on base. Alone and with the sun pouring through the thin curtains at the bedroom window, Ethel rose with her nightgown tangled around her knees. In the kitchen, she perked herself coffee, fried two slabs of bacon, and boiled a bowl of hominy grits for breakfast.

Deep down, she was much too excited about her day with the children to eat, but since she had no idea how long she'd be helping at the orphanage, she needed to fill her belly with something that would stick. After she ate and tidied the kitchen, she considered phoning Julia but knew she'd have a sleep hangover from being up all night with her infant daughter, who was colicky most evenings. As she fastened the buttons on her black-and-white tea dress, she noted that it would have been nice to take a friend with her, but every woman she knew had her own children to mind. Today Ethel had children to care for too, and this thought put a little extra pep in her stride. She slipped her feet into her most comfortable flatties and then pinned her beaver felt hat in place. Inside her crochet bag she stashed scissors, two combs, one brush, and a jar of Dixie Peach hair pomade. On the way, she would stop by the new commissary in Benjamin Franklin Village to pick up rubber bands, ribbons, and anything else she could find to make the girls feel lovely and cared for. As a last thought, she reached under the bathroom sink and grabbed Bert's barbering clippers in case any of the boys needed their hair fixed too.

When she arrived at the wrought-iron gate, Sister Ursula unlatched the lock and greeted her warmly. "Thank you so much for coming back." She patted Ethel's hand. As Ethel trailed Sister Ursula through the courtyard, she knew that she was in the right place.

"The older children have gone off to the local school, but they will be back for lunch." Sister Ursula pointed to a folding chair underneath a wide-branched tree next to a tiny milking stool. "I assumed you would prefer to sit out in the fresh air with the children. The breeze this time of day feels lovely."

It was then that Ethel noticed a small girl in a yellow sundress, around the age of three or four, watching her every move. When Ethel sat down in the chair, the little girl meandered up to her and raised her arms to be lifted. Joy swept through Ethel as she pulled the girl into her lap. She was so tiny and sweet in her arms and smelled like cinnamon. Ethel let out a long sigh as the girl twisted to get comfortable.

"This is Anke," said Sister Ursula. "As you can see, she enjoys a nice cuddle. Please start with her while I check on the others."

Warmth flooded through Ethel's chest as Anke placed her tiny head against Ethel's heart. Then Anke looked up at Ethel with squinty eyes and opened her mouth. "Hallo." She pointed her finger, then stuck it between her lips.

"Hello." Ethel smiled, and just like that, Anke squirmed back down to the ground.

"Come." Ethel beckoned while showing Anke the stool. When

Anke didn't move, Ethel reached into her pocket for a piece of strawberry licorice. It was quite early for a treat, but she gave it to Anke anyway, then propped her on the stool and ran her fingers through the girl's wavy hair.

Tender-headed herself, Ethel tried being as gentle as possible. Once Ethel had finished raking through Anke's hair, she swapped her out for the next little girl. Although the children were not bilingual, Ethel used a lot of facial expressions and hand gestures to communicate, and the candy helped. One after the other, the girls came for chewy licorice and a hairdo, all leaving the space between Ethel's knees with edges brushed, scalps oiled, and pink ribbons tied in elegant bows.

While Ethel parted, prodded, and massaged the kinks from matted hair, Anke played at Ethel's feet atop an old towel. Anke occasionally reached for the hem of Ethel's dress and twirled it between her fingers with her head resting on Ethel's shin.

Around noon, the older children returned for their afternoon meal, and Sister Ursula brought two girls over to Ethel's little salon under the tree. When Ethel looked up, she stifled a gasp. "What happened here?" she asked, nodding toward the two girls.

Sister Ursula's face blanched. "We didn't know what to do when it got knotted. We thought it best to cut it off."

Both girls looked to be around ten years old, and their hair was cut so short that they looked like boys. Nonetheless, Ethel nodded that she understood. That didn't make it right, but she understood.

"Sit, sweetie." She motioned to the stool and took her time with the first girl's hair, combing it and massaging her scalp before tying a ribbon around the base of her crown. Then she did the same for the second girl. Once she was finished, she held up a mirror so they could see themselves.

"See. Pretty," Ethel cooed until the girls grinned, and she saw that they were both missing teeth.

"Danke," the girls said in unison, and took turns throwing their arms around Ethel before lining up with the other kids for afternoon school.

When Ethel had styled as many heads as her hands would allow, Anke found her way back into her lap. She had found the edge of Ethel's sleeve and balled it between her fingers. The movement seemed to soothe her.

"She's taken a liking to you." Sister Ursula handed Ethel a cool glass of lemonade.

"How long do the children stay here at the orphanage?" Ethel shifted Anke to the crook of her arm.

"What do you mean?"

"Do their mothers come back for them? Are they adopted?"

Sister Ursula's face went slack. "Some mothers visit, but adoption is not common. It is hard for the brown babies. Unfortunately."

Ethel could feel the weight of the half-Negro orphans' fate, living in a country that didn't know what to do with them. Did the American government even know these children existed? Holed up here and hidden away? She rocked Anke, and as the little girl looked up into her eyes, Ethel knew that something needed to be done.

When the schoolchildren returned later that afternoon, Ethel had abandoned her comb and brush in favor of playing games during their free time before supper. The kids circled her like a new toy, and she taught several of the older children the hand games she had played as a child. "Miss Mary Mack, Mack, Mack," Ethel showed them while clapping and flipping her hands against theirs.

"She never came back, back, back, till the Fourth of July," she said, and then started chasing the group around the yard to loud squeals and peals of laughter. When Ethel saw that the sun had moved across the yard, she realized that she didn't want to leave, but she had to get dinner going before Bert came home.

Ethel left the circle of children and packed her crocheted bag to go. As she walked through the courtyard, at least ten children trailed behind her. At the gate, a few grabbed her by the arms, while others threw their small bodies to the ground and wrapped themselves around her limbs. Anke was one of the children at her feet and tugging on her dress.

"Mummy," Anke cooed. "Mummy."

Ethel felt her throat close, and tears strained against her eyelids. She patted the sweet girl on the head.

Sister Ursula appeared, talking to the children in German. One by one, they let Ethel go and stepped back to let her pass, but Anke had begun to wail. Three other children picked up the cry. "Mum. Mum. Mummy."

Then all the children at the gate shouted, "Mummy. My mummy." Over and over. Ethel could barely turn away. She searched Sister Ursula's face for help.

"They will be fine," Sister Ursula said to Ethel while grabbing the little children by the arms and pulling them back inside. "But since you've made such an impression on them, we do hope you will come again."

"Tomorrow?" Ethel croaked.

"We will see you then." Sister Ursula held her gaze with those startling blue eyes and then closed and locked the gate behind her.

As Ethel turned onto the street, she could still hear them singing to her: "Mum. Mum. Mummy."

Ethel rolled down her nylons and then changed into a flowered housedress before rummaging around in the kitchen. It had been nearly a week since she'd done the grocery shopping, so her dinner options were limited. She prepared a simple meal of toast with sardines, boiled eggs, and a cucumber and tomato salad. Just as she was draining the eggs from the water, she heard Bert enter the apartment.

"Ethel, that you, darling?" he called, like he did every day, which always made her chuckle, because who else would be banging around in their kitchen.

"Yes, it's me." Ethel removed her waist apron and touched her hair, then made her way into the living room. Bert stood tall with big shoulders and a kind smile.

"This is the best part of my day," he murmured as he closed the distance between them, folding her into the safety of his arms. Bert smelled hardy, and as Ethel held him around the waist, she gazed up into his eyes.

"Supper's ready. Hope you aren't too hungry, because it's not much."

"I'm absolutely famished, woman. So you better feed me something." He kissed her cheek.

"Well, come on, then." She patted his chest.

Bert removed his garrison cap and service coat. Once he sat down at the table in the kitchen, he loosened his necktie.

Ethel brought over their plates.

"Smells good," he said.

"Well, I promise to do the food shopping as soon as I can."

Bert reached for her hand and then led them in grace. He took a bite of his toast piled high with sardines and asked after her day.

Ethel could feel her breathing speed up as she recounted her time at the orphanage. "They were all so precious. You should have seen them." She put down her fork as her eyes glazed over. "Such beautiful children."

He chewed. "How many kids were there?"

"Too many to count. Something has got to be done, Bert. They look like us. All shades of beige and brown. They need an advocate."

"You said the Catholic nuns run the place, right?"

"Yes, and they are doing what they can. Don't get me wrong, but there is only so much they can do. It's terrible to see so many motherless children. Especially American children. It's not right."

"I'm sure there are programs . . ."

"There's nothing. Sister Ursula told me that it's hard for brown babies. No one wants them. All because of the color of their skin. That feels way too familiar, considering how far we are from the same madness at home."

Bert spooned another egg onto his plate and doused it with salt.

"Those kids, they were all so smart and lovable. We played, even though most of them didn't speak a lick of English."

Ethel stopped talking because she noticed that Bert was staring at her. "Albert Gathers, why on earth are you studying me like you don't have the sense God gave a chicken?"

"This is the most alive I've seen you look in a long time."

Ethel relaxed. "It was such a good feeling to be useful. Those kids needed me today, and I needed them just as much."

"It seems that you've found something here. When are you going back?"

"Tomorrow." Ethel smiled. "Maybe you should come with me. It would be good for the young boys to see a man who looks like them."

"Darling, I'd love to. Maybe once work slows a bit. We are in the process of planning our next field maneuver exercises in an abandoned town south of here. I'll probably be gone for a week or two, but I can join you when I return." He stood up from the table and carried his plate to the sink. "I love that you've found some purpose." He kissed her forehead, then trudged into the living room, where he turned on the television.

As Ethel slipped into her rubber gloves, she relived the savory sounds of the children crying "Mummy."

CHAPTER 11

Kitzingen Basic Training Center, August 1948

OZZIE

A week after Truman's order desegregating the military came down, Ozzie stood in the moist grass in Tent City, where he had been learning how to operate the telephone switchboard. When he looked up from the machine in front of him, Sergeant Marshall had marched toward him with his clipboard in hand.

"Philips, Lieutenant Hill would like to see you in his office."

Ozzie's hands went cold. "Did the lieutenant say what this matter was about?"

"Soldier, please report immediately." Marshall's face was unreadable.

Ozzie trotted back across the grass toward the main building, wondering if the heated exchange he'd had with the white soldiers at the club last week had reached the ears of the lieutenant. Even though Ozzie had not put his hands on the men, as he would have liked, he understood that they could drum up any charges against him. It would be their word against his. At worst, he could be charged with bad conduct, placed in confinement, and docked two thirds of his monthly pay. He walked down the corridor and located Lieutenant Hill's name on the last office door to the right. As he knocked on the open door, Ozzie told himself not to worry. If it came to their word against his, he had witnesses.

"Sir, Private Philips reports as ordered." Ozzie stepped into the office, stood at attention, and saluted the higher-ranking officer.

"Private Philips, please have a seat."

A map of Europe was drawn on the wall behind the lieutenant, and the American flag was propped on a stand in the corner. Ozzie lowered himself in the seat adjacent to Lieutenant Hill's desk as the lieutenant opened a manila file folder. A bright red stamp blazed across the piece of paper the lieutenant fingered. Ozzie exhaled. What would his mother say? He had been in the country only a week, and already he was in trouble.

"Philips, in all my years at Kitzingen, I have never seen anything like this." He pushed the ashtray overflowing with cigarette butts to the side and slid the packet of papers across the desk toward Ozzie.

It wasn't a bad-conduct report, it was his aptitude test.

"Not only did you pass the exam, but you got every answer correct." Lieutenant Hill's eyes widened.

"Thank you, sir."

"How on earth did you do it?"

Ozzie dropped his chin. "I like to read, sir."

"Clearly. Well, there is no point in wasting your smarts at this training facility. I'm recommending that you be transferred to a unit in Mannheim immediately. There are a few positions available in supply, maintenance, and transportation."

Ozzie tried to keep the frown from reaching his face. Then tilted his chin. "I'd like to work in Intelligence, sir."

The lieutenant crinkled his brows. "I'm not sure if there are any positions available there. Besides, for Intelligence, you need to speak an additional language."

"I've been studying German, and I know a good deal of Latin, sir."

"Well, I'll put you down for maintenance, and once you learn the ropes, you can try for branch reclassification. Now pack your things. You will move out in seventy-two hours."

Three days later, Ozzie arrived by jeep to Sullivan Barracks in Mannheim. Morgan, who had also tested high on the aptitude test, was at his side. Thornton hadn't received more than a Mississippi eighth-grade education and stayed in Kitzingen, where he was enrolled in high school equivalency classes in addition to basic training.

Sullivan Barracks was twice the size of Kitzingen. Ozzie and Morgan had been assigned to Building 201, and when they arrived, they were pleasantly surprised by their upgraded living accommodations. Instead of the communal sleeping quarters, the two shared a private room with two twin-size beds, a double wardrobe, and a chest of drawers for each of them.

"This is what I'm talking about." Morgan lounged on his bed with his feet up while Ozzie opened the weathered Bible his mother had given him and removed the one photograph he had of Rita. She was standing on her front steps with both hands on her hips, smiling, with her hair pulled away from her beautiful face. Ozzie wanted to tape the three-by-five picture to his mirror but thought better of it. Instead, he slipped it into his top drawer and reread his military orders. Ozzie was to report to the motor pool for training on inspecting vehicles and equipment. A no-brains position that couldn't be further from what he wanted to do.

"I'm telling you, Morgan, if they think I'm going to waste my time kneeling down to these hillbillies, serving them hand and foot, they got another thought coming. Desegregation must mean something, or what's the point."

"At ease, soldier." Morgan looked up from the edge of his bed, where he was tying his boots. "Progress happens in phases. All things in due time."

"But I had a perfect aptitude score? It doesn't make sense that I'm not in an Intelligence unit."

Morgan stood. "Maybe all the units were full."

Ozzie flagged his hand at him.

"Look on the bright side, you're still stuck with me. I have the same orders, so we can watch each other's back. Now let's report to duty and see what the position entails. Who knows, we might learn something useful."

Ozzie and Morgan passed their first two weeks attending PT drills in the morning, and in the afternoon, they learned the mechanics of the fleet of service vehicles they had been assigned. It did not take long for Ozzie to settle into the routine of maintenance and repair.

On Ozzie's third week stationed in Mannheim, two squads from his platoon were tasked with passing out care packages and supplies to local German residents. They loaded up two cargo trucks and drove west of the barracks. Since arriving, he hadn't spent much time off base, and as he peered out the window, the landscape changed dramatically. There were buildings with the entire roof blown to shreds, chunks of cement rubble, stacks of broken bricks, and piles of sewage debris, detritus and destruction from World War II. His platoon drove through entire villages that had been air-bombed and crumbled into concrete ruins. White dust covered everything. Ozzie knew many Negroes who lived below the poverty line, but this former war zone felt abysmal.

The three-axle trucks rumbled to a stop in an open field adjacent to a village slum dotted with tiny houses and gnome-size gardens. Ozzie noticed that most of the homes needed a fresh coat of paint. As the men unloaded boxes from the backs of the trucks, the villagers stood by in anticipation.

Germany was still coming off its worst hunger years, and many of the residents looked gaunt. Bony women hung thin babies on narrow hips, scrawny old men leaned gingerly on canes, a group of lanky boys kicked a ball. There was a slight breeze rustling through a patch of maple and English walnut trees, bringing with it the smell of soot.

First Sergeant Tom Petty, the company first sergeant, had pale skin and a thick neck. Once the men had climbed from the vehicles, he started barking orders on how to set up the supplies and distribute them. "Keep a tally of who gets what," he yelled. "One load per family. No seconds. Nothing extra. We need enough to go around."

The men lined up prepackaged loaves of bread, canned meat, butter, hazelnut paste, coffee, and small canisters of sugar, along with wool blankets, flashlights, and batteries because the power was known to go out in these parts of town. Ozzie stood behind the table piled with blankets, feeling proud to serve in his uniform. As he doled out provisions, he noticed a slender woman with saucer-shaped eyes watching him. Finally, she stepped up to the table. He handed her a blanket.

"This is not enough." Her voice was low, and she pronounced "this" like "zis," but Ozzie understood.

"It's all we have to give, ma'am."

"My papa is ill. Do you have pills?" The woman's hair was pulled back into a loose chignon, her small forehead on full display.

They were not a medic squad, but there was a first-aid kit inside each of the supply trucks. Ozzie didn't know what had come over him, but he asked the soldier next to him to keep watch over his station. "I have to take a leak," he said.

Ozzie walked back to the parking lot and rifled through the emergency pack in the truck. The woman followed and stood a few feet away.

Ozzie found the packets of acetaminophen, a few bandages, alcohol wipes, and cotton swabs. "What's wrong with him?"

"His head." She reached for the packet, and their fingers touched.

"What do you think you're doing here?" It was First Sergeant Petty. "This isn't the time for conversation, Philips." He turned to the woman. "Has this man harmed you?" he asked, his accent white and Southern.

She shook her head.

"Do you understand what I'm saying? Has he touched you in any way?" he said louder.

"First Sergeant, I was helping her."

"I didn't ask you, Private. Speak only when spoken to," he sneered, then turned back to the woman. "Ma'am, do you speak English?"

"I am fine." She turned on her heel and stomped away.

"Stay in the vehicle, Philips, until further instructions are given," Petty ordered before storming off. Ozzie ground his teeth. Within the hour, the soldiers had passed out all the supplies, and they were back on the road, heading toward the barracks.

The next morning, when Ozzie reported for PT exercise, Petty pulled him out of the line.

"What you did yesterday was unacceptable. Under no circumstances do you go off with a local woman without a battle buddy while on duty. It's against protocol."

"First Sergeant."

"Don't you dare interrupt me when I'm speaking to you." Petty looked down his nose at Ozzie. After chewing him out and calling him every vile word in the book, he ordered, "Report to mess hall duty for the rest of the weekend."

Ozzie turned his back without a word, but the anger that brewed inside of him alchemized into a funk, a sweat that oozed from nearly every pore. After cleaning pots and scrubbing floors in the kitchen, Ozzie returned to his room. Morgan stood at the mirror, combing his hair.

"Looks like you had a rough day."

"This is some bullshit. I didn't come all the way here to mop floors. Punk-ass Sarge just wants to keep a brother underneath his foot." Ozzie's hands were dry from bleach, and the small of his back throbbed from bending over the bucket.

"Come on out with us tonight, Philips. Blow off some of that steam."

"I need to brush up on my German."

"That's what Monday nights are for. Come on, it's Friday night, Square Pants. And it's blues night, which means we won't have no trouble with them white boys. They'll all be on the other side of town at one of those Billy clubs, listening to that country crap."

They had just received their month's pay. Ozzie had earned eighty dollars. He had wired thirty-five dollars to his mother and decided to live off ten dollars a week for the next month and put five dollars in the American Express for a rainy day.

"Sure."

"Okay, we walk over at twenty-one hundred."

The Federal Eagle Club was just east of the Benjamin Franklin Village, the new barracks still under construction. According to Morgan, the club was known for good music and great bratwurst, and hospitably welcomed Negro soldiers on blues and jazz nights. The best part was that it was located within walking distance of the barracks, since none of the men owned cars.

As they made their way to the entrance, Morgan passed out peppermints to Ozzie and the three others who had joined them. "Don't want your foul breath offending the ladies," he said, chuckling.

"Once I pull my harmonica out and play three notes, it's all over, turkeys," said a guy named Satchel. He was tall and reedy and never without his harmonica pressed against his front shirt pocket.

Inside, the lights were dimmed, and the sultry sounds of the blues immediately relaxed Ozzie.

Satchel clapped his hands together. "Philips, what's your poison?"

Ozzie opened his mouth to say club soda, but the thought crossed his mind that a beer wouldn't hurt him. After what he'd been through this week with his first sergeant and the mess hall, he deserved that much. He'd just stay away from the hard stuff.

Satchel brought over mugs of pils, a light golden beer that Ozzie had seen men drinking in Kitzingen. He tipped the glass to his lips and drank as the men exchanged gripes about work.

"I'm sick of these crackers thinking I work for them."

"Didn't they get the memo? Slavery is over."

"And with Truman's executive order to desegregate, you'd think these clowns would change."

"Things ain't changing. Least not for me. I had this one corporal-ass redneck ask me if I wouldn't mind polishing his boots. I looked at him like he was crazy, then walked away like I didn't even hear him."

"What's worse, they've taught the Germans to be afraid of us. They can't stand to see us with these women. That's why I'm about to get me one of these honeys tonight." Satchel stood, patted his pocket for his harmonica, and walked toward two women sitting at the bar.

"The system is pure bullshit."

"An abomination," Ozzie offered.

"You always trying to kill us with those big words."

"Right, you see why I told you he was like a damn professor. You know this fool wanted to stay in and practice his German tonight," Morgan teased, and the men at the table roared.

"Okay, okay." Ozzie toasted his mug to Morgan's. "I'm here now. You were right. Glad you got me out."

"You smell that perfume? That's my cue." One of the guys got up and the others followed, leaving Ozzie at the table alone. He drank while he watched Morgan show one of the German girls how to do the jitterbug.

A thin waitress dressed in a black short-sleeved dress walked by with a tray of shots.

Ozzie touched her arm. "Hey, I'll take one."

She spun around. "It is cheaper to buy the bottle."

Ozzie didn't like her tone. It reminded him of First Sergeant Petty talking down to him. In an instant, his good mood was gone. He'd had enough of white people telling him what to do.

"I didn't ask you all of that," he spat. "Mind your business and give me what I asked for."

Ozzie knew he was taking out his frustration on this woman, but he couldn't stop himself. The power felt good. He looked up into her face, ready to say more, but then he stopped. Those saucer-shaped eyes. They stared at each other. It was the woman to whom he had given the medicine in the village.

"You will regret it by the end of the night." She turned, but he brushed her arm again.

"We've met. The medicine for your papa."

She blinked. "You Americans are all the same," she hissed, and then huffed off.

Ozzie threw back the shot of brown liquor. He didn't even know what was in the shot, but it felt good coating his chest. Once it had settled, he felt awful about his encounter with the woman. He had treated her the way the white troops treated him, and she didn't deserve that. He got up to search for her, eventually spotting her at the side of the bar, restocking her drinks tray. Ozzie had to squeeze between patrons to get to her.

"Can I buy you a drink?"

"I told you, it is cheaper by the bottle." She drilled her gaze into him.

"Then give me the bottle and come have one with me, please." He placed his hand to his heart.

She looked at him long and hard and then walked away. Ozzie found the toilet. When he returned, the waitress stood with the liquor and two shot glasses next to his table. She popped it, poured, and held her glass up to him. "*Prost,*" she said.

"Cheers," he said, and then downed his.

While she gathered the glasses on the table, another girl nudged her, said something in German, and they walked away.

Maybe it was the effect of the alcohol, but Ozzie felt like the music was pulsing all through him. A shapely woman with rosy cheeks walked by him, and he patted her arm to dance. She smiled at him, and he let her lead him onto the floor. When Morgan saw Ozzie dancing, he gave him a thumbs-up.

Satchel bumped him. "Welcome to the party, my brother. The view is good from here."

Ozzie pressed against the rosy-cheeked woman on the dance floor. She was the first lady he had held since being deployed, and she smelled like he had imagined white girls did, kind of like strawberry shortcake. They swayed. When the song ended, everyone clapped, and Ozzie was thinking about getting another shot from his bottle. He moved through the crowd back to his table.

"What, I am good enough to drink with but not to dance?" the waitress said.

"I looked for you."

"You did not look enough."

He liked the direct way she spoke to him. No-nonsense, with her soft German accent.

"Want to dance now?"

"No," she said, and then marched off. Although she was slim, she managed to have hips, and the way she swung them sent a spark pulsing inside him.

The next morning, Ozzie woke up with an awful hangover, but it was the most fun he'd had in the six weeks since arriving in Germany. When the same guys mentioned they were going out that evening, Ozzie was in. When he stepped into the Federal Eagle Club, he found himself scanning the room for the saucer-eyed waitress. He didn't see her. Fats Waller's "Your Feet's Too Big" was playing, and once again Ozzie felt right at home. Morgan and Satchel wasted no time sidling up to two single women. All the tables were full, so Ozzie leaned against the wall, scanning the crowd.

"You came back for seconds?" she asked. She wore her hair loose around her shoulders, and a little smile played on her face. Had she been looking for him too? Without giving it a second thought, Ozzie took her hand and led her to the dance floor just as the music slowed down several beats. She wore another simple dress open at the throat, and Ozzie thought that she had a lovely collarbone.

As his torso moved against hers, the sweet, fruity fragrance of her overpowered his senses.

"You do not even know my name."

She was right. "Excuse my manners." He leaned back so that he could see her eyes. "My name is Ozzie. And you?"

"Jelka."

He pulled her back to him. "It's nice to meet you, Jelka."

"What kind of name is Ozzie?" Her "what" sounded like "vhat," and once again he found her accent endearing.

"It's a nickname."

She looked up into his face, confused.

"A name that my friends and family call me. My real name is Osbourne. Most of the fellas in the army call me by my last name, Philips."

"Osbourne." She rolled it around in her mouth. "I like that better."

"Are you working tonight?"

"No, it's my night off. But I can still get you a cocktail."

Ozzie had come with the thought that he wouldn't drink, but the moment she offered, he got thirsty. Once the song ended, Jelka led him to two high chairs at the bar.

"Two shots of Jägermeister," she said to the girl tending bar.

Ozzie raised his glass to her and then downed it. She did the same. The music sped back up.

"Will you teach me how to do that dance?" Jelka tilted her chin.

"You want to learn the Lindy Hop?"

She nodded.

Ozzie was a good dancer, and after another shot, he spun Jelka to her feet and showed her the step. When she didn't seem to get it, he grabbed her around the waist and moved her hips.

"Like this?" She smiled.

"You got it."

As the night wore on, Ozzie had waved off other girls as Jelka produced more drinks and they burned holes in the dance floor. The bartender shouted, "Last call," and Jelka leaned into Ozzie. "Osbourne, will you walk me home?"

Ozzie felt a warm sensation in his cheeks. He liked the way she said his name, and he dipped his head so she couldn't see him blush. "Of course."

He motioned to Satchel that he was going. Satchel pointed to him, signaling the universal *You the man.* Ozzie waved him off and held the door open for Jelka. The night air refreshed him as they strolled down the street.

"Do you like the moon?" she asked.

"How do you know?"

"You keep looking at it."

"When I was a kid, I thought the moon was my protector," Ozzie confessed, remembering long nights at his bedroom window watching it while he waited for his father to come home.

"I like the moon too. I pray to the moon."

"I don't pray."

"You should."

A gush of wind caught the collar of his drab coat, and Jelka stepped closer to him. Her trench was thin and didn't seem adequate.

"You warm enough?" he asked her.

"No."

"How can I get you warm?" He put his arm around her shoulders, and caressing her caused a familiar ache in his groin.

"Will you stay with me tonight?" She asked so directly that Ozzie stumbled, unaware that he had been lonely for a woman's comfort until she asked. Her delicate voice, her small fingers on his back, and her heady scent soothed him. Ozzie was hungrier for affection than he had realized, and Jelka's invitation turned a light on inside him. He didn't trust himself to speak, so he reached for the back of her head, brought her face to his, and kissed her slowly, threading his tongue into her warm mouth.

"Come with me." She grabbed his hand and led him down one street after another. They finally reached a large three-story house at the end of the road with a candle burning in the window.

Leading him up the front stairs, she knocked lightly until a thick woman with her hair tied in a scarf appeared. Ozzie watched as they exchanged words in German.

"Come." Jelka held his hand as the woman hobbled up the creaky stairs, down the dimly lit hall, and into a room on the left.

"Gute Nacht," the woman bade them before closing the door quickly behind her.

The bedroom was small and musty. The bed looked as if they'd barely fit, but Ozzie's insides were on fire. He reached for Jelka. She smashed her face against his, kissing him rough and deep.

"You are lonely. I can tell." She unbuckled his trousers.

"How?" He ran his tongue over her collarbone like he had wanted to do all night.

"Because I see myself in you."

Ozzie slipped her dress over her head and tossed it to the ground.

"Give it all to me." She grabbed his face. "I am here to make it all better."

They fell to the bed, and as Ozzie moved against her, Jelka grabbed his hips and pushed him to take her hard and fast.

Afterward, Jelka rolled from beneath him, breathing heavily. She opened her purse and pulled out a package of cigarettes. She lit one and offered it to him. Ozzie shook his head.

"First time with a German woman?" she said, puffing, her lips still stained a faint red from lipstick.

"What do you think?"

"So that is a yes." She moved back toward him and rested her head on his shoulder. "Maybe I am your last, Osbourne."

She took another puff, stubbed out her cigarette in the ashtray on the nightstand, and then trailed wet kisses down his stomach.

Part 2

We will be known forever
by the tracks we leave.
—**DAKOTA PROVERB**

CHAPTER 12

West Oak Forest Academy, September 1965

SOPHIA

When Sophia's eyes fluttered open, it was because Willa's alarm was blaring. Her roommate stretched her elbows overhead and then slammed her hand down to silence it. Sophia watched Willa throw her legs over the side of the bed and stuff her feet in a satiny pair of slippers.

"Rise and shine," Willa said. "Did you sleep okay?"

Sophia swallowed. "Yes, you?"

"Like a baby," she said, grabbing a tote bag of skin-care products. She shuffled out the door.

Sophia breathed a sigh of relief. She had slept soundly through the night and hadn't bothered Willa with her night terrors and screams. She looked up at the ceiling and silently thanked Walter's God.

Once again, she arrived early for all her classes. She said very little throughout the day. In physics class, Nancy lowered herself in the seat beside Sophia and then propped her forearm crutches against the wall. They discussed an upcoming project. In all her other classes, Sophia sat alone.

Halfway through her composition class, she realized that Thursday was only two days away, and she needed to learn the nuts and bolts of basketball before she reported to practice. There had to be more rules than what she had learned from playing two-on-two and H-O-R-S-E with her brothers. Before lunch, she made her way to the library with the hope of checking out a book that would help her.

The library sat in the breezeway between the boys' school, Donoghue Hall, and the girls' school, Campbell Hall, and was used by both genders. Inside, big windows were flanked by abstract paintings hanging from the walls. There was a big open common area with overstuffed chairs where students hung out with books opened in their laps. Sophia glanced at the rows and rows of library books and wondered where she should start.

"May I help you?" asked a woman with clear-framed glasses and frizzy white hair.

"Yes, ma'am. I'm looking for a book on how to play basketball," Sophia whispered.

The woman let out a hearty chuckle. "Ah, my friend Alastair has gotten to you too?"

"Excuse me?"

"The basketball coach with the British accent," she said, imitating his closed-mouthed way of speaking.

"Yes." Sophia relaxed. "I guess you can say that he did."

"I have just the book for you," she said. "Right this way."

Sophia followed the short woman to the section marked "Sports in Society." Halfway down the aisle on the middle shelf, she plucked out a book. "Try this."

Sophia took the book in her hand. *Winning Basketball Plays* by Clair Bee.

"This should at least explain the rules of the game to you. But you will also need to practice."

"Yes, I know." Sophia opened the book and scanned the inside flap. The book smelled vintage, like it hadn't had much use.

The librarian shifted on her feet. "How are you getting on here? I know this is all new for you."

When Sophia glanced in the woman's direction, she noticed that her gray eyes were kind. She reminded her of her counselor, Mrs. Brown at Brooks High, and before she could stop herself, she blurted, "It's been a bit overwhelming, trying to take in so much newness at once."

The librarian nodded. "I can imagine that things might feel strange around here. Change is never easy, but it's the only thing that's constant. I for one am glad that West Oak Forest has put in the effort for equality. It's high time we right some wrongs around here."

Sophia didn't know what to say. So far, the librarian had been kinder than all her teachers combined.

The librarian lowered her voice. "Listen, dear, the library can always be your refuge. It's a safe space under my watch."

"Thank you," Sophia said, clutching the book to her chest. "What's your name?"

The librarian smacked her hand against her forehead. "Silly me, for not introducing myself. My name is Mrs. Fordham."

"Sophia Clark."

"Pleased to meet you, dear. Now, there's a little room back here." She motioned for Sophia to follow her to a corner door. "If you and your friends ever need a little privacy, it's always unlocked. Leave no trace, and you'll never hear a peep out of me." She winked.

"Thank you, ma'am. That's so generous."

Mrs. Fordham erected her shoulders and smiled. "I participated in the March on Washington in '63. Set up a little table and handed out Dixie cups of water to those who wanted it. That day changed my life. I'm here if you need me." She reached over and squeezed Sophia's hand.

Sophia left the library with her book on basketball feeling empowered and pleased. She braved the cafeteria alone for the first time and enjoyed a chicken salad sandwich with carrot sticks. The carrots made her think of her brothers, Karl and Lu, and she wondered if Walter was making sure that they ate and got through their morning chores and to school on time. She thought about the farm animals, hoping that Unc had secured the help he needed to run the property without dragging her brothers out of school. She thought about Ma Deary and the Old Man, relieved that neither had come to get her. At least not yet.

She hadn't seen Willa or Louis, but she couldn't wait to begin eating if she was going to keep up her plan of arriving early to class. At the dessert bar, she wrapped a sugar cookie in a napkin and slipped it in her bag for later. Then she opened the book on basketball: It was a habit she had picked up on the farm, walking while reading. Page two had a drawing of a two-three zone defense that she studied. Before Sophia knew what was happening, she had collided into a mass of muscle. The book flew from her fingers and to the floor. As she stumbled after it, a strong hand grabbed hold of her forearm.

Sophia remembered the story of the boy being shoved around by the football players and braced herself for an angry outburst, but when she risked looking up into the boy's face, her breath caught in her throat. He was Negro and fine. His gaze was so magnetic that she couldn't turn away. What was this feeling that he had ignited in her?

"Sorry, I should have been paying more attention."

His gentle hand continued to steady her. "It's cool." His voice was deep.

He stood two inches taller than she did, so she had to tilt her face up to see him. He had a square jaw and dreamy pecan-colored eyes.

"You all right?" he asked. When he finally let her elbow go, she could still feel the electricity of his touch.

"Yes, sorry. I was just trying to do two things at once."

He reached down, lifted the basketball book off the floor, and snickered. "I can assure you that you can't learn how to dribble and shoot from a book."

Her cheeks flushed. "I already know how to play."

He looked her up and down. "I've been hooping all my life, and you don't look like a ball player." His attention made the back of her neck hot. Who was he?

"Well, you'll just have to see," she stammered, suddenly aware of the stray hairs springing loose from her ponytail.

"You new?"

She nodded.

"I'm Max McBay." He stuck his hand out, and she placed hers in his. The warmth from his touch traveled all the way down to her toes.

"Sophia Clark."

"Does this mean you're trying out for the basketball team?"

"I guess so. The coach cornered me at the sports fair and told me to show up on Thursday."

"Coach Fletcher?"

"Accent?"

"Yes, he's my advanced physics teacher." Max stepped closer and lowered his voice to a whisper. "He's one of the few teachers around here who isn't prejudiced. You'll like him."

"Good to hear."

"Well, if you don't discover what you need in that book, come find me. I'm always in the boys' gym." Max reached for the sugar cookie from the top of her bag and took a bite. Then he rewrapped it in the napkin and put it back. "See you around." He strolled into the cafeteria in the same airy way that Willa walked, like he belonged.

Sophia didn't have time to grab a fresh cookie, so she shoved the bitten one down into her bag. That boy had some nerve, sizing her up like that and eating part of her cookie. But as she walked through the quad, light-hearted and sweaty, she found it hard to be upset.

On Thursday afternoon, Sophia walked into the athletic center to the scent of sticky armpits and burnt rubber. The oversize lobby was painted canary yellow and showcased West Oak Forest Academy's pendants and posters. A wide glass case, centered on the back wall, displayed multiple awards, championship plaques, trophies, and photographs of boys' basketball teams stretching back over half a century. Sophia could hear dribbling, shoes sliding and screeching against the parquet floors. But there were two gyms, one on the right and the other on the left, and Coach Fletcher hadn't been specific. As the student athletes bounded into the lobby, Sophia pretended to study the trophy case until she could gauge which side was for the boys and which side was the girls.

She entered the gym on the right and found Coach Fletcher standing in the center of the court, wearing a matching blue short set. A whistle hung from his neck, and his sandy brown hair fell across his forehead. He clutched his clipboard to his side.

Sophia had worn her school gym uniform because she didn't have anything else and was relieved to see that the other girls had worn their uniforms too.

"Sophia." Coach Fletcher held up his list and checked her name off. "Good to see you. Find a ball and go warm up."

Some of the girls were dribbling; some caught the balls while others threw up shots. Sophia knew how to shoot a basketball. On the farm, Walter had fashioned a makeshift hoop out of a milk crate and nailed it to a dying tree. Though her brothers often drafted her for a game of two against two, she had never played in an actual gym. Brooks High only had a boys' basketball team, and while they were good, Sophia had never stayed to watch the games because she needed to tend to evening chores.

A ball rolled toward Sophia, and she stopped it with her foot. When she reached for it, the basketball felt firm in her hands. Not heavy and flat, like the balls Walter had brought home from the neighborhood dump. Sophia dribbled a few times to get the feel of the bouncy ball. It felt almost natural as she pressed her hand against the leather mound, and it sprang right back up to kiss her palm. She did the same motion over and over, and before she knew what was happening, she felt like the ball had become an extension of her right hand. The chatter and movement of the other girls in the room faded from her mind as she picked up her feet and started walking with the ball. When she realized that she remained in control, she jogged with the ball toward the basket. At the top of the key, she lifted the ball with both hands, positioned her wrist back, and let the ball fly. It hit the backboard and went through the hoop.

Swish.

That was what Walter always said when he made a shot. *Swish.*

Sophia ran for the ball, grabbed it, and then released it again and again. A few balls sailed through the hoop, while others bounced off the rim. Each shot she took felt good. She felt alive. By the time she heard Coach Fletcher's shrilly whistle, she was hot and damp all over.

"Gather around, girls," Coach Fletcher called.

"What is she doing here?"

Sophia had lost herself so completely in shooting and dribbling that she hadn't paid much attention to the other girls. But by now, she could pick Patty's whiny voice out of a lineup.

"I hope she's not going to be on the team," Opal said, snickering. She was Patty's friend who had made fun of Sophia's nightgown in the bathroom.

"And look at those shoes." Patty put her hand up to her mouth to hide her laughter. But everyone had heard her, and all eyeballs shifted to Sophia's feet.

Before class that morning, Sophia had no choice but to go to the administration building to rummage through the lost and found. It had been Ma Deary's solution for whatever items they needed. With only Ma Deary's Mary Janes and the donated loafers, Sophia had gone in search of a pair of tennis shoes for practice. But in the oversize rubber bin of forgotten items, there were no sneakers. She did manage an umbrella and a pair of rubber-soled oxfords that she had hoped would work for basketball. As she kept her eyes cast down, taking in everyone's feet, she saw that the girls wore either Converse All Stars or canvas runabouts, which made the oxfords stand out like a turd in a fruit bowl.

"Patty. Is there something funny?" Coach Fletcher called out.

"No, sir." Patty straightened.

Coach Fletcher pushed his bangs out of his eyes. "Break into two lines, girls." Sophia waited to see who would go where and decided on the line opposite Patty's, wanting to be as far from her as possible.

"We are going to do passing drills. Patty and Sophia, you are up first."

Patty rolled her eyes. "Can someone else go? I need to tie my shoe," she faked.

"We can wait." Coach Fletcher looked at her pointedly.

After retying her shoe, Patty stood, and Coach Fletcher threw her the ball.

"Now, shuffle your feet and pass the ball back and forth to get from one end of the court to the other. Next two, when they reach half-court, then you follow suit." He blew his whistle to signal that they should begin.

Patty threw the ball hard to Sophia, but she caught it. To Sophia's surprise, they made it down the court without once dropping the ball. After going over the passing drill several times, Coach moved on to dribbling skills. Fifteen minutes before the end of practice, he broke the girls down into teams of two. The returning girls wore red pinnies over their tops; Sophia and the newer recruits wore blue pinnies. Sophia and the girls in blue lost two to twelve to the red team. When Coach Fletcher blew his whistle to end the game, Sophia was out of breath, and her chest was soaked through.

"Huddle up, girls," Coach Fletcher called, and passed out the practice and game schedules. Then he took down the girls' uniform sizes and preferred numbers for their jerseys. As the girls headed to the locker room, Coach signaled to Sophia. "Hey, you played really well today."

"Thank you."

He lowered his voice. "Normally, we only allow trainers on the court. Do you need a pair?"

Sophia's mouth went dry. "I forgot to pack them, and I won't be going home for a while. I could ask my—"

"We have extra tennis shoes in the office, left over from previous gym years. Write down your size." He extended the clipboard. "Then arrive a few minutes early to practice tomorrow, and I'll have them ready for you," he said with a kind smile.

Sophia wanted to hug him.

"Go, Bears," he said, pointing to the mascot in the center of the court.

"Go, Bears." She smiled.

When Sophia hobbled out of the girls' gym, she heard loud voices coming from across the hall. A gang of giant-size boys streamed out of their gym in groups of three and four, bantering loudly and horseplaying. Max was pulling a windbreaker over his T-shirt when they spotted each other. Sophia tried not to let the delight of running into him reach her face.

"Did the book help?" He gave her a sloppy grin.

"Actually, it did. Too bad I didn't have enough energy to make it through practice because you ate half of my cookie," she teased.

"Seriously, you couldn't possibly be holding on to that cookie from the other day." Max chuckled. "You should carry a piece of fruit with you to eat before practice, anyway. That'll give you real energy."

Max held the door to the athletic center for her. The night air was cool, and she could see a sliver of the quarter-moon shining through the branches of the walnut tree. They walked in silence, and the cacophony of night creatures hemming and hawing reminded her of home. Sophia racked her brain for something to talk about.

"Where are you from?" she asked, remembering Louis's question to her.

"Silver Spring."

"In Maryland?"

He nodded.

"I'm from Prince Frederick. But that's way down south," she said. "Do you have any sisters or brothers?"

"Nope, only child. I have a bunch of cousins, though. An older cousin who is like my brother; we grew up in the same neighborhood."

They wandered through the quad. "What made you come to Forest?" she asked.

"My mom's a teacher. When she heard that Forest was opening their door to Negro students, she was first in line with my application."

"But did you want to come here?"

"I don't recall really having a choice, to be honest. How about you?"

Sophia shrugged. "I was selected through a program."

"So how did you learn to play basketball? I don't know many girls who can hoop."

"Blame that on having three brothers. They needed me for their games of two-on-two and H-O-R-S-E."

"You play H-O-R-S-E?"

They were almost to her dorm, and she could feel Max slowing his pace, so she did the same. Was he enjoying their conversation too?

"The boys didn't really give me a choice."

"Well, I'd like to see you beat me in H-O-R-S-E. It will only take about five minutes for me to take you out."

"Any time you want to get clobbered, let me know," she replied boldly.

"Cocky." Max wagged his finger at her. "I like that."

Sophia felt gooseflesh run up and down her arms.

"Has Coach told you what position you're going to play?" he asked.

"Not yet."

"You look like a shooting guard or small forward to me. I play the point. Which means I control the offense." He jumped up in the air and shot a pretend basketball. When he came down, he misjudged his footing and bumped into Sophia's shoulder.

"Dag, watch it," she said, pouting.

"I'm so sorry." He stopped moving. "Where did I hurt you?"

"Right here." Sophia pointed to the top of her arm. With his palm, Max rubbed it several times. He smelled like the outdoors, and his caress made Sophia's brain fill with static.

"Better?" He looked into her eyes, and the world around her stilled.

"Yes," she breathed.

They had reached the entrance to her dorm and fell into an awkward silence.

"I guess you owed me one for crashing into you the other day," Sophia said.

"I'd never hurt a girl on purpose. My mother raised me right," he said, then he started jogging backward. "Remember, if you ever want me to school you on the court, you know where to find me." He turned the corner and moved toward the boys' dormitory. She watched him until he was out of sight.

Sophia was still replaying their conversation in her head when she walked into her dorm room.

"What are you all giddy about?" Willa looked up from her notebook. She was sitting at her small desk, already dressed in her nightclothes.

"Just thinking about . . . basketball practice. It was actually way more fun than I had expected."

"Oh, goody. Tennis was cool too. Except for this upperclassman who thought she could shut me down. I just kept my lips tight and my eyes on the ball and beat her in three sets two to one."

"Congratulations."

Willa took a hair tie from her wrist and twirled her curls into a messy bun. "My father says I have the potential to be the next Althea Gibson."

Sophia kicked off her shoes and peeled back her socks. "Who's that?"

"Only the first Negro woman to win a Grand Slam title in tennis. She won a whopping eleven titles over the course of her career."

Sophia had no idea what a Grand Slam title was, but she didn't want Willa to think she was ignorant, so she didn't ask. As Willa continued with her tennis facts, Sophia found it hard to concentrate because her thoughts kept floating back to Max.

Unable to hold it in a moment longer, she blurted, "I met a boy named Max today." She hoped that her voice sounded neutral and unaffected.

"Max! Isn't he a dreamboat? We are practically going steady." Willa slapped the desk with her palm.

Sophia felt the wind being knocked out of her.

"What did he say? Did he ask about me?"

Sophia shook her head.

"He probably didn't realize that we were roommates. Have you met Claude yet? I was thinking that he'd be a good match for you."

“No, not yet.” Sophia picked at a ball of lint on her comforter so Willa could not see the disappointment on her face.

“Claude is also on the basketball team. I’m surprised he wasn’t with Max. They’re roommates.”

Willa started describing Claude, but all Sophia could think was that Willa was already dating Max. It was the first time she had ever liked a boy, and he was off-limits. She had rotten, stinking luck. Then she remembered what she had been holding on to.

Sophia reached into the small pocket of her school bag and pulled out the napkin-wrapped cookie. She hadn’t had the heart to throw it out. When she unraveled the napkin, Max’s bite mark stared back at her in the shape of a smile. Sophia brought the cookie to her lips, sucking on the bite until it dissolved into sugar on her tongue. Then she nibbled at it until she had eaten every stale crumb.

CHAPTER 13

Mannheim, Germany, June 1951

ETHEL

At the next monthly meeting of the Mannheim Officers' Wives Club held at Dorothy Hansen's house, Ethel turned out more sharply than usual, in a silk floral swing dress with a petticoat. This month's theme was pearls, so she wore a velvet tam with over fifty pearls sewn throughout.

"So good to see you, Ethel," Dorothy greeted her warmly; a flowing string of pearls hung down to her ribs. "We haven't bumped into each other in weeks. How have you been?"

Ethel removed her pearl-beaded gloves. "I've been so busy helping at a local children's orphanage. Is it okay if I add an agenda item to our discussion today? They could use our help."

"Certainly," Dorothy said. "Why don't you go in and make yourself comfortable. We will get started in a few moments."

Ethel said a few hellos as she made her way through the living room to Julia, whose daughter cooed softly and kicked her feet against her mother's lap.

"Well, look who decided to show up," Julia teased. "I thought we had plans to meet at the May Day luncheon?"

"Honey, I know, and I'll make it up to you. Promise." Ethel slid into the seat next to Julia and tickled the baby's feet. "I have some awesome news." She could barely contain her excitement.

"What?" Julia leaned forward in her seat.

"I'm going to be a mother," Ethel whispered in her ear.

"Oh my goodness." Julia touched her stomach. "Praise God."

"Shh," Ethel grabbed Julia's hands, not ready to share her news with the women in the room. "But it's not what you think. I'm not having a baby."

Julia's face fell, confused.

"We're adopting. A little girl. Her name is Anke. She's one of the children at the orphanage I told you about."

"The orphanage that has been taking up all of your time?"

Ethel nodded. "Bert and I are picking her up on Saturday."

"Oh my God! That's wonderful." She touched her cheek. "This is such a big step. Are you ready?"

"Who knows. I've been running around feeling like a chicken without its head attached, trying to get our little place together."

"How did all this come about?" Julia still looked dumbfounded. "And I better not be the last to know."

Ethel fanned herself as she caught Julia up. "The children there would melt your little heart, girlfriend. I wish you could come with me for a visit."

Just then, Dorothy tapped a glass with a fork. "Hello, ladies, and welcome. I think we'll go ahead and get started. We have a long agenda to get through today."

Ethel's eyes swept the room, taking in the same eight or nine faces of women who attended monthly. Then she saw a pair of women whom she had not met.

"We have new members." Dorothy gestured and prompted them each to stand and introduce themselves. Once they were finished, she said, "Please take time to welcome these ladies to our club and get to know them personally. Community is everything."

Dorothy called the meeting to order and then ran through the agenda. When she finally got to new business, Ethel raised her hand.

"Yes, Ethel, you have the floor." Dorothy motioned for her to come take her place at the front of the room.

"Good afternoon, everyone. I am Ethel Gathers, for those who don't know me. I have been volunteering at the St. Hildegard's children's orphanage, not far from here, and they are greatly in need of our support."

Ethel looked around to make sure all eyes were on her before she continued. "Apparently, with the war and occupation, there have been a lot of children born between American soldiers and German women. Unfortunately, the soldiers get reassigned, and the women are left with the children. In many cases, these women are ostracized for having children out of wedlock, they cannot afford to keep their children, and so the children end up displaced, some to local orphanages."

Ethel heard an audible breath. Many mothers were rocking babies on their laps or had toddlers playing at their feet.

"Sister Ursula, the gracious nun who runs the home, could use our help."

"This sounds like a worthy cause. What can we do?" Dorothy asked.

"There are a lot of moving parts." Ethel rolled her shoulders back. "We need to aid the German mothers here who are raising their children without support."

"For the mothers, maybe we could make gift baskets filled with baby supplies, perishable food, and blankets. I can head that up," offered Dorothy.

"That's a great idea," Ethel replied. "The children in the orphanage need our support as well. Most are mixed race, German mothers and American Negro fathers." She noticed a few of the women squirming in their seats. But she continued, "Being in Europe this past year has made me appreciate the privilege of being an American citizen. Wouldn't you agree?" She made eye contact with as many as she could. "I've made up my mind that these children, having American blood, deserve those same privileges. I'm working on a plan to have them adopted by American families, both here on military business and those back home."

The room was silent. Then Julia, the only other Negro woman in the room, spoke up. "Ethel, I had no clue. Those poor children. I think that's a wonderful idea. Anything I can do to help you, please let me know."

"Me too."

"I can help there too."

Dorothy stood. "Ethel, thank you for bringing us such a wonderful cause to throw our support behind. Ladies, why don't we break up into committees. We will need one for the German mothers on the ground, one in support of the orphanage, and the other for helping the children with clothes, shoes, and personal items."

Ethel walked Julia back to her apartment, carrying the baby's bag over her arm while Julia pushed the pram.

"That was something else. You sure know how to rally the troops." Julia cackled. "I just knew those white women would turn their noses up at helping our children."

"It's all in the way you present the information. Once Dorothy got on board, I knew the others would fall in line."

"So, tell me about this baby of yours. How old is she? Where's she from? What does she look like?"

Ethel couldn't keep the smile from her face. "She's three years old and took to me on my first visit. Head full of hair, bright eyes, an angel, really."

"I was going to offer you some of our hand-me-downs, but since she's older than my little bits, you'll be handing things down to us." Julia linked arms with Ethel, and they swung them back and forth like silly schoolgirls.

"My life is about to change. I've been wanting this for so long."

"You are blessed and highly favored. How could you not be," Julia ribbed her. "The saint that you are."

"I'm far from a saint, but adopting Anke does feel well with my soul. From the first moment I held her in my arms, I knew that she was heaven-sent."

They stopped at the intersection and waited for a line of military trucks to rumble by.

"But we still have a lot of work to do. Moving one child is simply not enough. There are so many others who need loving homes."

"Now that you have the Officers' Wives on board, that will lighten the load."

"That's a start, but we need to create a movement to find good Negro families stationed here in Germany willing to adopt, then get it done without being delayed by months of paperwork."

They had reached Julia's apartment building, and little birds chirped hungrily in the silver birch tree. A woman clutching a preschooler in each hand smiled as she passed them by.

"Every evening when I leave, they follow me to the gate, pleading, 'Mummy, Mummy, we want a mummy.' It's heartbreaking."

"I don't even want to imagine. But we'll get it done. Don't forget, we have the Negro Wives of Mannheim."

"But we voted to take a hiatus over the summer."

"You and I can divvy up the list and make phone calls to see who is willing to roll up her sleeves and help."

"You're right."

"Of course I'm right. Now stop worrying and go get ready to pick up your daughter."

At that Ethel smiled. Her daughter. She was about to become a mother.

On Saturday, Ethel set a fried egg over buttered grits with two pieces of toast in front of Bert, along with his black coffee. Although Bert had good intentions, he had been too busy doing fieldwork and conducting drills and training to find time to visit the orphanage until today.

After finishing, Bert pushed his empty plate away from him, satisfied. "Okay then, darling, lead the way."

They arrived at the gates of the orphanage to children's high-pitched voices, laughing and playing. When Ethel shouted out hello, boys and girls dressed in ill-matched clothing came running from every direction.

Sister Ursula unlocked the gate. Ethel and Bert stepped into the courtyard to children who waved and bounced on their toes, excited to see them.

"This is my husband, Albert Gathers," Ethel introduced him to Sister Ursula as two girls wrapped their arms around Ethel's waist. *"Hallo, meine Damen,"* Ethel cooed.

"Everyone just calls me Bert." He extended his hand to Sister Ursula.

"Nice to have you here, Bert." She smiled. "Your wife has been a godsend for us. Come with me."

As they followed Sister Ursula, Ethel noticed that two of the older girls had younger girls fastened between their knees, styling their hair. She had purchased extra combs, brushes, and pomade and taught them a few simple hairstyles. Watching them at work pleased her. Little ones rode tricycles, and a few had sticks and were digging holes in the dirt.

Two boys ran up to Bert but stopped right in front of him. Bert leaned down and put his hand up for five. The boys tapped his hand.

Then one produced a rubber ball, and within seconds, Bert had a game of catch going with several boys.

As Ethel moved deeper into the courtyard, she spotted Anke underneath the sycamore tree with one of the nuns, rolling a pram back and forth. When Anke saw Ethel, her mouth flew open, and she scooted in Ethel's direction.

"Mum, Mum," Anke said, holding her arms up to Ethel, and as Ethel held her against her heartbeat, all was right with the world.

Ethel and Bert stayed all morning, and Sister Ursula invited them to join the children for a simple lunch of vegetable soup and bread. Bert had taken a liking to one of the older boys, Franz, whose hair Ethel had cut on her second day of volunteering. Bert and Franz sat together during lunch. There wasn't much food to go around, so Ethel sipped on a cup of tea while the girls fought to sit near her.

After lunch, Ethel pried herself away from the children to tell Sister Ursula that she had proposed some of the army wives help with arranging gift baskets for the local mothers in need. "Could you help me locate the mothers?"

"We keep a log of addresses inside the office. I can share them with you."

"I'm also going to see if there are any military families willing to adopt. These children deserve parents."

Sister Ursula squeezed her hands in agreement.

When the sun dipped in the sky, Ethel motioned to Bert that it was time to go. Sister Ursula had packed up Anke's few things, and they had signed the necessary paperwork that gave Ethel and Bert permission to take her home.

Ethel carried Anke on her hip toward the gate, and as Bert followed, Franz was on his heels.

"Me too," the boy pleaded, latching on to Bert's palm.

Bert exchanged a sheepish look with Ethel. "What's one more?"

Ethel didn't give herself time to talk either of them out of adopting Franz too. She simply nodded in agreement. "Sister Ursula?"

The nun's hand fluttered to her veil. "Yes, of course. Go for now, and when you come back next week, Ethel, I'll have the temporary papers ready for Franz."

Anke rode in Bert's arms with Franz clutching Ethel's hand as they all headed home.

When Bert unlocked the front door to their second-floor apartment, there was a white teddy bear with a red bow sitting in the recliner. Anke rushed over to the bear and crushed it to her chest.

"Do you like it?" Ethel sat down in the chair and held Anke in her arms. Then she played a game of peekaboo with the bear, much to Anke's delight. Her peals of laughter made Ethel's heart swoon.

"Come on in, son," Bert said, his hand on Franz's back. Unlike Anke, Franz took timid steps around the living room with his eyes darting over the television set, sofa, and coffee table. The transistor radio seemed to catch his attention, and he meandered to where it sat on the bookshelf in the corner. Before touching it, he looked at Bert, who nodded encouragingly. "Let me show you how this works." Bert turned the dial, and when German folk music cranked out, Franz threw his hands up.

"You like this?" Bert said. "Let me see you dance," and he tapped his toes and snapped his fingers until the children imitated his movements.

Franz stomped and twirled, and Anke abandoned the bear and shook her hips. Ethel sat watching until Bert reached for her and pulled her to her feet. The four of them held hands and danced around the living room in a circle.

The Gatherses lived in a two-bedroom apartment, and Ethel had converted the spare room into a bedroom for Anke. All week she had dashed between the homes of the Negro Wives of Mannheim, picking up secondhand items. Pink drapes hung from the window, and she had spread a frilly comforter over the twin-size bed. Once the kids were settled with snacks and coloring sheets, Bert ran over to the barracks to see if he could secure a cot for Franz.

While Ethel prepared the sauce for chicken à la king, she heard Bert lugging in the camp bed with Franz quickly at his side. As the two rearranged the bedroom to make space for Franz, Ethel and Anke made a game of setting the table.

Over dinner, Bert said, "Once we have the official adoption papers, I can put in for a larger place. The kids sharing a room will work for now, but long term, they'll need more space."

Ethel nodded.

"Are you happy, darling?"

"Don't I look it?" She smiled back. "After all this time. We finally did it. It's not the way I pictured it, but the Lord sure works in mysterious ways."

When Ethel climbed into her own bed that night, she was so giddy from her day that sleep eluded her. She thought back to her hands on the grotto at the shrine of Lourdes and the words she had heard. Ethel closed her eyes and mumbled "Thank you" over and over.

CHAPTER 14

Mannheim, Germany, September 1948

OZZIE

At 0700 Ozzie and his company gathered around their battalion fleet to conduct "Motor Pool Monday," a standing weekly battle rhythm during which the troops facilitated preventative maintenance checks and service on their military vehicles and howitzers. Ozzie had his head in the guts of a Borgward B3000, replacing transmission fluid, when he heard First Sergeant Petty roar: "If a tire falls off because the lug nuts aren't properly tightened to the correct torque, then you're a sitting duck in the middle of combat. Leave no screw untouched."

"Yes, First Sergeant," the company replied in unison.

Tire irons, screwdrivers, pliers, and jack wrenches clicked and clanked as men changed tires, examined belts and loose cables, and replaced hoses. The transmission fluid smelled sweet, almost like candy, as Ozzie removed the dipstick, wiped it on a towel, and then reinserted it to check the levels. The night before, Ozzie had spent over two hours before bed studying technical manuals and reviewing inspection worksheets to assure that he wouldn't make any mistakes. Motor pool checkup was an essential part of his job. If any of his vehicles left base with faulty equipment, Ozzie's unit would feel the ass chewing.

Morgan was crouched down, checking the tire pressure on a cargo van. "Looks like somebody got lucky this weekend," he teased.

Ozzie tried keeping the smile from his face as he topped off the fluids.

"'Bout time our boy got that stick out his ass and had a little fun." Satchel knelt on the ground, changing the spark plugs to a generator. "Let me guess. It was that big-eyed waitress, wasn't it?"

"A gentleman never kisses and tells." Ozzie wiped grease from his hands.

"Well, I sure ain't no gentleman," Satchel sang as if it were the blues. "I gotta honey here, and a fine-ass woman back there." Satchel tapped the generator, keeping time with the rhythm. "Gave her a promise ring and everything. But shit, it's impossible to stay faithful over here, and that's as real as a chicken wing."

The guys all cackled at Satchel's song. "You ain't never lied," Morgan said to him, then turned solemn.

"It's the isolation that gets to me. We are literally on the other side of the world."

"Away from everything we know." Ozzie closed the hood to the truck.

"Being with men all day, every day. Shiiit, you need a touch from a woman to make life bearable."

Ozzie nodded in agreement.

"That's why Germany stays right here in Germany," Morgan piped. "Work hard, play hard." And all the men agreed.

During the days, Ozzie kept his nose clean at work; in the evenings, he practiced his German and brushed up on his Latin, so that when the opportunity came to be assigned to the Intelligence unit, he'd be ready. He had gone to the Federal Eagle Club for the past three weekends with his buddies and spent more money than he had intended on those nights with Jelka at the rooming house, which charged by the hour. When he had tried to negotiate with the thick woman in the scarf, she'd told him that her husband had been a local dentist but never returned home after the war. "This is how I make ends meet for my children," she said with sad eyes.

After patronizing the house a few times, Ozzie noticed it was only Negro soldiers with their German brides who rented rooms, and when he asked the woman, she told him. "The one time I let a white American soldier in led to trouble. I do not understand the hatred in them." She tsked her teeth.

Ozzie wanted to explain to her that the hatred had been bred, and at the root of it was fear, but when he was with Jelka, he didn't feel like thinking about America's race problem.

On his next Sunday off, Jelka asked him to join her at a small park a few blocks from the bar where she worked. The fall day was cool, and the orange and red leaves fell steadily all around them. Construction work could be heard on Käfertaler Street, the main throughfare, as buildings were being restored and roads repaved. Ozzie had worn a sweater under his army jacket so that he could offer it to Jelka if she got chilly. She had arrived first and was spread out underneath an oak tree on the wool blanket he had given her. She grabbed his face and kissed him gently on his lips. Out of habit, Ozzie looked around to see if anyone was watching them. He carried a brown paper bag with sandwiches from the mess hall, a tin of potato chips, and her favorite drink, Fanta. She smiled brightly when she tipped the drink to her fingers.

"Are you hitched?" Jelka tucked the Fanta between her fingers.

"No," he said, pushing thoughts of Rita away. He still had not received a letter from her. "Why? Do you have someone?"

The corners of her eyes drooped before she turned her lips into a grimace. "Once. But . . . I lost him to the war."

"I'm sorry to hear that." As if consoling her, he handed her a liverwurst sandwich.

"That was a long time ago."

"Do you want to talk about it?"

"No." She took a big bite and changed the subject. "This tastes good."

As Ozzie watched her eat the sandwich, he felt content. In the short time they had been seeing each other, he had come to enjoy taking care of Jelka. Last weekend, he had bought her a tube of lipstick and a bottle of fingernail polish from the commissary, and the look and kiss she had given him made him want to give her even more. She didn't require much, and he liked that about her. He knew that he wasn't in love, yet he enjoyed her company.

"Do you ever get time off from work?"

"If I want. Why?" She cocked her head at him, and he wiped away a bit of mayonnaise from the corner of her mouth.

"I have leave, a three-day weekend is coming up. I was thinking about traveling somewhere. I want to see more of Germany."

Jelka looked up at Ozzie. "We could go to Frankfurt. I have a cousin there. She can put us up."

"Really? You'll take me?"

"Of course," she said, sliding in closer to him and threading her leg with his.

On the second Friday in October, Ozzie had misjudged how far the Mannheim Hauptbahnhof was from his post, and by the time he reached the bustling station lobby for their trip to Frankfurt, Jelka looked flustered and red in the face. "What took you so long? I thought you were not coming."

"I'm sorry. Didn't mean to worry you. Just got a little turned around."

She grabbed his hand. "We must hurry."

They walked down the steps, through a long hall, and then up to platform four. Ozzie had only enough time to ask if she had the tickets when the train blew into the station. They found two seats together, and Jelka sighed.

"I have not been away from home in many years. The last time I took the train to Frankfurt, I was thirteen."

"How old are you now?"

"I am twenty-one."

Ozzie's eyebrows rose with surprise. The way the light hit her face, she looked seventeen.

"You?"

"Nineteen, but I'll be twenty soon."

"I am older than you. That means I get to tell you what to do?" She kissed him and then put her forehead to his so they were eye to eye. "And how I want you to do it."

When they got off the train in Frankfurt, Jelka hailed a taxicab. As they drove down cobblestone streets, the devastations of war were at every turn. What obviously once had been beautiful architectural structures now sat in ruins.

"This is Altstadt, the Old Town, destroyed by air raids." Jelka pointed to the rubble piled in places where timber-framed houses once stood. Then she instructed the driver to stop there. He parked across the street from a cathedral with entire walls blasted away and the roof collapsed in several places.

"That is what is left of the Kaiserdom St. Bartholomäus. The largest and most lovely church in Frankfurt," Jelka said once they were standing on the street.

Ozzie heard drills and hammers and smelled ammonia, burnt rubber, and concrete. "I can still see its beauty." He tilted his head.

"Come, the apartment is not far. We can walk the rest of the way to view the neighborhood."

"Careful," Ozzie said, and took Jelka's arm as they stepped over a broken sidewalk.

Strolling past piles of debris, Ozzie couldn't help but realize that he never could have imagined feeling at ease walking hand in hand with a white woman back home. As he and Jelka moved together through the streets, he noticed that none of the passersby even gave them a second glance. At a streetlight, he came across a group of Negro soldiers with German women sipping coffee at an outside café. Everyone looked relaxed, as if being together was the most normal occurrence, and Ozzie loved the sense of comfort he felt being away from work. With each corner they turned, the air entered his lungs, loosening the invisible noose that lived against his neck on base. His normal state of high alert subsided. Was this what white men felt every day? At ease and carefree?

They continued through a small park with a tiny stream, and on the other side, Jelka pointed to her cousin's building. It was banana yellow, and each flat had a small balcony with a silver awning.

Jelka led Ozzie up three flights of stairs. The smell of coffee wafted in the air as he brushed against a door pinned with a miniature pink pig. Ozzie touched the pig.

"*Glücksschwein,*" Jelka said, knocking harder. "The good-luck pig."

A woman as tall as Ozzie stood in the doorway. She grabbed Jelka and kissed her on both cheeks.

"This is Elga."

"*Willkommen,*" Elga replied brightly.

She was blond, big-boned, and sturdy. The flat was narrow and smelled like cigarettes and boiled meat. Ozzie could see everything except the bathroom from where he stood in the sparsely furnished living room. Jelka and her cousin exchanged a few muffled words, then more hugs. Elga waved to Ozzie and was out the door.

"What did she say?" Ozzie stood awkwardly. Just outside, he could hear a radio playing a talk show and a woman screaming at someone in German.

"That she was going to her friend's until we leave. We have the whole place." She opened the door to the bathroom. "I'm going to run us a bath."

Ozzie thought to object—it was midday and he was eager to see the city—but Jelka had already disappeared into the bathroom.

Once the tub was filled, Jelka beckoned him into the water. They had been naked together only in the darkness of the rented room. Ozzie felt shy as he undid his belt buckle. He turned his back to her as he let his pants fall to the floor. Jelka made space for him and then relaxed her head against his chest as the warm water surrounded them. Ozzie sighed.

Her cigarette burned in the ashtray that sat in the windowsill. Just outside he could see clouds parting.

"You make me feel good," she whispered, turning her face to kiss his chin.

"What do you want to be once Germany is restored?" Ozzie laced his fingers with hers under the water.

"Well, I was not so good in school. My mother said, 'You are not good in school. You are good for work.' So I got a job at a women's boutique."

"Will you do that again?"

"The shop was destroyed by the bombs."

"What would you like to do instead?"

Jelka picked up her cigarette, took a puff, and exhaled slowly; a few ashes fell in the water. "To stop being afraid."

"Afraid of what?"

"Everything. You do not know what it was like."

Ozzie felt her shiver against him. "Tell me."

She shook her head.

"Why not?"

"If I start talking, I will never stop. Just hold me."

Ozzie wrapped his arms around her. "You're safe now. You're with me."

She turned her body in the water until they were eye to eye.

"Promise?"

Ozzie nodded. "Promise."

After their bath, Ozzie convinced Jelka to take him to one of the few museums that had not been destroyed, but she was antsy and uninterested as they walked the halls and Ozzie studied the paintings and artifacts. After a walk along the river, they had dinner at a Turkish restaurant and then visited a private club that her cousin had told her about. The lights were low, the music American, the shots of alcohol cheap, and Ozzie and Jelka drank, danced, and then stumbled back to the apartment.

When Ozzie woke up, Jelka stood in the small kitchen, dressed in a short housecoat. Her lips were still stained with the crimson lipstick she'd worn the night before.

"Osborne. We need bread. Would you go to the bakery?"

As Ozzie dressed in trousers and a pullover, his hangover parked itself at the back of his head, the promise to his mother long forgotten. Jelka had pointed out the bakery and shops on their walk the day before, but Ozzie decided to take the long way around for a bit of exercise and fresh air. When he passed a small café, he stopped to see if they had any newspapers written in English. The small storefront smelled like butter and baked pastries mixed with the aroma of strong coffee. At the register, he flipped through the newspapers on the stand, disappointed to see that they were all in German.

"Philips?" He heard his name and turned.

"Clara?" he replied timidly.

She grinned at him, tossing a few loose strands of long hair from her face. "What are you doing here?"

He walked over to her table by the window, and she enveloped him in an affectionate embrace. She smelled like the talcum powder that he remembered she'd worn on the ship when she had nursed him back to health. That time felt like ages ago.

"I had a few days off, so I'm doing a little exploring." He stuffed his hands in his pockets.

"What have you seen so far?"

"Just got in yesterday, so not much. Where are you stationed?" He took the seat at the table across from her.

"A few kilometers from here, over at Rhein-Main. It's been a real learning experience on patience and persistence. That's the best way I can describe it." She pulled her shawl tighter around her shoulders. "You want coffee?"

"Yes, please," he said, knowing that Jelka would be waiting for him but unable to pass up the chance to connect with Clara.

"Ein Kaffee bitte," she ordered from the waiter.

"I'm impressed."

"I have found that when you try to speak the language, they treat you better." She pursed her lips. Then her face rearranged itself. "It's just been hard. The army won't give me permission to work on white patients. As if my degrees only work for one race. When there are no Negro patients, I'm stuck doing other things. Like cleaning and cooking, and it's frustrating."

Ozzie knew the feeling well.

"And it's not even coming from the Germans. They could care less about our stupid American Jim Crow laws. It's our own government. Intent on treating me like I'm stupid."

"It's the same for me," Ozzie confessed, telling Clara how he'd aced the aptitude test and still hadn't been placed in the Intelligence unit. "I spend most of my days with my head underneath a car."

"Are you homesick?"

"Sometimes."

"I miss my family terribly," Clara continued. "My sister had a baby girl, and she'll be darn near a year before I get to lay eyes on her." She sipped her coffee. "Where are Morgan and Thornton? You guys still together?"

"Morgan is stationed with me in Mannheim, Thornton is training in Kitzingen. Hopefully, he'll join us soon."

Ozzie's eyes shifted to the wall clock over Clara's head. More time had passed than he'd realized. "I better go." He downed the rest of his coffee.

"Who are you traveling with? Anyone I know?"

"A friend's cousin is putting me up."

Clara's gaze bored into him, and then she sighed. "They got you too?"

"Who?"

"You're with one of those Veronikas, then," she said with bite. Ozzie had heard the German women with Negro soldiers called many things. Veronika was a new one. But it wasn't hard to ascertain what Clara meant by the way her shoulders slumped. She was clearly disappointed in Ozzie for playing on the other side.

"She's a friend," he said hoarsely, not sure why he felt the need to explain to her.

"You know what's funny?" Clara squinted at him, her eyes now slightly red. "White men want white women. Negro men want white women. Black women are left out here to navigate on our own. In the slight chance that a white man does look my way, it's with lust. Or it's to get me a-scrubbing and a-cooking," she said flatly.

"Clara," he started, but she cut him off.

"I'm not asking for your pity, Ozzie. Just telling it like it is."

Her words dug deep into his skin. He had never thought about Clara or any of the Negro woman stationed in Germany and what it was like for them here. Ozzie searched for words to comfort her, but Clara stood with her navy coat in her arms. Ozzie reached for it and then held it open so she could slip into it. He fluffed her hair for her around her collar, then he reached for her right hand and brought it to his mouth for a short kiss.

"If you find yourself in Mannheim, I'm at Sullivan."

"Be careful, Ozzie. Not everyone out here can be trusted. Not even the chick you're with."

When Ozzie opened the apartment's door, Jelka was sitting on the floor between the sofa and armchair, rolled in the fetal position and shaking like a reed in a storm.

"Babe, what's wrong?" He squatted before her. Jelka kept rocking back and forth, muttering something in German that he could not understand.

"Jelka." He took hold of her shoulders. "Tell me what happened."

"What took you so long?" Her face was streaked with running mascara.

"I ran into an old friend."

"I thought they took you."

"Who?"

"They kill everyone." Her voice was shrill, and her eyes were wild and frantic.

"I'm right here."

"Men leave and they do not return." She cried harder.

It was the same thing Rita had said to him when she broke up with him, and his stomach sank. Ozzie took the edge of his sleeve and wiped her face. "Talk to me."

Jelka was quiet, rocking back and forth. "My brothers. I have lost two. They left for the war and never returned."

Ozzie hadn't known. He reached for her hands.

Jelka allowed Ozzie to help her to the sofa.

"When you didn't come back, it was like it was happening to me all over again."

Ozzie pulled her to his chest and shushed her. "You don't have to worry about me. I will always come back." He looked up at the ceiling and frowned. His words felt untrue.

CHAPTER 15

West Oak Forest Academy, October 1965

SOPHIA

It had been raining hard for two straight days. The campus's grass was soggy, and the pathways were lined with pockets of puddles. The students, though teenagers, pulled on colorful galoshes and happily splashed each other with water. Sophia, who had only her Mary Janes, miserably tramped through campus with damp water sloshing between her toes. The rain had fallen in such a relentless downpour that the roof leaked in the girls' gym and the janitors had to rotate buckets to keep the parquet floors from being damaged.

As a result, Monday's practice had been canceled. On Tuesday, Coach Fletcher had the girls meet him in his physics classroom, where he drew plays and game-day strategies on the blackboard. Today when Sophia arrived, there was a note tacked to the door that instructed them to report to the boys' gymnasium.

When Sophia stepped over the threshold of the boys' facility, she spotted Max with the ball in his hand, going up for a jump shot. His long legs were sculpted and tight, his Converse All Stars a gleaming fresh white. As Max shot the basketball around the world, Claude caught the ball and fed it back to him.

Sophia had met Claude at dinner a few weeks back, and despite Willa's best intentions of getting them together, Sophia felt nothing for him. The best way Sophia could describe Claude was that he was average. He slouched when he walked, and as a result, his back was bent. His skin was reddish brown; he was about Sophia's height, with long arms and buckteeth.

The girls clustered around Coach Fletcher.

"Ladies, I know this isn't ideal," Coach said as he opened the mesh bag of basketballs. "But we have our first game on Friday, so we can't afford to miss another day of practice. I've arranged with the boys to split the gym with us."

As the girls grabbed balls and started warming up, Sophia tried to forget that Max was in the same room, but she couldn't help sneaking furtive glances his way. Sophia had begun to find her place among the other girls, except Patty and Opal. Once a week, Coach Fletcher had conducted trust exercises in the form of three-legged races, willow in the wind, and human knots to help them form bonds and connect.

"Let's make two lines. Layup drills. Let's go," called Margaret.

She was the center, a senior, and the captain of the team. Margaret was over six feet tall and wore her straight hair pulled back into two braids. It was easy for Sophia to follow Margaret's lead, because from their first practice, it was clear that the most important thing to Margaret was winning, and she'd do whatever it took to uplift the team.

After their warm-up drills and conditioning, the girls broke into two teams. The blue team was the starters; Sophia played on the red team and found herself guarding Patty. Sophia kept her hands up in Patty's face, and when Patty went up for a shot, Sophia jumped and blocked it.

"Foul! You scratched me," Patty exclaimed, holding out her arm. "And gave me cooties!"

Opal and another girl laughed, and Sophia felt the skin around her neck heat up. Was Max watching?

Sophia sucked her teeth. "You're a liar. That was a clean block."

"Who are you calling a liar?"

"And a sore loser," Sophia added, and a few girls nodded.

Coach Fletcher blew his whistle as he rounded the two girls. "Enough." He looked from Patty to Sophia. "Now, listen up. To prepare for Friday's game, we are going to have a friendly scrimmage against the boys."

"Let's do this," Margaret called out, circling the team and high-fiving each girl. Her energy was contagious.

The girls formed a circle around Coach Fletcher while he drew out a play on his clipboard. "Anna and Sophia, I want you to play guard against McBay and Collins."

"What?" said Patty. "Why is she going in first? I'm the starter."

"Because this is my team. I make the calls, Patty," Coach Fletcher said frankly.

Patty crossed her arms over her chest and poked her lips out, sulking. Only Opal paid her any attention. The boys' coach blew the whistle, and the teams met at half-court.

"Let's play a fair game." The boys' coach tossed the ball in the air, and Margaret hit it to Anna. The girls ran their offense first, forcing the boys to play defense.

Max guarded Sophia. "You aren't touching that ball," he said, snickering, and his sloppy grin sent a tingling sensation through her chest.

"Watch me," she said, giving him a little elbow in the ribs before stepping out of his reach. Anna spotted that she was open and swung the ball in her direction. Before Max could recover, Sophia took the jump shot. *Swish.*

"What did you say?" she asked, toying with Max as she hustled to get back on defense.

They played three-minute quarters, and by the third quarter, Sophia was spent because she had played the entire first half without a substitute. At the top of the fourth quarter, the boys were leading by ten when Max came charging down the court with the ball. Sophia stepped in front of him to stop him from an easy layup, and he barreled right into her. She fell backward and slid on her bottom across the court.

"Es tut mir soleid. Moge Gott mit dir sein," Max said, his eyebrows furrowed.

His words covered Sophia, and she felt as if she were floating outside of her body. When he reached for her hand and pulled her to her feet, she stumbled. Where had she gone?

"I'm so sorry. Are you okay?"

"Yeah, sure." She wrung her fingers. "What in the world did you say to me?"

Max shook his head. "Sorry, I don't know where that came from."

"Sub," Coach Fletcher called, beckoning Sophia to get off the court. Sophia tried to hustle to the bench, but she felt off-center. Patty bumped her hip as she took Sophia's place.

After the boys beat the girls by fifteen points, the boys cheered while heading to their locker room. Most of the girls dressed and exited quickly, but Sophia had moved slowly, with her eye on the boys' door. Max was the first to bound out of the locker room.

"You sure you're all right? I didn't mean to charge you so hard." He looked her up and down for bruises.

"I have three brothers. Trust me, I've been hit much harder." She shifted her bag. "But what language was that? What did you say to me?"

"I said 'I'm so sorry, may God be with you' in German."

Sophia looked up. "How do you know German?" And why had her body reacted that way?

"They have German as a language here, you can take it next semester if you are interested. I've been taking it since last year."

"Wouldn't Spanish or French be more useful?"

"I was born in Germany," he revealed. "I came to this country when I was around five."

Something stirred inside her. Was it his words, or was it his nearness that was making her feel woozy, not at all steady?

"Tell me about Germany." She turned her body toward him.

"Oh, I don't remember that much. I lived in an—"

"Hey, wait up," Claude called while walking across the court. "Sophia. Nice game." He gave her a playful pat on the back.

"Thanks," she said, straining her face to keep her irritation from showing.

"Max, don't forget, we have Debate Club tonight." Claude slipped a small umbrella from his bag as the three walked to the exit. "Sophia, have you joined any clubs yet?" he asked.

"I haven't had much time."

"Well, you should join the Debate Club. We have a lot of fun."

"You have a lot of fun," Max corrected. "I just go because it will look good on my college applications."

"Whatever, man." Claude held the door open. The rain was coming down from the dark sky in sheets. Sophia yanked her jacket up and pulled it over her head.

"You don't have an umbrella?" Max turned to Sophia.

"I did, but the wind tore it to shreds this morning, so I threw it out." That was probably why she had found it in the lost-and-found bin in the first place. It didn't work.

"Here, take mine, and I'll share with Claude."

"I'll be fine."

"It's nearly a ten-minute walk to W5, and it's raining cats and dogs. I insist." Max removed the umbrella from his bag and held it out to her.

Their fingers brushed, and Sophia felt herself shudder. "Thank you."

Claude pushed his umbrella up and said, "I would have offered you mine too. We can't have one of our star basketball players sick before the game on Friday." He flashed her a wide smile, but it dulled in comparison to Max's.

"Star? You must be joking." She pursed her lips.

"Really, you played well," Claude said. "I was watching you."

Sophia frowned as she pushed Max's umbrella up over her head. She didn't want Claude watching her.

"Good night," she said as they went their separate ways into the rain. As she walked, careful to avoid the puddles, she revisited the words that Max had said to her.

Moge Gott mit dir sein. Where had she heard that phrase before?

CHAPTER 16

Mannheim, Germany, July 1951

ETHEL

There was a seven-year age difference between Anke and Franz, and each day Ethel searched for activities that would nurture a bond between them while Bert was away at work. Every morning after the breakfast dishes were clear, she taught them basic words in English, then, while Franz drew pictures, she got down on the floor and played blocks with Anke, using the wooden pieces to teach her to count. When Anke napped, Ethel sat with Franz while he drew and sketched.

During their first three weeks as a family, Ethel experienced every emotion from proud to profound joy, anxiety to crippling fear. Her biggest worry was that her love was not enough to fill the gaps of deep-seated loss that resided in her children. Anke was young enough that memories wouldn't plague her, but Franz, at ten years old, had been through so much. When Ethel had stopped by the orphanage to pick up the paperwork, Sister Ursula had explained that Franz's mother had fallen so ill with tuberculosis that she couldn't care for him and he was found begging for food in the American bars.

He was pensive most days, and Ethel fretted over what was going on inside his head, what he had seen on the streets, and how much losing his birth mother had affected him. But when Bert walked through the door, a light turned on inside Franz, and Ethel was happy to see that the boy had taken to at least one of them.

Three weeks passed before Ethel felt they had found their rhythm as a family, and she decided to surprise the children with a long-overdue visit to see Sister Ursula and their friends at the orphanage.

When they walked through the gates, Franz took off running, and Anke was scooped up by one of the older girls and carried to a circle of children sitting under the tree. Sister Ursula and Ethel walked to the office; it had a window that overlooked the courtyard. There was a tray with a pitcher of hot water, and Sister Ursula offered tea. "How are they adjusting?"

"Well enough," Ethel said, and then shared her concerns about Franz. "He's a different kid once Bert returns home."

"Franz is used to being in a pack of boys." Sister Ursula adjusted her glasses. "Once school starts and he makes new friends, he will be fine."

As they sipped their tea, Sister Ursula told Ethel about three new children who had been dropped off since she had visited last. "We are currently up to twenty-nine. We have enough space for them, but we could use more shoes as we prepare for school to start in the fall."

"I can ask around. Maybe I can organize a shoe drive on post."

They sat and talked until the bell rang for lunch. "We'd better go."

"Let the children eat with their friends first." Sister Ursula squeezed her hand, and Ethel obliged.

When the meal was over, Ethel called to Anke, but she could not find Franz. She looked all over the courtyard, and then a boy in cutoff shorts pointed to a small building that was used for storage.

"Franz," she called while pushing the wooden door open.

"Hallo," he said, down on his knees. He was pitching marbles with a boy who looked to be the same age.

"It's time to go." She pointed at the door.

Up on his feet, he took his friend's hand and put it in Ethel's. "Come home too?" His big brown eyes pleaded.

Then it all became clear. Franz had been drawing boys playing in the dirt in his sketches. Could this be the person Franz had been missing?

"Wie heißen sie?" She asked the boy's name.

"Ich heiße Heinz." Franz's eyes sparkled. "Come too?" he said again. "Please?"

Anke and Franz had already filled their home and her days, but it was apparent how special Heinz was to Franz. The boys threw their arms around each other's necks, and Ethel couldn't bear to wipe this rare smile from Franz's face. She knew she should talk to Bert about it first, but he was a man's man and would not object to having two sons. Rescuing two boys.

"Yes, okay." She nodded, and the boys cheered.

As they moved through the courtyard past the tree, Ethel was looking for Sister Ursula when Heinz clasped the hand of a young girl with a long braid.

"Meine Schwester," he said, and held her hand toward Ethel. The girl he referred to as Monika was a bit older than Anke, with pudgy cheeks. Ethel looked from Heinz to the girl, and right away she knew there was no way she would split up siblings. With an encouraging nod from Sister Ursula, Ethel's household went from a family of four to a family of six.

That evening when Bert came home to find four children around their kitchen table, with nowhere for him to sit, he didn't flinch.

"I guess we'll need more chairs." He kissed Ethel on the cheek.

"And a bunk bed," she added with a sigh of relief.

The boys slept in the small alcove in the living room; Ethel had draped a sheet to give them some privacy. Since she wasn't comfortable leaving them in the apartment alone, she asked Julia to come by and keep an eye on them while she ran to the commissary at Benjamin Franklin Village to do the grocery shopping.

The wide aisles held all the American staples and brands that families were accustomed to purchasing. As she placed cereal, bread, butter, and milk in her shopping cart, Ethel found herself tracking the total cost of the items in her head. Bert's paycheck hadn't changed, but they now had four additional mouths to feed, and though Heinz was a bony boy, he ate like he was squirreling away food in his belly for a hungry day.

She picked up a package of egg noodles and then rolled her cart back to the butcher in the far corner of the store. After securing two pounds of chuck beef, she'd stop by the produce section for onions, mushrooms, and garlic. While she waited her turn behind three well-dressed women, her mother's beef Stroganoff recipe flitted through her head. Ethel's mother had raised seven kids alone after the death of her husband, and she was the queen of a good hearty casserole. Ethel knew that Stroganoff was a meal she could stretch over two to three days, made new with a side soup or green salad.

"Ethel." Dorothy strolled toward the butcher's line. "Funny running into you here. Do you usually do your shopping on Tuesdays?"

"Thursdays, actually, but lately I've had to make some adjustments."

Dorothy stretched her red lips into a smile. "Well, you know good news travels. Congratulations, I hear you've adopted two children. A boy and a girl?"

"Four, actually." Ethel tilted her head.

Dorothy's gloved hand patted her heart. "From the orphanage you were telling us about?"

"Yes, and they have been a gift. All four are adjusting well."

After they exchanged polite small talk about Dorothy's summer vacation and Ethel's children learning English, Dorothy said, "I was able to secure additional care packages for the German mothers on our list this month."

The air around the butcher smelled metallic. Ethel pushed her cart up. "Perfect, I'm sure it will help get the women over the summer hump."

"I still have the last list you gave me, but if there are more in need, please let me know. I can't sleep thinking that any child would go to bed hungry."

"I was just at the orphanage, and there is a need for shoes, all sizes. Maybe we can add a back-to-school drive to the end-of-summer picnic. We can have a station where people can drop off gently used shoes."

"My children certainly have some laying around. That's a great idea, and I'll be sure to add it to our next meeting's agenda. Don't forget, our next theme is simply red, white, and blue."

They parted ways and Ethel hurried home. When she turned the key in the lock to their apartment, the girls came running toward her and hugged her like she had been away for a month. Ethel dropped to her knees and kissed them each on the forehead. "Hey, sweet girls, Mommy's home."

CHAPTER 17

Mannheim, Germany, January 1949

OZZIE

The year started off wet and cold. For the entire week, Ozzie had been assigned the deuce-and-a-half truck with the broken heater. It didn't matter how he layered his clothing, Ozzie never felt warm, and by Friday afternoon he was coming down with a cold.

On his last deliveries for the week, Satchel sat in the passenger seat with a blanket over his lap and a harmonica pressed to his lips. Ozzie felt a comfort come over him when he heard Satchel play. Ozzie's mother had sung whenever the mood hit, so Satchel's whiny harmonica reminded Ozzie of home, and a longing curled in his belly for that lima bean soup that always seemed to be simmering on the stove during the winter.

Six months had passed since he'd left home, and he missed his tiny one-way street with kids playing hopscotch and dribbling the basketball at all hours. He wanted his mother's fried chicken and potato salad and the banter of neighbors crowded together in the living room and kitchen, listening to Duke Ellington and Louis Armstrong on the nights she threw rent parties. From Rita, he had received a one-page letter at Thanksgiving and a glossy Christmas card with an "xoxo." Even though he had tried not to think about her, he missed Rita too. The honeysuckle smell of her and the way she tilted her head when she giggled at his jokes.

Ozzie's truck rolled past a line of pale-faced women with their lips painted and hair curled, waiting just outside the gates. They stomped their feet and paced to keep warm as they waited on their American sweethearts to bring them money and sneak rations so they could feed their families.

When Ozzie stopped behind another service vehicle waiting for clearance, he was surprised to spot Jelka among the women, smoking a cigarette. Ozzie and Jelka had been keeping company for four months, and not once had she ever come to the base looking for him on payday like the others.

Their eyes met. Ozzie killed the engine. "I'll be right back," he told Satchel. He walked toward Jelka, feeling unclean. He had avoided seeing her in his work uniform, which was covered in dirt and soot.

"Hey," he said.

"Hallo." She dropped her cigarette on the ground and stubbed it out with her foot. Then she kissed him on the cheek.

"What are you doing standing out here in the cold?"

"I need to talk to you."

"I'm still on the clock," he said, looking around to see who might be watching. Ozzie couldn't risk returning late. Being late was a serious offense, and he didn't want his CO to see him dallying at the gate and revoke his weekend privileges. "Can it wait until tonight? I can come by the club this evening, once I'm off."

"Sure. It will wait." She stood and touched her hand to his face, and he could see worry swimming in her big dark eyes before she turned and walked away.

"What was that about?" Satchel asked once Ozzie climbed back into the truck.

"No idea. You know women."

"It's payday."

"She didn't ask for anything. She rarely does. She just said she needed to talk."

"Better take some extra cash with you tonight. If she's anything like my girl, she'll have a story about needing money for medicine for her sick mother, or to repair a well for clean water. It's always something," Satchel said, and then blew out a tune on his harmonica.

When Ozzie, Satchel, and Morgan walked through the doors of the Federal Eagle Club, Ozzie scanned the room but didn't see Jelka anywhere. Chicago blues played, and four Negro women in uniform sat at a center table, giggling with one another. It was a rare sight to see Negro servicewomen in the bar, and Satchel and Morgan pulled chairs up to their table. Ozzie watched as they shot the breeze; he kept an eye out for Jelka while nursing a beer. He had decided that he would drink only one, maybe two beers tonight. He had Saturday-morning duty, and it was hard to take inventory hungover.

Jelka emerged from the kitchen with her hair twirled and pinned at the nape of her neck. She motioned him over with a nod. Ozzie downed his beer, then left the mug on the bar.

"Follow me," Jelka said, pulling on his arm.

An uneasy feeling came over him. If Jelka needed money, Ozzie wished she would just ask instead of keeping him in such suspense. She led him to a back room off the side of the kitchen; it held cleaning supplies, rolls of toilet paper, hand towels, and two slop buckets that she turned over, making seats for them. Before Ozzie could speak, she dropped her head in her hands.

"What is it?" he asked. Ozzie had grown used to her easy crying. "Talk to me. Is your mother ill?"

Jelka gazed at him with her face twisted in such anguish that in the moment, Ozzie realized he would do whatever she asked to take away her pain.

"Hey." He ran a finger along her cheek, blotting away her tears. "Tell me what's the matter so I can fix it."

The black lines under her eyes had begun to smudge. "I am pregnant."

Ozzie opened his mouth, but no words came out. After several long seconds, he managed to stutter. "I . . . I thought you . . . you were taking care of that?"

"Are you blaming me?" Her big eyes bore into him.

"No." *Yes.* "How could this have happened?" he muttered under his breath.

"Well, it takes two," she called back.

A baby. Ozzie put his hands on top of his head, and it was hard for him to breathe. A baby with a white woman on the other side of the world. His mother would whoop his ass.

"What am I supposed to do?" She raked her fingernails in her scalp, pulling loose ends from her hair twist.

What was he supposed to do?

Jelka stood and reached for him just as Ozzie started coughing. He hacked and choked and coughed until she stepped back. "Are you all right?"

He cleared his throat. "I'm fine." He wasn't fine. He needed some air. He was an American here on assignment. Eventually, he'd have to return home, and how could he do that with a child on the way. Ozzie's head fogged, and he could barely make out Jelka's voice.

"I thought we had been careful," she said.

"I did too."

Ozzie had made sure to use condoms, and when they didn't have one, Jelka had told him that she knew her body and it was all right. Had she done this on purpose?

"Well, you do not have to worry about me. You can go on with your life, like all the American men do."

"Why would you say that?"

"I have seen it in my village. The men get us pregnant and then leave us to deal with it." Jelka wrapped her arms around her belly. "I am ruined. The government will take my meager rations and make my life hell. I was already stopped by the police and sent downtown for a VD check last weekend."

"A venereal disease check? Why? What business is that of the law?"

She lowered her eyes. "The police officer saw me with you. Said we needed to be sure. They do it to us all the time. They get off on it."

Anger and embarrassment flooded him. "I'm sorry you went through that because of me."

Jelka just shrugged.

Ozzie's head swam, and even though he didn't have answers, he knew for certain that he would not abandon his child. He had watched his mother struggle without much help from his father, and he vowed to himself that he would never do that to his baby.

Ozzie pulled Jelka to her feet and squeezed her hands. "Give me some time. We'll figure this out."

All of a sudden, Ozzie felt exhausted. He knew a beer or two would not be enough to help digest this news.

Jelka moved to kiss his lips, but Ozzie turned, and she only got his cheek. She looked at him and then walked away. Ozzie shoved his hands in his pockets and went back to the table where his friends sat eating bratwurst.

The Negro women were gone. Ozzie's collar felt like it was restricting the airflow to his lungs, so he undid two buttons.

"Everything all right, lover boy?" Morgan teased.

"Have you seen our waitress?" Ozzie fidgeted. "We're going to need to order a bottle."

CHAPTER 18

West Oak Forest Academy, November 1965

SOPHIA

Sophia gasped and sat up in bed as cold water dripped down her face. When she opened her eyes, Willa was standing over her, holding a glass.

"What the heck, Sophia? You scared me half to death."

Sophia blinked. Her lashes were heavy with water, and her arms burned. It had happened. After nearly two months of wearing herself out at basketball practice, praying to Walter's God, and denying herself sleep, her secret was out. She was a freak.

"What in the world were you dreaming about?"

Besides Walter, Willa was the only person ever to ask her that question. On the farm, Ma Deary just yelled at her to get herself together and stop disturbing the peace with her nonsense.

"A fire," she answered hoarsely.

"Were you in it?"

Sophia nodded.

Willa picked up a face towel from her desk and handed it to her. "Sorry about the water, I didn't know what else to do. You were screaming and scratching your arms."

"It's okay." Sophia wiped her face. Water had dripped down into the neck of her nightgown, soaking her to the waist.

"Tell me about the dream."

Sophia closed her eyes. "I'm in a kitchen. In the back of a big house. Small children are eating at a table, two and sometimes three. And then all of a sudden there are flames. Everywhere. Lapping and licking. Hot. The smoke is choking the wind out of me and stinging my eyes. I try to reach for the children to save them, but just as I do, flames shoot up my arms. I've had this dream for as long as I can remember."

"Have you ever talked to anyone about this? Like a doctor?"

A snort puffed from Sophia's nose before she could censor it. Ma Deary never took them to the doctors. If they got sick, Ma would administer her own remedy. The only time anyone had ever gone to the hospital was when Walter fell out of a tree and broke his arm. But even then it was Unc who had taken him, not Ma Deary.

"No." Sophia got out of her bed, pushing the sheets to the side so they could air-dry.

"Well, my father is a doctor. Maybe when you meet him, he can help you."

"Maybe," she said, knowing that she would never ask Willa's father to fix her. It was one thing for Willa to know, but Sophia didn't want her parents to think their precious daughter was rooming with someone who was sick in the head.

The floor was cold as Sophia padded to her closet. She turned her back to Willa and slipped out of the wet nightgown and into her Wranglers and an oversize T-shirt.

"You do know the fall dance is approaching." Willa sat down at her desk and looked at her face in a hand mirror.

Sophia had seen flyers up all over school but had no intention of going.

"My mother sent me a picture of the dress she ordered for me. Want to see it?"

"Sure."

Willa reached into her desk drawer and pulled out an envelope, then unfolded a glossy page from a catalog. "What do you think?"

The dress was peach, with puffy sleeves. The bottom was shaped like a bell and looked expensive.

"It's gorgeous."

"You know the dance is called the Old South Ball. From the pictures I've seen in the yearbook, the girls wear dresses with petticoats, so make sure you have one. Have you phoned home for your dress yet?" Willa said, applying blush to her cheeks.

"I'm not going."

Willa's hand froze in midbrush. "Of course you're going. Don't worry about a date. I wasn't supposed to tell you this, but Claude's planning to ask you this weekend. So call home for your dress."

Sophia hadn't phoned home in the two months that she had been at Forest. Even if she had, there was no way Ma Deary would agree to send her a tube of toothpaste, let alone a dress for a dance. "We will see."

"Please, Sophia. It won't be fun without you. Don't leave me out there by myself."

Sophia didn't want to go to the dance with Claude, had nothing to wear and no one to ask for help, but the thought of disappointing Willa made her feel worse. "I'll see what Ma says and if she has enough time for a dress," Sophia lied.

"You're the best. I have to go. I'm meeting Max on the lawn." Willa took one last look at herself in the mirror. She looked well put together, as usual, in a pair of pedal pushers with bobby socks and a striped top that accentuated her full bust. Willa was as curvy as Sophia was slim. "I think he's going to ask me to the dance today.

I want to look good but not like I tried too hard. You know what I mean?"

Sophia nodded and closed the door behind Willa, pressing away the feeling of jealousy that had bloomed from the moment Willa said she was meeting Max. Deep down, she knew that it made sense for Max to like Willa. Not only was Willa gorgeous, but they also had the same air about them that said they belonged.

As Sophia gathered up her physics book and notepad, she wondered how she would get her hands on a dress. There certainly wouldn't be any stuffed in the lost-and-found bin.

She had time for a quick breakfast before she met her friend Nancy in the library to study for their physics test. As she moved through the breakfast line, piling her plate with pancakes, sausage links, and eggs, she spotted Miz Peaches, the lunch lady.

"Hey, sugar. Why the long face?"

The dining hall was mostly empty; students preferred to sleep in on Saturday mornings.

Sophia whispered, "The Old South Ball is coming up. Willa is insisting that I go, but I don't have a dress."

Miz Peaches arched her painted eyebrows. "Well, I just so happen to oversee the local Miss NAACP Pageant held at my church. I'm sure I can find something in your size."

"Really?" Sophia brightened.

"Sure, sugar." Miz Peaches took the pencil from behind her ear and started writing down notes. "Let me feel your waist." She came around the hot station and put her cool hands on Sophia's hips and her wrists and then did something with her red fingernails that started at the top of Sophia's head and moved to her feet. Sophia looked around to see if anyone was watching them, but the few students in the room were consumed with one another.

"Got your measurements."

"Just like that?"

"Sugar, dressmaking has been in my family for three generations. I've been sewing since I was knee-high to a spider. Let me see what we have at the church that might fit."

"I don't know what to say."

"Just know that when I'm finished with you, you'll be the talk of that ball."

"Thank you, Miz Peaches." Sophia beamed.

"Now, go and eat before your breakfast gets cold. You leave the rest to me."

On the evening of the Old South Ball, Willa's tennis team had planned to take pictures on the lawn before the start of the dance, and she left their room in a cocoon of eye shadow, hair spray, and perfume before Sophia had even started getting ready. Since she had arrived at Forest, Sophia had washed her hair sparingly, not wanting to disrupt the black dye, but even though the Ogilvie box read "permanent color," each time she shampooed, her hair faded. As she combed it through in preparation for the dance, she noticed that her hair was now a cherry brown and the roots had grown in. She wondered how much longer she had until she was fully a redhead again.

Orangutan, don't act like you don't know your name.

Sophia paced her dorm room floor. Miz Peaches was over thirty minutes late with the gown. Perhaps something had come up that was more important; after all, they hadn't known each other long. Sophia had not been in the habit of depending on people and chided herself for falling for Miz Peaches's enthusiasm to help her with the dress.

As soon as she had resolved that she would not go, she heard a knock at her door. When she opened it, Miz Peaches breezed in, smelling like citrus and carrying an armful of satin and tulle.

"Sugar, I'm so sorry to be late. There was an accident right at my exit off the highway. The darn lane was backed up for a full mile."

"I'm just grateful that you made it," said Sophia, relieved.

It was the first time Sophia had seen Miz Peaches out of uniform. She looked beautiful in a khaki swing dress. Her face was painted, and her hair was curled in the mushroom style that Sophia had seen on Diana Ross.

"Come on, sugar, let me get you in this dress."

She helped Sophia slip into the petticoat, tied her into a corset, and then slipped the seafoam green dress over her head. Then she pulled and tied and zipped and primped until Sophia was secure in the dress.

Miz Peaches whistled. "Honey, you look like a Southern belle. I feel sorry for those other girls."

Sophia faced the full-length mirror and gasped. She was taken aback. On the farm, they never dressed up for Easter or went to holiday parties.

"Now, let me just give you a little lipstick, 'cause you're so pretty, you don't need much else." Miz Peaches reached into her purse and pulled out a tube. "There. Now, who'd you say was your escort?"

"Claude."

"Honey, hush. Be prepared to give him a full-on heart attack."

Miz Peaches sprayed her down in perfume and then walked her to the lobby, where Claude stood in a black suit, two sizes too big, with a plaid bow tie. He did a double take when he saw her.

"You two have fun," Miz Peaches said with a wave. "My work here is done."

"Thanks again," Sophia called after her before turning to Claude. He cradled a pink and white corsage and held it out to her.

"Sophia. You look . . . beautiful."

"Thank you. You do too."

He stuck out his arm, and reluctantly, she linked hers with his as they walked out of the dormitory. The sun was nearly gone from the sky, and a light breeze shifted the air. They moved in silence for a few minutes before Claude struck up a conversation that at least helped them avert an awkward silence.

Up ahead was the Magnolia Clubhouse, the campus student center where the dance was being held. As they got closer, Sophia could hear rowdy voices, but she couldn't see whom they were coming from because it was getting dark. When they approached the clubhouse, she saw at least ten brawny boys dressed in Confederate uniforms standing on the lawn. A few twirled small Confederate flags as they posed for a picture. At the sight of them, Sophia felt Claude's arm twitch.

"You all right?" she asked softly.

"Yeah, I just don't want any trouble."

Sophia remembered the story that Willa had told her of Claude being pushed around and tormented by the boys on his first day of school. The trauma of that moment seemed to reactivate inside him, because she could feel his whole body shake as he pulled her along toward the clubhouse. When they reached the steps, Sophia could hear "Help Me, Rhonda" by the Beach Boys floating from the speakers inside. She thought about how much better she'd feel when they reached their friends.

"Well, would you look at who we have here," one of the Confederate-dressed boys said to their backs, but the two kept walking as if they didn't hear him. "It's Aunt Jemima and Uncle Ben. Boys, supper is ready. Now we can eat." He burst out laughing.

"What's on the menu?" another shouted.

"Chicken and watermelon," the other said, and cackled as the door to the clubhouse closed behind them.

In the foyer, Sophia turned to Claude, who looked like a cat stuck in a tree. "Don't pay them any mind."

"I'm not. I'm cool." Claude took her hand and led her into the large reception room.

Max, Willa, Louis, and Nancy from physics were sitting at a table next to the refreshments. Sophia could feel all eyes on her and Claude as they entered.

Willa stood and rushed to Sophia. "You look amazing," she exclaimed. "Come have a cookie."

Max stood when Sophia got to the table. "Hey, what took you guys so long?" He directed the question to Claude and then looked to Sophia for an answer. He was wearing a dark blue suit, tapered and fitted with a black bow tie. With his sloppy smile on her, Sophia's knees felt spongy.

"It was my fault," she said. "What did we miss?"

"Just foolishness," answered Louis, pointing to the decorations. The inside of the reception room had been made to look like a Southern plantation. The tablecloths were red and blue, with cotton stems arranged in olive buckets as the centerpieces. White stars seemed to be everywhere.

"And did you see the boys in those damn uniforms?" Louis gritted his teeth.

"Come on, guys, let's turn this party around." Willa grabbed Max's hand and led him to the dance floor.

The happy tune made Sophia want to clap her hands and let the nasty comments of the Confederate-dressed boys go. The teens found a hole in the crowd and shimmied their hips to "Twist and Shout" by the Isley Brothers. The music slowed with "Baby Love" by the Supremes, and Sophia shrank as Willa fell into Max's arms.

"I think I'm going to take a break," she said to Claude.

"Just one more dance? I really like this song," he pleaded.

Sophia sighed and let him put one hand around her waist and clasp her hand with the other. As they swayed, she tried not to look at Willa and Max over Claude's shoulder, but her eyes kept betraying her. Max had picked his hair out, and she wondered how his shiny curls would feel between her fingers. Just as the song came to an end, Max turned away from Willa, and his eyes found Sophia. Their gazes locked, and after staring for what felt like seconds too long, he smiled at her. She felt herself blush as she dropped her eyes.

They all returned to the table and reached for the paper cups filled with lemonade and the plate of assorted cookies. Sophia felt a bit sweaty, so she excused herself to the lavatory. Willa stood to come with her, but then one of her tennis friends pulled her back onto the dance floor. In the bathroom mirror, Sophia was amazed to see that she looked just as lovely as she had when she left her dorm, except for the perspiration on her brow, which she dabbed with a tissue. When she came out of the bathroom, her friends were up dancing again, but Sophia's feet ached.

Air. She could use some air, so she slipped out the back door. Couples were draped on the porch swings and wide comfy chairs. Sophia found an empty bench a few feet away from the building. The view of the parklike campus was stunning. What a turn her life had taken in just a few short months.

"Oh, what a night." It was Max.

"Hey." She looked up at him and then behind him for the others, but he stood alone with a paper cup in each hand.

"Would you like one?" he asked.

"As long as you didn't spike it."

"I was careful to avoid that punch, God knows what they put in it," he said, sitting down next to her. "Those kids over there are wasted. Look at how everyone is suddenly all handsy and falling down laughing. Telltale sign."

Sophia could feel the heat radiating off Max as he sat next to her. He smelled of cedar and spice, and she inhaled him slowly. Down the hill but in eyesight, a small crowd of students had started to gather. It looked like they were building a bonfire.

"Are they allowed to do that?"

"From what I've seen, the wealthy kids make the rules around here. Administration doesn't want to rock the boat because those families are their bread and butter. They get away with all types of crap."

They watched as a boy threw a big piece of firewood onto the growing pile.

"I see that you girls are having a pretty good season so far," Max said.

Sophia punched his arm lightly. "Are you making fun of me? We've won one game."

"That's a good start for Forest. It's only the second year the girls have had a team. Last year they went oh and eight."

"Meanwhile, you guys have won four straight."

"Well, what do you expect with me as the point guard." He chuckled.

"Okay, Mr. Conceited."

"Not conceited, just confident."

A small flame caught on the wood, but then it quickly sputtered out.

Sophia turned to Max. "So, you mentioned that you grew up in Germany?"

"I never really talk about this," he confessed. "My parents have done their best, smothering me with love, which I appreciate, but . . . it feels like they want me to forget."

"Forget what?"

"That I was adopted," he whispered. "No one at Forest knows this. I can't believe I'm telling you."

"It's okay, you're safe with me," she said.

Max looked off into the distance, contemplating for a long while, before he opened his mouth. "I lived in an orphanage in Germany before I came to America."

Sophia felt uneasiness come over her. "What do you remember?"

"A lot of things. I remember the women in charge wore black habits. Catholic nuns, I think."

"Those black robes with their hair covered?"

He nodded, and his eyes looked like he was traveling back to that place far away. "There was a play area. A patch of dirt, really, under the shade of a tree where the grass just didn't grow. I used to ride a tricycle, and there was a rope swing that I pushed my friend on."

As he described the swing, Sophia could feel her stomach drop, the feeling of going up and down and flying through the air. Silence passed between them as they watched the teenagers light the bonfire. A big flame went up into the sky.

"That looks so dangerous."

"I hate fire," he confessed.

"Me too." Then Sophia turned to him. "Why do you hate it?"

"I was caught in a fire once. When I still lived in the orphanage. Have you ever seen that dark mark on my arm?"

"No."

Max removed his suit jacket and started rolling up his sleeve. There was a dark mark just above his forearm, blistered over. Sophia didn't know what came over her, but she reached out and touched it. A spark surged from her finger to her elbow.

"Go on, finish the story," she pushed.

Max described the kitchen fire. Sophia closed her eyes, and as he spoke, her recurring nightmare flashed through her mind. She could feel the heat of the fire shooting up her arms. And then she remembered. Black skirts. There were black skirts in the dream but no faces.

"I have a burn mark too." She turned to him. "It happened when I was little, but it's on the back of my thigh."

"How'd your burn happen?" he asked.

Ma Deary had told her that she'd gotten too close to the fireplace and the logs had crackled and spat fire at her. She couldn't remember it and had always wondered if Ma was leaving something out.

"Here's mine." She turned to Max and lifted the skirt of her dress. Max pushed his finger in her burn mark. Sophia closed her eyes against his touch. She saw herself walking to a door in a dark room. She reached for the door and pulled it open. *"Auf Wiedersehen,"* she said softly.

"Goodbye? Have you been practicing German too? Your accent is perfect."

The words were just there and then oozing from her mouth. She couldn't hear the teens down by the fire or the music streaming from the dance. Just their breathing. Rhythmic. It seemed like Max was feeling something too.

"There you two are. I've been looking all over for you." Willa stood holding a plate.

Sophia dropped her skirt back over her legs, hoping that Willa hadn't noticed.

"I figured you'd want something sweet." Willa handed the pie to Max.

"Thank you," Max said, and Sophia watched him slip away from her and back to Willa.

"Now, what were you two talking about so intently?" Willa put her hands on her hips as Claude came up beside her.

"Basketball," Sophia replied.

"It's all this dude thinks about." Claude pointed at Max.

"Ladies, please say good night." Sophia turned to see Ms. Meacham, her physics teacher and the girls' dorm mother, clapping her hands and calling out, "It's time to return."

Willa reached her hand in Max's direction; he took her hand and kissed it. Sophia realized she was supposed to do the same thing to Claude and acquiesced. His kiss was wet, and she desperately wanted to wipe her hand on her dress but resisted the urge. As she walked to meet the other girls in line, she stole a look back at Max, and to her delight, he smiled and mouthed, *Auf Wiedersehen.*

CHAPTER 19

Mannheim, Germany, January 1949

OZZIE

Ozzie woke up on his twin bed, unclear how he got there. The last thing he remembered was ordering a bottle of bourbon. His head was so heavy he could barely lift it. Was it the cold? When he tried to open his eyes, the light was blinding bright, so he closed them. He moved his tongue around his mouth, which felt dry as cotton and his throat scratchy. Even though it hurt to move, he needed to pee. Ozzie rose up on his elbows and saw that he was still fully dressed, right down to his boots. When he stood, the room swirled like a toy spinning top. As he shuffled to the toilet, pops of memory from the previous night ping-ponged through his head. Drinks straight with no chaser, Chicago blues, Jelka.

Jelka was pregnant with his child. Ozzie had been in Germany for less than six months, and already he had managed to upend his life. The staunch warning from his mother echoed in his ears: *That liquor gon' be the death of you, son. You mark my words.* He aimed his pungent stream into the urinal and peed long and hard, the alcohol sweating from his pores. Unsteadily, he swayed and held on to the urinal with both hands until the feeling of nausea passed. Damn. Fuck. Shit.

"Philips, what the hell?" called a voice.

Ozzie zipped his pants and erected his shoulders to attention and realized it was only Morgan.

"Bro. You're fifteen minutes late. I woke you up an hour ago. Petty is calling you everything but a child of God. You better hurry to your post."

Taking time only to brush his teeth, put on his sunglasses, and slug down some water from his canteen, Ozzie hoofed it the ten-minute walk over to the motor pool. The other men assigned to the same fleet of vehicles were already buzzing around in motion. He had never reported to duty late, and he kicked himself for oversleeping. When Morgan spied him coming through the fence, he tossed him a rag and pointed to a spray bottle with vinegar hanging from the side of a bucket. Ozzie tried to slip inside one of the trucks without being seen, but before he could fit his body in the front seat, he heard his name.

"Philips!" roared First Sergeant Petty.

Standing against the jeep, Ozzie dropped his cleaning props, doing his best not to rock. Petty took one look at him and then ripped him open with a slew of F-you this and that while a shower of spit flew from his lips.

"From this moment forward, when I say jump, you say how high. Is that understood?" Sweat dotted Petty's forehead.

"Yes, First Sergeant."

"I don't need this extra bullshit from you. I have a lot on my plate. You have a job to do, and I expect you to do it." Petty sniffed. "And you smell like a distillery. Rough night?"

Ozzie didn't respond.

"I asked you a question, boy."

Ozzie had wondered how long it would take Petty to go for the jugular. The moment had arrived. A white man only a few years older than he was had called him a boy.

Ozzie took his time answering. Slow but deliberate. "No, I didn't have a rough night."

"Remove those sunglasses when I'm speaking to you, boy."

Ozzie clenched his teeth. Reached for his sunglasses and looked Petty dead in the eye.

"You didn't have a rough night, what?" Petty yelled; sweat now poured from his face. He was getting off on this show of power. The whole motor pool was watching the interaction. "Answer me."

Ozzie kept eye contact while forcing the words out. "First Sergeant."

"Well, since you don't know how to answer your company first sergeant with respect, can't get to work on time, and don't know how to enjoy your Friday evenings without disgracing yourself and the United States Army, you are forbidden to leave this base until I give you the all-clear. Understood?"

Ozzie flinched. "Yes, First Sergeant."

"Dismissed."

Ozzie picked up his rag and spray bottle and climbed inside the truck. By late afternoon, he'd cleaned the inside of a dozen trucks, taken them to the gas station to be refueled, organized the storage units for the vehicles, and checked inventory. The steady physical work had helped him to shake off his hangover, but he thought constantly about Jelka, the baby, and his new confined predicament on base. He ate half a sandwich and carried the other half back to the barracks.

When he reached the common area, there was a circle of men standing around the mail carrier, who wore a canvas bag slung over his shoulder. The men were eager, hoping that their name would be called, signaling that they'd received a box filled with sugary treats or a steamy love letter from a girl back home. Ozzie sat on the edge of the sofa and tipped his canteen to his lips. The cool water felt good going down his throat, and he wondered what he was supposed to do on the weekends when he'd be confined to base.

"Philips," the mail carrier sang, and held up a letter. "Oh, and it smells delightful too." He waved the envelope in the air, teasing Ozzie, which elicited chuckles from the other men.

Ozzie reached for the letter and carried it down the hall to his room. It was from Rita. It was only the second letter he had received from her, and he smelled her honeyed scent before he saw her beautiful cursive on the envelope. His heart sped up as his fingers went underneath the seal and broke it. She had written the letter on cream-colored stationery.

Dearest Ozzie,

How is Germany treating you? Life at Lincoln is decent. My classes are hard, but I really lucked out with my roommate. Her name is Frances, she's from Harrisburg and has been a godsend. She's both smart and sweet. We've decorated our room in pink and white but no matter what they promise us, the temperature is never right, and I often wake up freezing or sweating my hair out. I do have an amazing political science professor who has really been pushing me to think outside of the box. He calls me Miss Attorney in class. It really makes me feel like I can do anything, but the sad fact is that I'm already short on my tuition for the spring semester. I hate to ask you, and I am not trying to take advantage of our friendship. Please know that if I had any other options, I wouldn't. Do you think you could wire me thirty-five dollars? I know that's a lot but it's the remainder of what I need. Without it, I'll have to sit my second semester out and I really don't want to fall behind. Please consider it.

Yours truly,
Rita

Ozzie tucked the letter underneath his thin pillow and put his head on top of it while trying not to succumb to the emotions that welled inside of him. What would Rita say if she knew his predicament?

He could remember the last time he cried . . . Ozzie was twelve. His dog, Pebbles, was an active dog and was always running out the door when someone opened it. He had tried to train her not to leave the house unless he gave the command, but Pebbles ran out into the street and got hit by an ambulance speeding through his block. Pebbles was the first living being that Ozzie had loved and lost, and he howled and cried uncontrollably. It was on one of the rare occasions his father was home. Big Otis snatched Ozzie up by the collar and told him through clenched teeth, "Men don't cry. Only sissies. If'n I see you cry again, I'll give you something to cry about. Now go get yourself together, 'cause I ain't raising no sissies." Ozzie was shaken. He gulped and sniffled until his tears were trapped in his chest, making it hard to breathe.

He hadn't shed a tear since, and that was seven years ago. But in that moment with Rita's letter under his head and Jelka's news in his heart, Ozzie knew if he allowed himself the luxury; he would cry a kitchen sink full.

First Sergeant Petty had alerted his commanding officer, and as a result, Ozzie had been confined to base for six straight weekends for his behavior. By the time he was able to visit the Federal Eagle Club, it was the end of February. The moment Ozzie stepped foot into the club, Jelka ran up to him and threw her arms around his back.

"I've missed you so much," she whispered, then grabbed his face and kissed him. Ozzie hadn't realized how starved he was for physical affection until he felt her lips on his and her arms threaded around his waist.

He exhaled and pressed his forehead against hers. "It's good to see you too."

"What can I get you, *Mein Prinz?*"

"Ah, I've been upgraded to a prince in my absence." He squeezed her hand. Jelka's face had a rosy fullness to it, like she was a flower in bloom. "Club soda," he said.

"Is that it?"

Ozzie felt an itch in the back of his throat, but he nodded. He hadn't touched a drop of alcohol in six weeks, and he had decided that his drinking days were behind him. He was about to be a father and needed a clear head to navigate his next moves.

"What time can you leave?" he asked, looking around.

"I can try to go now, if you would like. My boss owes me a favor."

"Yeah, let's get out of here. I'd rather be alone," he whispered.

Snow fell lightly from the sky, and it felt good to hold Jelka's hand as they headed toward the rooming house.

"Have you told anyone about the . . ." He had a hard time saying the word.

"No. Only you."

"Have you thought about what you want to do?"

She stopped in her tracks and scanned his face. "What choice do I have?"

Ozzie didn't have the heart to say she should get rid of it. He didn't know how abortions worked in this part of the world, but it was a dangerous back-alley business in Philadelphia. At least that was what he had overheard from a conversation between his two sisters.

"I don't know."

They walked the rest of the way in silence. When they arrived at the house, the thick woman in the scarf welcomed them in. "By the hour or for the night?" she asked.

"The night," Ozzie said, and then paid the fee.

She led them up the stairs and pointed to the room on the left. The fever came over Ozzie as soon as the door was closed, and Jelka seemed to ignite too. They clawed and sank into each other with a thirst that took two rounds to quench.

Jelka panted, and then her breathing slowed. Ozzie had not thought about what was growing inside her while he tended to his needs, but now that they had finished, he turned and stroked her belly, still flat against his palm.

Jelka kissed his chest and placed her head in the crook of his arm. "Maybe you should take me to America with you. When you go."

Ozzie stretched his legs under the sheets. "I'm treated far better in Mannheim than I've ever fared walking the streets of South Philly. You can believe that."

"You have family who will understand our child. Not like here. I am afraid it will be teased and hated."

"Don't worry about that now. Get some rest." He rubbed her head. In an instant, Jelka fell asleep. But every time Ozzie closed his eyes, he kept hearing a child cry out, *Daddy*.

CHAPTER 20

Mannheim, Germany, August 1951

ETHEL

At the playground, Julia sat on the metal bench, rocking her daughter in her arms. While Ethel pushed Anke on the swings, she kept one eye on the other three children, who ran between the slide and the monkey bars. There was a soft wind whistling through the trees, and the clouds shading the sun gave the day a reprieve from the summer's heat.

"You seem to be handling this change so well. You're making me envious." Julia sighed. "I'm so sleep-deprived and a cranky mess."

"You have a right to be out of sorts, you have a newborn."

"Tell that to my husband." Julia snorted. "What are their ages again?"

"Franz is ten, Heinz eight, Monika just turned five, and this little one is three." Ethel tickled Anke's neck until she squealed.

Julia moved the baby from her chest to her lap. "How's finding homes for the other children going?"

Ethel gave Anke one last push and then wandered over to Julia. "Slow, but I've been in contact with the German youth welfare offices so I can get an accurate count of how many children need families."

"Well, hallelujah, the German government wants to help."

"They've been much easier to deal with than the American agencies, that's for sure. So far, I've identified fourteen families stationed between Mannheim and Stuttgart who are willing to adopt."

"Girl, you are making progress. That's got to feel good."

"Up," Anke called, and Ethel moved back to the swing. Once she'd located Franz and Monika on the slide and Heinz on the monkey bars, she turned to Julia.

"But there's a lot of bureaucracy and red tape with so many hands of approval needed. At this rate, it could take up to a year to place the children."

"That feels like forever, especially in little people's lives."

"Exactly, and I've been trying to find a legal loophole to get around these narrow-minded holdups while, at the same time, reaching more Negro families who are willing to adopt. On my own, I've identified children's homes in Heidelberg, Karlsruhe, and Stuttgart, all with mixed-race children. I don't have exact numbers, but there are hundreds, maybe even thousands."

Julia stood and placed her sleeping baby in the pram, then rocked it gently with her foot. The sun had drifted from behind the clouds, and she shielded her eyes with one hand. "Whenever my mother was upset about something, she'd write a letter. Aren't you a fancy journalist? Didn't you tell me that you interviewed Thurgood Marshall at the Waldorf Astoria, for Christ's sake? Maybe it's time to pull out those writing skills."

Ethel looked from Anke to Julia. Why hadn't she thought of that?

"Come push Anke for a minute," Ethel said, then moved to the bench for her purse. She pulled out her journal and ink pen, sat down, and started scribbling.

Ten minutes passed before she looked up. Then she shouted, "I can write an article—a step-by-step guide for American families on how to adopt these children abroad."

Julia pushed Anke and said, “I love that idea.”

“I’ll reach out to my editors at the *Baltimore Afro-American* and the *Pittsburgh Courier*. Maybe we can even get it on the wire.”

“Can you imagine the kind of response you’ll get?”

Ethel’s heart thundered in her chest. “I’ll tell individual stories of some of the kids I’ve met. Make them real in the eyes of the readers, not just names and numbers.”

“You saw how Dorothy took that idea of getting gift baskets to the single German mothers and got an ad posted in the *Stars and Stripes* army newspaper. Gifts have been pouring in like crazy. Imagine what you can do.”

Ethel looked at the words she had written on the page. “It has been nice seeing the relief on the women’s faces when we drop off the packages. But I always feel like we could be doing more.”

Julia stood with her hands on her hips. “Well, imagine what will happen when your how-to-adopt articles run in the American newspapers. Honey, people will be coming out the woodwork to help.”

“That’s all I want in the end.” Ethel gazed over at the baseball diamond, where her three kids were chasing one another in a game of tag. “For children to have families to love them.”

“Well, you better stop talking to me and get writing.” Julia wagged her finger.

“More!” Anke kicked her legs.

“Go on, while you have me to keep an eye on the children for you.” Julia ruffled Anke’s hair.

Ethel’s eyes narrowed as her pen scraped against the notebook page. She wrote August 23, 1951, and then scribbled the words “The Brown Baby Plan,” and started outlining her idea.

CHAPTER 21

Mannheim, Germany, September 1949

OZZIE

By the start of June 1949, the white petals of the common hawthorn hedges outside Ozzie's bedroom window were in full bloom. Each morning as he dressed for work, they made him think of Jelka, who had also flowered with the season. Since she could no longer disguise her bulging belly with layers of clothing, she had been fired from her job at the bar. She had no husband and carried an illegitimate child. Now, instead of Ozzie sending thirty-five dollars home to his mother, he had decreased it to twenty-five and sometimes twenty dollars, depending on Jelka's needs. He had very little savings left, because he had given most of it to Rita so that she could remain in school.

Sometimes Ozzie imagined that, by a stroke of luck, the pregnancy would go away. That the child wouldn't come. That he could somehow return to the States and pick up with Rita where they'd left off. Other times he thought about what it would be like to stay in Germany with Jelka and raise their child away from America's bullshit.

While he wasn't drinking and partying at the club, he had managed to get into a few craps games on post, and the wins from his gambling helped ends stretch until they met.

On the Tuesday after a Labor Day barbecue, a short guy from his platoon delivered the message he had been waiting on: "Philips, a girl is waiting for you at the gate."

Ozzie had been servicing the brakes on a truck and didn't know how he'd sneak away without Petty finding out. They had been in a place of neutrality, and Ozzie hadn't been in trouble since the Saturday morning when he had overslept. Jelka was so close to the end that he expected the messenger was from her. He spied Satchel replacing a windshield wiper and whispered his dilemma.

"Go, I haven't seen Petty around, but be quick. I'll cover for you."

Ozzie removed his oil-stained gloves and then jogged to the gate just left of his motor pool. When he reached the entrance, a girl of about ten or eleven stood at the curb, wearing Jelka's trench coat.

"Osbourne?" she asked. She had the same big eyes as Jelka.

"Yes."

"Jelka had the baby," she said in a monotone way that suggested she had practiced those words in English the whole way. "I will take you."

Ozzie felt joy tangled with fear well up in his throat. He looked down at his hands, and they were shaking.

"Okay, wait here." He motioned for her to stay put. As he clambered back to the motor pool, his belly flipped nervously. He had a child in the world. A baby with his DNA. How could he be a father when he was barely legal himself? Ozzie slipped back into his work station. "Have you seen First Sergeant Petty?" he asked one of his unit friends, who was carrying a bucket of rags to the laundry.

"It's late on a Tuesday. He's probably at the NCO Club, drinking himself silly. You know Tuesday is their midweek hangout. Two-for-one beers."

Ozzie had been so shaken by Jelka's sister's arrival that he had forgotten it was Tuesday. The club brought in live entertainment, and he had heard that the cheeseburger special was a crowd favorite.

Satchel slid from beneath the car. "Everything all right?"

"Jelka had the baby."

Satchel clapped him on the back. "Congratulations. We need to break out the cigars. You know Morgan's been saving them special."

The air around Ozzie felt surreal. "No, not now. I've got to go. She's waiting on me."

"Go. If anyone asks, I'll say you went to the infirmary or something."

"You sure?"

"I'll take care of it for you." Satchel shook his hand. "You just entered a whole new world, brother."

Until now, Jelka had never invited Ozzie to her home. They'd met either at the bar or at the rooming house. Ozzie had tried to start a conversation with her sister, but after a few words, it was clear that her English wasn't as good as Jelka's.

They walked for over thirty minutes before she turned off the road. The sky was gray, and he heard church bells ringing in the distance, one, two, three, four, five. It was quitting time at work. His friends would be heading to the showers and then to the mess for dinner. But Ozzie was going to meet his child. He suddenly realized that he didn't know if it was a boy or a girl. He started to ask Jelka's sister but decided to wait. Either way, he was a father. Either way, his life was forever changed.

They passed a pasture with cows, and the stench of manure hit Ozzie in the gut. He followed the girl down a narrow path through a wooded area that opened to flat land lined with four cottages. The girl turned to the green cottage on the far right. The brown wooden door was chipped and squeaked when she opened it. The front door opened into a cozy living room. Jelka sat on a pea-green sofa with a baby's torso and legs peeking from underneath her blouse. She peered up at Ozzie with a timid smile. She looked exhausted but also mature and matronly. He often forgot that she was two years older than he was. In that moment, she looked it.

"Come, *Mein Prinz*. Meet your daughter."

A girl. Ozzie had a daughter. He peeped at her face as she fell away from Jelka's pink nipple, and he took a seat next to them. Jelka dabbed the baby's mouth with a cloth and then placed her into his arms. When he looked down into her face, he felt a swell in his chest. She was pale with pink lips, and she had his mother's nose. They called it the Philips nose, a bit wide, with flared edges. Her hair stood up in little spikes. She was so fair, it seemed hard to believe that she was his child, but when he turned her ears over between his calloused fingers, he saw a tinge of brown on the tips. The older women on his block had always said that Negro babies needed a few days for their skin to bake fully.

"She's beautiful," he cooed.

"Her name is Katja."

"Katja." He loved it. He loved her. Ozzie was so focused on the baby that he didn't hear Jelka's mother shuffle into the room.

"Hallo."

"Hello." He handed the baby back to Jelka and stood. It was their first time meeting, and she looked like a plumper version of Jelka, with gray temples. Ozzie had stuffed some American rations in his bag and pulled out a tin of coffee and held it toward her.

"Danke," she offered with a smile. "Thank you."

Seconds later, Jelka's father entered the room wearing dark aviator sunglasses and a button-down shirt two sizes too big. He didn't look at anyone as he plopped down in the recliner adjacent to the sofa where Jelka sat. He began kicking the top of the table lightly, over and over.

"Hello," Ozzie said.

Her father didn't look in his direction; instead, he kept pounding his feet against the wood.

"He doesn't take those off." Jelka motioned to the sunglasses. "We have to remove them when he falls asleep."

Ozzie nodded, but no other explanation for her father's strange behavior was offered. He had brought extra cigarettes and placed them on the table in front of her father. Still he pounded the table with his feet.

There was a tiny kitchen off the living room, and Ozzie could hear Jelka's sister, Jutta, banging around in there. The noise from her father's feet slapping against the table was hard to ignore, but then Jutta returned with a tray, and Jelka's mother offered up cups of tea. It was a strong brew, and Ozzie was grateful for it. When her father reached for the teacup, he stopped banging and sipped quietly.

Jelka's mother looked from Ozzie to Jelka and then said something to her in German.

Ozzie could tell by Jelka's sigh and huff that they were discussing him. Her father put down his teacup, then added his baritone voice to the conversation. The three went back and forth until Jelka passed the baby to Ozzie and then waved her hand in a way that said *enough*.

Jelka's mother got to her feet and tugged on her father's arm, and together they walked out the front door, slamming it closed behind them. The sound startled the baby, and Ozzie rocked her in his arms.

"What was that about?" Ozzie whispered to Jelka.

"I work my fingers to the bone to provide for them, and they are still so ungrateful. You must get us out of here. I do not want to raise Katja like this." Her big eyes pleaded with him. "No one here will be kind to her because of her skin. My parents are embarrassed that she is illegitimate," Jelka said softly.

Ozzie looked down at his daughter, and a strong feeling of pride overwhelmed him. Nothing else mattered in the world except Katja. He would do anything and everything to keep her happy and safe.

"Would it help if we got married?" Ozzie blurted.

When Jelka's mouth flattened, he realized that he was going about it all wrong. If he was asking her to marry him, he needed to do it right and get down on one knee.

Ozzie shifted the baby in his arms, then knelt before Jelka and asked, "Jelka, will you marry me?"

Tears crowned her eyes, and in a split second her shoulders caved as she let out a long whine. It wasn't the response he had expected. Was she afraid? He was afraid too, but it was the only way he could protect Katja and give her legitimacy.

"Oh, Osbourne. I am already married." She shook her head. "I am so very sorry."

Part 3

The tortoise doesn't embark on a journey it is not ready to finish. The day you chose this path is the day you chose to be awake.

—**AFRICAN PROVERB**

CHAPTER 22

West Oak Forest Academy, November 1965

SOPHIA

On the walk back from the Old South Ball, Willa threaded her arm through Sophia's while babbling with apple-scented breath against her ear.

"Wasn't that just the most romantic time ever? I could have danced all night," Willa crooned.

"Yeah, it was fun. You were right to drag me."

"I knew it." Willa squeezed her arm. "And you had a nice time with Claude. I saw you cutting a rug," she said, her gown swishing around her ankles.

Sophia pressed back, but she was thinking more of her time with Max than with Claude.

As they turned through the quad in the direction of their dorm, Sophia saw Patty and her gang up ahead, cackling and stumbling. She watched as two girls caught Patty by the arm to keep her from tripping on the hem of her dress.

"What in the devil is wrong with her?" Willa tipped her head. Loose strands of hair had fallen from her updo.

"She's drunk."

"How do you know?"

Sophia had watched the Old Man stagger around on many weekends after he had finished his work. She knew the signs. "They were guzzling down spiked punch all night long."

"Just foolish." Willa giggled and then sighed dramatically.

"What?" Sophia asked.

"Max. He just smelled so good. Like fresh linen in a forest of pine trees. I was hoping he would try to kiss me, but he didn't."

Sophia tried not to grimace. "Guess he's just a gentleman like that."

"For crying out loud, it's 1965, women are no longer delicate little flowers. Surely there is no harm in a tiny kiss." Willa held Sophia's arm tighter as she continued, reliving how Max had hung his hand around her waist on the dance floor.

"His touch made me feel all squishy inside," she said, and while Willa gabbed, Sophia couldn't help but think of her time alone on the bench with Max as they watched the embers burn in the fire. His fingertips pressed against her burn mark. Their easy way with each other. Max revealing his most hidden secret.

Sophia couldn't stop picturing Max as a scared small child. Germany was a long way to travel for a family. And she had never even considered that there were Negroes living in Germany. How had his parents gotten together in the first place? And it was such a crazy coincidence that he had lived through a fire and she was constantly having night terrors of escaping one.

"Ladies." Ms. Meacham stood in front of the double doors to their dormitory. "I hope you all had a divine evening. Please go to your rooms silently. Those who did not attend the dance are fast asleep, so please be courteous. You have thirty minutes to prepare for bed, and then lights out."

The girls tried to obey Ms. Meacham's courtesy rule as they walked down the halls and disappeared behind closed doors. Inside their room, Sophia removed her heels. She could feel her pinkie toe throbbing from being squished against the leather of the shoe all night. Willa sat down at her desk that she used as a vanity and removed her clip-on rhinestone earrings.

"I'm so glad fall break is in a few days. I cannot wait to shower in my own bathroom."

"Like your own, own? Simply for you?" Sophia turned her back as she slipped her dress over her head.

"Yes, silly. Did you forget that I'm an only child? Who else would I share with?" Willa said, swabbing a cotton ball over her eyelids to remove her eye shadow.

Sophia thought about the one bathroom she shared with the whole family. Most times the pipes clogged, and nothing but rusted water poured into the blackened tub, too stained for her to even bathe in properly.

"What are you doing over Thanksgiving break?"

Sophia yawned. "Just hanging out here."

"You and your jokes." Willa laughed with her mouth open. When she noticed that Sophia had not laughed with her, she said, "You're kidding, right?"

"I . . . can't go home."

"But the entire school will be closed from Wednesday until Monday at four. You can't stay here. They won't allow it."

Sophia shivered. What option did she have? If she went home, there was no guarantee that Ma Deary would let her come back. Sophia could not take that chance. She was just starting to get the hang of things.

Willa picked up a clean cotton ball, dabbed it in makeup remover, and wiped away her lipstick. "Don't you miss your family?"

"It's complicated." Sophia dropped onto her bed with a thud. Christ, how had she missed the notice that the school was going to be closed? This threw a wrench in her whole plan. Sophia could feel panic well up in her chest. Maybe she could stockpile food and hide out in her dorm room. Miz Peaches had been so kind to her. Sophia could convince her to pack up a few meals under the guise of needing the food for a long drive home. Would the maintenance staff be on campus? She wouldn't leave her room except to use the bathroom, or maybe she could pilfer a bucket to relieve herself. She could dump it out the window under the cover of night. Peeing in a bucket would not be her lowest point. Nothing could beat that time Ma Deary had put a padlock on the refrigerator to teach them a lesson, and Sophia had gotten so hungry that she had plucked maggots out of half-eaten sandwiches from the trash can in the cafeteria at school.

Willa interrupted her thoughts. "Did you hear me?"

"No, what did you say?"

"That you can come home with me. I'm sure my parents won't mind."

"Are you serious?" Sophia looked at Willa.

"Sure. My father's favorite saying is 'The more the merrier.' There is always room at our table."

"Thank you," Sophia said. Comforted and slightly afraid at the same time.

On the Wednesday of fall break, all classes ended at eleven-thirty. The cafeteria staff had set up stainless-steel coffee urns, hot chocolate, and porcelain platters of crumb cake in the lobby of the dormitory. Sophia had wrapped several pieces of cake in a napkin and dropped them into her satchel bag for the ride.

"Let's wait outside. I want to see if I can catch a glimpse of Max before he leaves." Willa puckered her lips.

As Sophia stood with Willa in front of the administrative building, she watched shiny cars in shades of blue, red, and white glide through the roundabout with silver letters that declared Thunderbird, Grand Prix, and Starfire. Sophia felt a twinge of envy as her fellow classmates were reunited with mothers in silk dresses, under blond mink, wearing enough diamonds and pearls to decorate a Christmas tree.

"There's the car," said Willa excitedly. Her cape-collared coat was open, and as she waved, her miniskirt rose up her thighs, showing off brand-new opaque pantyhose. Sophia had worn her best hand-me-down drop-waist dress, which hung below her knees, and quilted coat. She tried not to think about how out of fashion she looked next to Willa.

A sparkling black Cadillac Fleetwood rounded the bend. The car slowed to a stop, and a tall, smooth-faced man exited the front seat in a crisp black suit with a midway cap. "Miss Willa, so good to see you." He beamed perfect white teeth.

"Lovely to see you too, Paulie." Willa motioned to Sophia and made a quick introduction.

Sophia smiled but thought, *A driver?* Just how wealthy was Willa? Sophia had seen chauffeured cars only on television, and the passengers were always white.

Paulie reached for the handle and opened the back door. A pair of patent-leather heels with interlocking C's on the toe touched the ground. As the woman emerged from the car, Sophia saw that her hair fell in loose curls around her face. She wore a purple tweed skirt suit with the same "CC" on the buttons. The woman looked posh and expensive but slightly older than Sophia had pictured Willa's mother.

"Grandma Rose," Willa squealed. "I didn't know you were coming to pick me up."

"Darling, I wanted to surprise you." Willa's grandmother opened her arms wide, and Willa fell into them. "Let me look at you." She took a step back and examined Willa. "You've grown, darling, and look at those rosy cheeks." She pinched.

Sophia shifted from one foot to the other.

"Grandma Rose, this is my roommate, Sophia. I've invited her to come with us. She lives too far to go home for such a short break. I hope that's okay." She batted her eyelashes in a way that conveyed she always got what she wanted.

Grandma Rose's nose tilted up in the air as if she had just sniffed something unsavory. Sophia watched as the woman's eyes took her in from head to toe.

"Hello, dear. I am Mrs. Pride." She stuck out her gloved hand.

Sophia pumped it. "Sophia Clark."

"Clark?" Mrs. Pride said. "Are you related to the Clark sisters? Detroit is such a long way to travel."

Sophia looked blank. "No, ma'am. I'm from Prince Frederick, Maryland," she said. Then noticed the look of disdain that passed through Rose Pride's eyes as she leaned in closer.

"Farmland, then?"

"Yes, ma'am." Sophia wrapped her arms around herself.

The way Mrs. Pride's eyes cast up and down Sophia's body, it was as if she could see the paint-chipped farmhouse with the missing shingles. What had Sophia agreed to? Was it too late to turn back? Perhaps hiding out in her dorm room wasn't such a bad idea after all. The uncomfortable look from Mrs. Pride was crushing her, and they had not even left school grounds yet. How would Willa's parents treat her?

"Well, let's do get a move on. We have a little ways to go, and I don't want to get caught in traffic." Paulie took Sophia's train case, which looked battered and bruised next to Willa's coral Samsonite set, and placed them in the trunk of the car. When Sophia moved toward the backseat, Mrs. Pride held up her gloved hand.

"Why don't you ride up front with Paulie, where there's more room, dear," she said to Sophia as she slid across the backseat and clasped Willa's hand.

As they pulled away from West Oak Forest Academy, Paulie slipped Sophia a peppermint. She rested her head back on the soft leather of the seat as she listened to Mrs. Pride coddle Willa with sweet words.

"Wait until you see the gorgeous dress I bought you to wear for Thanksgiving dinner."

"Grandma Rose, you shouldn't have."

"Yes, I should. Nothing but the best for you, my little dove."

While they giggled and spoke in what felt like a secret language, Sophia sucked on the peppermint and looked out the window as the highway miles passed. It didn't take long before the smooth kiss of tires to the road lulled her to sleep.

Sophia jolted awake as soon as the car stopped. She looked around to catch her bearings.

Mrs. Pride said to Willa, "Your mother has insisted that I drop you off at the library, but we'll take your bags to the house for you. Willa, go straight there, please. No dilly-dallying on campus."

"I know my way to the library, Grandma Rose," Willa said with a smile. "Come on, Sophia."

Once the car pulled away, Sophia looked around and asked, "Where are we?"

"Howard University. Have you never been here before?"

"No." She had heard about Howard University. It was where Mrs. Brown, her school counselor at Brooks High School, had attended college. Her diploma was proudly displayed in a thick wooden frame on her office wall.

As she followed Willa across the yard, she asked. "Your mother works here?"

"Yes, she's lead archivist at the library. I practically grew up on campus," Willa boasted.

While Sophia had been feeding chickens and milking cows, Willa had been surrounded by college kids and driven around in a chauffeured car. No wonder Max wanted Willa and not Sophia. Who would want a girl like her?

As they climbed the stairs to the library, Sophia wondered what an archivist did, but she didn't want to appear foolish for asking dumb questions, so she just took it all in silently. As soon as the girls passed through the heavy door, Willa skipped ahead to the front desk and wrapped her arms around the waist of a slender woman wearing a mint turtleneck and pink lipstick.

"Wilhelmina, welcome home, sweetheart," the woman said, pulling Willa into her arms and hugging her so tight that Willa opened her mouth and exaggerated trying to draw breath.

"Mommy, I can't breathe." She pulled away, grinning. "This is my roommate and best friend, Sophia."

Willa's mother turned toward Sophia, giving her a smile that started with her lips and danced around in her eyes. "Pleased to meet you, Sophia."

"It's a pleasure to meet you too, Mrs. Pride." Sophia extended her hand.

"Willa has told me all about you. And please, Ms. Eleanor is just fine. My mother-in-law is Mrs. Pride," she said good-naturedly.

"Mommy, is it okay if Sophia stays with us for Thanksgiving break?" Willa tugged on her mother's hand like a small child.

"I don't see why not. I'll just need to check in with your parents to make sure it's okay," she said to Sophia.

Sophia fidgeted with the cuff of her coat sleeve. She could feel heat rising in her throat. "Our . . . power is unreliable on the farm, so unfortunately, there is no way to contact them. I assure you that it is fine. I've told them all about Willa too, and they won't mind at all."

Ms. Eleanor tipped her head to the side, and Sophia could feel her looking at her inquisitively. But then she rolled her shoulders back and smiled.

"Well, girls, I have a few more things to do before we leave. But go explore the library, and we'll meet at the information desk at five to head home for dinner. I made crab cakes." She gave Willa's elbow a last pat and then headed up the stairs to the second floor.

Sophia chewed the inside of her cheek, feeling ashamed but also grateful that Ms. Eleanor hadn't pried further.

"This is like my second home." Willa waved her hands. "What do you like to read?"

"History." Sophia pulled her satchel up over her shoulder.

"Well, I'm more into romance. Boy-meets-girl type of stuff. I'll be in the novel section. History is over there." She pointed to the left.

"Okay, I'll go grab a few books."

"There's a lounge area in the back, near that window. That's where I'll be," said Willa, skipping off.

As Sophia watched Willa head in the opposite direction, she exhaled. Finally, a moment to herself. The library smelled like coffee grounds and morning dew. The earthiness eased the tension in her belly. Sophia walked in the direction that Willa had pointed but saw only books on politics, psychology, and religion.

"Ah, a new face. Can I help you, friend?"

Sophia turned to see an older woman with tight curls pushed away from her forehead. She wore a plaid dress with a high neckline and cap sleeves.

"Yes, ma'am. I'm doing a project for school on . . ." Sophia wasn't quite sure how to phrase it. "Negro children from Germany adopted in the U.S."

The woman looked taken aback. "Oh, my. Now, that's interesting. How did you come to that topic?"

"A friend from school. He's Negro but was adopted from Germany and brought here when he was little. He didn't know much, but I was wondering if there was any press surrounding it or any books I could read," Sophia asked.

The woman reached for the glasses hanging around her neck and pushed them up over her nose. "Well, you must be referring to Ethel Gathers and her efforts to move brown babies out of orphanages in Germany to the U.S. She's an extraordinary woman. Let me see what I can find for you."

Sophia felt something light up inside her. "Yes, maybe that's what I am looking for."

The woman smiled before heading off to find what their archives held. "I'm Dorothy Porter Wesley, and I oversee the largest collection of Negro history in the world. I'm sure I can find what you are looking for in *my* collection. Come with me."

Mrs. Porter Wesley took off at such a speed, Sophia nearly tripped over her own feet, trying to keep pace with her.

When they arrived on the lower floor, they entered a room that felt like someone had broken the thermostat at sixty degrees. Sophia shrugged back into her coat as Mrs. Porter Wesley led her back to a second room filled with wall-to-wall reel boxes. There was a big gray machine shaped like a boxy bell with a television-like screen in the center of it.

"Let's take a stroll through the microfilm and see what we can find for you," Mrs. Porter Wesley said, pointing Sophia to the two seats in front of the machine.

Mrs. Porter Wesley studied the reel boxes before taking a few off the shelf. Sophia sat next to her and watched as she expertly scrolled.

"Jackpot," she said. "I think this is what you are looking for." She made space closer to the screen for Sophia.

Sophia read the headlines. *Ebony*: "Homes Needed for 10,000 Brown Orphans." *Jet* magazine: "German 'Brown Babies' Arrive in U.S."

"Yes, this is perfect," Sophia said, feeling Max's story bubble up inside her.

"Wonderful," Mrs. Porter Wesley said. "What school did you say you attended?"

"I'm in high school. West Oak Forest Academy."

"Ah, you must be friends with our little Wilhelmina."

"Yes, she's my roommate."

"Well, the first opens the doors for the next. You remember that, and don't let them intimidate you. Always remember that you deserve that seat at the table. You've earned it, now do something amazing with it," Mrs. Porter Wesley said. "Now, let's get copies of those articles for you."

At the top of the stairs, Sophia thanked Mrs. Porter Wesley and then carefully shoved the articles into her satchel bag. She decided in that moment that she didn't want Willa to know what she was up to. It was Max's secret, and she intended to keep it close.

CHAPTER 23

Mannheim, Germany, September 1949

OZZIE

Jelka's words hung in the room heavy and thick, like gray clouds of smoke. Had Ozzie heard her correctly? He shook his head as if trying to clear water from his ears. He was still kneeling before Jelka, and his right foot had begun to tingle. Katja breathed evenly, her small body pressed against his chest as he cradled her in one arm like a football.

Ozzie pierced Jelka with his eyes. "What did you say?"

Her lips were dry and cracked, absent of the cherry lipstick she wore when they were out. "I am . . . married."

The three words needled Ozzie in the chest.

"Please do not be angry with me. I wanted to tell you." She reached for him, but he scooted back still on bended knee, out of her grasp.

The coral woven carpet was worn thin, and he could feel his kneecap twist under his weight as he looked down at Katja in his arms, then at Jelka, and then back at the baby. No, Ozzie had not been seeing things. Katja did have the Philips nose and enough melanin in her skin to belong to him. As if in answer to his question, Katja's face twitched, and she grinned at him in her sleep.

"Please, let me explain," Jelka pleaded.

He clutched Katja tight as he raised up off the floor and turned his back to Jelka, facing the tiny window, trying to calm down. The sheers were drawn, and Ozzie peered out into the darkness at the gravel road he had traveled just hours ago. Katja's arm jerked, and he rubbed her back to soothe her. She smelled like lilies, and Ozzie could feel her vines tighten around his heart. He was her daddy. What was he supposed to do now?

He had really made a mess of things this time. When he was younger and came home bruised from an alley fight, his mother would tease him by saying, "Boy, trouble sure seems to follow behind you wherever you go." Ozzie wished just once he could have made a liar of her.

He wanted to run. But if he did, he'd be just like his father. Leaving when things got hard. He had dug this hole for himself—the drinking, the woman, and now the baby. He turned back toward Jelka. She looked frazzled, stomach bloated, her big round eyes sagging with fear.

"Come sit, *Mein Prinz*."

"Don't call me that," he snapped. This was no fairy tale, and he had a hard time seeing a happy ending.

"Please. I will tell you everything." She patted the seat next to her on the sofa, but Ozzie moved to the chair that Jelka's father had occupied and lowered himself into it, careful not to wake Katja.

Jelka fidgeted with her hands. Folding her fingers over each other as if washing them clean. "I did not wish to get married. It was the middle of the war. Air raids. Bombs. They came, always in the night. I was afraid to leave the house." Her eyes bulged as she looked up at the ceiling. Ozzie followed her gaze to a long crack in the plaster that looked damp from years of neglect.

"My brothers were both dead. My father was fighting *der Krieg*. He sent what he could, but it was never enough. The rations got smaller and less adequate." She took a deep breath. "In 1944, as soon as I turned seventeen, my mother married me off. Gottfried was six years older but could provide."

"What did he do?"

"He managed the laborers at the local manufacturing plant. They made steel helmets for the Nazi regime."

Ozzie's jaw tightened.

"In the beginning, he went to work every day and came home at six." Jelka closed her eyes. "Then one day, he said he needed to go to Berlin. He was in charge of an important delivery. That was in October '46, and he never returned."

Jelka looked up, and Ozzie studied her face, searching for signs that what she was saying was true.

"More than a year went by before his sister discovered that he was being held as a prisoner by the Soviets. Word came sparingly and then silence. I thought he was dead before I met you."

"And?"

Jelka reached between the cushions of the sofa and held up a tattered envelope. "I received a letter from him last week. He is still alive. The Soviets will release him. He will return home soon."

Ozzie chewed the inside of his cheek but said nothing.

"I do not know exactly when he will be released, but I do not think he would be happy to see her. He has certainly beat me for less." She dropped her chin and her shoulders trembled.

Ozzie knew that she wanted his sympathy, but at that moment he had nothing to give. He felt trapped, and a sense of doom hovered over him. He rose and paced the floor. There was a family photo on the table. Ozzie peered at a preteen Jelka with two older boys flanking her. Her little sister was small and stood clutching the hand of her mother and father. Now Jelka's brothers were dead. Her father mentally unhinged. She had a violent husband on the loose, and Ozzie's newborn child was tied between them all. How had he gotten himself wrapped up in all of this?

"Osbourne, when I met you at the club, it was your kindness. The way you looked at me. For so long, I was dead inside. I felt empty. Your affection brought me back to life, and I will be forever grateful to you for that." Her bottom lip trembled as she moved across the room toward him. "You are *Mein Prinz*. No one has ever treated me as kindly as you have."

Katja began to cry. Ozzie rocked her a little, but she would not settle. Jelka reached for the baby. Her hand grazed Ozzie's arm as she took Katja, hushing her with sugary words in German. She sat with the baby on the sofa and lifted her blouse. Ozzie watched as she pushed her swollen pink nipple into Katja's mouth. Katja moved her head to and fro, smacking her lips like a guppy, trying to latch on. Jelka cooed until Katja found the milk flow and calmed down. Ozzie needed to be soothed too.

"You got anything to drink around here?" he asked.

"Look under the kitchen sink." She motioned.

Ozzie walked into the tiny U shaped kitchen. It was barely big enough for two people to stand in at once. He opened the cabinet and found a glass bottle with clear liquor. He assumed it was vodka. He found a small glass and greedily poured himself two fistfuls.

He returned to the living room with the intention of sipping it slow, but once the liquor touched his lips, he couldn't help gulping half of it down in one swoop. The burn in his throat relaxed him at once.

"What are we supposed to do?"

"I could try to divorce him, but that would take time and money, and there is no guarantee that it would be approved."

Ozzie had asked Jelka to marry him as a matter of duty but had not thought it all the way through. For Katja, he was willing to try anything to keep his daughter with him. More than anything, he wanted to raise her up and be a stable man in his child's life.

Jelka had placed Katja on her shoulder and started patting her back. Katja let out a loud burp. On her lap, Jelka swaddled Katja tight, tucking the edges of the blanket around her until she was wrapped like a mummy.

"She's so beautiful." Jelka met his eyes.

"Yes, she is. You did good."

Despite how her news had hit him, Ozzie couldn't make himself turn away. It was a tender sentiment, and it felt good to forget their troubles and share a moment, if only for a few seconds.

Jelka stood, then stroked his face with the back of her hand. "The only way to keep her safe is to run away."

He stumbled backward. "Run? What are you talking about? And go where?"

She leaned her weight into him. "I have a friend south of here," Jelka said. Then she told Ozzie about one of her schoolmates who had a brown baby and how her American sweetheart deserted his company. "They now live happily in a little village south of Ulm, and no one bothers them. They are content. Even had two more children."

Ozzie rubbed the back of his neck. The liquor had taken the edge off, so much so that he chuckled when he asked, "You wanting me to go AWOL?"

He had joined the army for stability. To make something out of his life. To be a proud American. To show America that the Negro man was just as capable as the white man. He didn't want to give up his dream of working in the Intelligence unit. Besides, since he had volunteered, it was the first time in his life that he'd had steady pay. It wasn't a lot, but it was damn sure more than he was used to making. How would he earn a living as a man on the run from the American government? His mother wouldn't survive it. And what about Rita's tuition? Ozzie bristled.

Jelka said, "I am just thinking about what's best for our daughter. With Gottfried returning, what kind of life do you think she will have here without you protecting her? He is a violent man."

Ozzie could not answer that, and Jelka's words were like a dagger through his heart. He knelt before Katja, who slept peacefully on the sofa. Already, looking at Katja was like looking God in the face. In just a few hours, he had discovered a love that he never knew existed. But Jelka was asking him to do the impossible. There had to be another way.

CHAPTER 24

Mannheim, Germany, September 1951

ETHEL

Ethel spent the remaining days of summer cloaking her four children in a mother's love. She taught them English, took them to the park, fed them well, and gathered them each night to pray before tucking them into their cozy beds. While they slept at night, she perfected the Brown Baby Plan and wrote how-to-adopt articles for the *Afro-American* newspaper.

Most evenings after Bert had gone to sleep, her kitchen light burned into the wee hours as she worked on the plans for her one-woman adoption agency. The single mission of the agency was to facilitate speedy placement for colored children with American families in Germany and the United States. Even though she worked hard, at every turn she found bureaucracy placing a wedge in her plans. For the past three weeks, Ethel had spent her days at city hall, petitioning the courts on behalf of the fourteen military families she had identified as prospective adoptive parents. The language barrier had proved a hindrance until two days ago, when a young law student offered to serve as her translator. After much back-and-forth, Ethel received her first win, and she couldn't wait to get to the Negro Wives of Mannheim meeting to share her good news.

On the next Friday, Ethel made her way to the basement of the yellow Protestant church at the front of the Benjamin Franklin Village, dressed in a floral A-line skirt and sheer blouse. When she entered the open room with Anke on her hip, she found the two women in charge of hospitality putting the finishing touches on the food table.

Glass bowls of potato salad and macaroni salad sprinkled with paprika, crispy fried chicken legs, juicy sliced honeyed ham, and green beans smoked with pork made Ethel's mouth salivate. There was also a pitcher of fresh-squeezed lemonade and a pineapple upside-down cake for dessert.

"Looks fantastic." Ethel waved to the two women as she placed Anke down with the other two children on a mat with plush toys.

Julia pulled Ethel into a tight hug. "Oh, you smell good. What's that you're wearing?"

"Just a little Jean Naté."

"Smells better on you than it does on me," Julia huffed. "Were you able to run off copies of the agenda for me?"

"Yes, Madam President," Ethel teased, then reached inside her purse and handed Julia a stack of papers.

"How did it go in court?"

Ethel perked up. "I finally made a little headway, but I'm going to need all hands on deck. Can I hijack a few minutes with the ladies to put out a cry for help?"

"Of course, just add it to your vice president's report," Julia said, reviewing the schedule. "I do hope the social committee has secured a location for our dinner/dance fundraiser. I already have a handful of people who are ready to purchase tickets."

The room filled with laughter and chatter as more women arrived, dressed in their Sunday best. Metal chairs tied with pink bows were set around rectangular tables covered in starched white linen tablecloths. After hugs and small talk, the women held hands, said grace, and piled their plates high before drifting to their seats.

Julia passed out the agenda and called the meeting to order. After she went through their social and membership outreach points of engagement, she turned the meeting over to Ethel.

Ethel stood, and as she walked, she could feel that the waistband of her skirt had tightened against her belly. She had treated herself to seconds of everything.

"Good afternoon, ladies. Protocol having been established, I am Ethel Gathers, vice president and community service chair. First, I want to thank all the women who prepared the food today. You really put your foot in it." She smiled, and many of the women chuckled. A few fanned their hands in the air as one lady shouted, "Say it again," and another called out, "Got me licking my fingers to the bone."

Ethel went on, "As many of you know, I have been working feverishly to place the half-Negro orphans living here in Germany in American homes. I am bringing this before our group to secure your help in locating families willing to adopt. Any way you can help, really."

A tall woman dressed in a flowy peach dress raised her hand. "Are you looking for families in America too? I have a cousin in Charleston who can't have children," she said.

"Yes. I've just penned an article that ran in the *Baltimore Afro-American* newspaper, letting folks know that these children need homes. I've asked the potential parents to send their inquires to the newspaper, providing a good description of what they are looking for, girl or boy, infant, toddler, school-age child. To be frank, that's the easy part," Ethel said, thinking about all the affidavits of support from the immigration authorities, financial records, and the long list of legal documents needed for the consulate in Germany to start the process.

"Are all the kids locked away in orphanages?"

"Many of them, but not all. Some are at home with their mothers until we can move them. Regardless of where the children live, we need the written consent of the mother to get the paperwork rolling. Once that happens, the child is separated from the mother and then placed in a *Wisenheim,* which is the German way of saying an institution."

"That sounds like the hardest thing to do for a mother," one woman said, wincing.

"How hard could it be? They're giving up their children anyway. The sooner the better," another snapped.

"And who pays for all of this?"

Ethel cleared her throat. "Once we identify a match, the family adopting the child is charged twenty dollars a month for the child's food, clothing, and medical care until his or her name reaches the German quota list." Ethel purposely left out the additional forty dollars it would cost to translate the documents into German, not to mention the cost of the long-distance calls to and from the States requesting documents. She didn't want the fees to scare away any potential parents.

"So what's the holdup? Seems like if the mothers don't want them, you should be able to move the kids in droves."

Ethel cringed. She had spent enough time with local German mothers to know that they didn't always want to give up their babies. Most times they had no source of income, no family support, and no other choice.

"The toughest part in all of this is proving the baby's nationality," Ethel said, repeating what her translator had just related to her in court.

"Aren't they all just German?" Julia asked.

Ethel shook her head and explained, "When a German woman marries, she automatically becomes the nationality of her husband. If she's not married, her nationality must be proved through her grandfather. She must produce proof before the passport of the child will be issued."

"Good grief. There are so many hoops to jump through while those poor children just have to sit and wait," Julia said, reaching for her daughter, who had started to fuss.

Ethel clutched the podium with both hands. "It could take six weeks to six months for the proof to be obtained and processed."

"What can we do?"

"Pray," someone shouted.

"Prayer always helps." Ethel chuckled. "But I need boots on the ground. I need you all to start chatting with Negro women in your networks, at home, here, and anywhere in Germany. Help me get the word out that these babies are available for adoption. As many of you know, I have adopted four, and they have been the joy of my life."

Words of congratulations rang around the room. Once the women settled back down, Ethel added, "My goal is to get as many of these children to America as I can, and for that we need resources."

"I can organize a bake sale," said the woman in the flowy dress. "I make a mean sweet-potato pie."

"That's a start," said Ethel as woman after woman called out ideas. Then, as if on cue, Anke stood in all her sweet stickiness, reaching her arms out to Ethel with the white bow slipping from her hair, shouting, "Mummy. Up." And the ladies oohed and ahhed as Ethel nuzzled Anke in her arms.

CHAPTER 25

Mannheim, Germany, March 1950

OZZIE

Two weeks after Katja was born, Ozzie won a Land camera off a white boy from Boston in a heated game of poker. The camera produced a glossy Polaroid photo in sixty seconds. Each weekend he wasn't on active duty, Ozzie visited Katja and would snap a photograph of her. Ozzie had to restrain himself to one picture each week because the Polaroid film was expensive. Only ten film sheets came in a pack, and he had to make them stretch. Ozzie liked the ritual of capturing her forever in a picture, and he wanted to hold on to her infancy as long as he could.

Jelka wanted her to look perfect in every photograph, but Ozzie's favorite shots were the ones when he caught her lying on the floor after a diaper change in a white tee, or on her stomach, eyes droopy from her nap or mouth wet with milk.

During the week, Ozzie carried the latest snapshot in his breast pocket above his heart. In the evenings, before he went to bed, Ozzie pulled out the pictures of Katja and lined them sequentially across his bed, marveling at her growth in just five short months.

"You got it bad," Morgan would tease him during this ritual.

"Ain't that something, got me wrapped around her pinkie and she ain't even walking," Ozzie snorted.

The rooming house where he had taken Jelka for most of their relationship was for lust, not for families. Now, on the weekends when Ozzie wasn't on active duty, he stayed overnight at Jelka's house, sleeping on the coral woven carpet on the floor, with Katja on his chest.

For every month's milestone, Jelka insisted on a small celebration for Katja. On the Saturday in March when Katja turned six months, Ozzie walked into Jelka's living room to the smell of soup boiling on the stove. Alpine folk music played from the gramophone, and a fire curled and crackled around wood in the tinplate belly stove. Katja was on the rug, rolling around on her back.

"She can crawl." Jelka pawed the air, mimicking the movement. Her dark hair was pulled back from her face, and her skin looked freshly scrubbed and oiled.

Ozzie removed his olive drab coat, scarf, and leather gloves and rested them on the back of the recliner. "When did this start?"

Katja heard his voice and turned her face toward him. Then she started to cry and kick her legs. Drool ran down her chin and dripped onto her white tee as Ozzie scooped her up in his arms.

"Hello, Kitten," Ozzie purred.

Katja went from crying to giggling as he blew bubbled lips on her tummy. A curl flopped down over her eye, and he massaged her scalp with his fingertips. Ozzie lived all week for this moment with Katja. He could deal with First Sergeant Petty talking down to him and assigning him menial tasks if, at the end of the week, it meant that he'd see the joy on his daughter's face. He had long since reached the point when he could not remember his life without her.

"Just a few days." Jelka stood, smoothing down her cotton dress. She had lost the baby bulge around her waist and in her cheeks. Only her breasts were still swollen.

She stood on tippy toes and kissed his jaw, then rubbed away the red lipstick with her finger. She smelled of the vanilla-scented Drene shampoo that he had brought her. "I missed you," she said, smiling.

The space that had grown between them since he'd found out that she was married had slowly dissolved. Somehow they had found a comfortable rhythm of pretending like her spouse did not exist.

"Yeah?" He grinned. "Well, I got you something."

Ozzie repositioned Katja in the crook of his arm as he rummaged in his jacket pocket for a package of Lucky Strikes and a Mr. Goodbar with peanuts, her favorite American candy.

"You are too good to us," Jelka said as her mother, Maria, shuffled out of the back room and nodded at him. Ozzie used his free hand to pass Maria the provisions he had bought for her. Coffee, sugar, and a few potatoes.

"*Danke.*" Maria patted his arm and carried the goods into the kitchen.

"Ma made pea soup with speck and dried beans," Jelka said. "Are you hungry?"

Ozzie nodded. "Always."

He propped Katja up on the sofa between two throw pillows. He had his camera draped around his neck and put the viewfinder to his eye to watch her through the lens. She was a lovely child. Long lashes and dark eyes that followed Ozzie around the room.

"You never take a picture of me," Jelka said, pouting. "Are you ashamed?"

Ozzie pulled the camera from his face. He had been careful with his film but realized that Jelka was right. He should have a picture of them both. "Okay, come hold her."

Jelka's face lit up. "Let me change her first." She swooped Katja up and disappeared into the back room. When she returned, Katja was wearing a white dress, and Jelka had reapplied her lipstick.

The mother-and-daughter duo looked beautiful, and the way Jelka held his daughter with tenderness melted Ozzie's heart. "Okay, ready?" he asked, aiming the camera.

"Maybe Jutta should take a picture of the three of us." Jelka smiled, then called to her younger sister in German before Ozzie could protest. "Show her how to take the photo, please," Jelka said.

Ozzie held the camera to his eye and mimicked what to do for Jutta, who nodded her understanding of the task at hand. Ozzie then sat on the sofa next to Jelka and put his arm around her shoulders.

"Teeth," Jutta said, and both Jelka and Ozzie chuckled. Flash.

"Take one more," Jelka said to Ozzie. "One for you and one for me?"

Ozzie nodded, and Jelka conveyed the message to Jutta. She held the camera to her eye again and snapped.

Jutta placed both Polaroid pictures on the coffee table, and all three of them watched as the photographs developed.

"Nice." Jutta pointed.

"Thank you," Ozzie said, patting the young girl on the hand, then he reached into his pocket and handed her two chocolate morsels.

The pictures developed, and he let Jelka choose which one she wanted to keep for herself. The other he slipped into his breast pocket until he could add it to his collection back at the barracks.

"Eat?" Maria clapped, then motioned a pretend fork into her mouth. That was the way she communicated with Ozzie, one or two words in English and a lot of hand motions.

Ozzie nodded. *"Ja, danke."*

By June, nine-month-old Katja was pulling herself up by grabbing on to the coffee table, and when she saw Ozzie, she babbled, "Dadadadadada." Slobber pooled at her chin as she showed off her four teeth.

Ozzie had made it a habit to read American books to Katja on the nights he was with her before bed. He had just finished reading his latest purchase from the commissary, *Curious George,* when Jelka walked into the living room carrying a basket filled with Katja's laundry. She sat next to him on the sofa and let her thigh rest against his as she folded the diapers, undershirts, and cotton dresses into piles on the coffee table. The radio was on in the kitchen, tuned to the local German news. Jelka's parents were asleep in the back room.

"I received another letter from him," she whispered.

Ozzie's shoulders stiffened. "Who?"

"Gottfried," Jelka hissed in a way that conveyed her agitation at Ozzie for making her say it. As if saying his name broke the fragile incantation that Katja's birth had cast between them.

"And?"

"He's fallen ill. He hopes that because he can no longer work, they will make his transfer back to Germany quick. It could happen at any time."

Ozzie looked down at Katja, sleeping peacefully across his lap. Her belly rose and fell as her sweet, milky breath curled against his arm. From his comrades in his platoon, Ozzie had heard stories about the radical behavior of German POW men returning from harsh conditions in Polish mines, Soviet camps, and war-ravaged France, only to find that their wives had betrayed their sacrifice by taking up with other men and bearing their children. Ozzie had done a little research and discovered that because Gottfried was married to Jelka, it was his legal right as her husband to make decisions as far as Katja was concerned, and that worried Ozzie. He would have no rights and no claim to Katja because Jelka was married. The last thing Ozzie wanted was another man in charge of his daughter. A scorned man who would no doubt resent Katja because she wasn't his and because she was Negro.

"I'm scared," Jelka whispered.

"You don't have to be." Ozzie reached for her hand, but she pulled away.

"My neighbor's son returned two days ago from a camp in the Soviet Union. He was the one who brought me the letter from Gottfried. He was so skinny and hunched over. His eyes had no life in them." Her lips quivered. "Gottfried is going to expect me to take care of him. Maybe he would try to get you arrested and have them remove Katja from our home. I lie awake at night thinking of all these things."

"Shh." Ozzie reached for her with his free arm. "It's going to be all right."

"You cannot know that."

"I said I will protect you, and I will."

Ozzie just didn't know exactly what that would entail. If he were to tell the truth, the horns of this dilemma kept him up at night too. He had witnessed the German women at the American bars on payday with their half-Negro children, hungry and begging for scraps. Katja deserved better, and he wouldn't let Jelka's husband lay harm to his child. But going AWOL? That was a different beast.

"Maybe you can take the baby down to your friend's house in Ulm and stay with her and her American husband for a while. Till we figure things out."

"I want you to come with me. I want us to be a family. I do not love him." She grabbed his chin, blinking back tears. "Now I am with you."

Ozzie didn't know what else to say, so he squeezed her hand. This was his family now, and Ozzie's first duty was to protect them at all costs.

CHAPTER 26

Mannheim, Germany, September 1951

ETHEL

On her way home from yet another day petitioning the courts on behalf of potential adoptive families, Ethel made a quick stop at the commissary to pick up a bag of flour so she could make cupcakes to celebrate the children's first day of school. Franz, Heinz, and Monika had returned to their German elementary school to start the year, but once their adoption paperwork was complete, Ethel would transfer them to Mannheim Elementary, the American school set up by the Department of Defense for an international education.

With Anke on her hip, Ethel arrived at the one-story school a few minutes early for the children. In the yard were three wooden benches set against the chain-link fence. While she waited on one of the benches, she pulled a coloring sheet and two crayons from her purse for Anke.

Three German mothers were talking to one another on the bench adjacent to Ethel, and she noticed that they kept glancing over at her. Then one woman broke from the group and strolled over.

"Hallo," she said, swooping her brown hair into a knot at her neck.

"Good afternoon," Ethel said, protectively laying a hand on Anke.

"The Brown Fairy?" the woman asked in a thick accent.

Ethel's cheeks blanched. An article that ran in the *Mannheimer Morgen,* the local newspaper, had reportedly dubbed Ethel "The Brown Fairy" for her work securing goods for the German mothers with half-Negro babies; it even gave a plug to her adoption agency.

"People call me that, but my name is Ethel Gathers."

The woman fidgeted with her hair again. "My baby. I can't keep. Will you help?"

Ethel looked up at the woman and nodded. It was not the first time a German woman had asked for her help. She had been cornered on the streets several times and asked to take half-Negro children home with her. She reached into her purse for a scrap of paper and wrote down the name and address of St. Hildegard's orphanage.

"Sister Ursula will help you," she said to the woman, who squeezed her hand in thanks as the school bell rang.

The elementary children were released by class, and eight-year-old Heinz bounded to Ethel first, holding up a math assessment. "One hundred," he said, smiling, showing off his missing front two teeth.

"Excellent," Ethel said, pulling him into a hug.

Then Monika ran toward her, showing off a picture that she'd drawn.

"It's lovely." Ethel patted her head, then sat the children on the bench next to her as she waited for Franz. Line after line of children poured from the school before she finally spotted him. He moved toward her slowly, expressionless.

"Franz, are you okay?" Ethel asked, holding him at arm's length.

He nodded and slumped out of the school yard. Even after three months together, Franz was still the hardest of the four children for Ethel to reach. As they walked the few blocks to their house, Heinz and Monika played a game that had them avoiding the sidewalk cracks, but Franz declined, walking behind them instead. Ethel decided to give him a little space.

When they reached home, she sent Franz to shower, while Heinz, Monika, and Anke sat around the kitchen table. Even though they did not have homework from school, she had obtained workbooks in English and now gave them two pages each to work on while she mixed the batter for the cupcakes. Once the cupcakes were in the oven, she sat down at the table to inspect their work.

As she was holding Monika's hand, teaching her to trace the capital letter B, Franz burst into the kitchen crying. His copper-colored face had red blotches on the cheeks and chin.

"My dear, what happened?"

Franz was sobbing so hard he could barely breathe. Ethel pulled him to her chest and rocked him. "Talk to me, please."

He took her hand and led her into the bathroom. In the sink was the scouring pad that Ethel had used to clean her skillet. Ethel looked at Franz's face and arms and then at the soapy steel pad in the sink. She was horrified, and her voice trembled. "Franz, did you use this on your skin?"

The boy looked down at his feet.

"Why, honey?"

"To get this off," he said, pinching the flesh on his arm.

"What off?" She examined him.

"The color. I want it pale like the others. Maybe *bleichen*?" He looked up at her with hopeful eyes.

Ethel's heart sank as she realized he wanted her to bleach his skin. She got low and looked him straight into the eyes. "Franz, God made you perfect. You were created in His image."

"But I do not want this. I want to be like them." He stomped his foot.

"But you look like Dad and me." Ethel grabbed his arm and placed it next to hers, fighting back her own tears.

Franz pulled his arm away from her and doubled over, howling in pain.

"It's okay," she soothed, while rubbing his back.

He slowly released his arms by his sides. Ethel reached into the medicine cabinet for some Vaseline and gently pressed the petroleum jelly to his battered skin.

Franz trying to scrub the brown off his skin haunted Ethel as they went through their bedtime routine. She read two books to the children, watched as they brushed their teeth, and led them down on their knees to pray the rosary. Once she had tucked them into bed, she placed her black Continental typewriter on the kitchen table and punched out the heartbreaking story of Franz and the scouring pad in an article for the *Afro-American* newspaper. In her write-up, she used Franz's shame and confusion as further proof of why these children needed to be placed in loving Negro American homes, and quickly.

She heard Bert's key rattle at the door, and then he was standing in the arched frame of the kitchen.

"Well, aren't you a vision of beauty." He clutched the mail. "Come here, gal. Give your man some sugar." Bert dropped the envelopes on the counter and opened his arms to Ethel. He was her ease and comfort, and just the smell of him dissolved the tension from her day.

"How are you?" she asked, touching her cheek to his.

"Better now." His hands slid from her waist to her buttocks, and Ethel patted his greedy fingers away.

"Let me feed you first."

The plate she had kept warm for him rested under foil in the oven. Bert unbuttoned his uniform shirt down to the waist, exposing a white T-shirt. "I'm hungry as a horse. They worked me like the devil today. We are planning our next maneuver. I'll be away for at least two weeks, training a platoon in land navigation." He flopped in his seat and dug his fork into the pot roast. "I'm not looking forward to sleeping in tents in the woods."

Ethel reached into the refrigerator and pulled out a cold bottle of beer that she placed in front of him.

He took a swig. "How are the children?"

"Mostly good," she said, and then sat across from Bert and told him the details of Franz and the steel wool pad.

"I can only imagine what that boy has been through." Bert shook his head. "Well, I'll teach him some Negro pride. I was thinking we can send for some of those Negro League baseball cards, let him get to know the players."

"That's a good idea. He loves baseball."

"In the meantime, I'll ask around the barracks and see if anyone has a set they wouldn't mind parting with."

Ethel fingered her rosary beads in her lap. "I've been looking into ways to get the children across the Atlantic once I get the adoptions approved. I've tried the air force, but the military furloughs are dragging along."

"Have you tried the major airlines?"

Ethel reached across the table for her composition book and looked over her notes. "I've made inquiries with TWA and Pan American, and they both said that they could not transport such young children to America."

"Try Scandinavian Airlines or Lufthansa. I'm sure they'd love the publicity of doing some charity work for brown orphan children."

"Good idea." Ethel scribbled. "When the American adoptions are approved, I don't want transportation to add to the delay. I want these kids in loving homes with their new families quickly."

Bert pushed his plate away. "I'm proud of you, darling."

"It feels like I should be doing more." Ethel lifted his empty dish, washed it, and placed it in the plastic drainer.

When she turned around, Bert had slid up behind her and put his mouth to her ear. "You are doing just fine. Now, put that pen down and that damn typewriter away and come on back in the room with me so we can enjoy some dessert."

"I made cupcakes. We can have them right here," Ethel whispered back, playing coy, but Bert didn't miss a beat.

"We can have those too," he said, pulling her close.

CHAPTER 27

West Oak Forest Academy, November 1965

SOPHIA

Willa's parents had activities planned on each day of fall break, and while Sophia had enjoyed her time with the Pride family, she never had a moment alone to read over the articles that Mrs. Porter Wesley had given her until she returned to Forest.

Back at school, Sophia made a beeline for the library and was happy to find that the little room Mrs. Fordham had told her about was unlocked and vacant. The room had a round table in the center with an overstuffed chair in either corner. There were no windows, but the air smelled of potpourri.

Sophia opened the folder and flipped through the magazine pieces, reading one after the other. When she had gotten halfway through the stack, she heard the doorknob turn. Christ, she had forgotten to lock it behind her. She quickly gathered the pages into a pile as the door pushed open.

Her face relaxed when she saw that it was just Max. She didn't know that it was possible, but in the few days they'd been apart he had grown even more handsome. He had gotten his hair trimmed and edged at his temples, and his skin glowed like he had been fussed over.

"Soph, I didn't know you were back." He stopped. "Your hair. It's red."

Sophia's cheeks flushed as she ran her fingers through her hair. Before they had returned to school, Ms. Eleanor had insisted that both girls stop in at Bernice's Beauty Parlor. Bernice had scrubbed Sophia's hair to a shine, and the last of the Ogilvie dye had drifted down the sink. Then she'd pressed it with the hot comb until it fell to her bra strap in a luster that Sophia had never known.

"Do you hate it?" she asked, tucking loose strands behind her ears.

Max stood with his mouth agape, tugging on the sleeve of his West Oak Forest Academy sweatshirt. "No, you look great. Was that dye before?"

Sophia nodded and then, eager to change the subject, said, "How did you know about my secret hiding place?"

"Mrs. Fordham told me I could use this room to get away from the racket. I was going to review for my calculus exam."

"I hope I'm not in the way."

"No, never. What are you working on?"

Sophia hesitated, and in those few seconds, Max reached for her pile of papers and scanned the headlines. "What's all this?" he asked, frowning.

"Your story piqued my interest. I was at Howard University's library over break with Willa, and I looked your story up."

"You told Willa?" The vein in his neck bulged.

"No."

"Damn." He dropped the papers. "I thought I could trust you."

Max grabbed his backpack and reached for the doorknob. Sophia pushed to her feet and jammed herself between Max and the door.

"Max, I promise. I didn't tell a soul. I had the papers all weekend, and I never even pulled them out of my bag. That's why I'm in here. I wanted to look them over in private."

"Why, though? What's it to you?" He gritted his teeth.

"I can't explain it. Your story touched me."

Max shifted on his feet. "My parents would freak out if anyone found out. It's not even something we talk about."

As she nodded, Max stepped into the room. She breathed a sigh of relief as he flopped down in the metal chair opposite her seat at the table. He reached for the first article.

"*Jet* magazine: German 'Brown Babies' Arrive in U.S." Sophia watched his face as he read it. "I didn't know there were so many of us. I'm not the only one?" He shuffled the papers, reading through the headlines.

"You are not. From what I can gather, there were at least thirty-five children who were adopted from Southwest Germany and brought to America. But that's only from these few articles. I bet there were more."

Max sat quietly. "So many of us. Maybe they feel like I do sometimes. Like a misfit."

"Well, you don't need to be adopted to feel that way. I've never felt as if I fit in anywhere."

Max cocked his head to the side. "But you know your family." He reached for the next page.

She wrung her hands. "My folks are not like most. I just spent the weekend with Willa's parents, who worship the ground she walks on. I've never had it like that. All I do back home is work."

"We all have chores, right?"

She shook her head, conveying that it was more than that. "Ma Deary and the Old Man feel more like employers than parents." She looked down at the table. Emotions were bubbling up inside her, and she was trying to tamp them down so she wouldn't erupt.

"I've never felt loved," she croaked. "No hugs. They never bought me a present. Heck, they didn't even remember my birthday. Never came to school when I won an award."

"I'm sorry to hear all this," he said, but Sophia was on a roll and couldn't stop her thoughts from flowing out of her mouth.

"If it wasn't for my school counselor, I wouldn't even be here. Ma Deary forbade me to take the scholarship." She laughed out loud. "What type of parent would do that? She said my job was to work the farm. My brother Walter stole her car and drove me. I forged her name on my documents. That's why I didn't go home for break. I was afraid that she wouldn't let me come back." Tears threatened to spill from her eyes, but Sophia willed herself not to cry in front of Max.

His eyes were gentle with concern. "I didn't know."

"No one does. I don't even know why I'm telling you," she mumbled. "Except it feels as if you'll understand or at least not make fun of me."

Max slid his hand across the table and covered her hand with his. His touch was so comforting, so soothing, it made Sophia want to crawl into his lap. When had she been touched with such tenderness? She couldn't even remember.

"I feel the same way too." His voice was husky.

"Your story, I just wonder. And it may sound crazy. But I wonder if I was adopted too."

There, she had said it, and the small confession to Max felt like a weight floating off her chest.

"Why would you think you were adopted?"

Sophia shrugged. "I don't remember much of my childhood. Whenever I've asked about our family lineage, Ma Deary's response was always 'Stop asking dumb questions, we the only family you need,'" Sophia mocked in Ma Deary's shrilly voice. "And there are no baby pictures of me or Walter in the house," she said. That realization hadn't hit her until she went to Willa's.

Sophia had been amazed at the many photos of Willa on the walls in her stately home. On Sophia's last evening with the Pride family, Ms. Eleanor had taken her into the family room. As they sipped hot cocoa, they flipped through several photo albums displaying Willa at every stage of her life. Sophia had cooed, but deep down she couldn't ignore the blinding pang of jealousy. Where was her life stored? Who was keeping track?

To Max, she confessed, "It has always felt like a part of me was missing. And then I heard your story. And . . . I know I'm shooting darts in the dark. But why did those German words just rush out of my mouth the other day? It feels like I need to try this out and see what I come up with."

"Well, if there is something here, I'll help you get to the bottom of it. I can study for calculus later. Where do you want to start?" Max was still holding her hand, and Sophia reluctantly pulled it away to retrieve her satchel. She pulled out three sheets and put them on the table.

"The woman who ran the Brown Baby Plan, the one who organized the adoptions of the mixed-race children from Germany, her name is Ethel Gathers. When I was talking to the librarian at Howard, she mentioned that Mrs. Gathers sat on some board with her."

"So?"

"So she's alive. And probably lives in D.C." Sophia held up the three sheets. "I tore these from the white pages when I was at Willa's house. All the Gatherses in D.C. I'm assuming that the telephone number is in her husband's name."

"Do you know his name?"

Sophia shook her head. "No, but I'm going to start with A and go down the list until I find her."

"You know this is bizarre, right?"

"It's all I have to go on."

Max picked up the newspaper clippings. There was one article with a photo of lots of children huddled together. "I'm still amazed that there were so many of us. I really thought I was the only one."

"This is our little secret. Promise you won't tell a soul about me, and I won't tell anyone about you."

"Ich verspreche." Max flashed his teeth. "That's 'I promise' in German."

"Show-off." She scrunched her nose up at him.

Max stood and reached for her hand again, and Sophia felt her breath stall as he clasped it within his. "You are safe with me, Soph. *Ich verspreche.*"

CHAPTER 28

Mannheim, Germany, December 1950

OZZIE

Ozzie's twenty-second birthday fell on the first Friday in December, and Jelka arranged for her mother to look after Katja so they could go out and celebrate. When Ozzie arrived at the cottage, fifteen-month-old Katja dropped her rubber blocks and toddled over to him.

"Hallo," Katja said.

"Hey there, Kitten." Ozzie crouched down so she could run into his arms. He held her against his chest, loving the way her delicate skin felt against his. She smelled like Jelka's vanilla-scented shampoo and baby powder, and her curls were damp from her bath.

Katja reached up and pinched his nose.

"Bonk," he said, pinching hers back.

"Bonk." She giggled. They went back and forth pinching each other's nose until Katja tired of the game and climbed down.

Jelka's father sat in his recliner, wearing his aviator sunglasses and pounding his feet against the table. Ozzie had grown used to his odd behavior and patted him on the shoulder in greeting. Katja brought a plastic ball to Ozzie, and he got down on the floor with her.

"Ready?" He had not heard Jelka walk into the living room, but when he looked up from Katja, she took his breath away. She wore a burgundy dress that dipped low and hugged her waist. Her hair was blown and bounced as she moved toward him.

"You look lovely," he said, and she lit up.

Maria came out of the kitchen, wiping her hand on her apron. *"Alles Gute zum Geburtstag."* She tilted her head.

"Danke." Ozzie clasped Maria's hand. "It has been a happy birthday so far."

"We better go." Jelka tapped his wrist.

When Ozzie patted Katja's head goodbye, she started to cry. Ozzie scooped her up and kissed her on both cheeks and then the forehead, but she wouldn't be soothed.

"Noooo," Katja called, grabbing him around the neck.

"Aw, Kitten. Daddy will be back."

"Nooooooo," she said again.

"Kitten, Daddy always comes back," he said, rocking her a bit.

"Ma will take care of her. We have to get going, the taxi is waiting." Jelka flicked her watch. "She's just tired."

Ozzie gave Katja one more cuddle and then handed her to Maria, who cooed into their daughter's ear. Ozzie looked back, and Katja with her wet face was reaching for him. It broke his heart to leave her so distressed, but he closed the door behind them, telling himself that she would peter out the moment they left her sight. But as they climbed into the taxicab, he could still hear Katja's high-pitched wail for him: "Noooooo, Da-da."

Jelka insisted they try a new nightclub that had just opened a few blocks from the Federal Eagle Club.

"It's your birthday, and I feel like dancing," she whispered before licking the soft spot behind his ear that made him weak for her. When they exited the taxi, Ozzie wrapped a protective arm around Jelka as they walked toward the neon sign that flashed "Soda Club."

"You know I can skip the dancing." He fingered her hair. It had been months since they had visited the rooming house, where they could be free with each other, instead of the quick humps in her parents' living room.

"There is time for both," she said, leaning into him and pressing her lips to his chin.

Inside the club, the hallway light flickered on and off, and the space was so narrow they had to walk in single file. Ozzie could hear "Rum and Coca-Cola" by the Andrews Sisters playing as they entered the horseshoe-shaped room. The dance floor spilled over with swaying bodies. He scanned the crowd: The patrons seemed to be more German than American. Then he spotted Morgan and Satchel. Morgan was the first to see him and raised his hand in greeting before patting Satchel, who waved.

"I invited them to celebrate with us." Jelka squeezed Ozzie's hand and then led him to the dance floor to meet his friends.

Satchel and Morgan clapped his back. "Happy birthday, brother."

"Thank you."

"First round on me," Morgan said, grabbing the barmaid and whispering, "Four shots of vodka, please."

After two dances, Ozzie leaned into Jelka. "I gotta take a leak." She nodded and made her way off the floor.

While Ozzie washed his hands at the bathroom sink, he caught his reflection in the mirror. Man, this was twenty-two. Gone was that wet-behind-the-ears look that he'd had two and a half years ago when he had first reported to Kitzingen for training. So much had changed. He was a father; he had Jelka and a few dollars in the bank. While he didn't have it all figured out, one thing was certain, he was a grown-ass man.

When Ozzie walked back into the club, he couldn't find Jelka. He looked on the dance floor, then to the tables against the wall. Finally, he saw her at the edge of the bar, standing next to a tall blond man who leaned in much too close. Jelka turned her face in disgust, but the blond man didn't catch the hint. Heat spidered up Ozzie's neck as he crossed the floor in a few wide strides. He slipped between a couple and came up on the left side of the man.

"Come on, pretty lady," the blond man pleaded. His voice was Southern, and his hair was cut close, signaling to Ozzie that he was an American and military. "Let me show you a good time."

"I am with someone." Jelka took a step back, prompting the man to step closer.

"You can dance with that uppity nigger all night, but you won't give me one dance?" he puffed.

"Please, go." Jelka turned, but the man grabbed her wrist.

"Don't be like that."

"The lady said no." Ozzie stepped up, placing himself between Jelka and the man.

The blond man snickered. "Fuck off, George."

"That ain't my name, and this here is my date. So you fuck off." Ozzie shot the words from between his teeth.

The blond man looked around, seemingly for backup, but it was just the two of them squared up. His laugh was chilling. "You niggers over here running 'round like park apes. You know better than to touch a white woman." His nostrils flared. "'Less you find yourself hanging from a tree."

Sweat broke out across Ozzie's forehead. "Take your Jim Crow bullshit and go somewhere with that mess." Ozzie stared the man down.

"You don't know who you're talking to," the man spat. "If I was you, I'd watch my mouth. Boy."

"Boy" bounced from the top of Ozzie's head and landed at his feet. He was sick and tired of these white dudes trying to keep their foot on his neck. Before he could stop himself, he shoved the man.

"Better back up with that dumb shit," Ozzie said.

Jelka grabbed his arm. "Osbourne. Let's go."

The blond man snickered again. "You better listen to your *Amihussy*—Osbourne, is it?"

Morgan appeared behind Ozzie with a hand on his wrist. "Everything good here, bro?"

The three men eyed one another, and then the blond man kissed his teeth and walked away.

"Can't even go somewhere and just have a good time," Morgan said.

"The Germans ain't even studying us. They could care less. It's always them white boys from below the Mason-Dixon Line."

"What happened?"

"Fool tried to get Jelka to dance and got pissed when she said no."

"I gotcha back," Morgan said.

"We're heading out anyway," Ozzie said, shaking Morgan's hand. "Be safe, brother."

The two men pounded fists.

Thirty minutes later, Ozzie had paid for a room by the hour, and Jelka wasted no time stripping down to her lace panties and matching bra.

CHAPTER 29

Mannheim, Germany, December 1950

OZZIE

Burger night! My favorite," said Morgan, picking up a tray as they moved through the chow line the next evening.

"Man, did you hear about the NBA?" Satchel said, his harmonica peeking from his shirt pocket.

They sat in their usual corner, at the end of a long dining table toward the back of the room, each with a plate heaped with food.

"They finally signed three Negroes to the league." Morgan pulled the newspaper from his back pocket and opened it to the sports section.

Ozzie read out loud: "'Chuck Cooper, Nathaniel Clifton, and Earl Lloyd Break the NBA Color Barrier.' Well, I'll be damned. They gonna wait till I'm over here to let us in?"

Satchel laughed. "What difference does that make? Your ass wasn't getting into the NBA."

"Whatcha talking about? They call me Sure Shot on the streets of South Philly. Ask anybody 'round there. They'll tell you."

"Man, whatever."

Mayo rested in the corner of Morgan's mouth. "First thing I'm going to do when I get back home is get tickets. I want to see them play against each other."

"Which teams?" Satchel asked.

"Says here Boston Celtics, Washington Capitols, and New York Knicks." Ozzie held up the paper.

"Never been to New York before." Morgan grinned.

"Let's make a pact, then. When we all return to the States, we gonna meet up in New York for a game."

"Deal."

They all raised their mugs of Coca-Cola, and as they toasted, the hairs on the back of Ozzie's neck bristled. He turned to see First Sergeant Petty and two other soldiers walking toward him. They stopped at Ozzie's table.

"Evening, soldiers," Petty greeted them, and then said, "Philips, come with us."

Ozzie looked from Morgan to Satchel as he stood and slipped on his coat. As he followed Petty out of the mess hall, he wondered if the shove in the bar had traveled. The three men walked two paces in front of him and said nothing more as they led Ozzie past the sports arena and into the three-story brick building that housed the offices.

They landed on the second floor, turned down the hall past the empty secretary's desk, and into a boxy office with the blinds drawn. Petty flipped on the light switch, and the overhead fluorescent lights gave off a light hum.

"You still need us, First Sarge?" asked the taller of the two men who accompanied them, standing in the doorway.

"I'll take it from here."

Being alone in a deserted office building with Petty was not Ozzie's idea of a pleasant Sunday evening.

"Please have a seat." The first sergeant motioned as he lowered himself into his chair.

The grease from the burger had turned sour in Ozzie's belly.

Petty clasped his hands in front of him on the desk. "Philips. You've been promoted to corporal, effective immediately. Congratulations." He stuck out his hand.

Ozzie's expression ferried from shock to pride as he reached for Petty's hand and pumped it.

"Typically, we'd have to wait for the CO to come back from leave to have a promotion ceremony, where we'd pin you your stripes. But since the battalion adjutant has already processed all the paperwork, consider this your ceremony." Petty clapped his hands together.

Corporal Philips. Ozzie liked the sound of it. And to receive the reward the day after his birthday made it even more special. His mother was going to be so proud. "It's an honor."

"You've earned it." Petty pursed his lips. "Now, we have a situation in Auerbach that needs immediate attention." He slid a file across the table to Ozzie. "You'll have a small team to manage, and you will leave for Auerbach at nineteen hundred hours."

The clock hanging from the wall ticked as the pride Ozzie felt in being promoted slipped from his face. "That's thirty minutes."

"I realize it's short notice, but we must be ready to answer the call at any time."

Uneasiness pressed against Ozzie's chest as he leaned forward in his seat. "May I ask, where is Auerbach?"

"It's about four hundred kilometers northeast of here."

That was a few hours away. What about Jelka and Katja? He wasn't prepared to leave them at all, certainly not without making arrangements.

"I have a daughter, First Sarge. Can we delay my departure so that I have time to give her a proper goodbye?"

Petty chuckled. "You men are over here spreading seeds like farmers with hoes. You're a noncommissioned officer now, you have to act like one. Besides, if I gave every soldier a chance for a proper goodbye, we wouldn't be able to get anything done. Be ready at nineteen hundred hours." He stood, dismissing Ozzie.

The matter was closed.

Back in the barracks, Ozzie stacked his possessions in a fog. Being ranked as corporal put him closer to seeking the position that he really wanted in Intelligence. It was a pay raise, so he'd have more money to support Katja, but he didn't want to go without saying goodbye. He hated the idea of being separated from Katja for an indefinite period.

Twenty minutes later, the jeep scheduled to transport him was waiting in front of his building. As Ozzie placed his footlocker in the back, Morgan walked down the path. "Brother, what's up?"

"I've been promoted to corporal."

Morgan pumped his fist. "But what's all this? You leaving us?"

"They are transferring me to Auerbach, effective immediately. Can you get a word to Jelka for me and give her this?" Ozzie handed Morgan an envelope.

"It's time to pull out, Philips," called the soldier behind the wheel of the jeep.

Ozzie and Morgan embraced. "Look after Katja for me," Ozzie said, and then stepped in the backseat of the vehicle.

CHAPTER 30

West Oak Forest Academy, December 1965

SOPHIA

Sophia skipped lunch in favor of making the telephone calls to locate Ethel Gathers. There was one pay phone in the basement of the girls' dorm. She had swapped the dollar bill Walter had given her with Miz Peaches for dimes, which afforded her ten calls at a dime apiece. Inside the telephone booth, she pulled the wooden accordion door closed and sat down on the cold steel stool. The torn-out white pages were on her lap, and she quickly counted the number of people with the last name Gathers. There were ninety-two. Where would she get enough money to try them all?

Baby steps, she told herself. There were fourteen Gatherses with names that began with A and only five that began with B. She would start at the beginning. Sophia reached for the receiver, put it to her ear, and dropped in her first coin.

"Yes, hello," said a sultry woman's voice.

"Good afternoon, ma'am. May I speak with Ethel Gathers, please?"

Pause. "To whom?"

"Ethel Gathers," Sophia repeated slowly, twirling the telephone cord around her finger.

"I'm sorry, but there is no one here by that name. You must have dialed the wrong number," the woman said.

Sophia crossed off Aapo Gathers. There was no answer at Aaron Gathers's home, and Abel Gathers's line had been disconnected. Twenty cents saved. The young girl who answered for Abner Gathers informed Sophia that she had reached the wrong number, as did the women at Abraham and Ace Gathers's homes.

On the call with Adam Gathers, she was pulled into such a lengthy conversation about the weather and holiday shopping that the operator prompted her to add five cents for an additional two minutes.

"Sir, does Ethel Gathers live there? I'm running out of time," she interrupted.

"Oh, never heard of her. But if you ever want to talk, I live alone. I'm home most—"

Beep. Beep. Beep. The operator had disconnected the line.

Sophia returned the receiver to the telephone base just as the school bell chimed, signaling the start to afternoon classes. She tucked the remaining fifty cents in the small pouch inside her satchel and left the booth.

Before basketball practice, she wasted three more dimes on calls to Adrian, Afton, and Aiden. Frustrated, she headed to practice with only twenty cents left. When she arrived in the gym, most of the girls were already dressed and taking warm-up shots at the basket.

"Sophia." Coach Fletcher tapped his clipboard. "Running late, are we, mate?"

"Sorry, Coach. I needed help with a math problem," she lied.

"Very well. Make haste. I want to show you a new offensive play."

Sophia shuffled into the girls' locker room. It smelled like a mixture of ammonia and hair spray. There were two rows of wooden benches with tan lockers on three sides. The white tiled floor squeaked beneath her Mary Janes. As Sophia undressed, she noticed her teammates' clothes, flats, and leather school bags with short handles tossed about with no regard to the locker spaces provided. As she sat down to tie her secondhand tennis shoes, a pink change purse carelessly left on an open satchel caught her eye. The kids at Forest tossed money around like paper confetti, and she could see by the shape of the bulge that the purse was full. A ticking started in her ear. It would take less than thirty seconds to rifle through the wallet and snatch a few bills that she could convert into coins later. She wasn't a thief, though she desperately needed the cash. Her breath quickened as she glanced around. There was no one in the locker room but her. Who would know?

Sweat gathered at her temples. She stood, looked over her shoulder, and then tiptoed. Just as she reached down for the abandoned purse, she heard footsteps.

"I'm so over James. I've given him so many chances, and he still hasn't gotten the hint."

"Maybe you should start flirting with Eliott. Bet that would get his attention."

A fit of giggles, and then the two girls rounded into the locker room.

"Hey, Sophia." It was Margaret, captain of the team. "You'd better hustle. Coach sent me in here to get you. What're you doing, anyway?"

"I was . . . um . . . tying my shoe. Ready." Sophia stretched her arms over her head while stepping away from the bag.

"Love the hair, by the way." Margaret grinned. "Ginger looks way more natural on you."

"Thanks," Sophia said, grabbing her ponytail.

What had she been thinking? If anything went missing in that locker room, she would have been the number one suspect.

Between studying for her midterm exams, basketball practice, and the poster board project on innovations that shaped the 1920s for her U.S. history class, three days passed before Sophia had a chance to make calls again. Even though her stomach growled and begged her to eat, Sophia skipped lunch in favor of sneaking in her last two calls.

When she reached the telephone in the girls' dorm, one girl was in the booth, and two other girls stood waiting their turn. The lunch period wasn't long enough for her to be third in line. Then she remembered that there was another telephone booth in the dining hall, next to the bathrooms. She had avoided that booth because it wasn't as private, but she took the steps two at a time and headed in that direction.

The smell of freshly baked bread made her empty stomach yearn as she passed the main dining hall. But she remained stoic. As she made a left toward the phone booth, the boys' bathroom door opened, and Max strolled out, drying his hands on a paper towel.

"Hey," she said, unable to keep the glee from her voice.

"Soph. What're you up to?"

She loved that he called her Soph. "Nothing. Just trying to sneak in a few more calls to you-know-who before class." She clutched her notebook to her chest.

"Oh. I'll come with you." He tossed the towel in the garbage can and fell in stride beside her. Sophia could feel the back of her neck heat up. Was it because she had jogged over, or was it her proximity to Max McBay?

His arm brushed against hers. "Any luck so far?"

"None. I have two dimes left, so fingers crossed that I get lucky."

Max reached into his pocket and pulled out a ball of lint and an eraser. "Sorry." He laughed. "I'm not much help either, but I'm here for moral support."

"Here goes nothing." Sophia stepped into the telephone booth and slid the accordion door closed. Max leaned against the wall, and she knew that he was close enough to hear. She dialed the next number on the list, Alan Gathers, and as the telephone rang, she held her breath that this was the one.

CHAPTER 31

Mannheim, Germany, May 1952

ETHEL

Ethel clutched the mail to her chest. She wanted to scream and stomp her feet but contained herself because Julia was in the girls' bedroom, putting her daughter and Anke down for their afternoon nap. Instead, Ethel reached into her apron pocket for her rosary beads, got down on her knees smack in the middle of her kitchen floor, and prayed a single decade of the rosary—an Our Father, ten Hail Marys, and a Glory Be.

Julia entered the kitchen just as Ethel was using the table to pull herself to stand.

"What in the world?" Julia reached for Ethel's hand. "Why are you down on the floor?"

"Just giving thanks. God is so good all the time." Ethel held up the correspondence.

"And all the time God is good. Now spill the beans, will you?" Julia put her hands on her hips.

"Scandinavian Airlines agreed to take four adopted children to America for mere peanuts."

Julia pumped her fists and then threw her arms around Ethel.

"Congratulations. You've worked so hard for this. What a blessing you are for those children."

"I'm speechless. I've only been harassing the airlines for the past seven months."

"Persistence is your middle name, honey. This calls for some celebratory sugar. What do you have?" Julia opened the pantry.

"Just a few ladyfingers and maybe a bit of ice cream." Ethel moved to the radio sitting on the kitchen counter and turned the knob. Big-band music played, and she set out glass bowls and silver spoons for their treat.

Once they each had a dish of vanilla ice cream and two ladyfingers in front of them, Julia asked, "Do you have the kids picked out, and how's the paperwork approval going?"

"I have selected the children, yes, but the authorized documentation is still up in the air."

"What's the problem?"

"Well, at my last petition, the judge was asking about the American fathers and why they can't support their children."

"He has a point." Julia waved her spoon.

"You'd think, but it's nearly impossible for a German woman to file paternity or child support against an American father. In the meantime, the German government does nothing to support her. Most of these poor women are fired from their jobs." Ethel clucked her tongue. "But don't get me started on that. This is supposed to be a celebration. And now we have a solid date with the airline."

"When are they leaving?"

"First week of August."

"Well, isn't that something? The babies will be delivered just in time for the holidays. Brava, Ethel! You have truly outdone yourself."

Ethel let the cool ice cream melt on her tongue, then she remembered the caveat and pushed the letter across the table toward Julia.

"There's one issue. The airline won't let the children fly alone. They need a guardian to accompany them."

Julia scanned the page. "Who better to chaperone than you? I don't see an issue at all."

"But what about my own children? I'm a mother now, I must think of them first." Ethel frowned.

"Honey, I will help. I'm sure we can get a few of the ladies from the Negro Wives club to pitch in as well. They'd be chomping at the bit to assist you, sweetie."

"I'll have to talk it over with Bert. I've worked so hard to build a stable environment with structure. I don't want the kids to feel as if I've abandoned them."

"How long would you be gone?"

"There is a flight returning to Frankfurt the very next day. A night or two."

"They will be fine. Probably won't even notice that you are gone." Julia clapped her hands together. "As my mother always said, it's done."

Deep down, Ethel knew that Julia was right. She had arranged for her first group of children to join loving parents in America. Everything else would fall into place. She just had to continue to put her faith in God.

The next day, Ethel walked the three older children to the schoolhouse. Once she'd dropped Anke at her half-day preschool, she headed to St. Hildegard's.

It had been two weeks since she had visited, and she was eager to share the news of Scandinavian Airlines's contribution with Sister Ursula. As Ethel turned the corner and moved toward the orphanage, she smelled burnt rubber, charred wood, and smoke. Then she saw the charcoaled roof on one side of the building had caved in.

"Oh, my heavens." She put her hand in her pocket and squeezed her rosary beads as she hastened her pace.

The gate to St. Hildegard's was unlocked, and she stepped over burnt planks, broken tables and spindles from chairs, chunks of broken dishes, and pieces of gassy debris.

"Hello," she called out. It was eerily quiet.

Then a wrinkled nun who did not speak English appeared with a baby strapped to her back. She motioned with her pointer finger for Ethel to follow her through the courtyard. Scorched cushions from chairs and pieces of drapes were tossed about, and the smell was sickly.

The nun ushered Ethel through the front door, past the office where she met Sister Ursula for tea. They continued down a long hallway and up a steep flight of stairs. The old nun knocked twice on the wooden door and then pushed it open. Inside, Ethel found a twin bed and a rocking chair, a chest of drawers, and a single cross hanging from the bare eggshell walls.

Sister Ursula was sitting in the chair. Her gray frizzy hair stopped at her ears. She was dressed in a thin pajama set with a knit blanket over her lap. It was the first time Ethel had seen her out of her habit, and she looked as if she had aged ten years in two weeks.

"Jesus, Mary, and Joseph. Are you all right? What happened?" Ethel covered Sister Ursula's hands with her own. They were cold and veiny.

Sister Ursula pressed her lips together. "Th—there was a fire," she stammered.

"Are the children all right? Anyone hurt? Why didn't you send for me?"

The old nun took her leave, and Sister Ursula gestured for Ethel to take a seat on the edge of her bed. "It started in the kitchen and spread quickly. Most of the electrical and plumbing in this place have not been updated since the First World War." She cleared her throat.

"Sister Proba was serving breakfast at the time. She is in the hospital. Too much smoke in her lungs and a few burns on her hands, shins, and ankles. Her habit caught fire as she tried to usher the children out."

Ethel made the sign of the cross. "Will she be all right?"

"It's in the Lord's hands." Sister Ursula took hold of the gold cross hanging from a black cord around her neck. But the look on her face was grave.

"The children?"

"Two with burns, but they have been bandaged, and besides being frightened, they will live. They have all been moved into temporary housing not far from here."

"What can I do?"

Sister Ursula shook her head. "Do you know, at one point we could house up to one hundred and twenty children here. It was tight and chaotic, but with the kitchen out, we will be unable to manage for a while."

"How many children reside here now? How many are in need of temporary homes?"

"We had twenty-six kids living here at the time of the fire. I've found shelter for ten locally, and ten are going to a children's orphanage in Stuttgart. That leaves six needing homes, and I don't want to send them to the *Wisenheim*. It is overcrowded. I know you've been working tirelessly, dear, but can you possibly place more children?"

Then Ethel remembered the nature of her visit. "I came with good news from Scandinavian Airlines. They've agreed to transport four children to New York City."

Sister Ursula smiled. "Excellent work, Ethel. Can you give them another push? See if they will agree to transport two or three additional children. You have several American families waiting to adopt, yes?"

Ethel had just received an inquiry from a family in Maryland.

If she could get the legal forms through quickly, she could make an adoption happen. “I do.”

“The frightened mother that you sent—Durchdenwald, I think is her last name. She’s worried about her child and has begged me for an American adoption.”

“Let me see what I can accomplish,” Ethel offered.

“Maybe you can tap your network for temporary homes locally for the rest of the children.”

Ethel gave Sister Ursula a pat on the shoulder and said, “I’ll do my best.”

“You always do.”

CHAPTER 32

Auerbach, Germany, January 1951

OZZIE

In the three weeks Ozzie worked in Auerbach at Camp Casanova, he tried his best to be a solid leader to his men, but it had been hard to bolster morale when he himself felt demoralized. He was no closer to landing a job in Intelligence than he had been on that hot day in May at his neighborhood block party in South Philly. Ozzie had assumed that with the title of corporal would come a bump in status, but he found himself side by side with his men, working in the trenches. Camp Casanova had been a prisoner-of-war camp, and their job was to pick the grounds and the adjacent two-story building clean. The rumor was that they were preparing it to be a headquarters for the relatively new CIA. Ozzie shoveled shit both human and God knew what else, cleared rubble, took waste to a nearby incinerator, and burned what they couldn't repurpose. They smoothed out ditches, repaired the roof, and painted the two-story building.

Every night Ozzie slept in a room that smelled like a bag of jockstraps, on a cot as flimsy as construction paper. He had to hold his nose when he used the latrine, and the water in the communal showers dawdled out in dribbles. And it was freezing. Mannheim had been cold, but Auerbach was downright arctic, and the lack of electricity only added insult to injury. What had worried him most was that Ozzie had not received word from Jelka.

It was bad enough that he had left them behind without a word, but worse, he didn't know Jelka's physical address. Ozzie had always been excellent with directions and had a photographic memory when it came to landmarks. From the moment Jelka's sister had led him to their home on the day Katja was born, he knew his way from the barracks. But without her address, he couldn't reach Jelka, and her family didn't have a telephone.

Ozzie had sent two letters to Morgan, asking him to find Jelka. He had even drawn a map from the barracks to her house, but he had not heard from Morgan either. What he did hear playing like a record on repeat was *With Gottfried returning, what kind of life do you think she will have here . . . ? He is a violent man.* Not being there to protect his daughter unnerved Ozzie from his teeth to his toes.

CHAPTER 33

Mannheim, Germany, June 1952

ETHEL

With the help of her translator, Vera, Ethel had secured an appointment in *Familiengericht*, family court, for six German mothers who were petitioning adoption by proxy for their half-Negro children. For the hearing, Ethel had dressed in her gray sheath dress with peep-toe heels, and a loose string of pearls dangled from her neck. It was a look that she hoped conveyed she meant business.

While the mothers stood around in the hallway, waiting to be called into the courtroom, they drank the complimentary coffee and bonded. Through Vera's quick translation, Ethel was able to follow along.

"I make only thirty marks per month," said the blonde called Frieda, and Ethel knew that only amounted to about six dollars and fifty cents. "I wanted to keep my child with me, but I cannot let him starve. I want him to have a good life."

Frieda had long fingers like a piano player, and she clutched her coffee cup with both hands and gulped it down so quickly, Ethel didn't see how she hadn't burnt her tongue. "My friends stopped speaking to me on the street. Behind my back, they called my daughter a freak." She spoke with her gaze on the floor. "I ran away to Frankfurt, where

I thought I could keep her with me, but after sleeping in the train station for a week, with no job, no food, no water, nothing to clean her with, I knew I could not do it." Tears sprang to her eyes.

"If I kept him, no German man would marry me. I would live a life in isolation. Alone," said Heidi. Her nails were bitten down to nubs.

Ethel's eyes fell upon a woman who called herself Jelka and held an unlit cigarette between her shaking fingers. The other mothers all looked at Jelka too, coaxing her with their silence to tell her story.

"I traveled to the place where I was told that her father was stationed in Auerbach, only to find that he was gone. I can't wait much longer. My husband said if I don't get rid of her, he will drown her in the river," she choked out.

Her tears seemed to set off a chain effect; two other women's shoulders shook with grief. Vera spoke softly to the women and then motioned to Ethel that it was time for them to enter the courtroom. Inside, the mothers sat together on one wooden pew, an unspoken camaraderie between them. One by one, each went before the judge. Ethel had instructed them to bring the official records that proved their nationality so the children's passports could be issued and the paperwork for the adoptions could move forward.

It was Jelka's turn, and she stood before the judge, hunched over.

"What is he saying?" Ethel asked Vera.

"Once she signs the papers and he seals them, she can never again lay claim to her daughter. He is making sure that she understands she is giving up all rights."

When Jelka was finished, she collapsed in the pew next to Ethel and silently sobbed. "I feel sick. But what other choice do I have?"

Ethel's heart ached over the costly decisions that these young German mothers had to make. She put her arm around the young woman and let her quiet tears soak the top of her sheath dress. Once the proceedings had concluded, the mothers were led into a small assembly room with stuffed leather chairs and a long wooden table that smelled of lemon polish. There was one window that overlooked the street, and Ethel could see that snowflakes had begun to flurry. Now the women had to prepare for the most painful part of the day.

The judge, a middle-aged man, deemed that once the paperwork was completed, the mother and child had to be separated swiftly. The courts believed that it was in the best interest of the children to break their attachment and get on with things, as if it were as easy as cutting the umbilical cord. Although the mothers had surrendered their children to the orphanage weeks ago, Ethel sat with them as they waited for the children to appear for a final goodbye.

The door opened and a curly-headed four-year-old boy bounded into the room. He was followed by a ruddy-faced girl who toddled into Jelka's arms. Ethel watched as some mothers tried to keep a brave face, while the others blubbered until their cheeks were damp and red, which caused the children to start crying too.

The officer in charge stood in the corner, and after several minutes passed, he held up his hand, signaling that it was time to go. Despite Sister Ursula's written plea to place the children with local families until it was time to fly to America, the children would be taken on a bus to the *Wisenheim,* where they would live for the next ten days as their "period of adjustment."

Ethel lifted her chin, trying to look impassive as Jelka's child howled, and then all the children started clinging to their mothers like life rafts. While the young mothers tried comforting them, they now needed succor themselves. As Ethel rubbed Jelka's back, Jelka whispered something into her daughter's little ear.

"She'll be fine," Ethel said to Jelka. "I have the perfect home all picked out for her. Don't worry. She'll have a charmed life."

Two months later, Ethel, Sister Ursula, and seven children under the age of five traveled in a passenger van to the Frankfurt Airport.

At the ticket counter, Sister Ursula prayed over all the children and wished Ethel good luck and safe travels to New York.

"You are truly doing God's work." She held Ethel's hand. "May God be with you."

"And also with you," Ethel said back.

Ethel lined up six children and paired them off to hold hands. She had baby Margit, the six-month-old and last addition to her caravan of children, in a baby carrier tied to her chest. Inside her canvas tote bag was their documentation, photographs, and passports, along with extra tissues, cloth diapers, ointments, and snack bags with shortbread biscuits, crackers, and *lebkuchen* gingerbread cookies. Once they arrived at Idlewild Airport in New York, the seven children would continue to their new homes with their adoptive parents in New York City, Washington, D.C, Maryland, California, and Arkansas.

Ethel counted and recounted the children every few steps, but as they waited at the gate to board, she couldn't help feeling like something was off.

When they took their seats on the aircraft, Ethel placed sleeping baby Margit in the bassinet attached to the back of the seat in front of her, then peered over at the children sitting in the row next to her and two rows in front of her seat. Satisfied, she reached into her purse for her rosary beads and realized that she had left them at home.

CHAPTER 34

West Oak Forest Academy, December 1965

SOPHIA

Sophia gripped the receiver so tight that her knuckles hurt.

Click.

Max slid the accordion door open. "Are you okay?"

She bobbed her head as feelings of defeat welled up inside her. "Why am I even doing this to myself?" She put her head in her hands. The last thing she wanted to do was break down in front of Max, but the emotions came from nowhere. "Before I met you, I was fine. Now it's like I've opened Pandora's box, and I can't get the lid back on. This is all too much."

Max touched her hands and pulled them away from her face. "Hey, it's okay. You are trusting your gut, and I admire that." He took his thumb and gently wiped at the stubborn tear that betrayed her. "Soph, please don't cry," he said, and the gentle way he cooed laid her bare. Max pulled her in a one-armed hug, and she could feel his heart thumping against hers. Sophia's mind went to mush, and her body felt a longing she had never known before.

"What's going on here?"

Max let go first. Sophia looked past him and saw Willa with an Echo scarf fashionably tied over her hair.

"Why were you holding each other like that?" Willa glared.

Shivering, Sophia gathered her school sweater tighter around her. She could see the questions in her roommate's eyes, and she couldn't bear it. She knew how his arms had felt and could only imagine how she and Max had looked to Willa. It wasn't what Willa thought, but Sophia couldn't tell Willa the truth. Not until she was sure of things. So she lied. "I just got some bad news from back home."

Willa crossed her arms over her ample bosom, looked from Max to Sophia, unconvinced, and then asked, "What?"

"My brother. He's fallen ill, and I hate that I can't be there for him."

"One of the twins?" Willa whispered.

"Yes."

Willa nodded with concern.

"I'm just feeling overwhelmed with everything, that's all. Max just happened to catch me."

From the corner of her eye, Sophia noticed Max looking down at his feet. He hadn't said anything to defend their behavior. The tension among the three of them was all too stifling on top of the fruitless phone calls.

"I gotta go." Sophia pushed through the two of them and walked out of the cafeteria. When she was out of their eyeshot, she took off running, just as it began to pour down rain.

Sophia hadn't missed a class since arriving at Forest, but she couldn't sit through her afternoon periods. She didn't have the energy it took for her to be invisible. Instead, she hid out in her dorm room with her head tucked under her pillow, listening to the rain. What was wrong with her? She had turned her world upside down and wished that she could forget it all and go back to her life before she'd discovered Ethel Gathers and her Brown Baby Plan. The hope and anticipation she put into each phone call only to be met with disappointment was draining her. Why couldn't she just leave it all alone?

When she gazed over at the clock, she realized that basketball practice started in an hour. If she left now, she'd have the entire gym to herself. She could run around until she was too tired to think.

The rain had stopped, but she was careful not to walk on the soggy grass in front of the Athletic Center. The smell of sweaty socks comforted her as she dropped her bag on a bleacher. There was a stray ball in the corner beneath the scoreboard, and Sophia picked it up and started shooting. She hadn't even bothered to change out of her school blouse and skirt. She just ran after the ball and shot, dribbled, shot until she worked up such a heavy sweat that the back of her blouse was soaked through.

Ten minutes before practice was scheduled to start, she heard voices outside the gym and scurried into the locker room to change. The tube light above her locker flickered on and off. Sophia spun the combination to her padlock and yanked the metal door open. Taped to the inside was a picture of a red fox with the eyes blacked out. She ripped the picture down and balled it to the floor. She knew only one person on the team would be so bold as to trespass into her personal space. Sophia gritted her teeth. The sound of footsteps rang out from the gym, and Sophia used the door of her locker to shield her as she stripped down to her underwear.

"Look what we have here," Patty croaked, seeming to appear out of nowhere.

Sophia didn't acknowledge her or her two flunkies. She hated being naked in front of anyone, especially the girls at school. But she couldn't ignore Patty, because when she reached for her gym shirt, Patty grabbed her wrist and thrust it up in the air.

"Get off." Sophia tugged, but Patty's grip was firm on her arm.

"Opal." Patty snickered with her friend. "Do you remember that book we found in the library about the girl on the auction block? Looks like someone is stripped down so that everyone can see what a fine field nigger she'd make."

Heat spread across Sophia's face. She abhorred that word, and Patty was the first person to ever hurl it directly at her. For a few seconds, she felt like the wind had been knocked out of her.

"Let me go." Sophia tugged, which made Patty hold on even tighter.

"How much would you pay for her? Look at these strong biceps. She'd do good work," Patty sang. "She already has experience working with livestock. Can't you smell it on her?"

Opal laughed. "I'd pay fifteen cents for her."

"I'd pay a quarter," said the girl who played small forward.

"Come on, now. This redhead must be worth more than that. Somebody give me fifty cents," Patty said, smirking.

"Go to hell, Patty," Sophia shot as Patty pulled her wrist above her head, exposing the patch of red hair beneath her armpit.

"Look at this beastly hair. Told you she was a savage."

"I wonder what's growing in her underwear." Opal clapped her hands.

"I've often wondered the same thing. Why don't we take a look-see?" Patty pressed her elbow into Sophia's stomach, pinning her against the locker. "Do it," she urged Opal.

Do what? Sophia's stomach dropped as she tried to flail her legs, but Opal put her hands on Sophia's knees to steady her.

"Stop it," Sophia called out. Opal's fingers felt clammy against her skin.

"I'm not playing." Sophia tried wrenching her arm free, but Patty was taller and stronger, and Opal had her pinned against the locker.

"I said do it," Patty said with a sadistic grin. "My daddy always told me to stay away from the nigger boys here on campus. Said they had tails."

"You think she has a tail too?" Opal said, wide-eyed.

"I'll give you a dollar if you find out," the third girl called out as Sophia thrust her torso and stomped her feet, trying with everything in her to wiggle away.

"Get the hell off of me," Sophia growled, and squirmed, but the girls just laughed.

"I was told that they had superhuman strength, but maybe that's just the boys." Patty tightened her grip as Opal grabbed the edge of her panties and started pulling them down her thighs. Sophia bucked her torso, but it didn't stop Opal from exposing a thick shock of red hair on her pubes.

"What the hell is wrong with you?" Sophia cried, still jerking her body.

"I told you she was an animal." Patty smirked. "Only animals have flaming red hair."

"Maybe she's the devil's daughter?" Opal cracked. "Look at those red welts on her arms. They look like fire."

"They shouldn't let animals into the school," Patty said.

Then the door to the locker room slammed open.

"What in the hell is going on here?" It was Margaret.

Opal let Sophia's knees go, and Sophia reached for her panties, dragging them up to her navel, shaking like a desert rat plunged into a bucket filled with ice water.

"Patty, get your hands off of her. Now!" Margaret's voice was loud and demanding. All the laughter stopped, and it was then that Sophia saw two other girls in the corner, watching the action. Had they been there the whole time and done nothing to help her?

"Pipe down, prom queen. We were just having a little fun." Patty released her grip on Sophia. "She doesn't need you coming to her rescue every time she gets a little paper cut."

As soon as Patty released her arms, Sophia shoved Patty into the locker with a loud thud. "You're fucking sick," she said. "I should beat your ass." Sophia pointed her finger in Patty's face and bared her teeth. Rage surged through her, and she felt like she could choke Patty with her bare hands.

"That's what animals do," Patty hissed back. "Go ahead, and you'll be out of this school and back in the mud so fast your head will spin." Patty flashed her teeth, and Sophia wanted to punch each one from her mouth and watch her bleed.

"Come on, Sophia, she's not worth the aggravation," Margaret said. It took all of Sophia's strength to back away. Her long-sleeve T-shirt was on the floor. She slipped it over her head and put on her shorts. The air in the locker room was thick.

Margaret put her hands on her hips. "Get out there and start layup drills. Coach will be here in five minutes, and I don't want him to know about any of this. We have a game to play tomorrow. Get your heads into it. Now go." She pointed to the door.

Sophia pushed past them. Feeling humiliated and more displaced than ever before.

Part 4

I swear to the Lord / I still can't see /
Why Democracy means / Everybody but me.

—LANGSTON HUGHES

CHAPTER 35

Philadelphia, PA, July 1952

OZZIE

As Ozzie stepped his spit-shined shoes onto the platform at the Reading Station in Philadelphia, it struck him like a blow to the chest that he could no longer conjure up Katja's soap and slobber scent. It had been one year, seven months, and four days since he had seen her last, and as Ozzie threw his B4 bag over his shoulder, he could acutely feel the hole she had left in his heart. Sometimes the hole whistled, other times it ached, and today as he walked down the platform it burned, because the forgetting felt like pouring alcohol on an open wound. Katja turned three in two months, and Ozzie didn't know the road back to her.

The train station's waiting area overflowed with men clutching briefcases, travelers checking timetables, and families reuniting. Ozzie crossed the station in his formal uniform, his garrison cap pulled to his temples, despite the way the hat made his head sweat. His uniform lent him an air of importance that he knew was infectious. Out of the corner of his eye, he spotted three women dressed in summer blouses admiring him.

There was no one at the station to meet him in the middle of the day. Uncle Millard was the only family member with a car anyhow, and shortly after Ozzie had arrived in Germany, he had moved up to Harlem with a woman named Tootsie.

Ozzie exited onto Twelfth Street to the sounds of horns honking and a stubby man with a pushcart shouting, "Peanuts, get your fresh peeee-nuuutts."

The pavement and cars were damp, and as Ozzie walked west, he could smell that he had just missed a summer rainstorm. He paused to take in the familiar thirty-seven-foot bronze statue of William Penn atop City Hall. He walked past Gimbels and Wanamaker's department stores, still with mannequins dressed in patriotic red, white, and blue for the Fourth of July. Ozzie had missed his neighborhood block party by three days.

Ozzie continued down the steps into the cave of the subway station just as the southbound train rattled to a stop. He sat next to the window and noticed appreciative glances from two teenage boys with thick hair, wearing white sneakers with red laces. One even saluted him. Yes, he had served his country well. Ozzie got off the subway at Tasker and Morris. When he didn't see the Tasker Street bus, he decided to walk.

At the square where he used to play basketball with his friends, four teenage boys in cutoff shorts were playing two-on-two basketball, and he could hear the shit talk between them.

When he turned onto Ringgold Street, the pavement was meticulously swept and all the front steps were scrubbed clean, but the block looked smaller than he had remembered it. Had the street shrunk, or was it that he had grown bigger? On the corner, Ms. Millie's front door was open, and he could hear the soaps she listened to through her screen door. Pigeons pecked the curb for insects as a light breeze caressed the back of his neck. He was home.

"Ozzie, that you?" his mother, Nettie, called from the kitchen.

"Mama." He dropped his bag and gobbled up the distance between them. They met in the small space between the front room and the dining room, and she smashed herself into his chest.

"Glad you made it home in one piece, son. Let me look at you." She touched his collar. "Dressed sharp as a tack. Just as handsome as the day you was born."

The fragrance of butter, cinnamon, nutmeg, and something else sweet wafted from the kitchen.

"What you cooking smelling all good?"

"My son's favorite dessert." She beamed.

"Sweet-potato pie?" His mouth watered.

"Even though it's way too hot to be in the house with the oven on, I done it for you." She put her arms around his waist and hugged him again, and he kissed the top of her head. "Gotta let it cool some. Come on back and sit awhile. Fixed some fresh lemonade for you and saved you a few pieces of fried chicken." Nettie turned, placed the food on a plate, and slid it across the wooden table to Ozzie.

He bit into the crispy skin and moaned. "Don't nobody make it like you, Mama," he said.

She smiled. "What can I say?"

Ozzie took another bite and then asked, "Where's everybody?"

"Sissy still working at the department store, they done made her a manager, paying her an extra fifty cents an hour."

"Ain't that something," Ozzie said, mouth full. His sister Sissy was the one person in his family light-skinned enough for a job in management. The rest of his family could only clean up the store after hours.

"Fannie finished beauty school. Got a job at a shop over on Wharton Street. Jonas, he working down at Mr. Timmy's tailor shop. Boy can cut a suit just as fine as them ones Millard wearing up in Harlem."

"What about John-John?"

Nettie sighed. "Running the streets with them hoodlums over on Oakford Street. You need to talk some sense in that boy. Else he'll be dead or in jail."

"I'll get him right." Ozzie pushed away his plate. Nettie kept up a steady flow of neighborhood gossip while she moved around the tiny kitchen, wiping down the stovetop and putting away the dishes.

"Big Otis been here?" Ozzie asked, hating the longing in his voice. He had heard only once from his father in the four years he had been gone. A letter asking Ozzie to wire him some money.

"I ain't seen him for a few weeks. Last I heard, he was staying over in the Black Bottom." Nettie cut him a slice of pie and put it in front of him. Then she grabbed a piece for herself and sat on the other side of the table.

"What about you, son? How was living in Germany? You ain't fall in love with no white woman, did you?" She looked at him pointedly.

Ozzie hoped his face was as blank as he urged it to be when he shook his head. "Naw, Mama."

"Good. 'Cause Melba's son just got back from England, bringing pictures of two white-looking kids. Talking 'bout trying to get married and bring them here. She got the whole church praying for her son's safety."

Ozzie gulped. He would have done the same thing for Katja if he could have. The hole in his heart burned as he opened his mouth to confess it all to his mother, but she cut him off.

"You ain't hot, dressed in that?" Nettie waved her hand over his uniform.

"No."

She cocked her fork at him. "Bet you wanting to stay all dressed up for Rita."

Ozzie blushed at Rita's name.

"After all this time, you still holding a torch for her?" She chuckled. "You seen her? How's she doing?"

"Just fine. Got a fancy job now. Walk out of her house every morning looking like money." She chuckled again. "She'll be home 'round five. She come up the street like clockwork."

Ozzie *was* hot in his uniform. He could feel the sweat beads gathering across his chest, but he wanted to look important when Rita laid eyes on him.

"You right, I'ma go sit outside."

Ozzie plucked his well-worn copy of *Native Son* by Richard Wright from the bookshelf in the front room and opened the screen door. As he took a seat on the top step, he heard a shrill, wailing meow from a stray cat coming from up the block. It sounded like the cat was in heat. Ozzie could understand the cat's pain. He could barely keep his eyes on the book; each noise made his eyes dart up the street in search of Rita.

Then, like an apparition on the breeze, Ozzie saw Rita dressed in a white-and-blue gingham button-down dress cinched at the waist. Her hair was twisted off her neck, and she wore silver at her ears and throat. The few pictures she had sent him over the years had not done her justice. Man, she was fine enough to make a blind man cry.

"Ozzie?" she called, fanning herself. "That you?"

Ozzie was up and down the steps, and they moved toward each other like magnets. He nuzzled his nose in her neck, and she smelled like the same honeysuckle scent that had fragranced her letters.

"It's good to see you, girl." She was light in his arms as he lifted her off her feet and spun her, then he pulled her tight against his chest.

With her feet on the ground again, Rita took a step back while eyeing him. "You lookin' damn good in that uniform. Why didn't you tell me you were coming home?"

"I wanted to surprise you."

She palmed his chest. "Well, I wish I had known. I would have fried you up some pork chops."

"There will be plenty of time for that."

"Have you seen your mama?"

He nodded. "Got the sweet-potato pie in my belly to prove it."

They stopped in front of her row house. "Why don't you go home and get me a slice. That'll give me time to freshen up. I sweat like a pig at work."

Twenty minutes later, Ozzie was sitting inside Rita's mint-green kitchen with floral wallpaper above the cabinets and behind the stove. Rita had changed into a pair of Bermuda shorts and a V-neck tee, and she padded around in her bare feet. Her toenails were painted a bright pink.

"I got some iced tea. 'Less you want something stronger."

"Iced tea is fine," he said, undoing the first few buttons of his uniform shirt. Ozzie hadn't had a drop of liquor since he'd gotten back into the States three months ago. He had been stationed in a rural town southwest of Little Rock, Arkansas, taking part in field maneuvers with the Second Army. The only way to stay sharp and alive during the maneuvers was with a clear head.

The house was quiet except for Rita pouring the tea over ice cubes and the wood mantel clock ticking in the front room.

"Where's Great-aunt Reese?"

"She hasn't been feeling well. Complaining of headaches. Doctor gave her something, but it makes her sleep too much, if you ask me." Rita placed a glass in front of Ozzie and then sat down.

"I got you something."

"Really?"

Ozzie reached into his pants pocket. "I was hoping to make it here in time for your graduation. It 'bout killed me to miss it."

Rita ran her fingers through her hair. "That's all right. Wasn't for you, I would have never made it. Thank you for sending me that money. I will repay you every penny."

"That's not necessary." Ozzie handed her a blue satin box.

Rita looked at him with big eyes and then slid the box open. Inside was a gold necklace with a square emerald pendant.

"Oh, Oz. It's beautiful."

"It's your birthstone. Found it in a little shop on a stop through Lancashire, England."

"Thank you." She reached across the table and squeezed his hand. "Here, put it on me." She passed him the necklace, and Ozzie's fingers burned as they grazed her warm skin. Once it was secure around her neck, she clasped the charm in her palm. "Tell me all about your time away while I taste your mama's pie."

"What do you want to know?"

"Everything. What was Germany like? How was the food? Did you fall for one of those tall blondes with big boobs?" Her eyebrows arched.

For a split second, he thought about sharing the truth. Telling her about Katja. But he didn't want her to see him as a man who walked away from his responsibility. Instead, he shared about his job in the motor pool, stories about Morgan and Satchel, being shipped off to Auerbach, and his few weeks in England before coming back to the U.S.

"What about you? I know those college boys were all over you. Fine as you is."

Flashing her teeth, she said, "College was a life-changing experience, I'm not gonna lie. The classes, the culture, the space to be with smart Negro students and focus without worrying about other things. It was liberating."

"Not one guy?" he asked, knowing that a confession from her would relieve him of his own guilt.

"Not one woman?" she shot back, but then waved her hands. "I thought we agreed not to talk about it."

They stared at each other.

Rita broke first, counting on her fingers. "Germany, England, then Arkansas. Which place did you like the best?"

"Certainly not Arkansas." He shifted. "Wouldn't send my worst enemy that far south. Them white folks harassed our black asses like it was a job they were getting paid to do."

Ozzie recounted how one of the men from his battalion had been cornered by an angry mob who insisted that he remove his United States Army uniform. "When he refused, they pulled garden shears from their pickup truck, held him down, and cut the uniform off of his back."

"But why?"

"Said he didn't deserve to represent this country because he wasn't a real man."

"That's awful."

"Yeah." He paused. "My time away wasn't all bad. There were a lot of good moments. But still, I'm done."

"And you're sure you don't want to reenlist? Seemed like the money was good. You took care of me." She skimmed her bare foot over his shin, and her touch made him lose his train of thought.

"I'm tired of being so far away from home," he said finally. "Planning on applying for a civilian job at the shipyard. Look into that G.I. Bill and see about going to college."

"College, now, really?" She leaned back in her seat with a smile that said she was impressed.

"People have been saying the G.I. Bill will let me go for free."

"What would you study?"

"Maybe economics or business." He rolled an ice cube around in his mouth. "Ma said you was working down at some fancy law firm. You big-time now."

She blushed. "I'm only a switch operator, but I'm learning things about the law in the process."

Rita told him how she'd landed the job at the Negro law firm as one of ten girls applying for the position. "I work for a lawyer named Sadie Alexander, and she is brilliant. She and her husband, Raymond, are both lawyers."

"They must be filthy rich."

"Negro rich for sure. Sadie is the only black female lawyer in the city of Philadelphia."

"You don't say."

"Did you know that there are only fifty-eight Negro women practicing in the whole country? I've really got my work cut out for me." She stood up and pulled the beaded string that turned on the window fan. Cool air blew into the tiny kitchen. "Sadie's been helping me apply for grants and scholarships to fund law school."

Ozzie knew that Rita was ambitious and smart, but law school was impressive. "I'm happy for you, baby, you've really made something out of yourself." He stood.

"I'm proud of you too, Corporal Osbourne Philips." She smiled, and the way she said his name made him think of Jelka.

Rita furrowed her brow. "What? Did I get it wrong? Is that not your title?"

"No, you got it right," Ozzie replied, shaking the memory of Jelka loose.

Rita pushed back from the table and carried her plate and fork to the sink. While she ran hot water over them, Ozzie put on his garrison cap. "I better get going." The sun had gone down, and he didn't want to overstay his welcome.

"It's good seeing you." She led him through to the front door, where Ozzie couldn't resist pecking her on the cheek.

The next day and the day after that, Ozzie was perched on his mother's front steps when Rita got off the bus. He carried her bags, she fried him pork chops, he brought her flowers. In the evenings that followed, Rita pulled out her backgammon set, and they played best out of three games.

Two weeks after Ozzie had returned home, he pushed back from Rita's kitchen table at the appropriate time and reached for his hat, but she put her hand on his wrist. "Where you always running off to?"

"Home. I don't want to be disrespectful."

"What if I don't want you to go?" She stood and leaned against him. The heat radiating from her body ignited all of Ozzie's senses. She craned her neck and pressed her lips against his ear. "I think it might be time for me to welcome you home properly, soldier."

Ozzie didn't trust himself to speak, so he pressed his mouth against Rita's. His lips swelled against hers while his eager hands found the mounds of her breasts straining against her soft cotton T-shirt.

"Come with me," she whispered, and then led Ozzie through the dining room and down the narrow basement stairs.

On the green sofa, Ozzie licked and sucked every inch of her body, leaving love bruises along the way. Then he fitted her into his lap, and she moaned into his ear, "Glad you found your way back home."

A month later, Ozzie was bent over the same green sofa, feeling around in the dark for his drawers.

"We getting too old for you to be sneaking out the back door before the sun come up, got me looking like a loose woman." Rita turned on her elbow. Even in the dark, he could see the silhouette of her curvaceous body, and it made his mouth water.

"Well, I could just move in." Ozzie ran his hand across her thigh.

"I don't intend to share property with no man who ain't my husband," she whispered matter-of-factly.

"So, let's get married."

She sat up on the couch, and the thin blanket fell away from her breasts. "You gonna have to ask me a little better than that, Mr. Philips."

Ozzie scratched his head as he pushed the thought of this similar moment with Jelka to the back of his mind. That time his proposal had been duty, but this was Rita, his heart.

Gingerly, he knelt between Rita's legs and took her hand. "Darling. I've adored you since I first landed eyes on you. You are my first love. Will you be my forever love? Will you marry me?"

Rita squealed. "Yes, yes, I will."

CHAPTER 36

Washington, D.C., July 1954

ETHEL

Dear Julia,

I hope this correspondence finds you well. We made it across the sea in one piece. After two weeks in god-awful temporary housing, we are finally settling into our brand-new four-bedroom home on Madison Street in Northwest D.C. You would love the house. It's located on a beautiful tree-lined street with a fenced-in backyard big enough for the children to play. It has the most glorious fireplace, and the front porch is wide enough for a few rocking chairs, ideal for sipping iced tea.

As life would have it, Monika's eighth birthday fell on move-in day, so we hardly had time to celebrate her. I did manage store-bought cupcakes, and after she blew out her candles, she told Bert that she had wished for him to build her a tree swing. Well honey, Bert has been walking around the yard, assessing which of the four trees could hold up her swing. That girl has him wrapped around her finger.

How are you faring without me? I must admit, it is odd to be back home, after three and a half years stationed in Germany, with eight children in tow. And you were wrong, by the way, there's really no difference between four and eight kids, other than three dozen extra eggs, five chickens, and four more gallons of milk a week! I can't help but chuckle as I put this on paper, but seriously, they love each other so much and play so well, were it not for the grocery bill and the extra laundry, I'd not notice the difference.

I do, however, miss the Officers' Wives and the Negro Wives of Mannheim dearly. Yet and still, I know being in the States is an excellent opportunity for our children. They are already amazed at all the sights and sounds of America. During our first week here I took them to the National Zoo, and I couldn't tear Mia and Anton away from the sea lions.

Next week I'm going to enroll Franz, Heinz, Leo, Monika, and Anke at the Nativity Catholic school on Georgia Avenue for the fall, and I'll teach little Oti, Mia, and Anton at home until they are old enough to start kindergarten.

You won't believe who called me. I would make you guess but you'd never get it. Lerone Bennett Jr. Yes, the writer from Ebony *magazine! He is coming to D.C. in two weeks and would like to do a two-page spread on our family. He has read my Brown Baby Plan articles, and he wants to do an in-depth interview, his words not mine on how Bert and I went from two kids to four and then returned to the States with eight adopted children to raise and love.*

When we hung up the telephone, all I could think about was how you and I used to share our Ebony *magazines, fighting over who got to read first. Provided all goes well, we will be featured in the November issue, so keep your eyes peeled. Better yet, I'll mail you a copy as soon as the issue hits the stands.*

Dearest Julia, I miss you so much. In the month we've been apart, it has really made me realize that you are more than a friend to me. You are my sister. Please kiss the girls and write soon. Oh, and send some lebkuchen cookies for the children. I've tried to bake them myself but they are never as good. I'm enclosing a recipe for curried spaghetti that I found in Good Housekeeping. *When I made it, Bert was practically licking his plate. See you later, alligator.*

With love,
Ethel

CHAPTER 37

Philadelphia, PA, September 1952

OZZIE

On the second Sunday of September, at Tasker Street Missionary Baptist Church, Ozzie stood at the altar adorned with pink and white carnations, dressed in his military uniform, holding Rita's face, as he kissed her on the lips and sealed their commitment.

As bride and groom, they feasted on fried chicken, chitterlings, pigs' feet, potato salad, collard greens, and corn pudding and then washed it down with cans of beer, jug wine, and Irish whiskey. The wedding reception had started in his mother's living room but spilled out on the sounds of Muddy Waters into Ringgold Street. When the liquor was gone and the music stopped, Ozzie officially dragged his footlocker and two duffel bags across the street to his new home with Rita, where they consummated the marriage in her back bedroom and not the green sofa in the basement.

The next morning, Rita was still grinning when Ozzie shuffled into the kitchen in a T-shirt and pajama pants. The harsh ceiling strip light intensified the banging that he had woken up with in his head.

"Can you turn that light off?" He slumped into the wooden chair and closed his eyes. It had been nearly six months since he'd had a drink. But it had been his wedding day, and everywhere he turned, people were shoving a glass of something in his hand. At first he had tried to refuse, but the men of Ringgold Street were relentless.

"Drink this, it'll help you stay up all night long."

"What, the army done turned you into a pussy now? Boy, you better drink."

"Welcome to the married club, son. Let's all drink to the bride and groom."

Drink, drink, drink.

He had tried to sip that first whiskey slow, use the same cup for each toast, but then one glass led to the next, followed by he didn't know how many beer chasers.

"Guess my new husband had a little too much fun last night." She kissed the top of his head. When he looked up, Rita was cracking open a white bottle and shaking two tablets into his hand. "Here, take these." She turned to the stove and poured him a cup of coffee from the percolator. "And drink this."

Ozzie did as he was told. The coffee was strong and sweet, just how he liked it. "Thank you." He looked up at her. Rita was wearing a periwinkle dress with big black buttons down the front. A matching patent-leather belt cinched her waist, showing off the sway of her hips.

"Damn, you look good," he blurted.

"And you look like shit, so drink up so you can make it down to the shipyard on time."

"I'll be good. Just need to get two of these in me," he said, slurping down more coffee.

Rita removed a plastic container from the icebox and placed it on the table. Then she assembled two egg salad sandwiches and wrapped them in waxed paper. "For your lunch." She slid one across the table. "Don't forget we have the appointment down at the Philadelphia Savings Fund Society. You remember where it is, right? Twelfth and Market. I only have an hour for lunch, so don't be late."

"What's the appointment for again?" He gripped the mug.

"A mortgage, Ozzie. It's one of your G.I. Bill benefits, and I want to take advantage. Can't live with Great-aunt Reese forever." Then she leaned over and whispered, "Not with the way we were going at it last night." She chortled.

Ozzie's body flushed with warmth as the memory of their wedding night rushed back through his midsection. Rita reached for her black gloves and hat and then kissed him.

After his second cup of coffee, the aspirin kicked in. Ozzie hopped the trolley down to the Philadelphia Navy Yard, where he had finally been called down for a job. His unemployment benefits had held him over for the past two months, but he was ready to get back to earning a living. He had applied for the management position of warehouse specialist. With his experience working as a corporal, U.S. Army, for maintenance and transportation, it would be an easy transition for him. A cakewalk, really, and as he entered the Navy Yard and caught a whiff of the fishy smell of the Schuylkill River, his morning headache was replaced with excitement. Inside a trailer marked "Security," a balding man wearing a light blue button-down shirt shoved forms across the desk.

Ozzie gave his name, and after producing his ID, he was handed a white name tag with a sticker adhesive. "Report to Building 620," the balding man said. "It's the main administrative building just to the left. Can't miss it."

Ozzie pressed the white name tag to his uniform. He had not been told what to wear, so he'd figured that showing up in his full-dress uniform would give him an extra air of respectability. There were about six men waiting, four white men and two Negroes. Ozzie was the only person in a uniform. Had he made a mistake? Should he have come in civilian clothes?

But then he remembered what his uncle Millard always said: "Dress your ass off, boy, and then nobody can't say you don't belong."

He picked up a copy of *True: The Man's Magazine* and flipped through it while he waited. The four white men were called into the admin office first, and after about fifteen minutes, they walked out with a bag and a folder each. They all smiled, but none made eye contact with him, not that he had expected it.

All the Negro men were called into the office together. Ozzie put the magazine down and brought up the rear of the group. The thick-necked man behind the counter looked up at Ozzie and blinked. Then he looked down at the list on his desk and read out each of their names. "You three will report to the warehouse. The job is receiving, hauling, and unloading materials. You will also be in charge of keeping the areas clean."

Ozzie felt heat trickle up his spine. Did this man even see him? Had he read his application properly? Ozzie was more than a mule fit for manual labor. This job was below his intelligence and skill level.

"The job pays seventy-five cents an hour. The attire is navy blue trousers with a navy crew shirt. If you head back down the steps and make a right and walk toward the river, you'll see the warehouse. Ask for Mr. Howell. He'll get you straight."

The other two men turned and left together. Ozzie stood in place. Seventy-five cents an hour? Was he serious? That was half of what Ozzie had expected to earn.

"Were my instructions unclear?" The man tilted his head.

"I served as corporal in the army in Germany. I managed men in maintenance and transportation. I applied for warehouse specialist."

"This is the job that's available," the man grunted, waving his hand as if Ozzie were a fly he was trying to get rid of.

"When will something else become available?"

"That's it. Take it or leave it." The man eyed him. "But if you don't take what's offered, I'll have to alert the VA. Let them know you refused employment."

Ozzie knew the rest. If he declined employment, he'd lose his unemployment benefits. This was unfair. He had served four years for his country, only to come back to this subpar position. But what choice did he have? He had a wife to support now. *And a child.*

Ozzie had mailed two American dollars to the Federal Eagle Club where Jelka had worked each month, in hopes that someone would find her and give her the money for Katja. Even though he never received a response, he had to believe that he was supporting his child. He couldn't help out if he wasn't earning a living.

"Fine," he said, and then turned on his heel.

Ozzie held the glass door to the bank for Rita as she walked out onto the street.

"Well, now that our application is in, all we have to do is wait," Rita said, slipping her black gloves onto her hands.

Ozzie looked down the street. "I guess."

"What do you mean, you guess?"

"The teller didn't seem all that interested in what we had to say." He pulled out the street map that the banker had given him. "Even if they do give us a mortgage, who wants to live in these neighborhoods? The houses are all run-down."

"I'll talk to my boss, Sadie, about that. Let's just focus on getting the mortgage. First things first." Rita grabbed his hand, and they started walking toward Broad Street. "The G.I. Bill is going to help us, and thanks to your service, we'll be living the American dream."

CHAPTER 38

Washington, D.C., December 1956

ETHEL

Miniature American flags were handed to each person as they entered the courtroom.

"Welcome to the naturalization ceremony, and congratulations. Please come in and stay standing for the Pledge of Allegiance," said the officer of the court, parked by the door with a jovial grin.

Men, women, and a few children shuffled in behind the Gathers family, donned in their best dresses, slacks, and ties. The room swelled to stuffy and full. Ethel could barely keep a straight face: Oti's six-year-old voice was the loudest and proudest as he recited the Pledge of Allegiance. She rewarded him with a pat to his head as they took their seats. Bert sat at one end of the spectators' bench, with all eight children sandwiched between them. The judge was only a few moments into his presentation about the rights and responsibilities of becoming an American citizen when Ethel touched Mia's foot to keep her from kicking the chair, disturbing the man in front of her.

As she scanned the room, she saw about thirty people present, all of European descent. Ethel could feel the electricity of their hopes and dreams, and the honor they felt in becoming American citizens. She told herself to breathe it all in too. It was just a few years ago that she had started the Brown Baby Plan with the vision that half-American children could have the same rights as all Americans, and here she was with her own receiving their certification of citizenship.

The judge ended his presentation by asking for persons over the age of fourteen to please rise for the Oath of Allegiance. Franz was the only of their children old enough, and Ethel watched as Bert smoothed down Franz's collar with a nod of approval. With his hand raised and his shoulders erect, Franz recited the oath that he had practiced all week.

Once the group finished, everyone clapped, and then a woman in a pleated dress stood at the podium with a pitch pipe to her lips and blew a note. When she opened her mouth, the most beautiful rendition of "The Star-Spangled Banner" sprang free, bringing tears to a few eyes. After more applause, the judge called out the names of the new citizens. Ethel held Anton's and Mia's hands, and Bert snapped pictures as the judge presented them with their naturalization certificate.

A lump formed in Ethel's throat as she watched each one of her children shake the judge's hand and take their certificate. They had done it. All eight of the Gathers children were official American citizens, praise be and hallelujah!

"Mommy," Anke said, interrupting her prayer. "Wave your flag."

Ethel looked around and saw that the new citizens and their family were all waving their flags as the woman belted out "America the Beautiful."

"Congratulations to you all," the judge said, and bade them good day.

Once they reached the curb, Bert took Ethel's hand in his. "I'm glad that I got to witness this and that it didn't happen while I was over in Korea."

"Me too. I couldn't imagine having the ceremony without you." Ethel stroked his cheek.

On top of all the thoughts rolling around in her head, she didn't want to add Bert being deployed to Korea to the list. Even though he was leaving in five days, she just wanted to relish this special moment with her family the best she could.

"Can we go get some ice cream?" asked Monika. "Please, Daddy." She squeezed Bert's hand.

"Or a hot dog with onions and sauerkraut," said Heinz, touching his belly. The boy ate just as much as he had when he first moved in with Ethel and Bert, and while he had grown taller, she still wondered where he put all the food.

"I think that can be arranged." Bert looked at Ethel, who rolled her eyes in a way that said, *You are such a pushover.*

"But ice cream first," said Oti, and they all burst out laughing.

Bert's flight to Korea was scheduled for the following Wednesday. He had left a two-page instruction sheet on how and when to pay the mortgage and all the utilities, and whom to call if Ethel had issues with the maintenance of any appliances, plumbing, or electricity. Even though he had left her many times in Germany for maneuvers and special education training, it was the first time he was going overseas without his family, and Ethel could tell he was uneasy.

"We will be fine," she assured him.

"Nine months feels like such a long time. They are going to grow so much while I'm gone."

"I'll send pictures, and we'll sit down to write you every Sunday."

Bert pulled Ethel into his arms and held her flat against his chest. They stayed like that, holding on to each other and swaying.

Three days later, a horn beeped, and Bert called to the children, telling them it was time for him to go. They all grabbed for their piece of him, wrapping skinny arms around his waist, his legs, his arms.

The horn tooted twice this time, and the kids shouted a slew of

"Goodbye" and "We'll miss you" and then scattered. Ethel walked him to the door.

"Oh, and don't forget to check the mail. There're a few pieces on the coffee table with your name on them."

"Got it." She kissed him one last time and then watched as the sedan pulled away from the curb.

Bert hadn't been gone longer than two minutes when Anke cornered Ethel in the kitchen. "Can you paint my nails?" She held up a bottle of Pepto-pink polish. Her hair was frizzy and loose from her braid.

"You can't wear nail polish to school."

"Emily does it all the time."

"Well, I'm not Emily's mom. I follow the rules." Ethel carried the Tupperware containing leftover cabbage and placed it in the fridge.

"What about my toenails?" Anke opened the bottle and sniffed. "I'll paint yours, and then you can paint mine."

Ethel smiled. "Come on here, girl."

They plopped down on the sofa in the family room with Anke's feet in Ethel's lap. While Ethel brushed pink onto her toes, Anke caught Ethel up on the happenings in her third-grade class. "Van had his name on the board with three strikes. Sister Therese took away his recess and sent him into the hall to clap the erasers. For the rest of the day, his blue pants had chalk on them, and he couldn't get it off."

"Well, hopefully, he has learned his lesson."

When Monika and Mia saw Anke getting her toenails painted, they took off their socks too. Ethel picked up the mail from the coffee table and fanned one envelope over each girl's feet. After ten minutes of Monika's fifth-grade gossip, Ethel declared, "All dry. Please make sure you say your prayers before bed." She tickled Mia and sent them each upstairs with a forehead kiss.

Exhausted, Ethel moved to the recliner. She had intended to read a few pages of the December issue of the newspaper *Freedom,* published by Paul Robeson, but then she looked at the letters in her hand. One was from the library with a red stamp that said "Overdue," and she racked her brain for which of the children's books she had forgotten to return. Then a pale blue envelope, postmarked from Germany, caught her eye. Ethel grinned: It was a new letter from Julia, and she ripped it open.

CHAPTER 39

West Oak Forest Academy, December 1965

SOPHIA

The rumor had spread quickly across the campus of West Oak Forest Academy. All the Negro students had monkey tails, and if you got close to any of them, you'd catch a tail too.

"This is childish and bizarre, and nothing more than leftover propaganda with roots in slavery," said Louis as the five Negro students crammed around a table in the corner of the cafeteria. "Anything to portray the Negro as something other than a person just like them."

"Simply ridiculous." Willa shook her lovely curls.

Sophia threaded her fingers together under the table. In front of her sat a plate full of mashed potatoes, meat loaf, and creamed spinach. None of which she had touched. It had been hard for her to eat anything substantial for the last few days. Her nerves just wouldn't settle after the incident with Patty. She told no one but Willa what had happened in the locker room but swore her to secrecy. The boys couldn't know the humiliation she had suffered. It was embarrassing. To have those girls auctioning her off like an animal, then exposing her private parts. The one silver lining was that the secret with Willa had wiped away any residue of her initial anger at finding Sophia in Max's arms at the telephone booth.

"Until this dies down, we move throughout campus with a buddy system. We need to have each other's backs," Max added. Sophia nodded as she watched how the light from the window sparked the irises of his eyes, remembering how his chest felt pressed against hers, how the pitch in his voice soothed her.

"Well, we have study hall." Willa tapped Sophia's arm, interrupting her reminiscence.

"Right, we better get going." Sophia stood and gathered her things, and when she chanced another look at Max, he was staring right back at her.

Christmas break was four days away, and Sophia was petrified that the moment Ma Deary saw her, she would chain her to her dugout room adjacent to the kitchen and forbid her to return to school. But what choice did Sophia have? Forest would be closed for two long weeks, and although she fancied herself a survivalist, she couldn't make it that long without food. Not to mention what would happen to her if she got caught.

"I hate school breaks," she mumbled under her breath.

Willa closed the lid on the jar of Pond's cold cream and stared at her. "You are really secretive, Sophia Clark. We've lived together for a full semester, and I still don't know that much about you. Why on earth don't you ever want to go home?" she demanded. Then she leaned forward. "Are you in danger?"

Sophia wrung her hands, unsure how much she could trust Willa with. "My folks didn't approve of me coming to Forest. They wanted me to stay back and work the farm."

"Can't they hire people to do that?"

"Yes, hopefully, by now they have. I don't know. I haven't talked to them since—"

"I thought you were on the phone with your brother and that he was sick." Willa's eyebrows raised. "That day with Max?"

Sophia had nearly forgotten her lie. "Yes, I talked to my brothers, but not my folks."

Willa moved from her desk to her bed. "If you are that frightened, I guess you could come home with me again."

"Willa, you are so kind to offer, but I don't want to impose."

"If you can't go home, you don't really have a choice, now do you?"

The sad fact was Willa was right.

"Then it's settled. My parents won't mind. We do it up really big for Christmas. Lights, eight-foot tree with all the trimmings, and a big feast. Oh, my mother makes a seafood gumbo on Christmas Eve that will knock your socks off. You'll love every moment of it. You'll see." Willa moved her comforter back and slipped between the sheets. "Don't forget to take those pills my father prescribed for you. Last night you were screaming like a banshee. I'm surprised the dorm mother didn't think that I was killing you."

Sophia had one last dime and pushed herself to make another call before leaving school for winter break. As a result, she had to run to catch Willa in the pickup line. When the shiny Cadillac Fleetwood arrived, Sophia was sweaty and out of breath. To her dismay, it was Willa's grandmother, Rose Pride, who again emerged from the backseat. She was dressed in a navy and crème bouclé suit, a matching scarf tied at her neck with "Chanel" in big block letters. Rose bristled when her eyes took in Sophia; then she turned and opened her arms to Willa and kissed both her cheeks.

"My darling Wilhelmina," she cooed.

"Hello, Grandmother."

Rose turned up her nose. "Sophia, I'm surprised to see you still here. I thought you'd be gone by now."

"She's coming home with us," Willa said brightly.

Rose took a step back, shaking her head. "Darling, she can't come with us. Didn't your mother tell you? We are going to New York City to visit Uncle Teddy for the holiday."

"Really?" Willa shrieked.

"Yes, we have it all planned, and there is simply no extra room." Rose turned to Sophia. "I'm sorry, but is there someplace that we can drop you off along the way, dear?"

Sophia knew the feel of a cold snub when she was slapped with one, and Mrs. Pride's was downright icy. It was obvious in the way she eyed Sophia that she was eager to get rid of her like yesterday's trash. *Think,* she said to herself. Sophia knew only two addresses by heart, and there was no way she'd have the Prides in their fancy Cadillac drop her off at their dilapidated farmhouse.

"Yes, ma'am. I do," she said to Rose.

"But Sophia, you said—"

"The decision is final," Rose cut Willa off. "Please give the address to Paulie."

Once again, Sophia rode in the front seat with Paulie, the Prides' driver. The Cadillac's ride was so smooth that despite the symphony of worries playing inside her head, once they hit the highway, Sophia couldn't stay awake. She slept until the city traffic slowed the car. When she opened her eyes, she recognized the Washington Monument. They had arrived in D.C., and her stomach churned with apprehension.

Through the rearview mirror, she could see that Willa was asleep in her grandmother's arms. Paulie took East Capitol Street and then pulled onto A Street, where Ma Deary and Unc's mother had left them a brick home that they'd turned into a rent-by-the-week tenement.

Sophia hadn't been to the house in over a year, but when she was younger, they had come often to collect the money on Friday afternoons.

As the car eased down the block, Sophia felt the weight of embarrassment pressing on her chest. They passed saggy porches, cracked cement stairs with missing railings, overgrown patches of weeds and grass, sidewalks littered with newspapers, shards of beer bottles, crushed soda cans, and fresh dog mess. Two alley cats dashed across their path as the car stopped in front of the house with well-worn green synthetic turf peeling at the edges on the front porch. Three plastic chairs pressed against the windowsill. A man dressed in a vintage wool coat stumbled in front of the car, then peered in the window. Paulie honked his horn, and the man continued on, clutching a brown paper bag.

Sophia's face stung, and she couldn't bear to look in the backseat at Willa or Mrs. Pride; no doubt both were wide awake and watching.

"Is this where you live?" Willa asked. "I thought you said you lived on a farm."

"I do. But my family owns this house too," Sophia said with a fake cheer that sounded hollow even to her own ears. "See you back at school. Thanks for the ride, Mrs. Pride." She opened the car door before Paulie could come around and do it for her. Sophia didn't want any more attention. She knew a big Cadillac like the Prides' had already drawn the neighbors' nosy eyes to the windows.

"Will you be okay for the whole break?" Willa asked, catching Sophia's eye.

"Yes, of course." Sophia made her lips smile. "Enjoy New York."

Rose motioned for the driver to pull off. Sophia felt the wind from the car in her hair before she reached the top of the front stairs.

Placing her tattered train case at her feet, Sophia crossed her fingers and pushed the bell. She waited a few beats and then pressed the bell again. Finally, she heard someone shuffling toward the door.

"Who is it?" a woman screeched.

"Sophia."

"Who?"

"Sophia."

The front door dragged open far enough for the woman to peep her head out. "Who you?" She wore a raggedy mushroom wig that made her look like a poor rendition of a background singer.

"Is Wayon here?"

"What's it to you?" Her red lips dipped into a frown. "Don't come 'round here asking 'bout my man," she snapped.

Sophia heard heavy footsteps, then Unc came around the woman and pushed the front door wide. "Rusty! Whatcha doing here, gal?" He ducked past the woman and pulled Sophia into a hug, crushing her to his wide chest. "I thought you were away at that fancy school."

"Who the fuck is this?" the woman howled.

"Gloria, go in the house and sit down somewhere 'fore I whoop your ass. This here is my niece."

"How I know she kin?"

"'Cause I just told you. Now get." He glared.

Gloria huffed off. Sophia stepped into the vestibule. The hallway was damp and smelled of pickle juice. The dull wooden floors creaked beneath their feet as Unc led Sophia down the narrow hall and back into the kitchen.

"You hungry?" Unc asked. He was tall, broad-shouldered, and chiseled like a boxer. He carried himself like a man who got respect on the streets.

"A little."

An off-white Formica table took up most of the room, with tan leather swivel chairs. A stack of papers sat on one corner of the table, so Sophia sat on the other side and shrugged out of her coat. The television blasted *I Spy* from the living room, and Sophia could make out Bill Cosby's voice over Gloria mumbling to herself.

Unc ignored Gloria. "How'd you get here? Deary know you out of school?" He turned on the pilot to the stove. It *tick-tick*ed, then he struck a match and fed it to the pilot until it roared with fire. Unc put a cast-iron pan over the eyelet, tipped in what looked like bacon grease from a mason jar on the counter, and then cracked three eggs. "Fried hard?"

She smiled. "You know it." It felt good to be with someone who knew her.

Once Unc put the plate of eggs and two pieces of jellied toast in front of her, he sat down and lit his Pall Mall. Sophia forked eggs into her mouth while Unc caught her up on the farm, the new workers, and the last time he'd seen her brothers.

Sophia ate the crust of her toast. "Unc, can I ask you something?"

"Shoot."

"Where did I come from?"

Unc choked on the smoke from his cigarette, pounded his fist against his chest, and then chuckled. "What the hell kinda question is that?"

"I *mean,* where did I come from? I don't remember much about my childhood. There are no pictures. Whenever I've asked Ma Deary, she says, 'We the only family you need to know.' That's not a real answer."

"Well, we are the only family you need to know. And we love you, girl. Stop asking stupid questions," he said, getting up from the table with his back to her and strolling out of the room.

Sophia finished her eggs as she heard Unc and Gloria whispering in the living room. Then Unc came back wearing a double-breasted leather coat with his lapel popped.

"I gotta make a run. Wash up them dishes for me. Damn roaches think they paying the bills 'round here."

"Where you going?"

"I gotta go see a man about a dog." He turned to the small mirror pinned to the wall and licked his finger. Then he ran it across his mustache.

Sophia knew he wasn't really seeing to no dog. That was Unc's way of saying "None of your business."

"But I'll be back in a few hours. You gonna have to stay the night here, and I'll drive you out to the farm tomorrow morning. I was going out there anyhow."

"I can't go to the farm."

"Deary ain't frontin' on you no more. She knows you did what you did so you could get that education."

Sophia looked at her empty plate, not feeling convinced.

Unc leaned against the doorframe. "You do okay up at that school?"

"I did fine." She tried smiling but knew it fell short on her cheeks as the memory of Opal pulling down her panties flashed through her mind. She shook the image away.

"Sit tight. We have four boarders upstairs. Don't talk to none of them. If they ask you any questions, tell them they gotta wait for me."

"Got it."

"Good to see you, Rusty," he said, patting her on the head, then he pressed his hands in the pockets of his leather jacket and strolled down the hall.

Sophia could hear the *click-clop* of Gloria teetering on her high heels behind him. "Who did you say she was again?" the woman called to him. "She too pretty to be roaming the streets, just showing up unannounced."

The front door closed shut, and she heard the seal of the double locks. Sophia went to the sink. Washed her dishes and scrubbed the pan clean. She waited a full ten minutes to make sure Unc wouldn't double back for a forgotten item. Then she reached up into the cabinet over the sink, pulling down the canister that said "Flour." She reached inside past a mess of pins, clips, pencils, and buttons for the nickels, dimes, and quarters. She put the money on the counter and dug deeper until she found what she was looking for. A copper-colored key, the spare to the front door. She opened her satchel bag, pulled out the white pages, studied the address, and then slipped the key and coins into her coat pocket and headed for the door.

CHAPTER 40

Washington, D.C., December 1965

ETHEL

Ethel's mother used to say that time was a thief that never got caught, and Ethel couldn't agree more as she gazed out the kitchen window at the yard dusted in a silver frost. It felt like just yesterday that they were all moving into the house on Madison Street, claiming bedrooms, posing for the *Ebony* magazine feature, hanging tree swings, preparing for confirmations, dressing for sock hop dances, and fitting into graduation caps and gowns.

They had been living in D.C. for nearly eleven years, and Franz, Heinz, Leo, and Monika had all left home, between enlisting in the military and attending college. Anke was in her final year at Dunbar High School, and the younger three were growing like stalks of bamboo. At times, Ethel wished she had a time machine to slow it all down. But the thing that had always been constant in her life was change.

Ethel looked from the window down into the apron sink, where she had been massaging butter into a plump roaster chicken. After sprinkling the bird with an array of seasonings, she pushed it into the oven. Ethel set the egg timer and then opened the door to the shed kitchen, where the Speed Queen wringer washer rumbled and gurgled. Using her poker stick, she turned the clothes round and round. The water was murky with dirt, and she decided to let the laundry spin for a little while longer. As she returned the wringer plate, the doorbell rang.

Ethel tsked her teeth. During this time of day—after lunch but before the children got home from school—was when Jehovah's Witnesses liked to visit. Despite her telling them that she was a devout Catholic who faithfully attended St. Aloysius Church, they pulled her into long conversations about their good news. It was either them or a street peddler trying to sell her Christmas lights, or a new set of encyclopedias that they didn't need. She touched her fingers to the pins holding back her hair, then removed her bib apron, running her fingers down the front of her housedress to assure that all the buttons were fastened.

"Good afternoon," Ethel said, peering down at the bushy redheaded teen standing on the steps, a respectful distance from the door. She had a satchel strapped over her shoulders. "Can I help you?"

"Mrs. Gathers?"

Ethel took a step forward, pulling the door close so as not to let out the heat. "Yes." She hoped the young lady wasn't here to sell magazine subscriptions. She had more than she could count.

"I'm Sophia Clark."

Ethel gasped and then drew back. It was the girl who had phoned just that morning, asking if she was one of the Brown Babies. Said something about reading about her in an article and locating Ethel with her last ten cents on a pay phone. What in the world was she doing on her doorstep?

"Young lady, you should not have come to my home unannounced. Barging in on me like this when I specifically suggested that you speak to your parents. Don't you have any manners?"

Sophia's bottom lip quivered. "Ma'am, forgive me for being so forward, but I am desperate. When I reached you with my final dime, I took it as a sign that I couldn't give up. Please. I promise not to take up much of your time."

Ethel saw tears rise in the young girl's eyes, and that cracked through her shell. She had received so many calls over the years, from disgruntled families unhappy with one thing or another, that she couldn't possibly take them on anymore. She had given her all and had done everything in her power for the Brown Baby Plan, and she simply could not intervene on every family's behalf.

But when Ethel saw the teen wrap her arms around herself, it was hard to turn her away now that she was here. "This is not the way I do things," she said in a voice that sounded flimsy to her own ears.

"I promise you that I don't mean any harm, ma'am. I just really need to know, and I don't have anyone else to turn to."

Ethel hoped she wouldn't regret this as she took a step back from the door. "Very well. Come on in."

The vestibule had black-and-white-checkered tile and a wooden coat rack where Bert liked to hang his hat. When Ethel offered to place Sophia's quilted coat on the hook, Sophia clutched the jacket to her chest. "It's okay. I'll keep it with me," she said. The girl had an athletic build and was taller than Ethel by an inch or two. Her shocking red hair hung just past her shoulders.

"Very well then, follow me." Ethel led Sophia through the living room and into the small library that doubled as an office at the back of the house. Ethel flipped on the overhead light. Inside was a rectangular desk with a pile of envelopes and folders that Bert had brought home from work. Two ladder-back chairs sat in front of the desk, and there was a velvet chaise in the corner where Ethel liked to hide out and read. She gestured to Sophia to take a seat in one of the chairs. "I was meticulous with the records for every child. I made two copies of each, giving one to the adopted families and filing one away for moments like this."

Ethel didn't know why waves of nerves kept sloshing through her; she hoped she was doing the right thing. In the past, it had been the adopted parents who had contacted her about this or that. Sophia was the first child, potentially. They weren't even sure at this point if she was one of her Brown Babies. This could all be one big misunderstanding. The girl could just have unkind parents; that wasn't uncommon in rural areas where money was tight.

"You really like to read," Sophia responded, still clutching her coat as her eyes traveled over the wall of books.

"In order to be a good writer, one must read."

"Are you a writer?"

"Yes, a journalist." Ethel paused and looked the girl over. She had kind eyes, and Ethel found herself drawn to know more about her. "What do you want to be when you grow up?"

Sophia coughed. "I'd like to work in an office, ma'am."

"An office doing what?"

"Anything that doesn't put me anywhere near a farm," Sophia retorted in such a way that Ethel could feel the tiredness down in the young girl's bones.

"Well, you are going to need to dream a bit bigger than that. You are at West Oak Forest, right?"

"Yes."

"Such a prestigious school. I read about the integration in the *Post*. How's that been for you?"

"Good, I'm learning a lot," Sophia said while dropping her eyes. Ethel watched how she fidgeted with the hem of her skirt and wondered what deep struggle she was enduring.

"Always remember that education is the one thing no one can take away from you." Ethel turned, and as she pulled open the file cabinet, she asked, "You said Clark, right? Norma and Frank?"

Sophia nodded. "With my three brothers. Walter, Karl, and Lu."

"One kid at a time."

Ethel flipped through the files before sliding a manila folder marked "Clark" from the cabinet. She studied the contents, closed the file, and then walked over to Sophia. "Do you pray, Sophia?"

"Sometimes."

"Let me pray with you before we go any further."

Ethel stood in front of the girl, took her cold, dry hands, pulled her to her feet, and prayed the Lord's Prayer, followed by the Hail Mary.

When she finished, she said, "Now, you should probably sit back down, Sophia Clark. This could be a lot to take in at once."

CHAPTER 41

Washington, D.C., December 1965

SOPHIA

Sophia did as she was told and sat down in the ladder-back chair. A square pillow rested at the small of her back. This was the moment she had been working toward since she'd learned of Max's origin, the fire that made sense of her nightmares, and read the stories of the Brown Babies coming to America from Germany. Her heart thundered in her chest, and she could feel heat gathering in her armpits as she opened the file folder.

There were four sheets of paper. The first one looked like a birth certificate, but it was written in German. She made out the name Schultheiß. Could that be her original last name? The next sheet was in English, an adoption petition form; and then what appeared to be an affidavit of facts. The last page was a medical form, also written in German, but in the top right corner a three-by-five photograph was attached.

Sophia had never seen a photograph of herself before the age of ten. She'd only ever seen one of herself, from the Easter Sunday when she and her brothers had dressed up in passable hand-me-down clothes and been taken to an Easter-egg hunt at a nearby church. It was the most fun they'd had in months, and Sophia had come away with the golden egg. The pastor of the church, a squat man with a silky voice, had taken a Polaroid picture of Sophia holding her prized egg, which he later gave her as a parting gift. But that was the only one she had, and her hands trembled slightly as she removed the paper clip, trying her best not to scratch the photograph.

She stared at her younger self without blinking. The photo was in black and white, and she wore a white bow in her hair, a dark cardigan over a ruffled blouse. A stuffed bear with floppy ears sat in her lap. Sophia took in every detail of the picture, unable to stop her bottom lip from twitching. "This isn't me?"

"What do you mean?" Ethel stood over her.

Sophia swallowed back a sob. "She has a birthmark on her cheek. And look at her hair." She lifted the photo up to Ethel. "This looks nothing like me."

The girl in the photograph was not her, that she knew with every fiber in her body. She had been wrong all along. She was not one of Ethel Gathers's precious Brown Babies after all. How foolish she had been, wasting so much time and energy on chasing a pipe dream. She had wanted some sort of explanation for her horrible life, but she had just been dealt a bad hand. Ma Deary and the Old Man were her parents. The Clarks, in all their dysfunction, were her family.

"I'm sorry for wasting your time, Mrs. Gathers."

It was a good thing she hadn't hung up her coat. It would be easier for her to leave without taking up any more of this woman's day.

Mrs. Gathers took the photo out of Sophia's hands. Her eyes drifted from the picture to Sophia and then back to the picture. Sophia noticed that her skin turned a shade paler almost instantly. The woman probably felt sorry for her.

"Why don't we go into the kitchen for some tea."

"I don't want tea. I just wanted to understand—"

Mrs. Gathers covered her mouth with her hand and gasped. "I never meant for this to happen. Dear God, what have I done?"

But Sophia didn't want her sympathy. She wanted to run out into the cold so she could lick her bleeding wounds in private.

"My aim was always to do good. To be useful and help those American children confined to the orphanages. All children deserve a mother's love," Mrs. Gathers said, and then she let out a strangled breath. "But even though I had the best of intentions, some things did go wrong."

A chilling shadow passed over Mrs. Gathers's face.

"Please, give me a moment to explain."

CHAPTER 42

Washington, D.C., December 1965

ETHEL

It was a good thing that Sophia had refused the offer of tea, because given the way Ethel's hands shook, she would have scalded them both.

Sophia's arms were once again wrapped around herself and she looked much smaller than she did when she arrived. Poor thing. Ethel's mission had always been to help the children, and she could not fail the girl sitting in front of her. She closed her eyes, reached into her dress pocket for her rosary beads, and took a deep breath. The cool feel of the beads between her fingers steadied her and gave her the courage she needed in order to forge on. When she opened her eyes, the day at Idlewild Airport slowly came into focus, like a Polaroid picture.

Ethel blinked. "I hadn't anticipated that the news of my arrival in New York city with the Brown Babies would cause such a ruckus. The Scandinavian Airlines flight had arrived at Idlewild ahead of schedule, and so we had to wait a few minutes before deboarding the plane." Ethel remembered her anxiety at being alone and in charge of seven German-speaking children under age five, including one infant whom she had to carry.

"Naturally, the children were cranky and hungry," she said. "And as we deboarded, it was raining, so I had to hurry the children down the airstairs, across the tarmac, and into the terminal."

Ethel had assigned all of the children a line partner, and they walked in pairs. Once inside the terminal, she did a quick head count and then hurried the little ones along, following the signs for Immigration. She carried a large canvas bag with a file holding each child's information. Every folder contained the name of the child and the birth parents, the date and place of birth, the alien number, a copy of the birth certificate, a passport, and a photograph of the child, as well as the adoptive parents' names. Ethel had decided on the photo at the last minute. She'd had a photographer come two weeks before and take portrait photos of each child. She had two copies made up, one for her files and the other for the new family.

"Transparency was always my aim. I wanted the children to know who they were. I gave the parents everything I had, with the hope that when the children asked, they would share their identity. I have always been up front with my own family. But I must admit, in hindsight, most parents have passed the children off as their own and never disclosed that they were in fact adopted.

"When we rounded the corner toward the Immigration line, bright lights assaulted us as photographers from all the major news outlets took flash photograph after flash photograph."

The lights made Margit fret in Ethel's arms, and she had to rock the baby to get her to settle down while, at the same time, ushering the other children through the line. One of the boys began to cry.

"Ethel Gathers, is it true that they call you the Brown Fairy?" one reporter called out.

"How did you manage to get these children to America? Are you sure they have American fathers?"

"What if the children get to their home and it's not a fit? What will you do then? Send them back to Germany?"

More flashing lights. More microphones. More reporters.

"All the children looked panicked. I tried to shield them the best I could and soothe them with the few German words that I knew."

Ethel looked around for help. Why wasn't there someone from Child Services, or the police holding these aggressive reporters at a distance? She felt ambushed as she continued to move the children through the line. Ethel handed over her passport and then the baby's paperwork. Stamped and processed. She handed the next two, then the next two.

"Oh my goodness. They're here. Our little darlings are here!" a woman shouted and then ran over to Ethel. "Which one is mine?"

"Just a second, ma'am. If you'd just wait over there. We are still processing the children," Ethel said, trying to hold her at bay.

The woman, taller and wider than Ethel, pushed her aside. "My goodness, look at all that good hair," she exclaimed.

By this time baby Margit was full-out crying, and Ethel fumbled in her pockets, searching for the pacifier. From the corner of her eye, she could see the cluster of families who had arrived to pick up their children and hoped that they'd have more patience than the large, pushy woman. *Rejoice,* she told herself. *This is what you wanted. To do right by these children and give them loving families.*

Ethel juggled the baby while she ushered the children through two at a time and handed the man behind the Immigration desk their folders. The two boys went first. As the next two girls were coming through the line, a bold reporter in a black pantsuit snaked her way to the Immigration table. Her photographer flashed the light and took a picture of Ethel as the reporter shoved the microphone in Ethel's mouth.

"Mrs. Gathers, surely this is going to be a problem. The children are speaking German. The parents are speaking English. You say they are American, but they are German too. How do you plan for these kids to adapt?"

Ethel said to Sophia, "At that moment, a television camera appeared in my face, and I just froze. I remember feeling attacked and wondering why this interview couldn't wait. But you know reporters, everyone is rushing to be first, they don't care about the people involved. Then I heard the clerk at the Immigration desk swearing."

Ethel saw from her peripheral vision that the Immigration agent had dropped the file folders on the floor. Before Ethel could move closer to make sure the files were sorted in the right order, the reporter grabbed her arm.

"This is a live broadcast, Mrs. Gathers, the American people who have helped fund this experiment of yours deserve an answer."

"Well." Ethel pulled herself together. "I can't understand why people think it is so strange for a colored couple to adopt these children. Don't they think we have hearts too?"

"Thank you." The newsperson lowered the microphone.

Ethel turned as the Immigration clerk stamped the files and passed the last group of kids through the line.

"The chaos made me uneasy. Before I had time to gather myself, a woman from Child Services who'd been sent to help finally appeared."

"Thanks, Mrs. Gathers, we will take it from here." The woman wearing gold-framed glasses reached for the baby in her arms.

"Each child had been given a small knapsack with the basics; some had an additional change of clothes. It was the noise that I remember. It seemed to be coming from every direction, all punctuated by a few of the children clinging to me and crying."

"Ethel Gathers! You look fantastic. Which one is my baby?" called Bertha, a woman Ethel knew from the *Afro-American* newspaper. Ethel remembered hugging her tightly, so happy to see a familiar face. Then another woman walked up to her.

"Hi, I'm Mrs. Clark. Here for the two children. A boy and a girl." Mrs. Clark smiled, showing off a gold tooth as she leaned closer to Ethel.

Something about Mrs. Clark seemed off. But Bertha kept talking, pulling Ethel's attention away. "I have turned a room right off the kitchen into a playroom. I can't wait to get my bundle of joy home."

Ethel wasn't listening to Bertha; she was busy craning her neck, trying to take in the woman who had introduced herself as Mrs. Clark. Then, like a vulture, another reporter swooped down on Ethel and shoved yet another microphone in front of her face.

"I was glad that I thought to include the photos of the children. I had anticipated it would be hard for the parents to communicate, with the children speaking German and everyone else English."

Sophia's eyes never left Ethel's face, but her hands fidgeted with her sweater sleeves.

"Parents were grabbing up their children and leaving before I could get away from the reporter to check that everything was in order."

Ethel remembered feeling like she needed to converse with Mrs. Clark and that quiet man, dressed in a too-big sport coat with his eyes on his shoes, before she released the two children to them. As Ethel gave yet another interview, she couldn't shake the gut feeling that she had misjudged their application in her haste to bring additional children to the States after the fire at the orphanage. She decided that she would question the Clarks further before letting the two children go.

"How can people reach out to make a donation to your organization to help more of these Brown Babies?" the blond reporter pressed. "Surely there are more?"

Ethel looked into the camera and gave them all the information they needed. Once the cameras finally turned off and the microphone was gone, most of the families had left, including the Clarks. Ethel scanned the lobby for the Clarks, to no avail.

"Why are you telling me all of this?" Sophia asked. "What's this all got to do with me?"

Ethel touched a lock of Sophia's red hair, then she rose on shaky knees, suddenly remembering that the wringer was still spinning the laundry. She needed to go turn it off and check on her roaster in the oven, but she had to do this first. Ethel walked over to her file cabinet and removed several folders. "There were four little girls with me on that flight from Frankfurt."

"And?"

"The Clarks were one of the families who received two children."

"Clark is not an unusual last name," Sophia replied, and Ethel could see from her slouched posture and the dark circles under her eyes that she had lost all the hope that she had come through Ethel's door with just an hour ago.

Ethel spread the four files across the desk. "Just look these over and see if anything sticks out to you," she said. She watched as the girl studied the pictures, then brought one closer to her face.

"Oh my God," Sophia shrieked. "This is me."

CHAPTER 43

Philadelphia, PA, November 1952

OZZIE

Two and a half months of marriage had passed faster than a greased pig at a country fair, and although Ozzie had settled into a comfortable newlywed rhythm with Rita, he was no closer to securing a mortgage from the bank and moving them out of Great-aunt Reese's home. In addition to the Philadelphia Savings Fund Society, he and Rita had put in applications at Fidelity, Girard, and Provident banks. What was frustrating was the banks never exactly told them no, but they were not saying yes either. Just more applications, more questions, more proof that led to nowhere. It felt very much like a stalemate. Meanwhile, he had read several articles in *The Philadelphia Inquirer* detailing how his white G.I. counterparts were securing large mortgages and moving out to the lofty suburbs.

Ozzie left his work boots at the front door and peeled off his uniform shirt, which he dropped on the sofa. His feet sighed through his cotton socks as he walked back through to the kitchen, which always seemed to smell of bleach and lemons. The Kit-Cat Klock hanging on the green wall above the sink rolled its eyes and wagged its tail as Ozzie reached into the icebox for a Schlitz. He flopped down into the kitchen chair with the cold can in his hand, feeling dog-tired. His foreman had called in his team for a quick haul, allowing him only a short amount of time to move steel, material, and lumber from the warehouse onto a ship that was being repaired. It was backbreaking work, and Ozzie felt like nothing more than a tool. But it was Friday, he had two whole days off away from the shipyard, away from a boss who could never seem to remember his name. Two days off from being nothing more than muscles, and he was looking forward to relaxing. As he popped the tab on the can, he heard Rita coming through the front door.

"Aunt Reese, it's just me," she shouted up the stairs, then, as she moved through the dining room, she called, "Hey, good-lookin', what's cookin'?"

Ozzie felt his pulse quicken at the sight of her. She stopped in front of him, wearing a wide grin, as he stood and pulled her into his arms. "Girl, you're always so soft." He snuggled against her.

"That's 'cause I wear lotion. Unlike you, ashy feet." Rita touched his chin and gave him her cheek. As she kicked her heels under the table, she said, "I know you ain't starting in early?" She moved to the sink, turned on the faucet, and let it run before dipping her glass for water. "Don't forget, we've been invited to the Alexanders' tonight at eight for a party. It's the first time I've been invited to my bosses' home, and I need you in your right mind."

Ozzie brought the beer to his lips and took a gulp. "That tonight?" He sighed.

"Yes, that's tonight. I've been reminding you all week."

Had she? If so, Ozzie had forgotten, and after the day he'd had, the last thing he wanted was to go all the way uptown to hang out with rich folks he didn't know.

Rita filled the teakettle and lit the pilot light. "I have already ironed your suit. It's hanging on the back of the closet door in the middle room." Then she moved next to him and sniffed. "You smell like a hard day's work, baby. Why don't you go wash up while I get Aunt Reese situated. I want to leave here by seven-thirty. You put gas in the car?"

Ozzie nodded. "Soon as I got paid."

"Good." She pecked him on the top of his head. "Go get ready. Make sure you wash your hair too."

Ozzie groaned.

"What was that?" Rita stretched her fingers over her hips, but Ozzie stood and replaced her fingers with his. Then he pulled her to him and rested his forehead against hers, peering down into her brown eyes.

"Just tired, baby. World ain't been treating me so good."

Rita rubbed the back of his neck. "Oh, love, I'll take care of you tonight. Give you something to look forward to."

"I'ma hold you to that." He kissed her eyelids, then her nose, and then pressed his mouth against hers until she murmured, "Go on now, 'fore we mess around and miss this party."

He rocked his hips against hers. "I'm okay with that."

"Later tonight, baby. Promise," she said, pushing him off her and out of the kitchen just as the kettle whistled.

At 7:35, Ozzie stood holding open the passenger door of his Chrysler Windsor for Rita. The car was ten years old, but he had bought it cheap and tinkered with it on the weekends until it purred. Rita's floral scent took up all the breathing space in the car, and he draped his arm around the back of her seat as he steered the car up Broad Street, past City Hall, and then into North Philadelphia.

The Alexanders lived in a three-story redbrick house at the corner of Seventeenth and Jefferson. Ozzie slowed the car, looking for parking. "Why don't you get out here, sweetie. I'll park and meet you inside."

Rita pulled the vanity mirror down and scanned her face. Then she turned to Ozzie. "How's my makeup?"

"You the prettiest thing walking." He kissed her hand.

"Okay, see you inside." As she lifted herself out of the car, Ozzie reached up and squeezed her behind. "Ozzie," she squawked, swatting him away.

Ozzie watched as her hips sashayed under her wool wrap onto the sidewalk and up the front stairs. Then he put the car in drive and circled the block until he found a parking spot two streets away. The slight buzz from his beer was long gone, and he slipped a peppermint into his mouth as he walked up the steps of the stately home pulsing with the sounds of jazz and boisterous laughter.

A young caramel-colored woman opened the door, balancing a silver tray of champagne flutes. "Welcome to the Alexander residence," she said, holding the tray toward Ozzie. He winced at the black-and-white uniform she was wearing. It was identical to his mother's.

Nettie had worked as a maid for a white family in Center City since Ozzie was a young boy, and now his wife worked for Negroes who had their own maid. What type of money did one have to earn in order to have personal domestic help? Ozzie and Rita couldn't even figure out how to purchase their own house, let alone the help to go with it.

He picked up a flute and swallowed down his unease with the bubbles of the champagne. A crystal chandelier hung from the ceiling of the foyer, and the woman with the drink tray pointed him toward the parlor. As he walked across the gleaming white oak floors, he scanned the room for Rita. Piano music played, and after a few beats, Ozzie recognized the album *The Amazing Bud Powell* playing from the phonograph. His shoulders relaxed a bit as he gave in to the familiar tune.

A ruby-colored settee hugged the wall, flanked by two overstuffed matching Queen Anne wing chairs. People stood in clusters with diamond-cut glasses in their hands. The women were dressed in silk and satin frocks that looked like they came straight from the display windows of Gimbels or Wanamaker's. Ozzie was wearing a black suit, one that he had bought from a secondhand store not far from work; it stood out against the gray and blue sharkskin suits most of the other men wore.

Ozzie could hear Rita's laugh and followed it into the living room, where a few nodded as he passed through to the dining area. Rita glowed like she was onstage in a magenta swing dress with a keyhole neckline. Ozzie recognized Raymond and Sadie Alexander standing next to her, but he did not recognize the white woman who completed their circle.

"My love." Rita smiled, making room next to her. As he slid in beside her, he felt beads of sweat on his forehead.

Mr. Alexander held out his hand. "Ozzie, right?" He was dressed in a textured double-breasted suit, and his jacket hit mid-thigh. Ozzie knew if he touched the man's lapels, they'd feel soft as butter between his fingers. The ensemble looked like it cost more than two weeks of Ozzie's salary.

"Mr. Alexander, nice to see you again." Ozzie pumped his hand with a firm grip.

"Please, call me Raymond."

"And you remember my boss, Sadie." Rita turned to Ozzie with a smile so radiant it almost knocked him off his feet. It was clear that she was in her element.

"If anyone's the boss, it's her." Sadie chuckled. Her hair was in tight curls rolled away from her face. "I don't know how we got anything done before Rita joined our team. And this is our dear friend Martha Markoe. She works at the law school at Penn."

"Nice to meet you." Ozzie tilted his head.

"Well, Martha has come with news." Sadie clapped her hands together with so much glee that it caused her husband to grin too.

Martha cleared her throat and tugged on the bow tied around her neck. "I was going to save it for later, but since we are all here . . ."

She raised her voice over the piano improv of the album playing from the next room. "Rita, we've reviewed your application for admission to Penn Law."

Penn Law? Rita had mentioned to Ozzie that she was applying to Temple and Drexel. University of Pennsylvania was Ivy League. He could barely afford to send her money for Lincoln.

"I am pleased to say that we are extending to you our very first Sadie Tanner Mossell Alexander Scholarship, named for yours truly." Martha pointed at Sadie, who stood beaming. "The scholarship will cover your full tuition and books."

"What?" Rita brought her hands to her mouth. Then her bottom lip started to tremble. "This can't be happening."

"You've earned it." Martha grinned.

"Oh, my." Rita reached for Ozzie's hand to help steady herself. Ozzie stood, just as stunned. His wife was going to Penn Law. She was going to become the lawyer she had always dreamed of being, and at one of the premier schools in the country. Suddenly, it felt like the collar of his white shirt was too tight on his neck.

"I knew well that the only way I could get that door open was to knock it down. Now it's your turn," Sadie said, pushing her gold-rimmed glasses up her nose.

"Thank you, thank you." Rita embraced Sadie, and they rocked.

Martha touched Rita's elbow. "I'm committed to helping deserving Negro students like you have the opportunity to break through these bullshit ceilings. This scholarship, named after our first Negro woman to graduate Penn Law, is just the beginning."

"Well, this causes for a toast," Raymond said, flagging down the woman with the tray of drinks.

Yes, a drink, Ozzie thought. He needed something to slow down the thumping in his chest.

"To Rita becoming one of the finest lawyers this city has ever seen." Raymond held up his glass. They all drank to that.

"I'd like to propose a toast too," Rita said. "To my new husband. Without him, none of this would be true." She held up her glass. Everyone looked at Ozzie, and as he held his glass to his lips, he realized that he was the only one who had drained his entire flute on the first toast. He leaned over and kissed her cheek instead.

"Congratulations, baby. Dreams do come true," he said, just as the music changed to a slow and somber tune.

"Oh, Rita, I want to introduce you to my soror. She is the current national president of our sorority. Maybe you will consider joining us one day." Sadie winked and whisked Rita away, with Martha following behind them. The two men were left alone.

"Ozzie," Raymond said. "Rita tells me you are working for the shipyard and that you volunteered for the army."

Ozzie straightened his back. "Yes."

"What do you do?"

"I'm a . . . warehouse specialist." The lie felt tart on his lips. "I'm in the process of going back to school also. One of the benefits of the G.I. Bill." He moved from one foot to the other.

"Wonderful. Which university?"

"I've put in applications at Lincoln and Cheyney State. I'm hoping to start spring semester," Ozzie offered, and as the schools that he had been so excited to attend rolled from his lips, he remembered that the Alexanders had both attended Penn, and that Raymond had attended Harvard as an undergraduate. All of a sudden, his dreams felt foolish and small.

"Ambitious, just like Rita. I love it." Raymond clapped him on the back. "Come, let me introduce you around."

The party was now in full swing, and Raymond stopped to introduce Ozzie to a dentist and an orthodontist who were arguing over whether eighteen-year-old Hank Aaron had made the right choice leaving the Indianapolis Clowns for the Boston Braves.

Then they stopped in the kitchen, where a bar was set up and a man in a black suit was pouring the real stuff. Ozzie felt his tongue salivate as Raymond got into a conversation with three men holding double old-fashioned glasses.

"Ray, I love this album by Bud Powell," said the man wearing a tweed sport coat. "It's one of his best, but whenever I hear it, it reminds me of how awful things got for the brother. He's one of the baddest piano players I've ever heard."

"Yeah, that beating he took on Broad Street by the railroad police changed the trajectory of his life," commented Ray.

"Don't it always."

"Friend of mine said Bud is up at Pilgrim State now. You know—the psychiatric hospital. Got him on shock treatments. Said the doctors don't even let him near the piano."

"That don't make no sense. That cat was a genius."

"Whitey sure knows how to break a man."

Ozzie nodded in the right places; while he had never been beaten down by the police, he'd had his run-ins with the authorities.

"Gentlemen," Raymond finally interrupted. "Where are my manners. Ozzie, these loudmouths are my dearest friends. John Francis Williams, Lewis Tanner Moore, and M. Hubbard. These men are the best damn lawyers in the City of Brotherly Love."

"And don't let no one tell you different." Lewis slapped Raymond five, and they all laughed.

"This is Ozzie Philips, Rita's husband. He's a manager at the shipyard, just got out of the army."

"Very honorable of you," John said, sipping from his glass.

"Make yourself right at home. Get a drink," Lewis pushed.

"Good to meet you," Ozzie said.

Then the men turned their backs and returned to their conversation. Ozzie couldn't find his way into their discussion, and unable to shake the feeling that he didn't belong, he slunk away and sidled up to the man behind the bar at the rear of the kitchen.

Once he had a fresh drink in his hand, he felt some of his power return. Raymond took hold of Ozzie again and introduced him to a doctor and a judge. Then a restaurateur and his wife. All the names blurred together. Each professional introduction felt fancier than the last, and as the night wore on, the liquor stopped giving him courage. Ozzie felt his confidence seep out of him like the helium from a party balloon. Echoing inside of his head was *You ain't shit, and you'll never measure up to these men.*

Raymond got pulled into a lengthy chat, and Ozzie excused himself for another stop at the bar, but the bartender had stepped away. Ozzie looked around and then helped himself to an aged Scotch that went down so silky smooth that before he had swallowed good, he was pouring another fistful. Then he found a stool just off the kitchen that was unoccupied. It had a full view of the living and dining room, but he was shrouded in darkness and out of sight.

As Ozzie watched the people laugh and dance, it was crystal-clear that this was a party of "who's who" in Negro society. Ozzie had not met another working-class man without a title or a degree, not unless he included the maid and the bartender. How had these folks gotten so financially far in life? What was Ozzie doing here pretending like he had anything in common with them? He moved materials down at the shipyard for seventy-five cents an hour. They lived in his wife's great-aunt's house. In that moment, he felt like he didn't have a pot to piss in or a window to throw it out.

Rita had invited him to one other work event since he had returned home. The Alexanders had held an NAACP fundraiser in their offices at Nineteenth and Chestnut streets last month. To that event, Ozzie had worn the same suit. He wondered now if Raymond Alexander had noticed and pitied him for it. Was Raymond looking down his nose at Ozzie, knowing instinctively that he didn't measure up? It was easy for him to introduce Ozzie around his fine home, because the job of the host was to make a guest feel welcome whether he was worthy or not. That was just good manners and did not mean Ozzie had Raymond's respect.

Perhaps Raymond's kindness had all been a hoax for Rita's sake, because the Alexanders were invested in her future with their law firm. They'd helped her get a full scholarship to University of Pennsylvania, for goodness' sake. Once she became one of them, and fully ascended into their world, what would Ozzie have to offer her? He couldn't catch up to these folks in the room right now, even if they gave him a pocketful of money and a head start.

"Hey, good-lookin', what's cookin'?" Rita had sneaked up on him. She smelled of champagne, and her cheeks were flushed. "Babe, this is simply the best night of my life. Are you having fun?"

This was the best night of her life? Not the night their wedding reception had spilled out onto Ringgold Street, where they had danced under the stars and then made love until the sheets were sliding from the bed?

The music playing on the phonograph had gotten louder. A horn was whining. It sounded like Miles Davis. Ozzie tapped his feet on the white oak floor as a strumming pounded in the back of his head.

"You been socializing?" she asked, sitting down in his lap.

He draped one arm around her waist while thinking: How long would it be before Rita's girlhood crush on him wore off, and these high-siddity men in suits got her attention?

"Of course."

"I saw Raymond introducing you around."

"Yeah."

Rita balanced herself on his thigh. "He's great and so supportive of Sadie's career."

"I bet he is, he can damn near pass for white. Doors must fall open at his command." The comment had floated through his mind and left his mouth before he could filter it.

"What did you say?" Rita turned her face toward his, her brows knitted.

"Nothing." He cleared his throat.

"Don't be rude. We're guests in their home."

"I know exactly where we are," Ozzie retorted.

"You talking like you ain't got good sense. Like you left the screws from your head in Germany." She sniffed, then peered at him more closely. "How many of those have you had?"

"Stop studying me, woman." His voice came out raspy. "I'm cool."

"Goddamn it. I asked you to pace yourself."

"You don't have to tell me nothing, I'm a grown-ass man." Ozzie could feel Rita stiffen on his lap, and then she stood up.

"Make that your last one," she whispered. "Don't be embarrassing me like that time you punched Harold in the face. This ain't no South Philly rent party."

"Why you gotta bring that up?"

"'Cause you don't know how to act once you get that liquor in you," she said.

Ozzie didn't like her tone. She didn't know the weight that was pressed down on him so heavy, it was hard to breathe at times like these. "I don't need you policing me. I get enough of that at the shipyard," he said the moment the music stopped. Rita shook her head at him just as Sadie's skirt swished around her knees at Rita's side.

"You lovebirds all right?" Sadie asked, and Ozzie couldn't tell if she had heard and was pretending that she hadn't, but he didn't miss the anger that flashed through Rita's eyes.

"I was just coming to say my goodbyes." Rita turned to Sadie and threaded her arm with hers. "Would you come with me as I thank Martha one last time?"

"Certainly," Sadie responded, and then they moved through the crowd.

Ozzie drained his glass and sucked on an ice cube. He needed to pee and found the powder room through a small door underneath the stairs. As he was moving back toward the kitchen, a man with a thick mustache stopped him. "Hey, fellow. Could you make me an old-fashioned on the rocks?"

Ozzie shook his head to clear his thoughts. "Excuse me?"

"With whiskey, not brandy, please." The man touched his pocket watch in his waistcoat pocket.

Then it dawned on Ozzie what was happening. "I'm not the help," he said, then pushed past the man and out the front door. As he was closing the door behind him, he heard Raymond call his name over the music, but he did not stop. He staggered down the front steps and into the fresh air, which eased the suffocating weight that had been sitting on his throat.

When he pulled the car around, Rita did not wait for him to get out and open her door. She plopped down in the passenger seat and said, "You sure know how to show your ass and ruin a good night."

He pulled away from the curb. "Why didn't you tell me you were applying to Penn?"

"What difference does it make which schools I apply to? The important thing is that I go."

Ozzie flicked his turn signal and then made a right turn onto Broad Street, careful to stay in between the white lines. "The Alexanders tell you to keep that from me?"

"What? No." Rita fumbled with her gloves in her lap. "It was a long shot. I didn't even think I'd get in."

"It would have been good to know what my wife was doing. I stood there smiling like a fool."

"You played the fool all on your own. Drinking like a fish, then sitting in the corner by yourself like a damn recluse."

He pulled to the corner of Ringgold Street and was glad to see a spot that he could slide the car into without needing to parallel park. Rita hopped out of the car before he could kill the engine. She had no reason to be mad. He should be the one upset.

He dropped his keys in the candy dish on the end table in the living room. The stairs creaked under his weight. When he reached their back bedroom door and turned the knob, he found it was locked.

"Sleep on the couch," Rita shouted at him.

He tried again, softening his voice. "Come on, baby. Don't be like that."

"If you wake my aunt . . ." Her voice trailed off.

Rita was as stubborn as an elephant's leg. There was no sense in trying to bend her. He shuffled down the stairs and then into the basement and flung himself on the green sofa.

As he tossed, he replayed Rita's comment. *You act like you left the screws from your head in Germany.* He hadn't left the bolts and nuts to his head, but he had left a chunk of his heart and a piece of his soul.

Katja.

His three-year-old daughter was lost to him, and that gutted him deep in his core. What kind of man was he?

And with Rita moving into this new elite world, he didn't know what he could offer her either. He was happy for her and so proud, but in the same breath, he was more unsure of himself than he had ever been in his life.

CHAPTER 44

Philadelphia, PA, December 1952

OZZIE

Contrition crept in as Ozzie relived the fight with Rita. *I behaved like an idiot,* he thought, folding the blankets and stacking them at the end of the sofa. When he came up from the basement, a pot of coffee sat on the stove, and Rita had left him a plate with scrambled eggs and three pieces of crispy bacon, still hot. Ozzie took that as a good sign. She didn't hate him, it wasn't over, and he would spend the whole weekend making it up to her.

After he ate, he slipped into an old pair of dungarees and coat and worked through the honey-do list that she had been after him to tackle for the past two weeks. He changed dead lightbulbs, replaced batteries, fixed the leak underneath the bathroom sink, checked the mousetraps, and sprinkled poison down near the cracks in the basement floor and wall. He was in the yard spraying insect killer around the perimeter of the back of the house when he saw Rita standing behind the screen door.

"You're back," he said, with the nozzle for the pesticide dangling from his hand.

"You almost finished out there?"

"Just gotta store this under the house." He held up the jug.

Once he'd put everything away, he stepped into the box-shaped kitchen. Rita stood leaning against the sink, her hair pulled away from her face.

"About last night," he said, removing his overcoat and draping it on the back of a kitchen chair. The rubber gloves, he peeled from his fingers and then tossed them into the metal garbage can next to the sink.

"What about it?" She fingered the button on the bottom of her sweater.

"I shouldn't have said those things about the Alexanders. They are good people. And I'm proud of you for getting that scholarship."

"I wasn't keeping secrets from you. I just didn't want you to be disappointed in me if I didn't get in."

"I could never be disappointed in you, baby. Do you realize how far you have come? You have a college degree. You are going to law school. It's me who should be ashamed." He dropped his gaze.

"Now you talkin' foolish."

He looked up at her, and she stared right back.

"I wouldn't be here if it wasn't for you. Your letters, the money you sent me. I would have dropped out. I would have been working at the Alexanders' house, not at their law firm," she said, and the skin behind Ozzie's ears prickled as he remembered the pocket-watch man asking him to make him a drink.

"I got a little intimidated is all. So many successful people in the room. Made me feel not good enough and out of place." He looked down at his feet. Rita was the one person in the world to whom he could confess his insecurities, but the words still scraped at his manhood as they left his mouth.

"That crowd can be a bit daunting, but you don't have anything to be ashamed about. I use their successes as fuel. People like that let me know that my dreams are possible. That we can reach high and come back with the stars too."

Ozzie wanted to look at it that way, but sometimes it was hard to see past his own circumstance. "Will you forgive my diarrhea of the mouth?"

"I guess I can get past it." She tilted her head. "Just don't drink so much. You've been emptying a lot of bottles around here lately. I need you to pace yourself. One, maybe two drinks, and then stop. Six, seven, and you start acting foolish."

"Okay, I'll do better," he said, and then reached for her hand, but she pulled away.

"I mean it, Oz. I work for these people. We are trying to advance right alongside them, and I can't have them thinking that I'm unfit because of you."

"I get it. I'm sorry, and it won't happen again." He lifted her chin. "And I'm proud of you. Last night showed me that you're really doing big things. A full scholarship to Penn, damn, girl."

Rita exhaled. "Now that I'm in the school, the real work begins. I'm going to need your support. I can't do this without you."

"You won't have to." He kissed her on the forehead. "We are in this together."

On Monday morning, Rita woke Ozzie up with twenty-four kisses to mark his twenty-fourth birthday. The nearness of her sweet-smelling body made Ozzie swell, but when he tried to bring her back to bed with him, Rita scooted out of reach.

"Put that away for now, cowboy." She moved toward the closet. "Sadie has invited me to court with her today, and I can't be late."

"Five more minutes for the birthday boy." He reached out his arms to her.

Rita slipped into a knit black dress and tugged up her zipper. "You know you'll want more than five minutes." She blew him a kiss and was down the steps in a whirl of perfume, lipstick, and promises of cake before he could give her a rebuttal.

Once Rita was gone, the room turned cold. The quiet of the morning gave his mind too much room to roam. To feel and remember. Despondency opened in the pit of his stomach as he swung his legs over the side of the bed. In addition to today being his birthday, it also marked the two-year anniversary of the last time he had laid eyes on his Kitten.

His Katja.

Her absence haunted him most days, and while he had managed to live with it, already this morning it felt unbearable. Ozzie knew he should have been in the bathroom ten minutes ago, but as he stared out the back window at the cloudy sky, he felt like a rudderless boat on a choppy sea. A soul sickness spread through Ozzie that hurt worse than being trampled by ten horses.

He searched for a recollection of a good moment with Katja, but all he kept picturing was her wailing bloody murder when he put her down on the rug so that he could leave the house with Jelka. Worse, he remembered hearing her crying as they had slipped into the taxi. It was like Katja had known something that Ozzie hadn't. As if she had sensed it would be their last time together, and he felt remorseful that he had not been able to change their fate.

The clock ticked on the side of the bed. Ozzie needed to get going so that he wouldn't be late for work. He dragged himself down the tiny hall but passed the bathroom for the middle bedroom. The room was so narrow that they used it only for storage. The closet with the wooden sliding door was all his, and he knelt on the shaggy carpet and slid out his army footlocker.

Inside, he opened the tin container with a German cottage hand-painted on the front. He sat on the floor with his legs stretched out in front of him and opened the box. Katja's face smiled up at him. Ozzie took each picture out and lined them up in age order. There were thirty Polaroids in the box, and he let his time with Katja play in front of him like a picture show. He took in her sweet face, her heart-shaped mouth, and her voluminous hair, the ones when she started to get teeth. Then he held up the photo that Jelka had insisted they take together as a family, one of the few pictures in which Katja had not smiled.

"Ozzie? You ain't left for work yet?" called Great-aunt Reese. "You know I like privacy when I'm in the bathroom." He could hear her standing in the doorway to her bedroom. The hall was short, and even though she moved with a limp, it would take her only four or five steps to reach him. He swooped the photos up quickly, shoving them in the tin, and pushed his footlocker back into the closet just as she made it to the doorway.

"What you doin' in here, anyway?"

"I was looking for a shirt."

"On the floor?" She looked down at him.

"I couldn't remember where I put it."

"Well, I need to get in the bathroom. Got a doctor's appointment at ten."

"I'll be quick." Ozzie got up.

"Happy birthday," Aunt Reese said.

"Thank you."

Ozzie scrambled into the bathroom, and when he stared up at himself in the mirror, he hated what he saw. The only idea he had come up with to find his daughter was to place an ad in the classified section of the local newspaper in Mannheim, the *Mannheimer Morgen,* with the hope that Jelka would see it. He didn't like that he had kept such a big secret from Rita, but as time passed, he didn't know how to tell her without looking like a complete loser. As he turned on the faucet, he heard the words *deadbeat, fraud, failure* echo over the stream of water. Then the thought of a tall, stiff drink—promising him that with a few sips, it would make his hurt, pain, self-doubt, and shame all vanish—seized hold.

CHAPTER 45

Washington, D.C., December 1965

SOPHIA

The photograph felt like cardboard between her fingertips. Even though the photo was in black and white, she could tell the hair that fell over her forehead was red in color. She traced her finger across her lips.

"This is me." Sophia was shaking all over. "I found me," she whispered, clutching the picture against her heart.

Mrs. Gathers reached over to pick up the files, and as she studied the papers, she rested her hand under her chin.

"Katja Durchdenwald," Mrs. Gathers mumbled. "Yes, this makes sense. Now I remember the little girl with the red hair."

"Katja?" Sophia said, breathless. "Is . . . that my real name?"

Mrs. Gathers nodded. "I believe so." Then she flipped over one of the forms in the file and blurted, "Yes, I recall meeting your mother."

Sophia couldn't get enough air in her lungs when she sputtered, "My mother?"

The woman who sat across from her had met her mother. Even though this was what Sophia had searched for, it still felt surreal. Was it really happening?

"Tell me about her," Sophia pleaded. "What was she like? Why did she give me away?"

Mrs. Gathers sighed, then looked up at the clock. "You've experienced a lot today, dear. Maybe it's best that we stop here. I have already trodden on your parents' toes, and my own children will be arriving from school any minute."

"Please, Mrs. Gathers." Sophia could hear the panic in her voice. "Just tell me what you remember. We've come this far. Just a few more minutes, please."

"Let me take the chicken out of the oven." Mrs. Gathers rose to her feet and then disappeared out the door.

Sophia picked up the file again. Her mother. She had found her mother. How long would it be before she could meet her in person? Was she still in Germany? How in heaven's name would she get to Germany to reunite with her?

Mrs. Gathers brought the scent of rosemary and thyme back with her as she crossed the room and sat behind the desk. "Where was I?"

"You said you met my mother."

"Well, I know she hadn't wanted to give you up for adoption, which was the case for many of the German women, but she didn't feel that she had a choice." Mrs. Gathers clasped her hands in front of her.

"What do you mean?"

"Her . . . family situation was unstable. She took you to St. Hildegard's orphanage because she knew that it was a place where you'd be safe."

Sophia felt the pressure that had been like a weight in her belly lift a bit. She had been right all along in knowing that she did not belong to the Clarks. They had brought her to this country more as a servant than as a child to love. She had known something wasn't right. But what of her brothers? Were they brought here too? Were they even related? But before she could ask questions about her brothers, Mrs. Gathers interrupted her.

"Dear, I really must let you go."

"But—"

"I realize that I made a grave mistake with the mix-up in your identity, and for that I am truly sorry. But you should talk to the Clarks. I've already said too much."

Sophia continued as if she hadn't heard Mrs. Gathers. "And my father?"

"I just know that he was an American. Negro."

Her father. Sophia let the thought of him settle over her and felt a pang in her belly for him too. "Did either of them visit me in the orphanage?"

Mrs. Gathers stood but then stopped in front of the office door. "Most of the mothers did as often as they could. I must stress that many of the women didn't give up their children because they wanted to. It was a different time back then, and they simply had no other choice."

As Sophia followed Mrs. Gathers out, the smell of the roast chicken made her mouth water. How much time had passed since Unc had served her the eggs? When they reached the foyer, Sophia stopped at the door and turned. "Mrs. Gathers, will you help me find her? My mother, I mean?"

"Oh, dear, I have given you everything that I have. I'm afraid the official records are sealed."

"What does that mean?"

Mrs. Gathers placed her hand over her heart. "It means that the reports have been filed away by the German government, and there is no way to access them."

"But you said you knew my mother." Sophia could hear her voice raising with panic.

"I did . . ." Mrs. Gathers stammered. "But I can't . . ."

"Please. I need to know who I am. Can you imagine going through life without knowing your true identity?"

"It's quite expensive to call Germany."

"Maybe you could at least write a letter to the orphanage on my behalf? Please, I've come this far."

Mrs. Gathers slowly nodded. "Let me see what I can do to make this right." She reached out her arms to Sophia, and Sophia fell against her breasts. The sobbing was instant, and as she wept, Sophia could feel Mrs. Gathers tracing comforting circles on her back.

Sophia stepped onto the bus and paid her twenty-cent fare. On the ten-minute walk from the bus stop to the rooming house on A Street, her pinkie toe had rubbed against the leather of her shoe until it blistered. At the corner of the block, Sophia searched for Unc's Chevy Impala, and when she didn't see it, she let herself into the house.

A baby wailed from a room on the second floor, and she could hear the bang of pots and pans and heavy footsteps overhead as she walked through to the kitchen. The canister that read "Flour" was where she had left it, and she reached for it, moved around the buttons and safety pins, and buried the house key. In the living room, she collapsed onto the brown burlap sofa, her mind reeling with all the things she had garnered from Mrs. Gathers, and from the pieces she could only speculate about for now.

What was she supposed to do with all that she had learned? Unc was going to take her back to the farm in the morning, and there was the perpetual worry that Ma Deary would forbid her to return to school. So many thoughts spun in her head that she felt like her ears were ringing.

Sophia pulled her coat over her for a blanket, rested her head on the scratchy throw pillow, and fell asleep to the thought of getting on an airplane for the first time and flying to Germany to meet her mother. She had hoped a picture of her real mother's face would come to her in her dreams, but she saw only legs and the flames from the fire, felt heat shooting up her thighs and her skin splitting. Her voice thundered in her ears. She was screaming.

A heavy hand slapped her across the face, and when she opened her eyes, she blinked them several times, hoping that she was still dreaming.

"Still carrying on like you ain't got good sense."

Ma Deary leaned over Sophia in her white uniform, smashing her big breasts into Sophia's face. She smelled of disinfectant, cigarette smoke, and sweat. "Come on here, so we can get home before first light. Cows ain't goin' to milk themselves."

Sophia pressed her hand against her throbbing cheek. Then she remembered where she was and what she had discovered last night.

"Rusty, I ain't got all day. I worked a double shift, and my dogs are tired. Now, 'less you want to walk your ass back to the farm, you better come on." Ma slung her pleated hobo purse over her shoulder and turned toward the hallway, and her footsteps reverberated out the front door.

Sophia found her Mary Janes, then picked up her train case and huffed after Ma Deary. It was dark out, and a frigid chill blew through her as she teetered behind Ma Deary. The red Rambler was parked three houses down at the curb. When Sophia slid into the front seat, the car was still warm, and the beige interior smelled like Ma Deary's lily-of-the-valley perfume, reminding Sophia of home.

"How'd you know I was here?"

Ma Deary flipped open a box of Lucky Strikes and slipped a cigarette between her faded purple lips. "How you think?" She flicked her red Winston lighter, closed her eyes, and pulled until the tip of the cigarette was bright orange. "Wayon called me on my job, and you know I don't like that shit. Talking about how you just showed up at the house."

"I didn't know where else to go."

Ma Deary released the brake, pulled on the clutch, and steered the Rambler away from the curb. "Why ain't you up at that fancy school? You done run away from there too?" She blew smoke out the side of her mouth.

Sophia waved fumes from in front of her face. "That's not it."

"I knew it." Ma Deary switched the clutch from third to fourth gear. "Got all the way up there and realized that your raggedy ass didn't belong, just like I said."

"School is closed for the holiday." Sophia bit her bottom lip.

She had belonged enough. Hadn't she? A cola bottle rolled around on the floor in the seat behind her, and she closed her eyes to the memory.

Looks like someone is stripped down so that everyone can see what a fine field nigger she'd make . . . How much would you pay for her?

Sophia did not want to think about Patty violating her in the locker room or feel the emptiness that had stretched inside her since leaving Mrs. Gathers's home. She had no clue what to do next. Sophia had thought Unc would drive her back to the farm, giving her time to think of what her next move would be. She wanted to confront Ma Deary, demand more information out of her, but each time she stole glances out of the side of her eye, Ma Deary's scowl stopped her in her tracks.

Sophia knew from experience that Ma Deary's anger was not to be stoked. Last summer, when Sophia had refused to go up to the garden to pick the vegetables because the news had declared that everyone should stay inside due to the extreme heat wave, Ma Deary had replied, "You worried about the heat? You should be worried about me."

Then she'd dragged Sophia to the shed and locked her in with no water for hours. Sophia had sat in the corner on the dirt, sweating and swallowing her saliva. When Ma Deary finally let her out,

Sophia's mouth was dry as cotton, her legs weak from lack of sustenance, and Ma Deary still refused her dinner until she went up to the garden and came back with the crop.

The memory haunted Sophia, but she realized that being denied food, working in the heat, even the strap that Ma Deary hung on a rusted nail in the barn to keep the kids in line, wasn't her biggest fear. What Sophia was most afraid of was Ma Deary preventing her return to school. Sophia's chest tightened at the thought of being confined to the farm again with no future in sight. She decided she would hold her identity close until she had a chance to talk it through with Walter. He had always been her voice of reason and would know what to do next.

The sun looked like an egg, sunny side up, low in the sky, as they turned off the main street and meandered onto the narrow tobacco road. The tires jolted over grit and gravel as the Rambler moved toward the farmhouse, while the rooster crowed and crowed, welcoming Sophia back home. Ma Deary pulled up to the front door and killed the engine. The bald spots in the roof where the shingles were missing still hadn't been repaired. Metal bumpers in varying sizes, left over from old vehicles and tractors, were scattered all over the patchy front lawn. The plastic that covered the front windowpane buckled and blew with the wind.

"How many hands you got working the farm now?" Sophia asked.

"Depends who shows. Today might be two or three." Ma Deary opened her car door and stretched her legs in front of her. "Go on and change clothes and give your brothers a hand. The twins don't seem to know their head from a hole in the damn ground without you."

Karl, Lu, and Walter. Sophia's heart fluttered at the thought of her brothers. *Biological or otherwise.*

As she walked along the side of the house, the early-morning chirp of crickets and the jug-a-rum of the bullfrogs relaxed her breathing.

Dead leaves cracked beneath her feet as she rounded the bend. In the distance, she could hear the horses, cows, and pigs waking, and the smells of fresh dew, earth, and manure unleashed a familiarity inside of her that she hadn't known she had missed. Just as she reached for the screen door to the kitchen, she heard "Rusty, that you?"

Sophia turned to see Walter, and her whole body smiled as he barreled toward her, swooped her up in his arms, and gripped her so hard that she was sure if he didn't let go soon, she would snap in two.

"Whatcha doing here?"

"We're on break."

"It's good to have you home." He smiled, a piece of straw resting at the side of his lips. He was wearing his Carhartt chore coat over bib overalls, and his hair had grown into a limp Afro.

"Somebody needs a haircut." She reached up and tousled it.

"You just ain't been 'round to cut it for me." He grinned.

"Well, you have an official appointment."

Walter chuckled as Ma Deary descended the stairs and tsked her teeth. She said, "Reunion over. Go on and wake the boys and get to your chores. And Rusty, after you pull the eggs, make sure them boys clean up that barn. Smells like hot piss and old cabbage in there." She let the door slam behind her.

Sophia and Walter exchanged looks and then burst out laughing.

"Welcome home, sis. You're going to have to tell me all about it."

"As soon as the boys are off to school and she's asleep." Sophia pushed her hair back. "Meet me at our spot near the cornfields."

Sophia pulled the sherpa blanket tighter over her coat and put her hands over the fire that Walter had built for them. They were out on the edge of the farm near the garden, in a patch under an ancient elm tree. Walter had skewered a sausage link on a sharpened stick and held it to the fire. Sophia watched as he concentrated on rotating the meat so that it wouldn't burn. The fire licked and crackled, and the smoky scent made her salivate.

"You let your hair go back to red," he said, looking up.

"I didn't have a choice. No dye at school." She pushed her hair back over her shoulders. She had let it hang loose under her wool skull cap.

"I like you better like that." He elbowed her.

Sophia tugged on her hat. "Walt . . . I gotta tell you something."

"Shoot." Walter pulled the sausage back from the fire, tucked it in a piece of foil, and then hung a second raw sausage on the stick and thrust it over the flames.

"I don't know where to start." She caught his eye.

"The beginning sounds like a good place."

"I met a boy."

"Oooh, Rusty has a crush," he teased.

"It's not that." She watched as the heat made the sausage sweat and drip. "There's a bit more to it."

She told Walter about the Old South Ball, finding out that Max was adopted from Germany, the shared fire, how the German phrase just came out of her mouth.

"What did you say?"

"Auf Wiedersehen," she said softly. "Which means 'goodbye.' It felt like it bubbled up from some place deep inside of me. A dormant place that I hadn't known existed."

Walter turned the sausage while she recounted going home with Willa for Thanksgiving break and meeting the woman in the library. "Mrs. Porter Wesley was her name, I think. She gave me these articles. Apparently, there were hundreds or thousands of children abandoned in Germany called 'Brown Babies' or 'War Babies.' They were children of German mothers and the Negro G.I.'s who were stationed there." She took a breath. "This woman, Ethel Gathers, adopted a bunch of kids of her own, I think she has like eight, and then helped other American families adopt the half-Negro kids so they wouldn't be stuck in the orphanage."

Walter lifted the meat from the fire as Sophia told him how she had found Mrs. Gathers in the white pages and shown up at her house.

"Why would you do that?" Walter wrapped the sausage in foil and handed it to her.

"There was something inside me that needed to know." She swallowed. "If I was one of those babies brought here."

She expected Walter to laugh, but he didn't. He held her gaze. "And?"

"Turns out I am. I was adopted, Walter. My real name is Katja."

Walter cast his eyes down to the ground. Sophia knew he would be disappointed that she wasn't his blood sister. But her brothers were all she knew, and she could never love them any less, bloodline or not.

"I know," Walter spoke up.

Sophia choked on her sausage. "You what?" He handed her his canteen of water, and she drank. "Walt? What do you mean, you know?"

"I've always known. I remember the long plane ride. Walking through the airport with the cameras flashing. Then us riding in the car with Ma Deary and the Old Man."

"So we came here together? You were the boy Mrs. Gathers mentioned?"

Walter nodded.

"How did I miss that?" She shook her head.

"When we first got here, you and I used to whisper in German, but Ma Deary put a stop to it. She said if she heard us speaking German, she would slap our faces. So we stopped."

"You knew? And you never told me!"

Walter looked at Sophia with droopy eyes. "I wanted to tell you on the drive to West Oak Forest, but I didn't want to burden you with too much."

"Before then, Walter. You could have told me years ago."

"Honestly, I had started to forget. As cruel as Ma Deary can be, farm life suits me. I'm at peace here, so I just never thought about it."

Sophia put her sausage back in the foil. If she needed any more proof that she was one of the Brown Babies, Walter had just given it to her.

"What do we do now? What about Karl and Lu?"

"We keep our mouths shut. No sense making a song and dance about nothing. We tell them when they are older."

"I can't live like this, not anymore. It feels like I'm just drifting, with nothing to anchor me. I have to find my real mother. I need answers."

Walter held his hands over the flame. "You sure about that? Ma Deary would blow a gasket if she caught wind of any of this."

"Mrs. Gathers said she'd help me. I've come so far in just a few weeks. I need to see this to the end." Sophia unwrapped the sausage again and took a bite.

"Okay."

"Okay, what?"

"If you want to see this through, I'll help you."

CHAPTER 46

Philadelphia, PA, April 1954

OZZIE

The kitchen smelled freshly scrubbed with bleach, and the transistor radio that sat in the window was tuned to the morning news. Ozzie sipped his second cup of coffee while listening to the daily reports.

Rita had come up from the basement in her housecoat and slippers. A basket of laundry rested in the crook of her arm. "Morning." She repositioned the basket, reached down, and kissed him on the top of his head. She smelled of Ivory soap.

Rita's first year of law school had taken up her days with legal principles, civil procedures, and moot court exercises. Ozzie didn't know how she still managed to get chores completed in between. The house was always spick-and-span.

"What time are you heading off to school?"

Rita placed the basket on the dining room table, which she often used as a laundry counter. "Once I sort these clothes and get dressed, I want to stop by the library to follow up on a case I've been studying."

"What's it about?" Ozzie turned toward Rita and watched as she folded a bundle of towels.

"You'd find it interesting. Back in 1924, two men were shoved onto a train. One of them dropped a package of explosives that caused a penny-weighing machine to crash down onto a woman passenger's head."

"Jesus."

"She was injured so badly that she became mute." Rita moved the pile of towels aside and picked up a fitted sheet. "We're having a debate about who was at fault for the woman's injuries, the man or the railroad company."

"Sounds interesting," Ozzie said as Rita carried the folded laundry upstairs.

In some ways, he envied Rita's studies. For the nearly two years he'd been home, he had little time for reading. He had only retained German well enough to mail his quarterly search ad in for the classified section of the *Mannheimer Morgen,* with the hope that Jelka would see it. The ad hadn't yielded a response yet, and beyond translating the notice, he hadn't stretched his mind in any capacity. He couldn't find the time. His favorite author, Richard Wright, had published a new book, *Savage Holiday,* and he hadn't even had time to purchase it, let alone read it.

Then Rita marched into the kitchen with such a heavy step that it caused Ozzie to look up from his coffee. "What's wrong?"

Her eyes blazed as she harshly whispered, "Great-aunt Reese just said you haven't paid her the rent yet?"

Ozzie's fingers tightened around his mug. "I know."

"Well, when do you plan on paying it? It was due two weeks ago. She said if she don't get the money from us, the electricity is liable to be shut off."

"I'll take care of it on Friday, once I get paid."

"You said that two weeks ago." Her voice cracked, and Ozzie felt shame bloom throughout his chest as he recalled his tab at Wally's, the local bar that he frequented after his shift. Ozzie scratched his head, unsure how his weekly bill had gotten so out of control that it had impacted the rent.

"Few things came up. But nothing to worry about." He stood, placed his cup in the sink, and then picked up the lunch pail she had packed.

Rita sighed. "Oz, I know it's a lot on you, paying all the bills while I go to school. But Sadie said my job at the law firm is always there if I ever need to return and make a few—"

"No," he barked. "You have enough to worry about with your studies. I'll take care of our finances."

Rita wrung her hands. "I appreciate it, you know I do. But this isn't like when I was in college. We have responsibilities now."

"Listen." Ozzie reached for her hands and brought them to his lips. "It's my job to provide for you, and I will."

The uncertainty in Rita's eyes would haunt him for the rest of the day. He tried to quell her concern by brushing a stray hair from her cheek and then giving her a swift kiss. "I gotta go."

As he moved past her into the front room, he had no idea where he'd get the back rent. He did know he didn't want Raymond Alexander to think that Rita had married a loser. They had already helped Rita get that full scholarship to attend Penn for free. All Ozzie had to do was keep a roof over her head and food in her belly, and he would do it come hell or high water.

When he reached the door, Rita called after him. "You haven't said much about returning to school yourself. Your acceptance letters to Lincoln and Cheyney are in the mail drawer, collecting dust."

Ozzie felt his posture collapse as he closed the door behind him. Outside, the clouds were rolling in, and he could smell the sweet pungent scent of an April shower on the rise. He kicked an empty soda can and then shoved his hands in his pants pockets as he walked down the street. Of course he'd like to go back to school, get a college degree, and work a career instead of just a job. But there weren't enough hours in the day. As it stood, he was going to have to ask his boss to put him on the docket for possible overtime, which was hard to get because the white boys always got priority.

Ozzie had applied for jobs at the Philadelphia Transit Company as a conductor and a bus driver, but he hadn't heard back. He had taken on a cleanup job down at the docks two nights a week, but most of that money he had sunk into new brake pads and tires for the Chrysler. Two dollars a month went to the Federal Eagle Club in Mannheim for Katja despite never hearing a word back. But as Ozzie stepped up on the trolley, he knew that the bulk of his money was being spent at Wally's on the evenings Rita was at school, and he'd have to stop drinking at the bar, at least until he caught up on things. When he slumped down into the plastic seat, he was exhausted, and he hadn't even gotten to work.

After much pleading, Sissy, his older sister, lent him the money and Ozzie paid Great-aunt Reese the following day, much to Rita's relief. For the remainder of the workweek, they went their separate ways, disappearing into their singular lives of work, school, hustle, rush, and haste. On Saturday afternoon, they took a stroll around the lake, and then Rita rolled out a blanket and they sat eating egg-salad sandwiches and potato chips while watching the ducks.

Every Sunday evening after the dinner dishes were clean, Ozzie scoured *The Philadelphia Tribune* and the *Inquirer* for notices that might be for him from Jelka. It was a long shot, but the search kept him from feeling useless. After he read the sports section, he folded *The Philadelphia Inquirer* lengthwise and worked on the weekly crossword puzzle to get his mind off what he hadn't found. An open can of Schlitz rested at his elbows.

"The first name of a politician whose last name sounds like 'raft,'" he mumbled to himself while readjusting the pillows underneath his head.

"William Taft," Rita called from the bathroom.

"Yes, that's right." Ozzie scribbled.

"Babe, what do you think of this?" Rita stood at the foot of their bed in a ruffled black-and-tan-plaid dress that hugged her hips.

The sight of her still took Ozzie's breath away. "Wow, pretty mama. Where you going, looking so fine?" The crossword puzzle dropped from his hand on the floor as he slid to the edge of their bed.

"I told you." She drew out the words. "Tomorrow evening I'm being presented with the Stout Legal Skills award at Penn."

"Remind me what that is again."

"Ozzie, you don't listen to anything I say," she said, pouting.

"Not true." He rose to his feet and placed his hands on her waist and pulled her to him. "You just have so much good news, it's hard to keep up."

"I need you to listen with your ears."

"Okay, tell me about this award."

"Well, it's presented at the end of the second year to the top legal-skills student, and that just happens to be me. It comes with a certificate and a cash prize."

He tipped his chin. "How much?"

"They haven't said, but knowing Penn, it'll be a good amount. I'm hoping we can set it aside toward our down payment on the house."

He let her go and reached for his beer, mumbling under his breath, "If the bank ever approves our mortgage."

"Patience, Ozzie. It'll happen. We just need to keep operating on faith."

He didn't want to go down that road with Rita again. They had gone back and forth with several banks for over a year, and nothing had come of his promise from the G.I. Bill. They were still crammed into the back room of Great-aunt Reese's house.

"You winning the award at Penn and outshining them white folks is enough for me." He drained the beer and then carried the empty toward the bedroom door.

"That your second beer?" Rita called as he moved down the steps.

"I'm done for the night, you don't have to worry."

Two beers for Ozzie was like drinking water. But she had put him on a two-drink maximum, and he knew if he wanted to keep the peace, he couldn't carry another beer upstairs. In the dining room, Ozzie listened for movement and then pulled open the bottom drawer of the buffet. Underneath a white tablecloth lay a fifth of Four Roses bourbon. Ozzie cracked it open and then took a few swigs, just enough to help him sleep, he reasoned. Then he lifted the glass lid from the dish meant for candy but which contained mixed nuts in the corner of the buffet. Ozzie crunched on a handful to mask the smell on his breath.

When he reached the bedroom, Rita had changed into her nightgown and was turning over on her side. "Penn don't operate on CP Time, baby, so please be on time."

Ozzie flipped off the lights. "I hear you, woman, and I'll be there."

CHAPTER 47

Prince Frederick, MD, January 1966

SOPHIA

On the first Sunday of the New Year, Unc picked Sophia up from the farm and drove her back to Forest. Much to Sophia's surprise, Ma Deary had grunted a simple goodbye, but she hadn't prohibited Sophia from leaving.

When he pulled up to the stately wrought-iron gates with "West Oak Forest Academy" stenciled in gold, Unc blew a long whistle through his teeth. "Woo-wee, this place is nice. Rusty, girl, you living like them Kennedys," he teased, and popped his collar.

Sophia smiled. "It's been a good experience so far," she said, trying not to think of Patty and the humiliation she'd suffered in that locker room.

Unc slipped from behind the wheel and grabbed her suitcase out of the trunk of the car. Sophia checked the front seat, making sure she had everything, and then stood beside him in the roundabout. Side by side, they remained in silence as they watched teary-eyed mothers in shearling, fox, and beaver furs hug teens goodbye before driving away in luxury cars. He handed Sophia her tattered bag.

"Thanks for the ride, Unc. I don't think Ma Deary would have driven me. She doesn't seem to have forgiven me for choosing Forest over staying home and helping with the farm."

"Any time." He put his hands in his leather coat pockets. "Don't be so hard on Deary. She'd never wish you any harm."

Sophia pressed her lips together. Ma Deary was his sister; he'd always see the bright side. Sophia stood waiting for him to get back in the car, but instead, he pulled off his sunglasses and took a step closer.

"That question you asked me back at the house? Where you come from and all?"

Sophia's eyes brightened. Did Unc know something more?

"Be careful digging up skeletons of the past. I don't want you getting hurt. Just forget about it and move forward. You've got a good opportunity here. Use that energy to focus on your schoolwork. Hear?"

Sophia nodded and then gave him a hug. "Unc, thanks again."

"See you on your next break." He walked to the driver's side of the car. "When is that?"

"April."

"Until then, be cool." He waved as he cranked the engine of his Chevy Impala. Then he turned up the volume to "The Girl's Alright with Me" by the Temptations. People stopped mid-conversation, and all eyes were on Unc as he pulled away from the school.

Sophia watched him go. She knew that he meant well, but she also knew she was going to find her birth mother no matter what it took.

When Sophia reached her dorm room, she found Willa, who was wearing a camel-colored turtleneck and a pair of slim-fit pants tapered at the ankle. Her hair had been cut into a stylish bob, and she squealed when she saw Sophia.

"You look fantastic." Sophia threw her arms around Willa.

"Thanks." Willa stepped back. "How was your Christmas break? Did everything work out with your family?"

"Yes, it turned out really well."

"And your mom?"

Sophia had forgotten that she had told Willa about being afraid to return to the farm. "She was fine. The boys were happy to see me, and my uncle drove me back. Why are you so dressed up?" she asked, changing the subject as she placed her suitcase on her bed with the notion of unpacking.

"Didn't you hear? There's a welcome-back social at the Magnolia Clubhouse. Lemonade and cookies, and I think they are even having music. Get changed so we can go." Willa picked up her blush brush.

Sophia had managed to snag a baby-doll dress when Walter took her by the local church for the annual rummage sale. She slipped that on and, after Willa insisted, applied a little rouge to her cheeks.

When Sophia and Willa walked through the double doors of the Magnolia Clubhouse on campus, kids stood in groups around the punch bowl, and a few swayed in place to the music. Claude and Louis were sitting at a table next to the assortment of refreshments with a deck of playing cards.

"Hey, boys," Willa sang, sliding into one of the empty seats. "Where's Max?"

"I haven't seen him," Louis said. "Want us to deal you in?"

"Whatcha playing?" Sophia plopped down.

"Gin rummy."

"Do you know how to play, Sophia?" Willa turned to her.

"Yes." Despite never having a full deck, she had played the game with her brothers on rainy days back on the farm.

Louis dealt the cards. "Did you hear about Sammy Younge Jr.?"

"Who's that?" Claude sipped his lemonade.

"A Negro student at Tuskegee Institute. Murdered for using a whites-only restroom at a gas station in Macon, Georgia."

"That's terrible," said Claude, and Sophia could see him visibly shudder. She remembered how the taunts from the white students had upset him at the Old South Ball.

"The man had served in the U.S. Navy. Even lost a kidney while serving, and this is how our country repays his service." Louis moved cards around in his hand.

"Goodness gracious, Louis. Can we please talk about something more pleasant?" Willa fanned herself.

"Like what?"

"Like what you got for Christmas?" she said, wide-eyed.

"Coal." He slapped the table and laughed.

"Very funny," Willa chided, just as Sophia spotted Max waving hello to a few teens as he glided toward their table.

Max wore a lime-green cardigan, slacks, and penny loafers, and his skin and hair glistened like a new copper coin. The sight of him made her fidget with the hem of her dress.

"Hey, what's shaking?" He slid into the only open seat at the round table, which happened to be right next to Sophia.

"Max." Willa beamed. "How was your break?"

"I spent most of my time being lazy in front of the tube. What are you playing?"

"Gin rummy," Claude piped up.

"Deal me in."

"You're lucky I didn't have a good hand." Louis picked up all the cards from the table and shuffled.

While Willa talked about her time in New York City with her family, and how pretty the Christmas tree looked in Rockefeller Center, Sophia found her knee against Max's. A sensation pulsed up her thigh as she waited for him to stretch away, but instead he sneaked a glance at her and smiled.

When the social was over, the five of them walked down the path toward the quad.

"I need to stop at the library for a book," Willa said. "Max, you want to walk with me?"

"I would, but I need to get changed and go shoot around before dinner. I've been sitting on my behind for two weeks, and I want to be my best for practice tomorrow."

Sophia could see disappointment flash across Willa's face, but she recovered and turned toward the library as the rest of them walked toward the Athletic Center. Then Claude and Louis both decided they were hungry and headed to the cafeteria.

"You want to shoot around?" Max asked Sophia.

"I'm not dressed for it." She held out her stockinged leg and Mary Janes.

"The locker room should be open. Come on."

Sophia followed Max into the Athletic Center.

"Come into the boys' gym once you get changed."

The girls' gym floor had been freshly waxed and smelled like turpentine as she passed through to the locker room and changed into her gym shorts and white tee. When she entered the boys' gym, Max was at the top of the key, shooting.

"Catch my rebounds. I'll go around the world first, and then I'll do the same for you."

"Okay," she said, planting herself beneath the basket.

Max shot. *Swish.* She threw him the ball. He dribbled a few steps to the left. Fired. Nothing but net.

"You aren't shooting like you were sitting around all break. 'Fess up," she said, chuckling.

"Well, you know me." He smiled. "I got a game in here and there with a few of my middle school buddies." Max lifted his arms, shot, and drained it. "What did you do?"

Sophia let the ball drop into her hand, then hurled it at Max.

While he shot baskets, she caught him up on riding to D.C. with Willa and then her visit with Mrs. Gathers. Max shot from the right corner, and when Sophia caught the ball, she gripped it with both hands.

"I found out the truth," she said, and Max stopped moving.

"What?"

Sophia took the ball and dribbled to the top of the key, leaving Max underneath the basket to catch the ball for her.

"I was right. I am one of those Brown Babies who came over from Germany," she said, shooting the ball and missing. Then she tossed the ball up in the air over and over while she recounted everything that she had learned.

"Unbelievable," Max said, joining her at the top of the court. "What if we came over at the same time?"

Sophia flopped down on the gymnasium floor, no longer able to hold herself up. "I've been wondering about the fire that I'm haunted by. Mrs. Gathers said that I lived at St. Hildegard's orphanage before I was brought here. She mentioned that there had been a fire a few weeks before we left."

Max dropped down on the parquet floor beside her.

"You told me that you remember nuns dressed in long habits and that you had been in a fire too," she said.

"Yeah, what are the chances?" The ball rolled toward Max and he gripped it with both hands. "Us being in the same orphanage in Mannheim, Germany, then meeting here at Forest."

"That's like a Hollywood movie." The ball slipped from his hands as she blurted, "A crazy love story."

Max turned and looked her in the eyes with such intensity, she could not will herself to turn away.

"You think this is a love story?" His voice came out husky.

Sophia could feel all her blood rush to her face. "Max, you know how Willa feels about you," she murmured just as he leaned in, with his face so close she could smell the lemon cookies on his breath.

"But what about how I feel about you?"

The eye contact between them was so intense that the gym faded away, and all Sophia knew in the moment was him.

"How's that?" she whispered.

Max pushed his lips toward hers until there was only a hair between them and breathed on her. "Like this."

His soft lips pressed against hers, and she melted into him. Then his hand caressed the back of her head as he opened her mouth with the warmth of his tongue. Every cell inside Sophia's body felt lit up, electric. It was her first kiss. She was kissing Max.

The sound of the gym door sighing open caused Sophia to pull back. When she turned her head, she saw Willa's reddened face staring back at her.

"Sophia, how could you!" she screeched. Willa stomped her foot and then ran back through the gymnasium doors.

Sophia exhaled all the air she had been holding in. "I better go."

"No, I made this mess with Willa. I should have told her a long time ago that I didn't feel the same. It's my responsibility to make this right." Max kissed her cheek, then scurried to his feet and jogged after Willa, leaving his cedar scent behind.

Sophia hugged the basketball to her chest and tried to hold on to the feel of Max's lips against hers, while hoping that her feelings for him hadn't caused her to lose her only friend.

CHAPTER 48

Washington, D.C., February 1966

ETHEL

It had been two months since Julia's family moved to Prince George's County, Maryland, but between getting her family settled and Ethel being swamped with the holidays, they hadn't managed to catch up in person, even though they lived only ten miles apart. After weeks of missed chances, their schedules finally aligned on the first Friday in February, allowing them to share a long-awaited date for tea.

They met in the lobby of the Willard InterContinental Hotel, falling into each other's arms.

"Oh, you smell so good." Julia held Ethel tight as they rocked.

"Girl, I'm still wearing the same old Jean Naté."

"I've always said that it smells better on you than it does on me." Julia removed her gloves and led Ethel past the marble columns to one of the bloodred tufted, U-shaped settees. Her hair was raked into a stylish side-parted bob, and her lips were painted plum.

Ethel didn't usually wear much makeup, but Anke had picked out a winter-white cashmere sweater for her the night before, and Monika insisted on a few swipes of cocoa-colored lipstick. Seeing Julia all gussied up made Ethel grateful for teenage daughters.

Grand twinkly chandeliers fell in tiers from the ceilings, and classical piano music made the large room feel cozy.

"You know right back there in that corner by the window is where Dr. King wrote his 'I Have a Dream' speech? The one that he gave at the March on Washington." Julia pointed.

"I didn't know that."

"Sure did. I read that a few Negro bellhops partitioned off the space so that he wouldn't be disturbed. Did you go to the march?"

Ethel shook her head. "I stayed back, but Bert went, and he took Franz, Heinz, and Leo with him."

"Wish we had been home, because I would have definitely been front and center."

"It was a hot day in August, I can't see you out there with all those people, melting away."

"The heat don't bother me none." She fanned herself, smiling.

"Well, Bert said that at some point, Dr. King's speech appeared to peter out. So much so that he started losing people's attention."

"Really?"

Ethel nodded. "It was Mahalia Jackson who shouted for him to tell them about the dream. He went off script, and that's when the speech came alive."

"Well, you know it's always a fabulous woman behind every good man." Julia cackled. "I sure did come back to the States at the right time. Now we have the right to vote, and white people have a law that says they must treat us civilly." Then she leaned in and whispered, "That's why I picked the grand Willard Hotel to meet: It's white-folks fancy."

Ethel snorted as the waitress took their tea orders, and Julia requested a plate of sandwiches, scones, jams, and clotted cream.

"How are the girls?" Ethel asked.

"You know how the teenage years are. Boys sniffing around. Sid keeps the shotgun by the door." She laughed.

"You must bring them over for dinner. I make a mean bone-in ham."

"Honey, trying to get my Sid to do anything social has been like pulling teeth. He is such a homebody. After work, he opens a beer and stays in front of that television box until it's time for bed."

"But he's always liked spending time with Bert. Let's pick a Sunday afternoon so they can watch the baseball game."

"I'll put it on our calendar."

The waitress returned with the pots of tea.

"But how are you, darling? You seem so busy."

Ethel poured cream into her teacup. "I had an interesting visitor right before Christmas," and then she told Julia about Sophia. How the girl just showed up on her doorstep only to uncover the huge mistake that Ethel had made. Fresh shame and guilt washed over her. "Words can't describe how terrible I feel."

"Honey, you did the best you could. If it wasn't for you, those children would be stuck in Germany in an orphanage. God only knows what would have happened to them."

"But it was my responsibility to get them here, sorted and safe."

"And you did that, even left your own children behind to bring them across the Atlantic Ocean."

"But a switch in identity? I should have been more careful. She's been celebrating the wrong birthday, for goodness' sake. Can you imagine what that must be like? To find out that you have gone through your whole life as another person?"

"You said she was a teenager, which means she still has her whole life ahead of her. This is just a tiny blip in the big picture." Julia reached for her hand. "Now, stop this. If my memory serves me right, I talked you into taking that flight with the children to New York. Any chaos that ensued, you can blame it on me."

But Ethel had stewed in her private shame for so long, now that she had voiced it to Julia, she couldn't stop the words that bubbled to the surface. "Do you know about all the phone calls and letters that I've received from parents over the years? People have even accused me of rushing the process of the proxy adoptions. Condemned me for not vetting the families properly. I could handle that from unhappy adults, but this is different. She's a child." Ethel's bottom lip quivered.

"You did your best."

"Stop saying that and just admit it. I made a damn mess!" she hissed, and Julia's head whipped back.

"Ethel Louise Gathers, I have never in my life heard you swear. That's my job, to cuss people out. And I'll be damned if I'm going to sit here and allow you to cuss yourself, especially when I know that you have a heart of gold." Julia reached into her purse and snapped her handkerchief in Ethel's direction.

While Ethel dabbed her eyes and blew her nose, she muttered, "I'm so sorry for my outburst. I don't know what just came over me." Her chest heaved up and down as she looked around to see if anyone was watching, but no one even blinked in their direction.

"Stop apologizing. You're human, and you are entitled to your feelings. But feelings are not facts." Julia brushed a hair out of Ethel's eye. "The bottom line is that you have always fought for those children abandoned in Germany. And heck, for the German mothers who couldn't keep their babies, and the American mothers who couldn't have their own. You've changed the face of history."

"Oh, Julia." Ethel felt her cheeks warm.

"Honey, I am certain that when it's your time, all of heaven will be right there to meet you at the pearly gates."

"Stop trying to make me smile."

Julia cocked her head. "Shucks, I'll be first in line petitioning the pope to start the canonization process. I've already picked out your name: St. Sarah."

Ethel shook her head, and her lips turned up in a half grin. "You are too much."

"I'm serious. What does this girl expect you to do?"

Ethel let out a long sigh and then took a sip of her tea. "I've reached out to Sister Ursula to see if she can dig up any information. Sophia is set on finding her birth mother."

"Well, that's all you can do."

Then Ethel told Julia that the girl was only a sophomore in high school and had tracked her down through the telephone book. "She has chutzpah, that's for sure, and I'm going to help her make things right."

The food arrived, and Julia plated a crustless sandwich and a scone with jam and handed it to Ethel.

"Now, the pity party is officially over. I want to eat this treat while you fill me in on all the army wives' juicy gossip. Don't leave out a single detail."

"Well, Dorothy Hansen's husband has been stationed in Saigon for more than a year. Poor thing, the few times I've heard from her, she's been worried sick about him and all the soldiers fighting in 'Nam."

Julia lifted her knife and spread a heap of clotted cream on her scone and took a bite. "Well, I'll keep her in my prayers. But I said juicy gossip. Isn't Wanda getting a divorce?"

Ethel smirked. No one could make her comfortable like Julia, and they sat with each other sharing stories until their tea was stone cold.

CHAPTER 49

West Oak Forest Academy, January 1966

SOPHIA

Sophia was at her wits' end on how to make it up to Willa for kissing Max. Willa had given Sophia the silent treatment for a full week, even going so far as waking up an hour early so that she would be gone from their room before Sophia opened her eyes. When Sophia ran into her around campus, Willa pretended not to see her. "Awful" wasn't a strong enough word to describe how Sophia felt. Crushing Willa was never her plan, their friendship meant the world to her, but it had been impossible to ignore the connection she shared with Max.

Sophia and Max were from the same place, and they had found each other across the distance and against the odds. It was a miracle, really. But on the other hand, Sophia had never had a friend outside of her brothers. Let alone a friend as kind and giving as Willa. If Willa had never invited her home, Sophia wouldn't have read those articles in the library that had connected her to Mrs. Gathers. There had to be a way to remedy things.

"Cafeteria is now closing," called the woman removing tin pans from the hot-food station. Sophia grabbed two sugar cookies from the dessert station and headed out.

Willa was lying across her bed facing the wall when Sophia entered the room. The new radio that she had brought back to school after Christmas was on low.

"Can we please talk? The silence is killing me." Sophia sat on the edge of Willa's bed and dug her nails into the down comforter.

"There's nothing to discuss. Max already told me."

"I want you to hear it from me, Willa."

Willa sat up and turned her face toward Sophia. "What?"

"For starters, I'm not who I thought I was."

"What does that even mean?"

Sophia took a deep breath. If she was going to get Willa back, she had to be honest. But she had to do it without incriminating Max.

"I found out that I was adopted," she said slowly, and then told Willa about the Brown Baby Plan, going to Mrs. Gathers's home and discovering the mix-up with her identity. When she was finished, Willa's mouth hung open wide enough to catch a fly.

"That's bizarre. Why didn't you tell me you were going through all of this?"

Sophia shrugged. "I just had this gut feeling but no proof. I didn't know for sure until I met Mrs. Gathers over winter break."

"What have your parents said about all of this?"

"I haven't told them that I know."

"Seriously? This is a lot for me to take in. I can't imagine how you feel." Willa's face softened.

"And then with Max . . . our connection to basketball . . . it just happened. I'm sorry for hurting you, Willa. I truly am."

Willa pulled her knees to her chest and was quiet for a long time.

Then she said, "Do I feel like you betrayed me? Yes. Am I hurt? Absolutely."

"I'll do anything to make it up to you."

Smoothing her hair back from her face, Willa took a hair tie from her wrist and made a ponytail. "It's fine. If I'm honest, Max never seemed that into me anyway. He's a guy that my parents would like for me, so I pursued him."

"You are my one and only friend. I would never intentionally hurt you."

"I said it's fine."

Sophia looked up at the ceiling. "Our chemistry . . . it's just been—"

"Ugh, spare me the details, please," Willa blurted. "Just don't be all mushy about it. That's a surefire way to make me puke."

"Deal," said Sophia.

"But do you want to talk about the other thing? I mean, finding out that you were adopted? It's gotta be rough." Her green eyes were kind.

"Maybe later," Sophia said, reaching into her bag and pulling out the two sugar cookies. "Peace offering?"

"It'll take more than sugar to win me back." Willa snorted. "But it's a start." She took a bite.

At the end of January, Sophia's basketball season ended, with the girls making it to the first round of the playoffs. They lost at home in overtime when Patty missed a buzzer-beating jump shot. The starters said they could have won if Patty had thrown the ball to Sophia, who was all alone under the basket.

Sophia moped out of the locker room to find Max waiting for her on the bleachers. His smile made the details of the game turn murky, and when he draped his arm around her shoulder and said,

"Don't worry about it, Soph, you played well," the loss was all but forgotten.

Once basketball season ended, Sophia and Max were inseparable. They took all of their meals together in the cafeteria and studied in the library with their limbs linked under the table. Max kissed her on the bench behind the Magnolia Clubhouse, carried her books through the breezeway between the boys' and girls' schools, and on Saturday nights, they'd sneak into the belfry tower to watch the sunset while he made her laugh until her belly ached.

At the end of February, Sophia finally received a letter from Mrs. Gathers. Max had gone off campus with the Debate Club, and she would not allow herself to open it until he returned to Forest. She watched for the school van from the cafeteria window, and when the club members piled off, she waved him over.

"Hey there," he said.

A light snow had begun to fall, and Sophia flicked the flakes from his hair.

"I've been waiting for you all day to open this." She held the letter up. "Come inside."

Max followed Sophia to a table inside the cafeteria. "Should we get some cocoa or something?"

"Afterward. I need to know what Mrs. Gathers found out," she said, slipping her finger beneath the seal. Her eyes darted over the page, and Max scooted his chair in closer so that he could read over her shoulder.

Sophia put the letter down. "It says my mother's last known address is in America. She's not in Germany but here in the States."

"I didn't see that coming," Max said as he took the letter from her hand and read it again more closely. "What are you going to do now?"

"I'm going to find her. Mrs. Gathers said she'd help. She wants me to call her; she said I could reverse the charges."

February melted into late March, and before Sophia knew it, she was studying for midterms and then packing for spring break. For once, she didn't need Willa to save her. She had her own plans. True to his word, Unc was there in the roundabout to pick Sophia up and drive her back to the farm for her final break before summer.

At home, she found Walter behind the shed with his head under the hood of an old Ford Six.

"She ain't much to look at," he said, gesturing to the mismatched doors and parts. "But she's enough to get me around town."

"Do you think she could get us to Williamsburg and back?"

"What's in Williamsburg?" Walter sneezed.

"Allergies?" Sophia reached into the front pocket of her dress and held an envelope out to him.

"You know spring's not my season." He sneezed again, then reached for the cloth hanging from his overalls pockets and wiped the grease from his hands. He skimmed the letter. "Your birth mother is in Williamsburg, Virginia? That's only a state away. Rusty, when you put your mind to something . . ." he said, reading the letter again.

"I already tried the telephone number, but it's been disconnected."

"What do you want to do?" He handed her back the letter.

"You think this pretty baby would make it down to Williamsburg and back?" She patted the hood of the car.

"I reckon all we can do is give it a try." Walter smiled at her in his easy way. "What do we have to lose?"

Sophia could list a whole bunch of things, but the biggest obstacle would be Ma Deary finding out and sabotaging their plan. She didn't want the twins to know either; she couldn't disrupt their lives as hers had been. Not yet, not until they were a bit older and could understand.

"Ma Deary has been working doubles on Thursdays. She leaves

like five in the morning and doesn't return until the middle of the night. Thursday would be our best shot," Walter responded as if reading her thoughts.

"And the Old Man?"

"He's in D.C. delivering the eggs on Thursday, remember? Lately, he's been stopping off to catch up with old friends and not returning till late."

She relaxed a bit. They had a working plan. Sophia just hoped her mother still lived at the address that the German orphanage had provided to Mrs. Gathers. That she hadn't moved or, worse, that she wouldn't take one look at Sophia before turning her away.

CHAPTER 50

Philadelphia, PA, April 1954

OZZIE

Ozzie whistled to himself while he stood waiting his turn to punch the quitting clock at work. His stomach growled, and he wondered if Penn would offer snacks tonight at Rita's awards ceremony. Maybe he'd splurge for the occasion and take Rita over to Niecy's Rib Shack for a celebratory dinner. *Rita would like that,* he thought. He'd even buy a few roses from the flower cart on Broad Street to show her how proud he was of her.

In the employee locker room, he unlatched his locker, and just as he reached for his stingy-brim hat, he heard "Sure Shot, that you?"

Only guys from South Philly called him Sure Shot. Ozzie spun around and saw Slim, a fellow from around the way.

"Brother man." Ozzie clapped Slim's hand. "When'd you start working here?"

"About a week ago." Slim was over six feet tall, with a thin frame and small eyes.

"Which department?"

"I'm over in receiving and maintenance."

"That's where I started too," Ozzie said. "Now I'm over in material control, we supervise the deliveries and distributions. It's a slight upgrade."

"That's good to know. 'Cause hauling this heavy shit is for the birds." Slim fitted a porkpie hat on his head. "Whatcha doing tonight?"

"Got plans with the Mrs." Ozzie closed his locker.

"Well, it's my birthday."

"Happy birthday."

"Thanks, man. You remember Bill and Tiny who lived over on Wilder Street?"

"They work here too?"

Slim nodded. "Think you could at least stop in at Wally's and say hello?"

Ozzie looked down at his watch. He had sworn off Wally's, the beer garden around the corner, but he hadn't seen those guys in years. He could spare a nickel for a Coca-Cola and thirty minutes for a quick hello. If anyone asked why he wasn't drinking, he'd say he was recovering from an infection and on strong antibiotics.

"Lead the way."

Three hours later, five men were crowded around a square table meant for four. Slim, who had always been the class clown in high school, told stories of his time in the marines, and Ozzie laughed so hard that his sides hurt. The dark bar smelled of wood chips and cigars. The jukebox was loud, and the barmaid, in a black dress with a plunging neckline, stood balancing a tray on one hand.

"Five Canadian Clubs," she said, placing the fresh rocks glasses in front of them and quickly picking up the used ones.

Ozzie had meant to refuse the next round. He needed to get

to Rita, but then Bill pushed the glass toward him and stood with a toast.

"Raise your glasses to Slim," Bill slurred. "May all your dreams come true tonight and every night."

"Hear, hear." The men raised their glasses, and the brown liquor slid down Ozzie's throat in one gulp.

The guilt of having picked up those first few drinks had eased its way into the back of his subconscious. Now all he felt was loose. Then he thought, *Rita's ceremony.* He looked down at his watch. Where had the time gone?

"I gotta head on out." He swayed when he stood, and grabbed the table for balance.

"Sure Shot, thanks for coming." Slim stood and gave him five.

When Ozzie turned his key in the front door, he could hear *Hancock's Half Hour* playing from the radio, which meant it was somewhere in the ten o'clock hour. Rita was sitting on the Queen Anne camelback sofa in her nightgown with her hair tied up in pink curlers. The lamp on the end table gave off a soft glow.

"Well, at least you aren't dead," she said.

He dropped his keys on the end table. "Why would I be dead?"

"It's the only reason I could come up with to justify you missing my awards ceremony. Because I'm such a fool for you, I couldn't allow myself to believe the truth." She blew air through her nose.

"Baby, I'm sorry. It's not what it looks like."

Rita pushed up from the sofa and marched over to where he stood just beyond the front door. She grabbed him by the collar, sniffed his neck and mouth, and then sucked her teeth. "It's exactly what it looks like. You're drunk. It's a freaking Monday night, for Christ's sake. And I reminded you over and over again about the ceremony."

"I'm sorry."

"Do you know I was the only Negro in the whole entire auditorium? Up there onstage, I could barely concentrate on what was supposed to be a joyous moment because I kept looking for you to walk through the damn doors."

He shifted on his feet, hating that he had ruined her big night. "Let me explain."

"You're full of shit, you know that?" Rita's eyes blazed red. He parted his lips to speak, but she held up her hand to silence him.

"I'm pregnant."

The temperature in the room dropped. "What?"

Rita stared at him pointedly.

"I thought you wanted to wait until after law school."

"Yeah, well, this baby had other plans. And I can't bring our child into the world with you drinking like a fish and not showing up for your responsibilities."

A baby with Rita. Ozzie stood in shock.

"You've been hiding liquor and lying about our two-drink agreement." She reached under the coffee table and set two empty whiskey bottles down with a thud. She had found his secret stash. His stomach turned sour.

"Those bottles are from before."

"First you embarrass me at the Alexanders', then you shame me by being late with the rent, and now you've humiliated me in front of my entire law school cohort by standing me up."

"Rita, I ran into an old friend, it was his—"

"You aren't the man I married," she shouted, and those words were like poison-tipped arrows through his heart.

"Baby."

"Don't you 'baby' me, Oz. I can't go to law school and take care of our child and your drunk ass too. If you don't get it together . . ." Her bottom lip quivered.

"It won't happen again." He reached for her waist, but she pushed him away and then pounded up the stairs.

Ozzie knew the doghouse drill and made his way down to the basement. What was he thinking, stopping into Wally's? He should have known that once he started drinking with those guys, it would be hard to leave. Rita was having his baby. How would he shoulder more responsibility when he was struggling to take care of them now? His heart raced as the worry of it all consumed him, but then he thought of Katja, and his breathing slowed.

She would turn five in the fall, and if she were with him, she'd be starting kindergarten. He wondered how tall she was now and what toy she loved best. Did she still have the Philips nose, or had her features changed? Then, like a tidal wave, the U-turn that his life had taken the moment he'd left Germany without her pulled him under. The booze had worn off, and in marched the pain. He had screwed over so many moments in his life that he was beginning to think this was just who he was now. Long gone was the young, optimistic fellow who volunteered for the army with the goal to work in Intelligence and show America what the Negro man could do.

Rita's voice echoed in his ears, *You aren't the man I married,* and shame wrapped around him like a second skin. Even in the dimly lit basement, he could see his hands twitching. Withdrawal. The alcohol was doing a number on him, and he had no idea how to make it stop. Ozzie had gotten so far away from the man he had set out to be, he no longer knew how to find his way back.

CHAPTER 51

Prince Frederick, MD, April 1966

SOPHIA

On the afternoon before their trip to Williamsburg, Sophia found Walter with his feet dangling from beneath the Ford Six.

"I can't stop picturing the look on my mother's face when I ring the doorbell. Do you think she'll be there? We haven't considered that she might have a job," she whispered as he rolled from underneath the car.

His overalls were covered in grease and soot. "Rusty, we have a problem."

Sophia froze.

"I don't trust this old gal on the road for such a long haul. I looked at the Old Man's map, and Williamsburg's more than two and a half hours away."

"So."

"The furthest I've driven her is over to Dares Beach."

"No, please don't back out now, Walt," she whined.

"I'm sorry, but it's an old car, and I can't put that much pressure on her. It's not safe."

Sophia slouched down on the grass next to him, picking at a hole in her overalls. Every time she took a step forward, she was hit with two giant steps back. If she didn't get to Williamsburg over spring break, then she'd have to wait until the summer. The knowledge that she could be so close to solving her life's puzzle was killing her.

"Isn't there someone you could call? Maybe Mrs. Brown at Brooks."

"My old school counselor?"

"She got you into West Oak Forest, maybe she'd help you with this too."

Then it hit her, and Sophia stood up and dusted grass from her backside. "Not Mrs. Brown, but I have another idea." She made her way back toward the house.

"Fingers crossed," Walter called after her.

The sky was still purple as Sophia lay awake in her bed, listening to Ma Deary hum along to "Precious Lord" by Aretha Franklin as she bumped around in the kitchen. It was a song that Sophia had always loved. Aretha crooning, along with the rumble of the bass and the rich fingering of the piano, brought her a semblance of hope. Today she would embark on a life-changing moment, and she needed courage.

"That uppity school done made you lazy." Ma Deary poked her head into Sophia's dugout bedroom, breaking the sweet spell that Aretha Franklin had spun. "Get on up, girl. The hens waiting on you to get those eggs."

Sophia pushed herself up. "Coming, Ma Deary." After shrugging into her West Oak Forest Academy sweatshirt, she made her way into the kitchen, fragranced with the aroma of coffee.

Ma Deary wore her white uniform that stopped below the knee. "Pile of laundry out back for you to wash." She scowled, then slipped into her blazer and let the screen door slam behind her.

Once Sophia heard Ma back the Rambler down the road from the house, she returned to her bedroom and changed into the khaki A-line skirt with attached suspenders that she had picked out of the lost-and-found bin, and her school blouse. Then she brushed her hair back into a ponytail.

Walter was waiting for her on the back porch in a rusted chair next to the broken icebox. "Ready?"

Yesterday Sophia had phoned Mrs. Gathers, and she had agreed to take Sophia to Williamsburg to reunite with her mother. Given the circumstances, Sophia couldn't meet Mrs. Gathers at the farm and chance a run-in with Ma Deary or the Old Man. That would put a stop to this whole expedition, not to mention Sophia's continuing shame over their poor living conditions. Instead, Sophia had given Mrs. Gathers the address of Brooks High School, with instructions to meet in the parking lot.

Walter had agreed to drop Sophia off on his way to purchase feed for the animals. As she slid across the cracked leather seat, she asked, "Will you double back and give the twins a ride to school?"

"They're used to walking. Quit babying them." Walter backed up the Ford Six and then turned the nose toward the road.

"I promised to bring them back cherry sours and Bazooka bubble gum." She passed Walter a boiled egg, peeled and salted.

Walter gobbled his down in two bites while Sophia ate hers slowly. Once it was in her belly, she worried that she'd smell like hard-boiled egg when she met Mrs. Gathers. She put her hand in front of her mouth and blew out her breath to smell it.

"There's a handful of peppermints in the glove box," Walter said.

Sophia wrenched it open. "I hope all this candy isn't an indication that you're still fooling with Mary Ellen at the General Store?" She popped a piece into her mouth.

His cheeks blushed. "We've been spending time together when she can get away."

"Have you lost your mind? Sneaking around in the woods with a white girl."

Walter grinned. "We're going steady."

Sophia turned in her seat. "You can't be serious."

"As a heart attack."

Sophia touched her brother's arm. "You know those brothers of hers smoke pot and are always up to no good. Not to mention that it's illegal."

"We're cautious," he said, pulling into the school's parking lot. "Don't worry about me. You just focus on finding your mother."

There was a blue Chevy parked over by a tree, away from the other cars and still running.

"That must be her," said Sophia.

Walter sidled up alongside the Chevy, and Sophia hopped out before he could kill the engine. "Mrs. Gathers," she rushed to say, "I can't thank you enough for coming."

Mrs. Gathers stepped out of her car wearing a plaid skirt, a button-down blouse, and flats. "It's my pleasure, dear." She opened her arms, and Sophia fell into her friendly embrace. "Is this your brother?"

"Yes, Walter, meet Mrs. Gathers."

He shook her hand.

"It's nice to see you, Walter." She squinted. "I sort of remember your face. I think you were the boy who was most well behaved on our flight to America."

Walter beamed. "Thank you for everything and especially for what you are doing right now for my sister. It means a lot that she knows who she is."

"I couldn't agree more. That's why we had better get a move on." Mrs. Gathers tapped her watch.

Walter grabbed Sophia's wrist and whispered, "Be careful. And no matter what or who you find, I will always be your big bro."

Squeezing his fingers, she thanked him and then climbed into the passenger seat beside Mrs. Gathers.

It wasn't until they had found I-64 heading east that Mrs. Gathers asked Sophia about her semester at school.

"It's going well. I have all A's."

"That's amazing, at an institution as prestigious as West Oak Forest. Have you given any thought to college?"

Sophia fidgeted with the hem of her skirt. "Not more than knowing that I want to go. I can't end up back at the farm."

"Well, there are guidance counselors at your school who will point you in the right direction when the time comes."

Sophia thought about the teachers at Forest. Most hadn't had the decency to pair her face with her name. At least twice a week, one of them confused her with Willa. In the beginning, Sophia had worried about her missing birth certificate, but after a month, it became apparent that no one in the office would cast another glance at her file. She looked out the window as the trees passed by. It was a beautiful sunny day, but the anticipation of what was to come planted a knot in her stomach. Rubbing it, she turned toward Mrs. Gathers, still a bit stunned that the woman had agreed to chaperone her on this harebrained trip.

"What made you get involved in this adoption thing to begin with? It seems like a huge undertaking."

As she signaled and changed lanes, Mrs. Gathers responded, "It's a very long story, but the crux of it is . . ." Then she paused for so long that Sophia thought she had changed her mind about answering. "I couldn't have children of my own, and I so desperately wanted to become a mother," she said finally, both hands gripping the wheel. "I fell into a bit of depression, but discovering those sweet children living in the orphanage brought me out of it. When I saw them, it felt like God was speaking to me. Telling me that I had been placed right there in Germany to be of service. They gave me purpose."

Sophia felt a burst of reverence for Mrs. Gathers. "But you have children now, right? I saw the family photographs around your home."

Mrs. Gathers smiled. "And they have been the joy of my life. To help children like you find loving homes, and women like me who couldn't conceive, have the chance to become mothers has been my life's calling."

"That's really admirable."

"Thanks." She chewed her bottom lip. "Lately, I've been thinking a lot about what's next for me. The adoption agency has slowed down to a halt, and my own children have grown faster than you can say 'Mississippi.' Half of them have already left the nest."

"Is that why you are helping me?"

Mrs. Gathers fell quiet again. "I can admit when I've made a mistake, and your determination is unlike any I have ever seen in a young person. I started you on this journey, and I'm duty-bound to help you finish it."

They stopped once to use the restroom and then drove into Williamsburg shortly before eleven. Once they exited the highway, Mrs. Gathers stopped at the gas station to get directions.

"We're just five miles away." She slid behind the wheel and tossed Sophia a banana.

Mrs. Gathers dropped her speed as she eased down Little John Road. The street was quiet, and all the houses had manicured bushes with identical spacious front lawns. When Mrs. Gathers put the Chevy in park and turned off the engine, Sophia reached for her hand.

"Thank you for coming this far with me, Mrs. Gathers. But this part I have to do alone. Don't drive off without me."

"No matter what you find on the other side of that door, know that I'll be right here waiting for you."

A damp spring breeze swept across Sophia's face as she stood on the curb and stared up at the house. It was an impressive home. Tudor-style with brick on the bottom, ecru stucco on the top, and big sweeping windows. As she glanced down the block, she thought it looked like an upscale neighborhood that she could picture her classmates from West Oak Forest living in. It was a stark contrast to her home on the farm.

Her knees trembled beneath her skirt. Her mother might very well be on the other side of those walls. This was the moment she had been waiting for, yet she had a hard time making her feet move.

The iron railing was loose and wiggled from side to side beneath her hand as she made her way up the winding staircase. Sophia stood on the top landing and pressed the doorbell. It echoed through the house, and then she heard footsteps. Pulling herself to her full height, she plastered on her best smile as the door hissed open.

A pale woman with sandy brown hair loose down her back and eyes hooded under false lashes stood behind the screen door. She was thin and sprightly.

"Hello," she said with a smile. "May I help you?"

Sophia fumbled with the sheet of paper in her sweaty palms. "I am looking for Jelka Durchdenwald."

The woman touched her hand to her throat and took a step back. "What is this about?"

This wasn't the reaction Sophia had planned. She assumed that her mother would take one look at her, recognize her instantly, and swallow her in her arms.

"My name is Sophia—I mean—" She felt faint and reached out for the shaky banister to hold her up. "My birth name is Katja, and I'm looking for . . . my mother," she rushed out.

"Oh, dear God." The woman unlatched the screen door and stumbled back so that Sophia could step inside the foyer. Under the light, she could see the woman better. They had the same cheekbones.

The woman stared at her, looking her over from head to toe. Then she touched the crown of Sophia's head. "My goodness, it is you." She thrust her arms around Sophia and rocked.

Tears sprang to Sophia's eyes as she inhaled a scent of strawberry shampoo. She had found her. When she released Sophia, she touched her face. "After all this time." Then she mumbled words in German that sounded like a prayer.

"Jelka?" Sophia croaked, just to be sure. She didn't want to call her "Mother" in their first meeting.

"No, I'm Jutta. Jelka's younger sister," she said. "Come in."

Her sister.

Jutta led Sophia down the hall. The floors were brick veneer, and the ceiling had a popcorn texture. Jutta turned into the living room and motioned for Sophia to take a seat on the gray plaid sofa. There were floral drapes hanging from the big bay window. An upright piano sat in the corner of the room, and Sophia could smell something piney.

"How on earth did you find me?" Jutta said. "Oh, where are my manners. Would you like something to drink?"

"No, thank you." Sophia shifted in her seat. "Mrs. Ethel Gathers reached out to St. Hildegard's orphanage in Mannheim. Jelka had left her address with the nuns, and a phone number, but it was disconnected. That's why I didn't call first. Sorry for dropping in like this," she said, feeling sheepish.

"How far have you traveled?"

"From southern Maryland. I just found out that I was adopted a few months ago, and I've been looking for my birth mother. Is she here?" Sophia asked.

"Tell me about yourself," Jutta said, crossing her legs in front of her. There was an ashtray beside her, and she lifted the silver cigarette holder to her lips.

"I'm in the tenth grade, I go to boarding school in Maryland, first year. My family lives on a farm in Prince Frederick, Maryland, and I grew up with three brothers."

"No sisters?"

Sophia shook her head.

"Pity. No one to play dress-up with or show you how to fix your makeup." Jutta's eyes glazed over. "Tell me more."

Sophia didn't know what Jutta wanted to know. So she told her how she had discovered the Brown Baby Plan and connected all the dots along the way to get to this moment. To meet her mother.

Impatience seeped from her voice when she asked again, "Is she here?"

Jutta put the cigarette holder in the ashtray. "You sure you don't want anything to drink?"

"No, thank you."

Jutta stood and adjusted her stirrup-foot stretch pants. "Well, you can follow me."

Sophia breathed a sigh, of what she didn't know. Relief, anxiety, joy? She was finally going to meet her mother, and it took everything in her not to push Jutta up the stairs more quickly. At the top of the landing were two gold-framed paintings of flowers on the wall. Jutta paused in front of the bedroom door to the right and turned the knob. When Sophia entered the bedroom, her heart stopped beating for a full two seconds.

The room smelled like hair spray, and the walls were covered in floral wallpaper. In the center of the room was a queen-size bed made up with a lace quilt. On the dresser was a cluster of perfumes and skin creams, and a brush-and-comb set. But otherwise, it was empty.

No Jelka.

"Is this your bedroom?" Sophia wrung her hands.

Jutta took Sophia's arm and guided her onto the edge of the bed. "It's for guests. I sleep here when I'm visiting."

"Where is she?"

"Your mother, Jelka . . ." Jutta hesitated. "Died nearly two years ago."

"No!" Sophia shrieked, clutching her heart.

"I'm so sorry."

The room started to spin, and Sophia's ears rang. She shook her head to make the nightmare stop. This couldn't be true. Not after all she had done to find her.

"What happened?"

Jutta was quiet for a long time. Then she said, "I blame myself. I should have been here for her. I was supposed to be keeping an eye on her, but I went to a Sonny and Cher concert with a jerk who I thought was my boyfriend. Turned out he was married. When I got back here, she wouldn't move."

Sophia didn't recognize the sound of her own voice when she asked, "Was she sick?"

"You can say that."

"How . . . did she die?"

"Pills," Jutta said. "Took too many. Her doctor had prescribed them for her sadness. He called it Mother's Little Helper. Made her like a zombie to me."

"Did she take too many . . . on purpose?"

Jutta nodded.

Sophia was quiet. Then she asked, "When did this happen?"

"September '64. The week of your birthday was always the roughest time of the year for her."

"My birthday is in March."

Jutta tilted her chin. "I was there when you were born. Your birthday is September fifth."

Then Sophia remembered that *Sophia* was born in March. Her

entire life was one big lie. She put her hands to her face and let the tears fall. Jutta put an arm around her shoulder and pulled her close. Even though Sophia had just met the woman, she felt familiar. Jutta rubbed her hair and soothed her.

"Did she talk about me?" Sophia smeared snot away with the back of her hand and wiped it on her skirt.

"Oh, Katja, your mom missed you every day of her life."

"But she gave me away. Didn't she love me?"

"More than anything. She regretted giving you up for that horrible husband of hers. At the time, it was the only way to keep you safe. But in the end, that decision cost her her life."

Jutta dabbed at her own eyes, and Sophia could see that she was trying not to smudge her makeup.

"When Jelka finally got away from him, she married Chuck. He's American and a good man, but she refused to have any more kids. She brought me with her to the States."

Then Jutta popped up suddenly. "I almost forgot why we came up here. She left you something." She stood and reached for the top drawer of the vanity. Jutta held out a small tin canister with a cottage painted on the front.

It was cold, and heavier than Sophia had expected in her hands. But she didn't move to open the tin. She wasn't ready to see what was on the inside. Instead, she asked another question. "My father? Did you know him?"

Jutta smiled, showing all her teeth. "Yes, he was very kind to our family. You have his forehead and eyes."

"Do you know how I can find him?" she asked.

Jutta tapped the tin box. "This is all I have. I must confess that I've never looked inside. Jelka always told me that she was saving it for you."

"May I take it with me?"

"Of course. Hopefully, it will answer some questions for you."

Jutta glanced up at the clock. "Shit, I have to go. My shift at the restaurant starts in thirty minutes. Did you want to stay the night? Chuck is away in South Carolina for work. I'm house-sitting and watching the cat until he returns."

"No." Sophia got to her feet. "A friend is waiting for me outside. We need to get back tonight."

"Well, I hope you'll come again." Jutta led Sophia back down the steps and into the foyer. Then she bent down and wrote her information on a piece of paper. "This is the number to my apartment over by the College of William and Mary and my telephone number at work. Please, keep in touch. I want to get to know you."

Then she pressed her lips to Sophia's cheek. *"Auf Wiedersehen,"* she said, and opened the front door for her.

"Until we meet again." Sophia squeezed Jutta's hand, then clutched the tin can to her chest as she descended the stairs.

CHAPTER 52

Williamsburg, VA, April 1966

ETHEL

Ethel watched Sophia stumble down the stairs and into the car, gripping a box so tightly that her knuckles looked white. Her face was tear-streaked, and she looked disheveled.

"What on earth happened?" Ethel asked as Sophia threw herself into the front seat of the car.

"My mother. She's dead."

Ethel reminded herself to breathe. How could this poor child have discovered her mother and then lost her all in the same day? Ethel reached into her skirt pocket for her rosary and started moving her fingers over the beads. "Can you tell me what happened?"

"She took her life. Because of me."

"Oh, dear. When?"

"September '64."

"How did you find all of this out?"

"Her sister, Jutta." Sophia crumpled against the car door. "If Ma Deary had told me the truth, I could have found Jelka before she was gone. Maybe meeting me could have brought her some peace, and she wouldn't have killed herself."

"Don't you dare blame yourself." Ethel slid across the seat and took the girl into her arms. Sophia shivered against Ethel like a puppy caught in the rain. "I'm so sorry for your loss."

Ethel rocked her as Sophia sniffled and cried. They sat like that for a long time, and Ethel traced circles on her back to help her calm. It was how she had soothed her own children, and it was working on Sophia.

"I feel so useless," Sophia said.

"Hey, there's nothing you could have done to prevent this. You are the child in all of this. You can't control what grown-ups do."

Sophia's eyes looked vacant.

"Let me get you home."

On the ride up I-64 West Ethel continued to talk, in an attempt to quell Sophia's pain, but after a while she could see that the girl needed to rest. With one hand on the wheel, she reached the other into the backseat for a blanket and draped Sophia with it. "You've had a long day. Why don't you close your eyes, and I'll wake you when we get close."

Sophia clutched the tin box to her chest and fell asleep in an instant.

The ride home always seemed faster to Ethel. When they arrived back at the high school parking lot, the sun hung low in the sky. She rubbed Sophia's arm until the girl opened her eyes. "Honey, we're here."

Sophia stretched and mumbled a thank-you. But Ethel didn't feel comfortable letting her out of the car. She was from the school of driving children up to their front door, watching them go into the house, and not pulling off until she knew they were safe.

"Sweetie, I'd never forgive myself if something happened to you this late in the day, walking down the side of a road alone. Where do you live?"

It was obvious from the look Sophia gave her that she wasn't used to being mothered.

"I can't let you take me all the way home. Ma Deary would . . ." She shuddered. "How about you drop me off at the little dirt path that leads to the farm?"

Ethel agreed and followed Sophia's directions to the path. The area was nothing but trees and bushes, wide-open and rural. She could hear the crickets and nocturnal creatures settling into the evening. "Are you sure you are going to be all right?"

"Trust me, Mrs. Gathers, it's a short walk. The house is right past that clearing. I've been doing it all my life."

"Please call me whenever you can. I'm home most days before three. We'll figure out what's next together." She reached down to the floor and passed the tin canister to Sophia out the window. "What's this?"

"Something my mother left for me. I'll open it when I'm ready." Sophia attempted a smile, but it landed as a grimace, and then she turned down the narrow path.

Ethel sat and waited, listening for any noise that would tell her the girl was endangered. When she felt satisfied that Sophia was fine, she steered the car back toward the highway and headed for her home in Washington, D.C. If she wasn't attached to Sophia before, she certainly was now. As she drove, she racked her brain for what she could do next.

CHAPTER 53

Philadelphia, PA, January 1955

OZZIE

Ozzie paced the halls of the maternity ward at Mercy-Douglass Hospital. His nerves were thinner than piss on a plank, and the thought that a shot of whiskey would calm him down fluttered through his head, but he dismissed it as he turned into the waiting room. Against the wall was a Kwik Kafe vending machine, and his hands were shaking so badly that he dropped the nickel three times for the cup of coffee he tried to purchase.

On the television fastened to the wall was an episode of *I Love Lucy,* and the noise of Lucy and Desi's shenanigans further irritated him. Ozzie was so wrapped up in his anxiety and agitation that he hadn't noticed the man sitting in the corner until his voice reached him across the room.

"Where do you hide the booze so your wife doesn't know how much you really drink?"

Trembling and startled, Ozzie looked up from where he knelt on the floor with the nickel in hand. "What did you say to me?"

The man released a hearty chuckle. "I always hid mine inside the toilet tank, behind the pump and lift chain. My wife would never look there."

Dusting off the knees of his work trousers, Ozzie said, "I don't know what you're talking about, man."

"My hands used to shake like that too. Worse was waking up drenched in sweat while shivering at the same time. I kept a fifth under the bed, within arm's length, for those times in the middle of the night when the beast would demand to be fed."

Every muscle in Ozzie's body straightened. "Do I know you?"

"Name's Joe." He stood and took two long strides over to Ozzie and pumped his hand up and down. His grip was firm and his eye contact intense. The blue pullover he wore was bright and his twill pants were pleated.

"Ozzie," he said, feeling dull in comparison to the man, who seemed to glow before him.

"Nice to meet you, brother. Let me help you with that machine." Joe pulled a nickel from his own pocket, popped it in, and while waiting for the coffee, he asked, "Is this your first child?"

Ozzie didn't answer.

"We are on baby number three. Praying Peggy gets her girl this time. We have two knucklehead boys at home, six and three. What are you hoping for?"

He thought of Katja, as he always did when people asked this question. He couldn't bring himself to wish for another girl. "A boy."

"Looks like you already had a few tastes today. Drink the coffee, so that when you see your family, you've sobered up some."

Placing the cup to his mouth, Ozzie did as he was told.

Joe motioned for Ozzie to take a seat across from him in the gray plastic chairs against the wall. "I had my first drink when I was nine years old. Down in the backwoods of Amherst County. My daddy used to make corn liquor. Bootlegging was how he kept a roof over our heads. All nine of us. I'd sneak in the shed when he was away making deliveries and have myself a belly full. Till he caught me and tried to beat the black off me." Joe grinned.

Ozzie didn't even crack a smile. This man was a complete stranger, why was he telling him his personal business?

"It started off as fun. Especially when I got good at the guitar and started hanging at the juke joints. I was only fifteen when I played my first show, down in Richmond. Have you ever been?" Joe asked but didn't wait for a response.

"Man, I was more scared than a whore going to church on Easter Sunday." Joe clapped his hands. "But then one of the fellows slipped me a glass of bourbon, and I downed it. My nerves were gone, and I got up on the stage and played like somebody possessed. Got a reputation as the little fella who could hold his liquor and play like Bo Diddley. So I had to live up to it."

Ozzie's skin itched. As Joe went on to describe nights when he'd wake up and not be able to remember how he got home and who the woman next to him was, Ozzie realized that he could relate. Days and nights were missing from his memory as well. Though lucky for him, he had awakened only next to Rita, except on the nights she had banished him to the basement, which in the past few months had been more often than not.

"I woke up with the shakes and went to bed with the runs. It all became too much, and a deep sadness had strangled me till I didn't want to live no more. Ten years went by without me drawing a clean breath. I lost my home, my woman, and only worked enough odd jobs to keep my mouth from getting dry. Alcohol had become my master; it was the only thing that mattered."

Joe spoke with an honesty that resonated intimately, gnawing at a truth buried deep within Ozzie. A lump formed in his throat as a wave of emotions rose to the surface.

"I don't know who I am anymore," Ozzie choked out. "We finally got an appointment for a mortgage after trying for two years, but I messed it up. Drinking on the job. By the time I arrived, the bank had closed, and my wife's been distant ever since."

"Trust me, I've done worse."

Ozzie looked at Joe. "So how'd you control your thirst? 'Cause it's ruining my life."

"A friend invited me to attend a meeting with him. I went and met men who had struggled with drinking just like me. I did what they told me to do. That was eight years ago, and I've been living a sober life ever since."

"You mean to tell me that you haven't had a drink in eight years? Don't bullshit me."

"Not a single drop. Best part is that I don't even think about it anymore. It has lost its power over me."

Ozzie didn't know if he believed him. Then Joe reached over and covered Ozzie's jittery hand with his.

"This isn't who you are, brother. Let me help you the way my friend helped me."

Those words opened something inside Ozzie, but he had trouble identifying the feeling. Was it hope?

"Mr. Philips?" called a thin nurse, dressed in white from head to toe, clutching a clipboard in the doorway.

"That's me."

"Your wife and baby are ready for you." Her smile was reassuring.

Ozzie stood. "It was nice meeting you."

Joe put out his hand and pulled Ozzie into a one-armed hug and whispered in his ear, "First order of business is to start with twenty-four hours. No matter what happens, don't pick up that first drink." Then he slipped Ozzie a business card with his telephone number on it.

The hospital room had two beds, and Rita's was on the left, closest to the window. Beside her bed was a woven bassinet. On a slip of cardboard scrolled in cursive were the words "It's a boy." Ozzie held his hat in his hands, in awe of this tiny miracle. He had a son.

"Hey." Rita's voice was hoarse, and her hair had been brushed away from her face and swept into bobby pins.

"You did good, baby." Ozzie touched her foot. "And you look beautiful," he said, even though he could see in her eyes that she was beat.

"You see our boy?"

Ozzie stood over the bassinet. As he watched the child's belly rise and fall, he couldn't help comparing this moment to the first time he had laid eyes on Katja. She'd been smaller and had twice as much hair, and her skin was so pale he remembered checking her features to make sure she belonged to him. Throughout Rita's pregnancy, Ozzie had wondered if it would be possible to love another child. But when he lifted his son and cradled him against his chest, his heart burst open with more love than he knew was possible.

"I want to name him Maceo, after my uncle Maceo," Rita said proudly. "If it wasn't for him losing his life voting in Georgia, I wouldn't have moved to Philly and met you."

There was a loving tenderness in her eyes that had been absent for months, and it further unraveled Ozzie. Joy, sorrow, and regret clipped his words so that they came out staccato.

"Thank you. For giving me a son. I know. I have disappointed you. The drinking. Late rent and missed appointment at the bank. But . . ." He looked down at Maceo, and it was once again like looking God in the face. His eyes crowned with tears. Joe's words had been a revelation. He owed it to his family and to himself to be better.

Rita beckoned him to sit on the side of her bed, then took her fingertips and caressed his tears. "I don't want to raise Maceo without you, but don't make me choose," she whispered, her face wet. "I need you to come back to me, Oz. Be the man I fell in love with, booze-free."

A surge of love, shame, and pain welled up inside Ozzie as he cradled the baby with one arm and Rita with the other. He didn't know why he was being granted this second chance, but he knew that meeting Joe had set something in motion, and he couldn't let it slip away.

CHAPTER 54

Prince Frederick, MD, April 1966

SOPHIA

When Sophia ambled up to the farmhouse, Ma Deary's Rambler was parked in its usual spot. The discovery of her mother's death and the time away with Mrs. Gathers had lit something fierce inside Sophia. She wanted answers, and she wanted them now.

Shoving through the back door, she tramped toward the snores coming from Ma Deary's bedroom and started tapping the woman's arm until she awakened.

"What the—? Rusty." Ma Deary looked surprised. "Girl." She sighed. "The devil has gotten into you? You know better than to wake—"

But Sophia cut her off. "Why didn't you tell me?"

"Tell you what?"

"That I was adopted."

Ma Deary fluttered her eyes several times and then sat up in bed. She felt around on the night table for her cigarettes. With one dangling from her lips, she said, "Girl, where are you getting this cockamamie shit from? Why would you say something like that?"

"'Cause it's the truth." Sophia plucked the cigarette out of Ma

Deary's mouth and threw it to the ground. "I'm old enough now. No more lies."

Ma Deary glared in the way she used to scare her, but Sophia would not be moved. Not after the news she had received today.

"It's always something with you, you know that?" Ma Deary picked up a fresh cigarette and pointed it at Sophia. "You better not touch this one, not if you want me to tell you anything."

Sophia stood taller. "Talk."

"Go put on some coffee for me, and I'll meet you in the kitchen. Let me get my head together, please, and brush my damn teeth."

Sophia relented. "Fine."

Ten minutes later, Ma Deary scuffed out of the bedroom, wearing her bathrobe tied around her waist. Sophia placed the cup of Maxwell House on the dining room table and took the seat across from her.

Ma Deary blew on her cup and then took a sip. "When I was eleven years old, I had a fever so hot that it burned up my ovaries. 'Least that's what the doctor told me. When I met Frank, I told him that I wanted to be a mother but couldn't carry no babies."

She shifted in her seat. "Then one day I was in the break room at work and came across an article in the *Afro*. It had photographs of all these pretty light-skinned orphans with that good hair. I knew I had to have me one. I followed the instructions on how to adopt the kids from Germany, and that's how you got here. Satisfied?"

Sophia crossed her arms. "You should have told me."

"Oh, girl, that's all water under the bridge now. Get over it. What matters now is that you here, that you ours."

"Get over it? I'm not some little pet, I'm a real person. With a heritage and family lineage that I deserve to know and understand. Sophia isn't even my real name!" Her chest heaved.

"What are you talking about?"

"I found my birth mother," Sophia roared.

Ma Deary's eyes widened. "Well, I'll be damned. How could—"

"She's dead. She killed herself. She was sad because she gave me up. If you had told me, I could have located her before she did it. Maybe she would still be alive."

"Why would you go stirring shit up? And after all we've done for you."

"Done for me?" Sophia raised her voice, appalled. "You mean how you have exploited me, worked me to the bone like free labor."

"Little girl, you gotta earn your keep."

"I've done more than earn my keep." Sophia slammed her hands down on the table, making the coffee cup rattle.

"You better watch it, Rusty. Don't get too big for your britches or else."

"Or else what?"

"I won't allow your ass to return to that fancy school."

"Oh, really." Sophia got up from the table, feeling like she had acquired the strength of three grown men. "You go ahead and try to stop me, and I will tell the twins and anyone who'll listen."

Ma Deary pushed back in her seat and began to stand but froze at the sound of Sophia's voice.

"Don't. Test. Me." Sophia pointed her finger and then stormed out the back door.

Two days later, Sophia was back at school. Willa had traveled to Disneyland in California for spring break and wouldn't return to campus until Monday. After living in cramped quarters on the farm, Sophia was grateful for the privacy.

Ma Deary hadn't fought her on returning to school, nor had they said much to each other, but she had worked Sophia like a mule. Before Unc arrived to pick her up, Sophia had to pull weeds, plant tomatoes, peppers, and lettuce, then scrape the roosting bar clean in the henhouse. The worst job had been mucking the horse stalls with a pitchfork, and she had gagged repeatedly over the putrid smells of urine and manure.

Now Sophia breathed in the sweet scent of the lavender sachets that Willa had placed around their room, and examined her hands in front of her. They looked dry, and her nail beds had dirt beneath them, even though she had picked them with an index card.

Then her eyes fell on the tin canister sitting atop her chest of drawers. She still had not opened it. On the farm, it had not felt right to bring her mother's memory to life in the home that had caused Sophia such strife. But even now that she was alone, she wasn't ready. What would she find? What if it was more than she could handle alone?

Sophia stood, placed the tin in her satchel, and decided to take a walk over the school grounds for a bit of fresh air. When she walked down the steps of her dorm, she saw Max and Louis playing catch with a baseball on the lawn. Her breathing slowed down at the sight of Max. He wore a Forest T-shirt and a pair of shorts that strained against the muscles of his thighs.

She strolled to a wooden bench and called out, "Hey, guys."

"Sophia." Louis palmed the ball in the air. "How was your break?"

"Uneventful." She shrugged as she made eye contact with Max. His eyes twinkled in the sunlight as he made his way toward her with Louis in tow. The boys flanked her on the bench.

"What'd you do?" she asked.

"Nothing much," responded Louis, stretching his legs in front of him.

"I was bored, quite frankly," Max said. "I'm happy to be back." He let his thigh rest against hers.

"I'm going to get a jump start on calculus," Louis said, standing. "Give you two lovebirds time to catch up."

"I was just going to the library," Sophia said.

"Okay, Lou, I'll catch up with you later." Max turned toward Sophia and cupped her chin. "Why the face?" he asked.

"I found my birth mother."

"For real?"

"She's dead."

Max put his hand over his mouth. "Soph, I'm so sorry."

"Me too." Sophia patted her satchel. "But she left me something. Will you come to the library with me so that I can open it? I didn't want to do it on the farm. Now that I'm here, I don't want to do it alone."

"Of course." Max stood, reached for her hand, and pulled her to her feet.

On the walk to the library, Sophia filled him in on her ride with Mrs. Gathers, meeting her aunt, and all that had transpired. "I wish I had asked Jutta for a picture of Jelka, alive and happy."

"There's time for that, since she told you to stay in touch."

Max held the library door open for Sophia, and the vanilla woodsy scent of the countless shelves of books eased her. There were two or three huddles of students in the main lobby, but none seemed to notice them as Sophia and Max headed back to their special room. Once inside, Max locked the door behind them and then pressed his lips against hers and kissed her slowly, shooting little sparks up her spine.

"I've been waiting to do that since the moment I saw you," Max said breathlessly.

His forehead was pressed against Sophia's, and as she gazed into his eyes, it was hard for her to think of anything else. She had been reeling for the last few days, and it was nice to slow down with him. Then she remembered why they were in the room, and she reached for her satchel, placed it on the table, and removed the box.

Max ran his hand over the letters on the tin. "*Prost!* That means 'cheers,'" he said.

"Yes, I know. Do you pray, Max?" Sophia asked, remembering Mrs. Gathers praying before they opened the files at her house.

"My mother made me go to St. Ambrose Catholic Church every Sunday. I was an altar boy from fifth through eighth grade. I know more than my share of prayers." He grinned.

"Will you pray for me?" Sophia's lips trembled.

Max reached for her hands. "How about the Lord's Prayer? That always brings me peace," he said, and Sophia closed her eyes while Max prayed the prayer.

When he was finished, she reached for the tin, pushing her thumb against the lid until it gave way and popped open.

At the top of a pile was a photograph of a younger woman who Sophia presumed was Jelka because of the resemblance to Jutta. She sat next to a Negro man in uniform. A baby of about four or five months was in Jelka's arms. Sophia held the picture close to her face. "I'm assuming this is me and my parents." A knot welled up in her throat as she showed the photo to Max, who studied it.

"I can see you in both of them." He handed it back.

Sophia peered at her parents. The people who made her, both in one place. She could feel love radiating in their smiles, in their closeness. She was one of them. They had belonged to each other, if only for a short time.

Next there was an index card, with "Katja Durchdenwald, September 5, 1949" scribbled in black ink.

"I'm technically six months older than I thought," she told Max.

"That's wild." Max scooted his chair closer until their elbows met.

Sophia didn't know who she felt like most. Was she Katja or Sophia? Which name would she keep? Which identity? After all this time, was it possible to be both?

Inside a handful of yellowing tissue paper, she found a gold heart locket. She opened the heart and found a miniature snapshot of her. She was older than in the family photo, maybe two, with big curls and a bright smile. From the looks of the photo, she had been happy with her mother. Then there was a small plastic bag with a lock of her hair.

"That's probably from your first haircut."

Sophia stuck her fingers in the bag and felt the texture. It was soft, and she closed her eyes, trying to transport herself back in time. But all she could see was the farm.

"I really wish I could remember," Sophia confessed.

"Memories sometimes take time. They'll come back. Just be patient."

Sophia put the baby hair aside. Next there was a rock, and underneath was a standard-size white envelope, stretched by its contents so that it would not close. The envelope was addressed to Jelka Durchdenwald, c/o the Federal Eagle Club. Sophia's heart quickened, and she pushed back the triangular flap and pulled out a stack of handwritten letters. In the center fold was a heap of two-dollar bills.

Sophia scanned the first letter, and then the next, and the next, until she turned to Max.

"These letters are from my father."

Her fingers trembled as she flipped the envelope over again. Then she saw it. The return address was printed in a neat scrawl. Osbourne Philips, Ringgold Street, Philadelphia, PA.

"Oh my God," she croaked as a prickly sensation traveled up her arms.

"Your father is in Philadelphia," Max said. "I think you've found him."

"Please, God, please, let him not be dead too."

CHAPTER 55

Philadelphia, PA, January 1955

OZZIE

At quitting time, Slim stood by Ozzie's locker. Ozzie had already punched out and was planning to head to the hospital to spend time with Rita and Maceo before visiting hours were over.

"I hear congratulations are in order."

Ozzie flashed his teeth. "She had a boy."

Slim clapped him on the back. "Let's head over to Wally's for a drink and a cigar. We gotta celebrate you, man," he said, loudly enough for a few of their drinking buddies to hear.

Ozzie opened his mouth, but then he heard: *Don't pick up that first drink.*

He bit back that itch in his throat. "I can't. Visiting hours will be over soon. Another time," he said, and then put one foot in front of the other until he was nearly running out the door.

When he arrived at Mercy-Douglass Hospital, he went straight to the nursery. He stood at the big window looking at all the infants in hues of brown, resting in identical wicker bassinets. He spotted Maceo right away, swaddled in a blanket with a blue knit hat on his head.

"Which one is yours?"

Ozzie turned. It was Joe, the man he had met in the waiting room.

"Second row on the left."

"Cute little fellow." Joe pressed his hand against the glass. "That's our baby girl next to him on the right."

"Congratulations."

"Thanks, man." They stood in silence, and then Joe asked, "So, how did you do?"

Ozzie knew what Joe meant, and even though they had known each other only a day, he already felt like he could trust the man. "I didn't pick up the first drink, like you said. Even though I couldn't sleep. I sweated all night and vomited twice before work."

"That's your body trying to detox itself. It'll get better. Remember the meeting I mentioned?"

Ozzie nodded.

"Why don't you come with me tonight. It starts at eight, and it's right here in the hospital. All we have to do is take the elevator down to the bottom floor."

"I don't think I need to do all of that."

Joe turned to face him. "Do you want to live or die?"

"What?"

"It's a simple question. To come with me tonight to the meeting is to live. To keep trying to do it by yourself is to die. What's it gonna be?"

Ozzie looked back at Maceo, who had started to fuss, and remembered his promise not to let this second chance at fatherhood slip away. He thought about all the ways in which he had failed Rita in their marriage. He wanted to be better for them and show up for Maceo in all the ways he couldn't for Katja.

"Okay."

"What room is your wife in?"

Ozzie told him.

"I'll meet you right in front at ten to eight."

The meeting was held in a drafty room with no windows in the basement of the hospital. Ozzie could hear the pipes hiss and rattle, and he smelled coffee and cigarette smoke. There were folding chairs set up in a circle, and the room buzzed with boisterous voices and deep laughter. On a plastic card table sat an assortment of cookies, Dixie cups, sugar cubes, and a pot of coffee. Ozzie watched the men greet one another with such pleasantry that it felt like he had entered a family reunion. How were these men supposed to help him control his drinking?

"This here is Ozzie," Joe introduced him around the room, and the men greeted Ozzie with the same enthusiasm.

Then someone rang a hand bell, and they all moved toward seats.

"Let's have us a meeting," said a husky man with gray hair at his temples. He introduced himself as Earl. "We have a new fella with us tonight. So why don't we talk about what it was like for us in the beginning."

One by one, the men in the room begin to share their stories.

"Every morning when I woke up, I asked God why the hell was I still here. My family didn't want me around. I was a disgrace."

"Doctor diagnosed me with liver disease, but even the threat of death didn't stop me from picking up."

"Alcohol was my best friend. I didn't know how I would function without it. I mean, how do you go to a party—hell, watch the fight on a Saturday night—without a drink?"

"It wasn't until I came in here with you men and learned that I have a disease, that I couldn't control my drinking . . . then I understood I had to stop completely."

Each share was more honest than the next. For close to an hour, Ozzie listened; they were all telling pieces of his story.

"Thank you for your vulnerability, gentlemen," Earl said. "In the early days, Sister Ignatia of the Sisters of Charity of St. Augustine would give her alcoholic patients a medallion. She asked only that before that person took a drink, they return the medallion. Is there anyone here who wants a medallion?"

Joe nudged Ozzie. "You should take one."

"But I'm scared," Ozzie said. "What if I can't do it?"

"I'll go through it with you." Joe stood.

Ozzie rose on shaky knees and followed Joe up to the front of the room, where Earl placed the medallion in Ozzie's palm. It was cool to the touch but weighty at the same time.

"Welcome home." Earl gave him a hug, and Ozzie had to tamp down the emotions that threatened to show on his face.

Rita and Maceo stayed at Mercy-Douglass for seven nights, and each evening when visiting hours ended, Joe and Earl were waiting for Ozzie outside of her hospital room.

The first time Ozzie saw them waiting, he was surprised and asked what they wanted.

"A sheep can't get lost if he is in the middle of his herd," Earl answered matter-of-factly.

The official meetings were held on Monday, Wednesday, and Friday evenings. On the other nights, Joe and Earl met Ozzie down in the hospital cafeteria, where they took turns reading to him from the literature that governed their program of recovery. Each night before he left for home, Joe would say, "Pray to God to keep you sober. Meet me back here tomorrow night at seven-fifty."

Although his work buddies peppered him with pleas to go to Wally's, Ozzie resisted. On his eighth day sober, Ozzie pulled the Chrysler Windsor up through the circular driveway and gave Rita's name to the front-desk clerk. It was twenty-eight degrees and breezy, so he kept the car warm and running.

When the same nurse who had been on duty the night Maceo was born wheeled Rita with Maceo in her arms out to his car, Ozzie stood tall with pride at the sight of his family. Rita was draped in a tan wool coat, and the white turban that covered her hair made her look regal. Maceo was bundled in a snowsuit.

"Baby, you two okay?" he asked.

"Ready to get home and sleep in my own bed." Rita smiled and handed the baby to the nurse. Ozzie scooped Rita up in his arms and carried her the few feet to the front seat of the car.

"You know I can walk."

"Not on my watch." He kissed her cheek, lowered her into the front seat, and then moved aside so the nurse could place Maceo in Rita's arms.

When Ozzie rounded the car, the nurse touched his arm and said, "Joe told me to tell you that he'll see you tonight, seven-fifty."

"I'll be there."

Rita had been given strict orders to avoid steps in her first week at home, so Ozzie lifted her up the stairs and into their back bedroom. He had already put together a wooden cradle, and Great-aunt Reese had dressed it with a heap of blankets. Once Rita and Maceo were propped up with pillows, Maceo started to kick his legs and fuss.

"You hungry?" Rita cooed, and Ozzie sat on the edge of the bed and watched as Rita removed her enlarged breast and pressed it against Maceo's face. The miracle of a woman's body never ceased to amaze him.

"Will you be okay for a little while? I need to run back to the hospital for my meeting." Ozzie had briefed Rita on his acquaintance with Joe and their fellowship in the basement.

"Sure, long as that's all you're leaving here to do?" Her eyes went dark. Ozzie knew that Rita had every right not to trust him.

"That's it." He moved to kiss her on her forehead, but he wouldn't make her another promise with his words. Now he had to show her with his actions.

At six months sober, Ozzie's head was clear, and he had the energy of a teenager. Rita had stopped questioning his intentions when he left the house for his nightly meeting, and she had started nudging him to resume their quest to obtain a mortgage from the bank.

"Sweet Maceo has sucked up the breathing space in this back bedroom. There is no place to move," she complained with the baby on her hip.

On his lunch breaks, Ozzie made his rounds to the banks again. He filled out another stack of paperwork and pleaded his case to the tellers.

In the seventh month, Joe told Ozzie that it was time for him to sift through the wrongdoings of his past. Ozzie made an inventory list, and Joe listened to him with patience. When he finished, Ozzie walked lighter, like he had shed ten pounds of guilt, secrets, and pain.

Now they were preparing for Maceo's first birthday party, and he and Rita were blowing up balloons. The fragrance of the chocolate cake that Rita had set on the rack to cool wafted into the living room, making him hungry. But he was too nervous to eat.

Paper streamers were draped across the wall, and a big "Happy 1st Birthday" sign was taped to the living room wall. The party wasn't scheduled to start for a few hours, and to give them time to prepare, Great-aunt Reese had taken Maceo with her to church for a morning social hour.

Ozzie's hands sweated, and his mouth was dry. "Rita, I need to talk to you."

A flicker of worry flashed through her eyes as he joined her on the sofa.

"I want to make an amends to you."

Her face relaxed. "I don't need any more apologies. You've been doing fine by me, baby." She put the balloon to her lips and blew.

"It's not that." He took a deep breath. Ozzie had already practiced what he was going to say to his wife with Joe, but somehow the words seemed to have vanished from his mind.

Rita tied off the balloon. "Well, what is it? Are you sick?"

"When I was in Germany. I was in a relationship." The nerves had given him a stomachache, but he pressed on. "From this union. A child was born."

Rita sat as still as a statue. "Are you saying you have a child?"

"Her name is Katja. This past September, she turned five. I haven't seen her since she was fifteen months old." Ozzie looked at the floor. "Over the years, I've sent money each month to the last place her mother worked. But I've never received a single reply."

Rita finally turned her body toward him. Her skin was ashen, and her eyes scanned his face, bewildered. "You've been holding this in all this time? How come you didn't tell me this before now? Does your mama know?"

"I didn't tell anyone."

"Why? Oz."

"Because I left her in Germany. I didn't mean to, but I did, and I was ashamed. Being an absent father made me feel like Big Otis, and I didn't want you to look at me differently."

Rita reeled in her seat. "Ozzie, that secret has been eating at you. Tearing you down for years. My God. A daughter?"

They sat in silence, then Rita stood and went into the kitchen. Ozzie knew from experience that it was best not to follow her. He heard pots and pans banging around in the sink. After what felt like an eternity, she walked into the living room and sat back down next to him.

"I wish you would have told me from the start. I can't say that I truly understand your reasons for keeping something so big bottled up inside for all this time. But what's done is done. If Maceo has a sister out there somewhere, then I will help you find her. What's yours is mine."

A sigh from deep in his belly escaped his lips. Rita was still by his side. Confessing his deepest secret to his wife had cracked a hole in him. A hole that he could already feel filling him with peace.

"Thank you." He squeezed her hands.

"Look, I can't sit here and play Little Miss Innocent. I had some relationships and situations while you were gone."

He looked at her, but she waved her comment away.

"We won't get into all that now. But these moments of honesty are a step in the right direction for us. I don't know what's happening in those meetings you go to each night, but they're working."

"Thanks for being okay with this," he said.

She looked into his eyes, her expression still baffled. "I'll talk to Sadie on Monday and see if she has any resources we can use to help find her."

Ozzie tipped Rita's chin toward him and kissed her. In that moment he felt lucky. He had his wife and son; Rita knew the secret of Katja and didn't hate him because of it. On Monday, he would celebrate one year of sobriety. In two weeks, he would finally begin his first semester at Lincoln University, albeit part-time. It was a start.

CHAPTER 56

West Oak Forest Academy, May 1966

SOPHIA

By the middle of May, Sophia's sophomore year at West Oak Forest had ended, and unruly teenagers sprinted across the lawn, hugging friends, and singing the lyrics to "California Girls" by the Beach Boys while their fathers lugged trunks, suitcases, and boxes of books to their cars. Sophia stood with Willa in the roundabout, clutching the same tattered train case she had arrived with in September. Willa talked nonstop about her summer plans in New York City with her uncle and then a trip to his summer house in Sag Harbor.

"There's the car." Willa waved as the shiny Cadillac pulled through the roundabout. When the driver opened the door, it was Ms. Eleanor who stepped out of the backseat, in a pair of windowpane culottes and a sleeveless shirt. Her hair bounced around her shoulders.

"Mother," Willa shrieked.

Ms. Eleanor hugged Willa and kissed her cheek. Then she reached for Sophia and squeezed her too. "How are you, darling?"

"Very well, Ms. Eleanor. It's good to see you."

Ms. Eleanor pushed a loose strand of hair from her eyes. "What are you doing for the summer?"

"My aunt is picking me up." Sophia couldn't keep the smile off her face, liking the way "aunt" sounded from her lips. She was so excited to see Jutta again. "We are taking a little road trip to Philadelphia."

"Mom, Sophia found out that she was adopted," Willa cut in. "Her mom sent her over to America from Germany because she couldn't keep her. She's just discovered a whole other family. Isn't that amazing?"

Sophia's smile slid from her face as she watched Ms. Eleanor's skin pale as if she'd seen a ghost. Did she feel sorry for Sophia? She had always been kind, unlike Mrs. Pride, Willa's grandmother.

"Congratulations, Sophia," Ms. Eleanor said. She urged Willa into the backseat of the car. "Baby, we had better go. You know how traffic is this time of day." To Sophia she offered "Good luck, and have a good summer" before slipping into the car.

"Thank you."

The big Cadillac pulled out of the circle just as Max came up with a duffel bag hanging down his side.

"Hey you," he said, letting his fingers graze hers. "Are you ready for this?"

"Yeah, I just wish that Willa hadn't blurted all my business to her mother. Now she's looking at me like some poor little orphan child."

"Don't be silly." He draped his arm around her waist, making her warm all over. "You are going to meet your father for the first time. Let that be your only concern." He gave her the sweetest smile.

"Hopefully," she said as the cars continued to move through the line, not wanting to give voice to all the things that could go wrong again. Sophia touched his chin. "I'm going to miss you."

"I'll miss you too, but we'll write, and you can call me." He reached into his pocket and pulled out a slip of paper. "Here's the number to the house in Martha's Vineyard. Reverse the charges if you need to."

"Your parents won't mind?"

"I'll worry about them." He kissed her temple.

A two-toned Dodge La Femme pulled up, and Jutta waved to Sophia as she got out of the car, wearing a bright yellow headband that matched her pedal pushers.

"Impressive school. I almost thought you gave me the wrong address," she said, sweeping Sophia into her arms. They had met only the one time, and spoken by telephone, but Jutta's embrace comforted Sophia in a way that said they belonged together.

"Jutta, this is Max. The one I told you about."

"Hello, handsome," Jutta said, taking him in.

Max replied, *"Guten Tag!"*

Jutta ribbed Sophia as she and Max exchanged pleasantries in German. "Wow. I'm impressed."

"I told you he speaks well."

"It's a passion of mine." Max beamed.

"Come on, we had better get a move on." Jutta walked to the driver's side.

Max grabbed Sophia's hand and placed a kiss on her cheek. "Call me. Soon as you can. Promise?"

She nodded, not wanting to let go of his hand.

On the highway, Jutta popped in an eight-track, and as the car roared up I-95, Sophia removed the letter she had received from Mrs. Gathers in her satchel.

"What's that?" Jutta asked, glancing at her sideways.

"The confirmation for our hotel in Philly, courtesy of Mrs. Gathers."

"I'm so glad she's putting us up."

"We lucked out. She's in Philadelphia this week, covering the call to desegregate Girard College for *The Philadelphia Tribune*."

Sophia didn't envy those students fighting for integration, not after the school year she'd had among the first at Forest. The violation in the girls' locker room, malicious rumors, monkey chants, derogatory name-calling: *Look, it's Uncle Ben and Aunt Jemima* had stained her.

Jutta cracked her window, and a sweet-smelling breeze rolled in. "That's a relief. I had reached out to an old boyfriend who lives in East Falls. He said we could crash on his sofa, but I had been worrying about it being awkward. Since I technically broke up with him."

"So, you're a heartbreaker," Sophia teased.

"Not hardly. But he was way too needy. Stay away from possessive men." Jutta laughed and then told Sophia about the new guy she was dating, and her job at the Ox and Fox Tavern, where she worked as a hostess and sometimes as a waitress. "It's not bad, my boss is fair, and it pays the bills." She reached for a cigarette.

While she fumbled with the lighter, Sophia asked the question that had been nibbling at her since she'd received the tin canister. "The letters from my father. Did Jelka ever write him back?"

Exhaling the smoke, Jutta responded, "No."

"Why not?"

"She never spent the money either. I'm sure it's all there in the envelope that she saved for you." Jutta tipped the ash from her cigarette in the metal ashtray.

"When she got to America, why didn't she try to find him? I don't understand why she wouldn't spend the money. Didn't she need it?" Sophia turned toward her.

"It was because she was ashamed that she gave you away to the orphanage. You were her pride and joy and the light of your father's world." Jutta's eyes glazed over. "He used to come to our little cottage every weekend and would barely let you out of his sight. Jelka thought he'd hate her for giving you away, even though she was trying to keep you safe."

Sophia looked out the window at the passing cars as Jutta's words sank in. Jelka had given her up to keep her safe. Her mother had thought she was doing the right thing. Even though her life on the farm had been miserable, and Ma Deary didn't have a mothering bone in her body, she had grown up with her brothers relatively secure, however unloved.

Jutta replaced one eight-track with another and then tapped the steering wheel. "I love this song. Do you know it? 'A Fool in Love'?"

"Of course." Happy for a change in mood, Sophia stretched her arms in front of her and mimicked the swinging dance she'd seen Tina Turner's backup singers do on the show *Hollywood a Go Go*.

"Look at you. You've got it." Jutta bobbed her head and rotated her shoulders.

When they reached the Delaware line, Jutta offered her a sandwich. "It's called *Stramme Lotte,* which is basically ham with a fried egg on top."

Sophia took a bite. "It's good."

After they finished the food, Sophia shared the sugar cookies that she had packed from the cafeteria at school. The folded map was slung against Sophia's lap, and once the road split and they merged onto I-495, Jelka stopped at the filling station to top off the gas.

They passed the Philadelphia Airport, and as they drove over a bridge, Sophia caught a glimpse of a tall skyscraper with the letters "PSFS." The city streamed through Sophia's car window like a picture show, vibrant and loud. Jutta turned the car down Dickenson Street, and they passed by a park square with young brown-skinned teens on the court, playing basketball. A stray cat meandered around the corner, and Sophia spotted the sign for Ringgold Street.

"That's it," and Jutta made the right turn.

At the nose of the one-way street, Jutta parked the car behind a blue Chevy. Before she turned off the engine, the driver's-side door of the Chevy opened, and out stepped a woman in a belted polka-dot dress. Sophia blinked several times. "Oh my goodness." She brought her hands to her mouth.

"Who is that?" Jutta asked.

"Mrs. Gathers, the woman I was telling you about." Sophia scrambled from the front seat.

They all met on the curb, and after a quick introduction, Sophia threw her arms around Mrs. Gathers and squeezed. "I thought you were meeting us at the hotel."

"My first interview ended early, and it was only ten minutes from here. I'm so glad I thought to ask you for the address."

"Me too. I'm really scared." Sophia looked down the block at the tidy row houses. "What if he turns me away?"

Mrs. Gathers looked Sophia in the eyes. "You've worked extremely hard to get to this moment. Trust yourself."

"I'll be right there with you." Jutta took Sophia's hand.

Sophia was thick with feelings as she looked from Mrs. Gathers to Jutta. Just nine months ago, she'd been stuck on the farm with no future, and then Mrs. Brown had helped her get into Forest, and now Mrs. Gathers and Jutta were here supporting her through this major life event.

"Okay, let's get this over with." She turned and then stopped when she realized that Mrs. Gathers hadn't moved. "Aren't you coming in too?"

"Why don't you and Jutta do this part together. I imagine it will be healing for both of you." Mrs. Gathers touched Jutta's arm. "And I'm sorry about your sister. I bet she's pleased that you are here for Sophia."

Just then a flock of birds flew overhead, and Jutta smiled with her eyes on the sky.

"I'll meet you back at the hotel. Good luck." Mrs. Gathers turned toward her car, and Jutta gripped Sophia's hand.

As Sophia walked across the sidewalk and up the limestone stairs, a warm feeling caressed her cheek. She heard gospel music and smelled the savory scent of fried fish.

CHAPTER 57

Philadelphia, PA, May 1966

OZZIE

Ozzie dropped his Samsonite attaché case, heavy with the midterm papers, by the front door. For the past four years, he had worked as an assistant professor in the Economics Department at his alma mater, Lincoln University. This semester he had taught two sections, and as per usual, his students had waited until the eleventh hour to submit their final papers. One student had even cornered him in the faculty parking lot to hand over work.

Untying his wing tips, he slipped the pair into the shoe rack in the hall closet, as was Rita's rule the moment they had purchased their new home on Twenty-Third Street. The beige carpet was soft under his tired feet as he padded around Maceo's *djembe* drums and past the reading corner down through to the kitchen at the rear of the house. Inside the refrigerator, he snapped up a cold cola, his after-work drink of choice.

Ozzie took his sobriety one day at a time, but sometimes, when he looked back, he was amazed at the progress he had made. The first two years had been like riding a bicycle with training wheels, and Joe and Earl had kept a steady hand on his back. By year three, Rita had trusted him to be involved with their finances again. Now, at eleven years, they had moved into an easy rhythm that only time could teach.

The telephone rang, and when he reached for the receiver hanging from the kitchen wall, he had a feeling that it was Rita, telling him that she was working on a brief and that she'd need him to pick up Maceo from baseball practice.

"Hello."

"Ozzie?" It wasn't Rita, it was his mother, Nettie.

"Hey, Mama. How you doing?"

"I need you to come on over here."

He frowned. "Why your voice sounding like that? What's wrong?"

"Ain't nothing wrong. I just need you to do as I say. Now, come along."

"Ma, just tell me what it is."

"Shouldn't take you but ten minutes to get here." And with that, she hung up the telephone.

Nettie was getting mulish in her old age, and Ozzie knew he couldn't do much but obey. After he scribbled a note for Rita, Ozzie changed into a 76ers T-shirt, sweats, and his Chuck Taylor All Stars. The weather was nice, and after teaching all day, it felt good to breathe in the fresh air. As he moved swiftly through the five blocks between his house and his mother's home, he hoped she wasn't summoning him for the bad news that someone was in the hospital or, worse, had died. Nettie was old-school-like, she never discussed anything of importance over the telephone.

The black-and-white front door to his childhood home was open, and the screen door scratched against the step, announcing his arrival. When he stepped into the living room, on the sofa sat a woman who looked familiar, and the sight of her made his mouth parch.

"Jelka?" he croaked, and in those few seconds, he could feel all the air drain from his lungs.

Nettie wore a red and yellow kaftan, and the material rustled as she lifted her arms and clasped her hands together. "Now, honey, I thought you said your name was Jutt-a."

"It is Jutta," she said to Nettie, then pushed herself up. "Hello, Osbourne." Jutta crossed the room and threw her arms around his neck.

"Oh my God." Ozzie hugged her back, unable to believe it. "You look just like your sister. How did you find me? It's been so long." He stepped back, taking in the woman before him but still seeing in her eyes the twelve-year-old girl he had left behind.

Before Jutta could answer, Ozzie saw a figure coming down the stairs. He released Jutta just as his knees started to buckle. Was it? Could it be?

"Katja?" he breathed.

The long-legged redheaded girl stopped at the bottom of the stairs, and the rest of the room disappeared. She was a combination of his mother and Jelka. Same pink lips with a sprinkle of freckles on her nose. The Philips nose.

"Hi, I go by Sophia," she said softly. "I just found out that my real name is Katja."

"And I just found out that my grandbaby goes to a hoity-toity boarding school in Maryland. Who would have thought it?" Nettie clapped her hands.

"I take it you are Osbourne?" Katja smiled, and that was when he saw Jelka come alive on her face. It was that smile, the way her lips curled and her cheeks rose.

All Ozzie could do was nod as he strode toward her, closing the distance between them. The girl reached into her front dress pocket and held out a Polaroid to him. He took it. It was one of the two photos that Jutta had taken of the three of them, the one he had given to her. He looked from the picture to Katja; she had grown, and she was stunning. His daughter. His Kitten was standing in front of him after all these years.

"Thank you, God," he mumbled as he pulled Katja into his arms and held her tight, tears drizzling his cheeks. "I can't believe it is really you."

Ozzie shook uncontrollably, and he wasn't ashamed. For he had been faithful, had done what Joe had told him to do. He had worked his recovery program, attended his weekly meeting without fail, and now his daughter was in his arms. Katja had found her way back to him. The promises of living a clean and sober life had come true.

Ozzie let go, then stared at Katja. She was only a few inches shorter than he was, tall and lanky, like his older sisters.

"Words can't even begin to tell you how sorry I am. I never meant to leave you behind in Germany."

"It's okay. I understand," she offered.

"I've searched for you." He grabbed both her hands. "I'll be here for you for the rest of my days, if you will allow me."

CHAPTER 58

Philadelphia, PA, May 1966

SOPHIA

The Divine Lorraine Hotel loomed on the corner of Broad Street and Fairmount Avenue. It was dark out, and Sophia dragged herself from the car, bone-tired. When they reached the fourth floor and knocked on door 444, Sophia didn't know how she had made it through the lobby and onto the elevator.

Mrs. Gathers ushered them into the spacious hotel room.

"Wow, this is bigger than my apartment." Jutta whistled. "Thanks again for putting us up."

"Certainly, how did it go?" Mrs. Gathers wore a satin pajama set, and her face was scrubbed clean.

"I met my father, Osbourne Philips," Sophia said.

Mrs. Gathers raised her hands in the air. "Praise God!"

"He was so happy to see me. The whole family was ecstatic. I'm still overwhelmed, to be honest."

"It was a lot to take in at once," Jutta admitted. "But I was really glad to be there."

Sophia was exhausted and needed a moment to herself. "Where's the restroom? I'm going to take a shower."

"Right down the hall, dear."

As Sophia headed toward the bathroom, Jutta kept up a steady stream of chatter with Mrs. Gathers, but the only voice that Sophia heard was Ozzie's. *I've searched for you. I never meant to leave you behind.*

Her father was alive, and he had tried to find her. But why had he left her in the first place? There had been too much commotion in the house, Nettie peppering her with questions, introducing her to aunts and uncles while stuffing her belly with the flakiest fried fish that she had ever tasted, to get any answers. When she had asked Jutta, she'd said she didn't know.

The heat and steam from the shower felt good. After slipping into her only nightgown, she found Jutta and Mrs. Gathers sipping tea on the settee.

"Are you okay, love?" Jutta asked.

"It's been a really long day." Sophia wrapped her arms around her waist.

Mrs. Gathers said, "Why don't you get some rest. You and Jutta can sleep in the room to the left of the bathroom. I heard you were having breakfast with your father tomorrow."

Sophia grinned. "He invited me to his home. I can't believe this is all happening."

"I knew God would provide."

Jutta lifted her mug to her lips. "Sleep well."

The bedroom had a full-size bed, two nightstands, and a chest of drawers. Under the covers, Sophia tossed and turned but couldn't fall asleep. It was too late to phone Max or Willa, and the high of her day had made it impossible for her mind to settle down. She swung her legs over the side of the bed and then tiptoed across the floor and reached inside her satchel. Tucked between two books was a crossword puzzle that she had scavenged from the Saturday newspaper at school. The grating of her pencil on the page scratched a part of her brain that she couldn't otherwise reach. After filling in half the puzzle, she was relaxed enough to doze off.

Sleep took her to the place that, no matter how much she willed it, she couldn't avoid. She was in the kitchen, and the heat from the flames started moving toward her. But just as she felt the flames shoot over her, a woman pulled her away from the fire and into her arms. The embrace felt familiar in her bones.

"*Schatz.*" The woman kissed both her cheeks, and when Sophia looked up, she was gone.

When Sophia opened her eyes, it was daylight, and Jutta was sitting up in the bed they shared. "Are you all right? You were trembling like a leaf."

As bad as it seemed, there was some good news. Despite not taking the pills, Sophia hadn't screamed or ripped the flesh from her arms with her nails. That was a first. She searched her memory. "What does *Schatz* mean?"

"It's a term of endearment. It means 'darling,' 'honey,' 'sweetie.' Something like that. Why? Are you dreaming in German now?" Jutta gave her a sloppy smile.

Sophia hugged her knees to her chest and told Jutta the recent iteration of her recurring nightmare.

Moving to the window, Jutta opened the curtains until full sunlight bled into the room. "Maybe it was Jelka. She called me *Schatzi* sometimes. Maybe it was how she called to you too."

A longing curled up in Sophia's gut.

Jutta peered out the window. "I talked to my ex, Danny. He wants to meet for coffee while I'm in town. I hope it's okay for Mrs. Gathers to drive you to your father's house. I promised him that you'd be there by ten."

Mrs. Gathers parked in front of a house with a lime-green awning. "I know you were expecting Jutta to bring you. I hope I'm not intruding."

"Are you kidding me? You're responsible for all of this. Getting me to America, helping me find my parents. It's only appropriate for my father to meet our Brown Fairy." Sophia smiled.

On the porch sat two railing planters filled with purple and white pansies stretching their petals toward the sun. Before Sophia reached the top landing, Ozzie pushed open the screen door. He was dressed in a green and yellow dashiki paired with dark Levi's, his short Afro glistened, and he smiled showing all his teeth.

"Katja. I'm so glad you came." He held the door open as he looked from Sophia to Mrs. Gathers.

"Hello, Mr. Philips, I'm Ethel Gathers, the one who organized the adoptions of the war babies out of Germany." She held out her hand.

"It is an honor to meet you."

"Mrs. Gathers has been a godsend in helping me find you." Sophia fidgeted with the sleeve of her sweater.

"Words can't thank you enough. Please, come on in."

They followed Ozzie into the living room. The walls were covered in African art, and the matching sofas were burnt orange with striped throw pillows. A curvy brown-skinned woman dressed in a floral pantsuit stood in the archway that separated the living room from the dining room. A boy about the same age as the twins leaned into her, squirming in a button-down shirt that clearly was not his outfit of choice.

"Katja?" The woman stepped forward. "I'm Rita. It's such a pleasure to finally meet you. You are absolutely beautiful."

"Thank you." She blushed.

"Sorry we missed you last night. I got caught up at work. Can I give you a hug?" Rita opened her arms and flattened Sophia against her bosom. "Your dad and I have been scouring the earth for you. He told me the story, and I'm amazed that you found us first." Then she turned to Mrs. Gathers. "Pleased to meet you too, ma'am."

"Ethel Gathers." They shook hands.

"I'm Maceo." The boy waved in a way that said, *Remember me?*

Sophia bent down until they were eye to eye. Here was another brother, and Maceo was the spitting image of her father. Deep mahogany skin, white teeth, and kind eyes. "Nice to meet you."

"Why don't we all sit down for a few minutes." Rita gestured to the sofas.

After a bit of polite small talk among the grown-ups, Sophia reached into her satchel and pulled out the tin canister with the German cottage painted on the front. "This box provided the final clue."

"Oz, don't you have the same box up in your closet?" Rita touched Ozzie's thigh.

He said to Sophia, "We bought them from a street vendor shortly after you were born at a little stall in the central square in Mannheim."

Rita glanced over at the table clock and exhaled. "Goodness gracious, I hate that we can't spend more time getting to know you, Katja, but Maceo and I are off to a fall cotillion interest meeting."

"We can skip it," Maceo piped up.

"You know better than that. I'm one of the organizers." Rita stood. "Mrs. Gathers, thanks again for bringing Katja to us." Her eyes sparkling, she said to Sophia, "Sweetheart, I am looking forward to getting to know you. Come back real soon."

Rita picked up her leather pocketbook and motioned for Maceo to give Sophia a hug goodbye, which he did. Then Sophia watched the tenderness among the three as Ozzie kissed Rita's cheek and exchanged a fist bump with Maceo. This was what she had been missing: genuine love.

"Why don't we go into the kitchen. Do you two like pancakes?"

"I do," Sophia said.

"Rita left us a batch in the oven, along with some bacon."

Mrs. Gathers stood. "Mr. Philips, I'm in the middle of writing an article for *The Philadelphia Tribune*. Do you mind if I use your desk in that corner to work on it? I'm sure you two have a lot to catch up on."

"Absolutely," he said, and then moved a few books around and pulled out her chair.

The kitchen was painted a bright yellow, and every surface was immaculate, not a dish in the sink or a crumb to be found.

"Do you drink coffee?"

"No, just water or milk if you have it." Sophia slipped into the wooden chair adjacent to the refrigerator. The round table was covered with a checkered tablecloth, and two places had been set.

Ozzie sat the platter between them and then served the food. "I didn't sleep a wink last night. Kept thinking about you coming back. Hoping that you wouldn't change your mind."

"Why would I do that?"

Ozzie shrugged, and a few silent moments passed between them.

"This is a really nice house," Sophia said, thinking about how dilapidated the farmhouse was in comparison.

"Thanks. It took a lot to get us here, but it's home. You're always welcome." Ozzie slipped a slice of pancake into his mouth, then put down his fork. "I placed ads in the local papers in Mannheim, and I never heard anything back. How in the world did you find us?"

Sophia told him about meeting Max, the German words flying from her mouth, and then about tracking down Mrs. Gathers through the white pages.

He said, "I had read about her in *Ebony* magazine years ago. But it never dawned on me that you could be one of the children she brought to America. I had always assumed that you were with Jelka in Mannheim. That's why my trail always went cold."

"That makes sense." Sophia chewed. She went on to tell Ozzie how Mrs. Gathers had retrieved Jelka's information from the St. Hildegard's children's orphanage and learned that she had moved to America.

He choked. "You lived in an orphanage?"

Sophia nodded. "But I don't remember much." She kept the nightmares of the fire to herself. "Jelka's second husband was an American stationed in Mannheim. Jutta said when Jelka came over, she brought Jutta too. With Mrs. Gathers's help, I found their address in Williamsburg, Virginia."

"You are way more resilient than I was at your age." Ozzie stood, then cleaned off the table and poured himself a second cup of coffee. "What are your adopted parents like?"

Sophia didn't want to tell him that they were mean, worked her like a dog, and lied to her. Instead, she said, "I never felt like I fit. It always seemed like a part of me was missing." Then she could feel her cheeks warm with delight as she told him about her three brothers.

"And you grew up on a farm? In southern Maryland?"

She nodded just as Mrs. Gathers entered the kitchen.

"Are you two all right?" she asked, looking at Sophia, who said that she was fine.

Ozzie rose to his feet and reached for another mug. "Please join us and at least have a cup of coffee with me."

Mrs. Gathers sat on the other side of the round table. "Black is fine."

"Sophia was just telling me that we were only living a couple hundred miles apart from each other all this time. Unreal."

Then he got really quiet, and Sophia wondered what part of their lives he was reliving.

To ease his mind, she said, "Jutta told me that Jelka took me to the orphanage because her first husband was a dangerous man. She left me there, even though she didn't want to, for my safety."

But it had the opposite effect: She could see the blood drain from his face. "It was my job to protect you. I'm so sorry that I failed. Not a day went by when I didn't think of you."

She looked from Mrs. Gathers back to Ozzie and asked the question that had burned inside her since this quest began. "Why did you leave? How did we get separated? Jutta said she didn't know."

Ozzie leaned back in his seat. "I received my reassignment orders with a thirty-minute notice. Couldn't even let your mother know that I was leaving or where I was going. Once I got to my new post, I had no way of getting in contact with her. I sent letters and money to the Federal Eagle Club, where she worked, but I never received a response. Now I know why she never wrote back. Because she had given you up."

"Mr. Philips, if I may interject," said Mrs. Gathers, "I've worked with hundreds of German women, and it was my experience that many of the mothers wanted to keep their children, but they had no support in raising them."

Ozzie nodded. "Even though Germany appeared to be more color-blind, I guess the truth was a lot more complicated." He reached for Sophia's tin canister. "May I?"

"Of course."

Sophia watched as he fingered the letters that he had written. Then he pulled the family Polaroid close to his face. "How is Jelka doing? I bet she lost her mind when she saw you."

Sophia looked up at him and then blinked several times. "You don't know?"

"Know what?"

"She died. Jutta said . . . she took her own life," and the words still felt surreal as they left Sophia's mouth.

"Oh my God." Ozzie brought his hands to his heart. "No. Jelka." He dropped his head, and his chest heaved. After a few moments, he pushed back from the table and went to lean over the sink. "When?"

Mrs. Gathers spoke up. "According to Jutta, it happened in September '64."

He turned to face Sophia. "So you never reconnected?"

Sophia told him that they hadn't. "I have no memory of her."

"I'm so sorry. God knows if I could rewrite history I would."

Another moment of silence passed between them, and then Ozzie reached for a napkin and wiped his nose.

"Do you need some privacy, Mr. Philips?" Mrs. Gathers asked.

"I'm fine."

Sophia waited until Ozzie sat back down at the table before continuing with her questions. "Could you tell me about her? Please. What was she like?"

Ozzie's eyes were sad, but his lips pulled back into a smile. "She was kind, took really good care of her family and you. She liked to dance. I taught her how to Lindy Hop and jitterbug."

As Ozzie talked about Jelka, Sophia watched his posture straighten and the memories flood out of him. He went on for over an hour, telling her about her infancy and early toddlerhood. The things they did together, how he spent every weekend with her, his time in the army, and what it was like living in Germany, away from his family, at such a young age. And she hung on every word as he gave her the missing memories of her history, what she had always known was absent from Ma Deary's rendering.

"As you were talking, Mr. Philips, I just realized that I hadn't actually considered the men in this story. I have always been so focused on the women and children," Mrs. Gathers said. "I've never reflected on what it was like for the Negro men to also lose their children."

"Not a day went by when I didn't feel Katja's absence," Ozzie said. "I wanted her with me."

To Sophia's delight, he recounted her young milestones, from the first time she crawled, to her first tooth, to the books he read to her as a little girl. Sophia clung to his every word like a life raft.

"Jelka was always speaking German to you, so I read you English books, and you loved them. *Curious George* was your favorite."

This man was really her father. Her flesh and blood. They shared the same DNA.

Ozzie straightened up in his chair. "I know some men left kids behind without a second thought. But that's not me. I've spent the better part of my life suffering the loss of my daughter. It sent me down a spiraling road—"

Sophia wondered what that meant, but before she could ask, Mrs. Gathers pressed on.

"I write a column in the *Baltimore Afro-American* newspaper. Usually, I recount the first year of the adopted child's life in the new, happy American home. But your story and perspective of losing contact with your child, seemingly against your will, needs to be told. I've never written a story from that perspective before."

"I'm not too sure that people will care about the story of a black man. Especially in these times of race riots and civil rights leaders being gunned down."

"I disagree. Oftentimes I feel like the Negro man in America needs a publicist. I'd love to be the one to showcase a veteran's love and commitment to find his lost daughter."

"She's really good," Sophia added. "I've collected as many of her articles as I could find."

"Really?" Mrs. Gathers turned to Sophia.

"Yes, I admire what you do," she said sheepishly, and then to Ozzie she said, "I think you should do it."

"Well, let me run it by my wife first," he said, winking, "but I'm sure she'll be all for it."

The day had gotten away from them; the hours Sophia spent with Ozzie and Mrs. Gathers passed like minutes.

"We had better get going. I'm sure Jutta is wondering where you are." Mrs. Gathers got to her feet. She carried her mug to the sink, and when she reached for the sponge to wash it, Ozzie waved her away.

"Rita would have my head if she thought I let you lift a finger in our home. Just leave it."

They walked back through the living room, and when they got to the door, Ozzie touched Sophia's shoulder. "I can't tell you how much this visit means to me. If you'd prefer that I call you Sophia, I will, but you'll always be Katja or Kitten to me."

On the farm, they called her Rusty; at school, she was simply Sophia. "That's fine."

He blew out a nervous chuckle. "I know that I have missed a significant portion of your life. But I promise you, as God is my witness, I will be there for you from this day forward. That is, if you will let me."

"I'd like that. To get to know you and your family better."

"Oh, darling. Between Rita and my mother, I'm going to have to hold them back from hijacking you. They're your family too."

Her family. Her real family. Those were the sweetest words her ears had ever heard.

"In that case, *Auf Wiedersehen.*" She smiled.

"Until we meet again."

CHAPTER 59

West Oak Forest Academy, May 1968

SOPHIA

Senior year for Sophia came and went. Willa had been sulking for days: Since she was a year younger than the rest of their crew, Sophia, Max, Louis, and Claude would soon graduate from Forest, breaking up their tight-knit quintet and leaving Willa behind.

"You'll still have Henrietta and Marion," Sophia said, making mention of the two Negro sophomore girls who lived down the hall.

"It's not the same, and you know it. You're going off to college in Philadelphia, and while you are living it up with your new friends, I'll be stuck here in twelfth grade. I'll never see you again." Her green eyes darkened.

"Don't say that. You can come and stay the weekend with me and even longer on your spring break. Penn's campus is beautiful, you'll love it."

But her words did nothing to improve Willa's mood, and Sophia was grateful for the distraction when she heard the swift knock at the door. "Mail for Sophia."

An envelope skated across the linoleum floor. Sophia reached down to retrieve it.

"Who's it from?"

Turning the letter over in her hand, she recognized Walter's neat handwriting. "My oldest brother."

"Well, I'm going to meet Marion at the library. I promised to share my notes from last year's advanced world history class to help her study for the final."

"I'll meet you at dinner."

"Only six more dinners with you to go." Willa gave Sophia a pouty expression, then breezed toward the door.

Sophia took the envelope to the vanity and tugged on the folded paper.

Dear Rusty,

I received your note, and I understand your concern. Unc has promised me that Ma Deary will be on her best behavior and not embarrass you in front of Ozzie and his family, Jutta, and Mrs. Gathers. Ma is a lot of things, but I know deep down she's proud of you and she wouldn't want to miss you walking across that stage. Last week, I overheard her on the telephone bragging about you to one of her friends from work, talking about how you were going off to college on a full scholarship. Then, yesterday, I caught her down in your bedroom looking at that old picture of you from the Easter-egg hunt when you found the golden egg. I think she's getting sentimental over everything, so cut her a little slack. And don't worry, I'll be there to help you put out any fires.

Mrs. Brown and the staff at Brooks High held a car wash to raise money to help with your college books. Since you're leaving for Philly right after the graduation ceremony, I'm tasked with making sure you get the check, so don't let me forget to give it to you.

Oh, and Mary Ellen sends her love. I was going to tell you this in person, but I need to tell someone, or I'll blow the whole thing.

Drumroll, please. Pat, tat, tat! I'm going to propose to Mary Ellen next month! Don't you tell a soul, but I'm going to get down on my knee on June 12, the one-year anniversary of the Loving v. Virginia Supreme Court ruling that makes our union legal. I know what you're thinking, and yes, I'm still a hopeless romantic. But please, keep it under your hat. I don't want anyone to get wind of this and ruin the surprise. When we see each other, I'll show you the ring.

Well, the cows need milking and the grass mowing, so I'll end here. The twins say hello, and we all look forward to seeing you soon.

Love your big bro always and forever,
Walt
5/3/68

Sophia closed the letter and placed it against her heart.

On the evening before graduation, Sophia was in the cafeteria by herself when Miz Peaches walked over to her table with a dishrag.

"So, are you really going to Penn?"

"I'm still in awe myself."

"Honey, hush." She whistled between her teeth. "And I know that school cost a pretty penny."

"My father's wife graduated law school there, and once I was accepted, she petitioned wealthy donors and all but moved mountains to convince them to give me a scholarship."

Miz Peaches smiled. "What're you majoring in?"

"I've decided on journalism."

"Why?"

Sophia thought back to the first time she had met Mrs. Gathers and seen all those books in her personal library. Over the years, she had collected copies of the countless articles that Mrs. Gathers had bylined in her quest to give American homes to children like her. The reason was simple: "I want to be able to help people. Give those a voice who might be overlooked and can't speak for themselves."

"That's admirable, and I'm going to miss you. I brought you a little something." Miz Peaches pulled an index card from her apron pocket. "Here's my sugar-cookie recipe. I know how much you like them. Whenever you start missing us around here, make yourself a little taste of home."

Sophia stood, and they rocked in each other's arms. "Thanks, Miz Peaches. I wouldn't have made it these three years without you."

"Just doing my job." Miz Peaches's face lit up. "And you, sugar, have made it worth it."

On the night before graduation, it was tradition for the seniors to break curfew. While most of the students ran amok and partied in the lower woods, Sophia and Max met on the bench behind the Magnolia Clubhouse. They sat in the same spot they had on the night of the dance when she'd discovered that he was from Germany. Max straddled the bench, and Sophia leaned back in his arms.

"I'm going to miss this." She circled his wrist with her fingertip.

"My parents have agreed to stop through Philly on our way back from Martha's Vineyard in August so that I can see you. Where will you be staying?"

"Precollege lasts for four weeks, so I'll be on campus. I think there is a week between that and when school actually starts, and Ozzie invited me to stay with him."

"You still call him Ozzie?"

"For now, and he's good with it." Sophia smiled, and then she placed her fingertip on his burn mark and enjoyed that exhilarating feeling of their early connection. In response, Max let his hand brush over the scar on the back of her thigh. Then he put his lips against hers and kissed her slowly at first, then with urgency.

Sophia came up for air. "I hate that this is it."

"It's not goodbye, it's just so long for now." He cradled her face, and she got lost in his eyes.

She placed her head on his shoulder, and they sat gazing up at the moon. The pair had gotten to the place where they didn't need words to convey their hearts' intentions, and Sophia liked that about being with Max. Even though tonight was the end of an era in her life, it was also the beginning.

"I've made a decision," she said to Max. "Going forward, I'll only be known as Katja. It's my birthright. I've fought hard for it, and I'm taking it back."

EPILOGUE

Arlington, Virginia, 1968

ETHEL

It felt like the coldest day of the New Year to Ethel, and she couldn't understand why the reporter from *Good Housekeeping* had chosen this location outside of Arlington Hall to do the interview. The entire Gathers family stood in clusters. Ethel had wedged herself between Anke and Monika, looping an arm with each.

Both of her eldest daughters looked so impressive in their full-dress army uniforms. Monika's was decorated with stripes and ribbons; she looked so grown up with her new bob haircut under her flight cap. Heinz and Franz, also in their service uniforms, flanked Bert, as usual. Leo was their college boy, while Oti, Mia, and Anton, all teenagers, looked about ready to go home. It had been a long day but an important one for Ethel and Bert, and she was glad that all of her children were present to witness such a global honor.

The lanky reporter stood a few inches taller than Bert. "Mr. Gathers, what is it like for you and Mrs. Gathers to receive the Papal Humanitarian Award from Pope Paul VI for your extraordinary work in placing over five hundred mixed-race children with U.S. families, and adopting several children of your own?"

Bert cleared his throat. "It is an honor and a privilege to be presented with this award, but I would be remiss to take much of the credit. My wife, Ethel, has always lived by the motto 'Do more.'

"The Brown Baby Plan and the adoption agency were her calling, and it was for all intents and purposes a one-woman show. It was Ethel who met with the nuns at the orphanages in Germany and found a way to move the children into loving homes, even when she had to tear down the bureaucratic red tape with her own hands. She churned out article after article reporting on the dire situation of these children and found American families to step up and adopt them. It was because of Ethel's faith and her refusal to take no for an answer that we stand here before you today with this award."

"Thank you," the reporter said. "Mrs. Gathers, some have referred to you as a Keeper of Lost Children. Would you like to add to this?"

Ethel touched her pillbox hat, then fingered the rosary beads in her pocket as she remembered the raspy voice that she'd heard at the shrine of Lourdes all those many years ago, when she was at her lowest point.

You have much to offer others.

"This award is an amazing honor, and I thank Pope Paul VI for recognizing our work. In the words of my late mother by way of the Book of Isaiah, 'A little child shall lead them.'" Her eyes roamed over each one of her kids, and she smiled. "Those beautiful children in the German orphanages demanded with their love and affection that something be done to improve their circumstance.

"So I did it."

Author's Note

While researching maternity homes and adoption for my novel *The House of Eve*, I stumbled upon a documentary film called *Brown Babies: The Mischlingskinder Story* by Emmy Award–winning journalist Regina Griffin. Through this film, I learned that there were thousands of biracial children born during WWII in Germany, products of Black American servicemen and German women. Many of these children were abandoned to orphanages because their German mothers feared the public scrutiny that came with having a mixed-race child out of wedlock. Many of the Black soldiers who wanted to marry their German girlfriends couldn't get approval from the U.S. Army commanding officers. Some wanted to return home to girlfriends and wives without bringing children, admitting their infidelity. As I watched the interviews in the film of the adults who were once labeled "war babies," I was introduced to Mabel Grammer, an unsung hero who made it possible for these bicultural and biracial children to be adopted by African American families.

There's a tingling sensation I get in my body when I stumble upon a trailblazing woman—someone whose role in our historical narrative has been marginalized, forgotten, or untold. From the way the hairs rose on the back of my neck, I knew I was being called to shine a light on this overlooked moment in our collective history. When writing historical fiction, I weave truth, intuition, and imagination together to tell a story that will delight, entertain, and educate. Here are a few of the real inspirational people you meet in *Keeper of Lost Children.*

Ethel Gathers was inspired by Mabel T. Grammer, an adoption champion and civil rights worker who was born on December 23, 1913, in Hot Springs, Arkansas. She was the granddaughter of enslaved African Americans and one of Pearl and Edward Treadwell's seven children. Her father, a bellhop, died when she was a child, and the family became impoverished. Tragically, she contracted peritonitis, which resulted in a ruptured appendix. She was left with scar tissue that prevented her from ever producing children.

After graduating from Ohio State University with a degree in journalism, she began working at the Baltimore-based newspaper *Afro-American*, penning a column called Mabel Alston's Charm School from 1938–43. When her second husband, Army Warrant Officer Oscar G. Grammer, was deployed to Mannheim, Germany, in 1950, she followed him there.

A devout Roman Catholic, she made a pilgrimage to the Sanctuary Our Lady of Lourdes shrine in France where, according to a close relative, she was moved to rededicate her life to "help others instead of focusing on herself." When she returned to Mannheim, Grammer was approached by a group of distraught young German mothers whose children were half African American, the consequence of wartime and postwar romances between these ladies and African American troops. She and her husband adopted twelve of these children and later established the Children Worldwide Organization, a private adoption agency that functioned for eighteen years. By the mid-1960s, Grammer had aided in the placement of 50 Afro-German children in Black American homes and more than 450 in African American military families' homes in Germany.

Mabel and Oscar received a papal humanitarian award from Pope Paul VI in 1968. Mabel died on June 5, 2002, and is buried at Arlington National Cemetery with her husband.

The documentary film *Brown Babies: The Mischlingskinder Story* was instrumental in helping me paint the picture of Ethel Gathers, Sophia Clark, and Ozzie Philips. The scene where Ozzie meets Jelka at the bar and she says "It is cheaper by the bottle" was inspired by a Black GI's story from the film. I also learned that some of the orphans tried scrubbing their brown skin in an effort to make it white, which Franz, one of Ethel's children, did in the novel. The film also introduced Sonja and Daniel Cardwell, who were taken from Germany and ended up performing farm labor in Maryland. Their journey inspired Sophia's hard life on the farm. Daniel Cardwell's book *A Question of Color: A Brown Baby's Search for Identity in a Black and White World* inspired the mix-up of adoptive parentage in Sophia's story.

Mrs. Brown, the counselor who helps Sophia go from Brooks High School to West Oak Forest Academy, was inspired by Harriet Elizabeth Brown, a Black teacher who represented Calvert County in a legal court suit that asked for equal pay for Black and white teachers. She contacted NAACP attorney Thurgood Marshall, who worked with her to sue the county based on a violation of the Fourteenth Amendment to the U.S. Constitution, and they won their case in 1937.

The Prosser Foundation, which allowed Sophia to attend boarding school tuition-free, was loosely based on the work of the Anne C. Stouffer Foundation. In 1967, Anne C. Forsyth, heiress of the R.J. Reynolds Tobacco Company, created the first foundation that provided African Americans with full scholarships to attend elite Southern boarding schools. Ms. Forsyth funded the foundation with one million dollars from her late father's fortune and donations received during the foundation's tenure. Over the ten years the foundation existed, 142 Stouffer scholars attended schools in thirteen Southern states, ranging from Virginia to Alabama to Florida. After high school, a majority of the scholars attended top-tier colleges with academic scholarships from their respective schools. By 1976, the Stouffer Foundation leaders felt they had accomplished their goal of integrating prestigious Southern boarding schools and they discontinued their scholarships to prep schools.

Sophia being one of the first to integrate a prestigious private boarding school was also influenced by the integration of the Westminster Schools in Buckhead, Atlanta, Georgia, that I read about in *The Atlanta Journal-Constitution* and *The New York Times*. I also found the book *Transforming the Elite: Black Students and the Desegregation of Private Schools* by Michelle A. Purdy a helpful resource in depicting Sophia's time at boarding school.

The scene when Sophia is in the locker room and Patty thinks it's funny to auction her off like her enslaved ancestors was prompted by a similar scene that happened in River Valley High School's football locker room (Yuba City, California) in October 2022.

The character of Ozzie was born in a conversation that I had with my great-uncle Edgar at a family reunion. He had served in the air force during the Double V campaign, and I had a longing to know what life was like for these Black men liberated from America's Jim Crow laws, living abroad with the taste of freedom. I was also gifted photographs by Ernest Gibson that helped me visualize what it was like for Black GIs in Germany during the occupation.

In researching Ozzie's story, I devoured *Half American* by Matthew F. Delmont, *Race after Hitler: Black Occupation Children in Postwar Germany and America* by Heide Fehrenbach, and various online articles about William Gardner Smith.

Clara Thompson and her Black nurse friends were modeled after the many Black women who were a part of the war effort. The Six Triple Eight Central Postal Directory Battalion was an all African American women's unit who went to England to sort the mail in 1945.

In Rita's world, there are quite a few inspirations from history. Rita's "uncle" Maceo Snipes was indeed murdered for trying to vote in Georgia. Also, in Rita's world, we meet Sadie Tanner Mossell Alexander, the first African American female lawyer in Pennsylvania. Later, she helped author President Harry Truman's report on civil rights. Sadie was the first Black woman to graduate from Penn Law, and the first in the nation to get a PhD in economics (and only the second Black female PhD recipient in the country; two of her five eventual degrees). In 2021, inspired by her legacy, the University of Pennsylvania Law School launched the Sadie T.M. Alexander Scholarship program. It was created to support incoming law students committed to racial justice, but because of this administration's elimination of DEI, at the time of publication the scholarship has been paused.

When Ozzie returns to Philadelphia, he struggles with receiving all that was promised under the GI Bill and instead is shunted into an unskilled job. I learned of all he encountered from articles in *Mother Jones* and at History.com. Second Lieutenant Lonnie W. Hill, assistant adjutant of the Kitzingen Basic Training Center, was a true person. I used photos from Getty Images to describe the Kitzingen Basic Training Center, which was initially established as an experimental training school exclusively for Black troops in early 1948, prior to President Truman abolishing segregation in the armed forces later that year.

This is a book of fiction. Throughout the novel, I have taken a few liberties with dates and timelines to make the story fit. Any errors are my own. My hope is that this book may open your heart to one woman's strength, one young man's longing to right his past wrongs, and one teenager's determination to find the truth. Thank you for allowing me the pleasure of sharing this story with you.

For a deeper dive on my research, I have included the following online publications for your reading pleasure:

Mabel Grammer: Robert Fikes, "Mabel Treadwell Grammer (1913–2002)," BlackPast, July 27, 2021, https://www.blackpast.org/african-american-history/people-african-american-history/mabel-treadwell-grammer-1913-2002/.

Alexis Clark, "Overlooked No More: Mabel Grammer, Whose Brown Baby Plan Found Homes for Hundreds," *The New York Times*, February 6, 2019, https://www.nytimes.com/2019/02/06/obituaries/mabel-grammer-overlooked.html.

Robert Fikes, "The Black Fairy of Mannheim: Mabel Grammer's Good Work in Post-War Germany," Afropean, July 17, 2021, https://afropean.com/the-black-fairy-of-mannheim-mabel-grammers-good-work-in-post-war-germany/.

Being bicultural and mixed-raced in Germany: Damian Zane, "Being Black in Nazi Germany," BBC News, May 21, 2019, https://www.bbc.com/news/world-africa-48273570.

Integrating boarding schools: Mosi Secret, "'The Way to Survive It Was to Make A's,'" *The New York Times Magazine*, September 7, 2017, https://www.nytimes.com/2017/09/07/magazine/the-way-to-survive-it-was-to-make-as.html.

Maureen Downey, "These Students Walked onto Westminster Campus and into History," *The Atlanta Journal-Constitution*, January 9, 2019, https://www.ajc.com/blog/get-schooled/these-students-walked-onto-westminster-campus-and-into-history/zZt776u8nu5mDMPi9jyIUJ/.

High school students portray a slave auction: Alexandra E. Petri, "California High School Football Team Forfeits Season after Players Staged 'Slave Auction,'" *Los Angeles Times*, October 3, 2022, https://www.latimes.com/california/story/2022-10-03/slave-auction-high-school-football-team-forfeits-season-yuba-city-river-valley.

Michaela Harris, "Student: 'I Did Not Want to Do It': River Valley Varsity Football Players Apologize for 'Slave Auction' Incident," *The Appeal-Democrat*, October 18, 2022, https://www.appeal-democrat.com/news/urgent/student-i-did-not-want-to-do-it-river-valley-varsity-football-players-apologize-for/article_1d27d572-4f5d-11ed-9feb-b3a6e473066b.html.

Harriet Elizabeth Brown: "Dec. 27, 1937: Harriet Elizabeth Brown Case Settled," Zinn Education Project, https://www.zinnedproject.org/news/tdih/harriet-elizabeth-brown-case-settled/#:~:text=Brown%20contacted%20NAACP%20attorney%20Thurgood,of%20white%20and%20Black%20teachers.

The Six Triple Eight: Alexis Clark, "The 'Six Triple Eight' Army Unit Made Sure U.S. WWII Forces Got Their Mail," History.com, February 1, 2019, https://www.history.com/articles/black-woman-army-unit-mail-world-war-ii.

Maceo Snipes: Erica Sterling, "Maceo Snipes," The Georgia Civil Rights Cold Cases Project at Emory University, https://coldcases.emory.edu/maceo-snipes/.

GI Bill and Black Veterans: Erin Blakemore, "How the GI Bill's Promise Was Denied to a Million Black WWII Veterans," History.com, June 21, 2019, https://www.history.com/articles/gi-bill-black-wwii-veterans-benefits.

Matthew F. Delmont, "How a Hostile America Undermined Its Black World War II Veterans," Mother Jones, November/December 2022, https://www.motherjones.com/politics/2022/10/black-world-war-wwii-veterans-denied-gi-bill-restoration-act-benefits-half-american-matthew-delmont/.

Kitzingen Basic Training Center: "Kitzingen Basic Training Center," Getty Images, https://www.gettyimages.com/photos/kitzingen-basic-training-center.

For more, visit my website, www.sadeqa.net.

Acknowledgments

I would like to thank God for constantly showing me how to be the Light as I walk in mastery of His plan and purpose for my life. My ancestors for constantly watching over me and whispering your stories into my ear. For my parents; Dad for your guidance, Mom for your love, and Francine for your constant support. You three believing in me is my superpower. To Uncle Edgar, for being an early reader and consultant—thanks for letting me poke around in your memory. I couldn't have written this without you. My favorite sibs: Tauja, Nadiyah, and Talib for always letting me be myself without judgment. My amazing nieces and nephews, cousins, aunts, uncles, and in-laws for always rallying the troops and supporting little ole me. I love you all.

I have the best friends on the planet, best sister circle, best Jack and Jill chapter moms, best trail boos, best belles—thank you all for your constant love and support. Ena Berry, thank you for being consistent, and Zurn Porter Isaac and Ilov Grate for grounding me with your 12 West love.

A special thank-you to Kellye Walker and Werten Bellamy, sponsors of the Freedom Writers Retreat at beautiful Great Oak Manor, where I wrote and was replenished. Lauren Francis-Sharma, thanks for the invitation (twice). To the Rowland Writers Retreat sponsored by Pleasant Rowland and the Rowland Reading Foundation, thank you for the time to create and commune. To all my retreat writing sisters who listened to my works in progress and graciously shared pages with me, bless you. Katherine Kezon, thank you for breathing life into my U.S. Army scenes, and April Gibson for sharing your father's military experience with me.

My dearest agent and day-one believer, Cherise Fisher, for your fierce protection, steady hand on my back, and for always being the one I can trust and rely upon. I so enjoy curating stories with you; our future is so bright—get ready! Agent Wendy Sherman, the ultimate boss lady and visionary who constantly shows me how to elevate and level up. All good things from here! To the best editor in the land, Dawn Davis, thank you for bringing out the very best in my work and pushing me beyond what I thought possible. It means so much that I can trust you with my heart. And Maria Mendez for connecting all the dots.

Jonathan Karp for your wisdom and support; I hope your mom likes this one too. Hannah Bishop for being an outstanding publicist and the one who I can depend on to take care of business. Ingrid Carabulea and the entire marketing and sales team at Simon & Schuster for making me shine bright. Christie Hinrichs, my incredible team at Authors Unbound, and Emily Varga: thank you for keeping a mic in my hand. To my Hello Sunshine family, thank you for amplifying our books and voices.

To all the independent bookstores, book clubs, bloggers, influencers, sororities, reviewers, and readers who lovingly show up for me, read my novels, and are ambassadors at spreading the word, thank you. I could not do any of this without you. It takes a village; thank you for being a vital part of mine.

For my beautiful children: Lena for seeing me at my core. Don't be afraid to be a Creative. Walk into it, it's your birthright. Your only assignment is to be true. Zora, you are strong, you are intelligent, you are powerful. Be brave, boss girl. Miles, my first. You've grown up beside my career, so you know that whatever you desire is possible. Go get your blessings. To Glenn, my beloved husband and partner in everything. You are the definition of marrying well, and I couldn't love you more if I tried. Thank you for being my forever partner and loving me when I forget to be kind to myself. There's still so much more to come, buckle up.